WRATH OF THE FALLEN

STEVE GILMORE

LIQUID MIND PUBLISHING

Liquid Mind Publishing

MORE FROM STEVE GILMORE

Heaven's Dark Soldiers

Rise of the Giants

Wrath of the Fallen

Rage of the Heavens

Dawn of the After Days

Ride of the Horseman (Coming Soon)

Sign up for Steve's newsletter for updates on deals and new releases!

https://liquidmind.media/steve-gilmore-newsletter-sign-up-1

For Sherrie. My best friend.

And those who led astray the world will be bound in chains and shut away in the assembly-place of their destruction, and all their works will pass from the face of the earth.

- The Lost Book of Enoch

PROLOGUE

THEY SAY time is the great equalizer. The unforgiving universal constant that dictates the terms of our existence. Infinite in nature, yet terrifyingly discrete. Although it flies or crawls, depending on your particular set of circumstances, it never stops. Not even for a damn second.

Within the proverbial blink of an eye, our present becomes our past, as we inescapably race toward an unknowable future. And if you have half a friggin clue, you make the best of every waking moment you have at your disposal because when it's up — it's just up. There's no getting it back.

Conversely, Einstein said that time was nothing more than an illusion. That no separation existed between the past, the present, and the future. That there was but one, single existence. A concept I used to consider complete and utter bullshit until something rather unexpected happened to alter my perspective.

I died.

In the year 1998.

On my friggin birthday.

Worst birthday ever, for the record.

But inexplicably, after a short stint in the Heavenly realms — during which fourteen years passed on the Earth — I came back.

But I digress. More on that in a moment.

While the concept of time was not quite as rigid for the dead, or pseudo-divine undead as it were, it still possessed the ability to kick you square in the ass.

For example, seems like an eternity ago when I thwarted the plans of a megalomaniacal fallen angel who was hellbent on destroying life as we know it by unleashing his legions of oversized, angel/human hybrid miscreants on mankind.

But in all actuality, it was only last week.

Adding insult to injury, it also seemed that my adversary's apocalyptic scheme was not exactly thwarted. It was merely postponed.

Epic letdown on both fronts. Bit of a time-inspired double whammy, if you will.

Don't get me wrong here — I *did* put a monumental beat down on a veritable shitpot of giant beasties. I even sent their entire friggin bizarro world to the north end of oblivion in a smoking torrent of judgment fire.

But, evidently, there was more.

A lot more.

The game was still very much afoot.

Damn the bad luck.

It was quiet for a few days, though. A few days, that is, before the giants started popping up at various locales around the globe. At first, folks thought it nothing more than a very elaborate hoax as blurry cell phone videos of impossibly large man-like figures started to flood all facets of social media until the entire internet buckled with the traffic.

Then the conspiracy theories started. 'Mutated Super Soldier Program Goes Horribly Awry' was amongst the most popular. Most countries pointed the finger at the United States. The rest blamed the Russians. North Korea tried to take credit, but nobody really took them seriously.

Bigfoot enthusiasts, however, took the opportunity to make a plea that the giant creatures were agitated sasquatches tired of being the subject of bad reality TV shows and beef jerky commercials.

The ancient astronaut theorists touted that a 'Race of Titanic Alien Beings Were Reclaiming the Earth - We Told You This Would Happen!'

Oddly, the doomsday preppers weren't surprised at all. Instead, they were pissed that it was *giants* and not *zombies* at the root cause of the apparent global meltdown. But they still happily retreated to their elaborate fallout shelters with machetes, sawed-off shotguns, and collector's edition *Night of the Living Dead* DVDs. Typical.

At any rate, it was all a bit of fun — until the giants started breaking shit and eating people. Then it became real. Impossibly real.

In life, I was a soldier. An elite product of the U.S. military. Upon death, I became something else. No longer human but not quite an angel, I was something conceived of mankind but no longer part of it. Something blessed and cursed with the power of God's wrath. A warrior of the light that existed in the shadows.

My name is Dean Robinson, the Seventh Deacon of the Seventh line.

I am to maintain the Balance.

The time of reckoning was upon the race of man.

I

"Is that *all* you've got?" He growled in a nightmarish, gravelly voice, slowly circling me like a brazen predator toying with a wounded prey.

I was bleeding. Badly.

Everything was blurry.

Muted.

Dark.

A deafening buzz of screeching static filled my ears.

My head pulsed with repeated crushing swells of unknowable pain.

I couldn't keep this up.

The deep gash running across my midsection stung like a raging wildfire as blood trickled down my already sullied jeans and pooled at my feet.

He was too strong.

Too fast.

I had to end it — now.

There was no other way.

He'd left me no choice.

That goddamned son of a bitch left me no choice.

Mustering all my strength, I pushed myself off the ground. Not quite ready to get to my feet, I just sat there on my knees and despondently stared at the ground for a long second. This shouldn't be happening but it was.

"Don't make me do this!" I barked, burying my emotions as I summoned all my unnatural ability and defiantly stood to face him. "I'm begging you."

In response, the mouth of the infernal, fifteen-foot monster standing opposite me curled into a harrowing smile proudly displaying row upon row of barbed, blackened teeth. Seething streams of viscous, ashen drool bubbled from the corners of its massive jaw and steadily oozed down its veiny, sculpted chest like snaking rivers of unnatural lava.

Fixing me with a poisoned glare, the creature's unnerving red eyes danced with a fiery madness as every chiseled, sinewy muscle making up its hulking red frame flexed and bulged from the mocking, guttural laugh that boomed from somewhere deep within its massive throat.

"The *great* Dean Robinson," it taunted, "*begs* me."

His mind was muddled.

Broken.

The man I knew had slipped into the ether.

Only the beast remained.

Tightening the grip on the hilt of my otherworldly gladiator sword, the cloak flared about my shoulders, sending rippling waves of divine Wrath coursing throughout my being like an electric current.

"You're not thinking straight," I grunted, as my wounds instantly healed themselves and argent metal gauntlets encased my hands in a spectral flash. "Remember who you are."

"And *who* is that?"

"My friend. You're my friend."

"*Friend*," the creature scoffed. A fine layer of orange flame silhouetted the scaly, blotched skin pulled tautly over a freakish skeletal frame.

"Stand down, goddamn you!"

"*God* has not damned me, my *friend*. Quite the contrary. It is you who are damned."

Holding out one of his impossibly large hands, he proceeded to mockingly admire the ghastly trio of razor-tipped talons jutting out from its clenched fist. Composed of jagged ashen bone and stained deep with streaks of haunting crimson, the grim instruments of eviscerating death forbiddingly gleamed in the moonlight as he loomed over me like an eager executioner waiting to carry out his appointed duty.

"Now, tell me," he growled. He was frothing at the mouth like a craze-stricken animal. "Is that *all* you've got?"

"Not everything. Not yet."

Letting out another barrage of guttural laughter, he said, "Then let us finish the game."

"Don't do this," I pleaded.

"I am going to end you now, Dean — but take solace in the fact that the rest of our *friends* will not be far behind. I *promise*. They cannot hide from me."

As his words hit me like a raging tidal wave, every muscle in my body tensed in anger. Feeling the mental switch flip to the on position, I slowly pulled in a long, deliberate breath.

Cleared my mind.

Focused my thoughts.

Found the Balance — the perfect balance between wrath and clarity.

As the unfathomable power welled up in the deep recess of my soul and the expected sensation of calmative awareness washed over me, I grumbled, "I really wish you hadn't said that."

And it was right about then when shit got real.

Without so much as another word, his gangly, talon-tipped claw swung toward my head in a blur of motion as he launched at me with a grace and precision that should not have been possible for a creature of such mind-blowing size and strength.

Unfortunately, it no longer mattered.

He was too far gone.

I knew what had to be done.

Floating to my left, and safely out of the arc of the death blow, his overgrown fingernails ripped into the cobblestone street as he let out a harrowing, primal scream in clear frustration that I was no longer standing there. Taking full advantage of the fact that he was bent over, my face curled into a dark scowl as I focused all my supernatural strength and thrust my sword squarely into his massive, heaving pectorals only to forcefully rip it down the entire length of his scaly midsection.

Like the opening of a macabre faucet, a steady stream of black, mucus-like blood spewed from the son of a bitch's exposed chest cavity as he grunted and flailed in protest. Leaving my sword lodged in his rib cage for the moment, I pummeled his kneecaps with my metal fists until they were nothing more than a bloody pulp.

Unable to stand upright anymore, he crumbled to the ground as I yanked my sword free and held it to his mighty neck.

Locking gazes with the unnatural creature, he again began to laugh a horrible, throaty laugh as his eyes erupted into flaming orbs of fiery apocalypse.

Saying nothing, he just gazed at me with a placid stare.

Almost like he wanted me to do it.

To restore what remained of his humanity.

To quell the madness.

To end him.

Lowering my head in defeat, I muttered, "I'm sorry, John. I truly am."

And then I cut Rooster's head off.

2

Twenty-Five Hours Earlier

Stepping through the arcane portal, I found myself standing in the deep shadows of the familiar alleyway tucked neatly behind Symphony Hall in Boston's Back Bay.

It was an unnaturally cold January evening, and the typical collection of city-goers scrambled to the nearby T-stop while bundled in ridiculous variations of layered overgarments. As the gateway snapped shut behind me, I did a quick scan of the area, making sure my rather peculiar entry was unobserved.

Satisfied that I didn't have any fanfare, I willed my otherworldly cloak into retreat, and it melted from existence in a spectral flash. Now looking a bit more like your average Joe, sporting faded Levi's and a black peacoat, I stepped from the quiet darkness of the alley into the flickering onslaught of Massachusetts Avenue in rush hour traffic.

More than anxious to get out of the weather, I wove like a ghost through the droves of disgruntled people bustling along the sidewalk. Hooking a quick left onto Westland Avenue and nearing my destination, I was pelted square in the face with a howling gust of frigid air that ripped through the surrounding buildings like a pissed off tornado.

"Awesome," I grumbled under my breath. My face instantly stung. "That's friggin perfect."

Just as I was about to dart across the street and finally call it a day, the faint clamor of a slurred fifties song I couldn't quite place stopped me dead in my tracks. Glancing downward at the snow-crusted curb, it appeared an unusually jovial street person was trying his very best to ward off the cold with a fifth of whiskey, a badly chewed cigar, and one hell of a spirited tribute to Elvis Presley.

"Hey, buddy," I said, reaching down to help the rather heavyset, side-burn-laden songbird to his feet. "Too cold to be out here. Even for the King of Rock and Roll. You need to get inside."

"Don't need your damn help. Thank you. Thank you very much." He batted my hand away as he took a big swig from his paper bag-wrapped bottle and belted out the chorus to "Jailhouse Rock."

"I'm not asking. Get your ass up. You're going to freeze to death out here in your blue suede shoes."

"All right, all right." He begrudgingly took my hand and staggered to his feet without making eye contact. "Goddamn do-gooders. Wish you'd mind your own damn business."

"Let's go, Mr. The King," I grumbled back at him as a solid waft of his liquor-drenched cigar breath penetrated my nostrils. "There's a shelter down the street. You can get some food and hopefully a breath mint or twenty."

Now completely on his feet and somewhat coherent, I expected him to say something else of a snide nature. But instead, he stood there gawking at me through bloodshot, widened eyes. Almost like he was trying to figure out if I was real. Or not.

"Good God almighty," he gasped. "What the hell ... What the hell *are* you?"

Interestingly, I seem to have this effect on most *normal* humans. Even those that hadn't consumed enough alcohol to drown a small village. I'm told it's because my presence on Earth wasn't exactly 'natural' anymore. Something about the fact that I died, crossed into the heavenly realms, and came back. Subsequently, most folks won't even acknowledge my presence because I evidently existed on the very edge of their perception.

However, on the rare occasion I spoke to somebody or made physical contact with them, it typically went one of two ways. The first of which was that they figured me for some kind of benevolent, guardian angel. The second, and much more unfortunate, was that they mistook me for an infernal, really scary—

"Demon!" A look of absolute terror washed over his sullied face, and he took a few steps backward, dropping his bottle of booze on the frozen sidewalk. "You're — a demon!"

And it seemed that Frumpy Elvis was going with scenario number two. Typical.

I shrugged. "Now that's just hurtful."

"Stay back — Hellspawn!" He did his very best to form a cross with his gloved, index fingers. But, as he was piss drunk, it actually looked more like a lazy V. Or a jacked-up L.

"Look, pal, relax. That's not going to work, okay. I'm not a demon. I'm a Deacon. And despite the fact that I've had a really shitty day, I'm trying to help—"

"A what?" he blurted out, continuing to backpedal while his eyes tried their damnedest to pop out of his head.

"Can't believe I'm about to have this conversation again," I muttered. "Okay. Even though you won't remember this in five minutes, it's like this — I'm a Deacon. One of forty-nine souls blessed and cursed with the power of God's wrath. Along with a secret society of supernatural side-kicks, I maintain Balance on the Earth by casting divine Judgment on the unspeakable, and often giant, evil miscreants that have been skulking around mankind since the beginning of time. Blah, blah, yadda, yadda. And you're not even listening ..."

"Get the hell away from me!" He spun around in a cloud of cigar smoke and bolted toward the traffic lights of Massachusetts Avenue in the not-so-far distance. "Demon!"

"Deacon! And you're welcome!"

As my new buddy drunkenly maneuvered down the street while screaming his muttonchops off, I just shook my head. "Sorry, folks, but Elvis has left the building."

Although not exactly to plan, I figured my good Samaritan quota was met for the evening, and it was high time to cut my losses and get on with it. More than ready to get inside, I made a determined beeline toward the rather nondescript, metal door sandwiched tightly between two sizable Victorian brownstones across the street.

Given the ornate nature and close proximity of the surrounding structures, any logical human being couldn't help but think the dilapidated doorway led to nothing more than a narrow stairwell. And compliments of a nifty veiling spell, that's exactly what they'd find if they happened to open it. Now, to those of us on the more arcane side of existence — it was a different story.

Reaching my destination, I focused my will on the faint collection of Enochian glyphs carefully etched into the dented panels and watched as they began to systematically emit a spectral bluish glow. Upon completion of the pattern, a bold symbol manifested in the door's humble center. Encased in a triangle and bound within a perfect circle, it was a peculiar 'X' with a prominent 'P' struck through the middle.

A symbol that I knew all too well. The Chi Rho. The representation of Balance between the light of mankind and the darkness of untold, unnatural evil lurking in the shadows.

Carefully placing my left hand on it, the door swung open, and my face curled into a wide grin as the impossibly large, candlelit room on the other side came into focus.

And by impossibly large, I meant like football field kind of big.

Maybe two football fields.

To be fair, it was honestly hard to gauge because the ginormous oak tree growing out of the floor obscured the view a bit.

Doesn't make any sense. I know.

Just as I was about to step inside, the distinct sound of someone clearing their throat caused me to stop dead in my tracks. Scanning the surrounding area, an exceptionally frail elderly man bundled in a burly black wool coat and tweed touring cap emerged from the deep shadows of the bordering brownstone.

"Binkowicz," I grumbled.

Sucking on an old-ass pipe clenched tightly in his teeth, he disdainfully muttered, "Hello, schmendrick."

"How's my least favorite prophet of the Lord doing this evening?"

"I *was* doing just dandy," he replied, blowing an impressive smoke ring at me. "Right up until you showed up."

"Tell me something, Fred."

"What's that?"

"Why the hell do you sit out here?"

"Because, schmendrick, I'm supposed to. Been sitting here — *right* here — for longer than I can remember. Every day. It's my job."

"Your job, eh?"

"Are you deaf or just stupid?"

When I offered him nothing in response besides a spirited finger gesture, he said, "We all have a job to do. Maybe you should try doing yours."

I smiled. "Thanks for that. Any chance of you calling me by my actual name anytime soon?"

"Not unless you plan on changing your name to schmendrick."

"And what exactly is a schmendrick?"

"A *schmendrick,* schmendrick, is a moron — a putz — an incredible dumbass. Basically, it's you. Any more questions?"

"Yeah, one more. Is there any particular reason why you're a cantankerous son of a bitch or should we just chalk it up to having a bad century?"

Shooting me an icy glare, he said nothing and resumed his usual perch on the foldout chair. I smiled again for good measure. "Okay, good talk. Always a pleasure. Yours, not mine. Just so we're clear."

Leaving Fred Binkowicz to go on about his business of being a crotchety bastard, I crossed the threshold of the battered doorway. The warm sensation of primal energy washed over me as I pierced the veil and stepped foot into the Quartermaster, my new home and otherworldly outpost for the Seventh Realm of the Guild of Deacons.

And although the QM was primarily the command center for our earthly exploits, it also housed the best damn bar in Boston. Granted, it wasn't actually in Boston, per se. It sort of existed in a nether region between Earth and Third Heaven in perfect dimensional alignment with one of the seven heavenly gates. But you get the point.

While the general motif was something between 'medieval castle meets an Irish pub decorated by inebriated hobbits,' the Quartermaster was powered by ophanim class angel technology and had more kick than Starfleet Command on crack.

All that aside, I was just damn happy to be back. It had been a long couple days.

"Giant *men* or, more likely, a *giant* hoax?" the smarmy, designer suit-wearing newscaster spouted from one of the hundreds of throneView screens lining the wall above the dark wooden bar. "Good evening and welcome to the Cold Hard Truth. I'm Rex Buckley, and as usual, *the Buck* — stops here. Okay folks, it's official. In the past twenty-four hours, unsubstantiated reports of '*giant,* man-like *creatures*' have originated from *all* fifty states. There's no shortage of alleged *evidence,* with more and more *eye witnesses* providing fuzzy pictures and conveniently out of focus video by the literal minute. I mean, can we seriously put any real stock into this *phenomenon*? Is this merely a malignant photoshop campaign gone viral? Come on, people. There's— no — such— thing as *giants.* Am I right? Of course, I'm right. Trust me on this one—"

"Change the channel," I muttered, as I maneuvered through the buzzing crowd of clerics and acolytes taking a well-needed respite. "I can't stand that asshole." Pulling up a stool, I happily parked myself next to a familiar face at the bar. "How the hell are ya, Coop?"

"Howdy, howdy," replied Cooper Rayfield with a thick southern drawl and cheek full of tobacco. Slugging back the remnants of a man-sized beer, he waved his hand at the screen and it instantly faded to black. "You look like death on a cracker, hoss."

"Thanks for that. Wish I could say you looked any better. When'd you get here?"

"About three beers ago." He looked exceptionally weary as he slid the empty pint glass across the bar and ran a couple fingers through his scraggly red goatee. "Maybe four."

"So not long, eh?"

"Have I become that predictable?"

"It's actually one of your better qualities." I looked around for the rest of my arcane strike team. "You the first one back?"

"Reckon so," he replied. "Haven't seen Big A yet. Caveman and Duncan are finishing their sweep in California. Stoner's in Utah. Rooster's still running around Washington, D.C. Crockett's combing through the upper Midwest. And I think Tango's in Vegas."

I nodded. "They should be back soon. Debrief's in thirty minutes. In the meantime, think I'll join you for a frosty beverage. Or several."

"The new barkeep should be along anytime now. I think she ducked into the kitchen."

"She? Rooster's got a chick watching the bar?"

"Durn skippy." He perked up a bit as he said it and carefully adjusted his signature maroon hoodie complete with sleeves haphazardly cut off at the shoulders. "And she's easy on the eyes, hoss. Think I might be in love."

"That a fact?" I chuckled. "What's her name?"

"Don't know her name. But I'm pretty sure she wants her some country boy."

"Of course she does, Coop." I slapped him on the shoulder. "She probably thinks you're Bo and Luke's lesser known, follicly-challenged step-cousin. No woman in their right mind could say no to that."

"Damn, hoss. If I had feelings, they'd be hurt."

I grinned. "No, they wouldn't. Switching topics, I take it you didn't have any luck in your travels, eh?"

"Nossir," he grumbled as he hacked a healthy wad of tobacco juice into his plastic spittoon. "Spent the past day and a half chasing every dagum lead originating south of the Mason-Dixon and nothing to show for it. I can't figure what the biggins are up to, but they're covering their tracks better than a Georgia swamp fox running from a pack of castrated hounds. How about you, any luck up north?"

"Negative," I replied, trying to put the latest Coopersim out of my mind. "Followed up on every sighting reported between Maine and Montana. No trace of the bastards. No indication of what they were doing either. Seems they've got us on a wild goose chase."

"Looks like somebody knocked your beer over again, Cooper," said an unexpected female voice from behind the bar. "Either that or you inhaled another one in the fifteen minutes you've been sitting there. I take it you're in for another round?"

"Little darling," Coop said with his very best redneck charm. "The only thing I'd like more is if you'd join me for it."

Looking up to find a striking vision of brown eyes, olive skin, and a smile that would make you forget your name, I blurted out, "Doc?"

"Hi, Dean," Erin Kelly replied with a rather content grin. "Surprised to see me?"

Surprised?

No.

I was not surprised.

I was downright, double dumbfounded, might've-just-pissed-myself friggin shocked.

3

So, Erin and I kind of had a thing. But it was...complicated.

In fact, up until a few short days ago she thought I'd died fourteen years earlier — which in all actuality, I did.

But then I came back.

And she found me.

And for obvious reasons, I didn't exactly tell her the truth surrounding my current unnatural state of existence.

So, in retrospect, complicated may be a gross understatement.

But you get the point.

"What the hell are you doing here?" These were, unfortunately, the first words out of my mouth as I gawked at her like a dope.

"Slinging beer," she said. "Rooster asked me to fill in while he was out hunting giants — or anakim — that's what you guys call them, right?"

"How do you know that?" Her response caught me completely off guard as my mind raced to catch up. "And how do you know Rooster?"

Her mouth curled into a smug grin. "Let's just say that I've learned quite a few things since our chat the other night."

"Wait a goddamn minute," I grumbled, turning to Coop. "Is this the new *'wants her some country boy'* barkeep you were just rambling on about?"

He shrugged. "Ah, maybe? Y'all know each other?"

"Yes, *Cooper,* we friggin do. This is Erin Kelly."

"Erin Kelly," he repeated, tugging on his goatee. "The doctor from the thing in Bosnia a while back?"

"Yep."

"Ah, *that* Erin Kelly."

"Yep."

"Well, that's dagum awkward," he grumbled, looking a bit sheepish. "My bad?"

"Why don't I get you boys a drink," Doc cut in, holding back a smirk as she retreated to the row of kegs at the far end of the bar.

Still glaring at the redneck Romeo, I felt a skulking presence to my immediate right and turned to find a familiar cleric standing there with a pair of Mossberg shotguns crossed on his back and decked out in his signature ghillie suit. Which, as I understood it, wasn't actually a ghillie suit but more of his *natural* form.

"Hey, Dean," he muttered, in a subdued, gravelly tone as his animalistic gaze swept back and forth like he was stuck in perpetual surveillance mode.

"Crockett? I thought you never stepped foot indoors."

"Making an exception." He gazed up and down the bar like a consummate tracker. "I need a beer. And I heard something about a hottie behind the bar."

And before I had the opportunity to tell him to shove it, I felt a solid slap on my back followed by a familiar gruff voice. "Hey, ladies. Just got back. Didn't find shit in Utah except a bunch of freaked out Mormons. Need a damn drink. Where's this hot bartender everybody's talking about?"

Saying nothing, I jumped off my stool and shot Stoner, our resident magus, a scowl that would stop a train. As a divine purveyor of the more arcane nuances of the Forbidden Knowledge, a magus was kind of like the pseudo-divine version of a wizard. Regardless of the fact he could supposedly turn me into a newt, I was still a bit miffed with his snarky ass.

Happily plopping on the stool between me and Coop, he carefully propped his glyph-inlaid staff against the bar. "What's the matter, Robinson? Somebody take your lunch money?"

As I stood there shaking my head, Coop leaned over and evidently explained that everyone should quickly move off the whole 'hot bartender' subject with great haste, as it was a bit on the sensitive side.

Anxiously clearing his throat, Crockett muttered, "That's awkward."

"Awkward," Stoner confirmed. "But funny."

More than ready to end the conversation, I sat back down and eagerly anticipated the arrival of my well-deserved frosty beverage when Tango pulled up next to me.

"Hey, guys. Vegas was a shitshow," he said, taking off his faded jean jacket and draping it over a stool. "I need a beer. Crockett told me that Rooster's got a hottie working the bar."

"Ah, no I didn't," Crockett protested, slumping down on his stool.

"Yeah, you did."

"Totally didn't."

Pulling out a comb, Tango meticulously ran it through his hair a few times. "Quit screwing around. Where's she at? I'm a' thirsty — if you know what I mean."

"Son of a bitch!" I barked.

As the wonder twins sat there chuckling while Crockett melted toward the floor, Tango asked, "What's wrong, Dean?"

"Tell you what, hoss," Coop said, collecting his long bow and quiver of peculiar broadheads. "Me and the boys will head on up to the Reliquary and get ready for the debrief. Meet you there in a couple."

"What about my beer?" Tango protested. "And the hottie?"

"Let's go, Tiberius," Stoner grunted. "Robinson evidently has his panties in a wad. Besides, I've got enough Rooster Rum in my pack to make you forget the fact you're wearing pastel pants. Where the hell do you get those things anyway?"

As they headed off into the crowd and faded from sight, Erin showed up with a couple beers. "Here you go." Her lips curled into a wide smile.

It was the kind of smile that made you want to slap your momma. A smile that made everything wrong with the world instantly melt away. If I were more of a romantic sort, I'd probably have some incredibly eloquent prose to tack on here. But, I'm not. So just trust me. It was friggin amazing. And although I was elated to see her, I was completely befuddled as to why she was here.

"Ah, thanks." I grabbed the man-sized mug of RoosterBragh Honey Orange Ale as she slid it across the bar.

"You okay? You look pissed."

"I'm good. Just having a little trouble adjusting to the fact that you're here — tending bar at the Quartermaster."

"Well, if it's any consolation, I'm having a little trouble adjusting to the fact that you're *not dead*."

"Fair enough," I muttered, nursing the beer. "Look, I didn't exactly know how to tell you this the other night, but—"

"It's okay," she said. "I know."

"You know? You know what?"

"I know what happened fourteen years ago. What really happened. I know what you — are."

"Wait, what?" I scoffed. "How?"

"That's simple, Buballah," answered an unmistakable female voice with a distinct Brooklynesque inflection coming from my immediate rear. "I told her."

"M?" I spun around on my stool to find a familiar principality class angel looking like an uncanny cross between Barbara Streisand and Sarah Jessica Parker smirking at me.

"Of course it's me," she replied, adjusting her low-cut, royal blue dress adorned with enough sequins to make you go blind. "And you're in my seat. Scoot your tuchus over. Move, move, move. I don't have all day here."

"Here you go, M," Erin said, sliding a steaming mug of black coffee across the bar.

"Oooh, that's wonderful! Thank you, Buballah!"

"Wait, I thought I was Buballah," I protested.

"You've been replaced," she said, taking a dainty sip.

"That's just hurtful. So, you two have met. That's really not awesome."

Erin shook her head. "Mariel visited me a few nights ago after I found you here — not dead."

"Of course she did." I glared at M. "And why exactly did you do that?"

"Erin and I have been long overdue for a chat. I've simply been waiting for the right *time*."

"M filled in all the blanks I've had since Bosnia," Erin said. "I understand now, Dean. For the first time in fourteen years — I get it. The giant, Goran Petrovich, the babies. I get it. All of it."

Not really sure how to take that, I sat in silence for a long moment. "And you believe it?"

"I do." Her gaze drifted to one of the throneView screens displaying the latest news broadcast of 'giant man' sightings from across the globe. "And it seems I'm not the only one that should. The anakim aren't hiding anymore, are they?"

"No." I fixated on her mesmerizing brown eyes. "They're not."

"Don't get all messhuggina," M chided. "Nothing you can't handle."

"Yeah," I grumbled, thinking that was one hell of an oversimplification of current events. "So, just to be clear, am I Buballah or is she Buballah? Seems like you're taking some serious Buballah liberties here."

"I will *Buballah* whom I choose to *Buballah* when I choose to *Buballah* them."

Shaking my head, I made the mental note that I'd really like to figure out what the hell Buballah meant at some point in the near future. "Moving on. Why bring Erin into this shitshow? Why now?"

"I've already told you. It was time."

"What the hell is that supposed to mean?"

"Mariel explained my purpose, Dean," Erin said.

"Which is?"

"Well, among other things, I'm evidently supposed to keep you out of trouble."

"Well, good luck with that, Doc." I slammed home my beer and took a healthy gulp from another one sitting on the bar.

She smirked. "Easy there, Robinson. Don't think I won't cut your sorry ass off."

"Look at you. First day on the job and already throwing your weight around. Think I need to have a discussion with Rooster about his hiring practices. Not sure you're going to work out here."

"You could only be so lucky."

"Yeah," I muttered, taking another pull of the divine ale as I gazed at Erin still somewhat in disbelief that we were having this conversation in light of the impossible circumstances. "Lucky."

"Speaking of Rooster," she said, "he asked me to tap another keg of cider before he got back. Don't go anywhere. M said you'd tell me about the different kinds of heifers."

I did a spit take. "*Nephers.* Nephers are the race of angel-human hybrid beings. *Heifers* are female cows."

As Erin gave me a 'piss off' sort of glare and headed to the other end of the bar, I shifted focus back to M. "So, you planning on telling me what the hell's really going on here? What's the deal with Doc?"

"Erin has always had the Sight," she replied, placing her coffee carefully on the bar. "And she's now opened her eyes."

"What the hell does that mean? And why the hell hasn't she aged in fourteen years? I mean, I'm not complaining. She looks amazing — especially in those jeans. But it's not natural."

"It's all part of her journey."

"Her journey? That's all you're giving me?"

"For now."

"What about all that crap about *her purpose*?"

"To do what must be done, you will need Erin Kelly and she will need you. You'll understand, Buballah. In due time."

"Awesome."

"There are more pressing matters," she said, transitioning to a somber tone. "I, as with all my kind, are to return to the Heavens, and I fear it will be some time before we speak again."

"Anakim are popping up on headline news and all the angels are bailing? What the hell?"

"We mustn't interfere in the coming events. For the time being, the Earth must make do without us."

"And what about me?"

"As I've told you before, you walk a path of destiny — and one that I can no longer walk with you."

"More with the destiny bullshit, eh?"

"You're missing the point." Rising from her stool, she peered at me over the rim of her naughty librarian glasses. "Destiny is like Gefilte fish. It may look like a pile of schlock, but it's delicious! Especially with a little horseradish and matzo."

I shrugged. "Is that supposed to be helpful?"

Grabbing my arm, she said, "When all else fails, remember this,

Buballah. Only by embracing mercy will the fate of destiny's design be witnessed."

And just like that, she was gone.

"Awesome," I muttered, yet again finding myself in a state of total bewilderment at the hands of a celestial being. "Mercy and gefilte fish. Sounds like a Hebrew boy band."

Figuring I needed to put the latest M revelation out of my head for the time being, I started toward the Reliquary to debrief with the crew. My team, as with the rest of the Guild, had been literally canvassing the country for the past two days trying to pick up the trail of our oversized adversaries.

By the sheer magnitude of sightings, all indication was that some really serious shit was about to go down. Where and to what end seemed to be the pertinent questions.

We needed a plan.

At the moment, we didn't have shit.

Although I was still a bit in the dark as to why Erin was at the Quartermaster, it was probably the safest place for her to be until we sorted everything out. For that, I probably needed to thank Rooster. Either that or punch him in the face for not telling me what he was up to.

"Dean, you're here," said a familiar voice with a detectable hint of anxiety from behind me. "I, ah, thought I'd make it back before you. You didn't happen to see—"

"The newly appointed *hot* bartender?" I turned to find my enigmatic ginger colleague looking more than a bit apprehensive. "Sure did."

"Right," Rooster muttered. "Awkward?"

"You think?"

"Sorry, buddy. It was M's idea. She said it's important that we keep Erin close. I wanted to tell you but figured you'd get all whiny about it."

"So I've heard. And what's with this whiny crap?"

"Hate to tell you this, but you get whiny when it comes to Erin."

"Whatever," I muttered, making the mental note to revisit this particular topic at a later time when a horde of unnatural giants wasn't on the cusp of a global incursion. "How'd you make out in D.C.? Any luck?"

"No." The frustration flashed across his face. "Followed up on every lead. No discernible pattern. It's just like before except they don't seem to be eating people — yet. Feels like they're on some kind of massive recon mission. I need Skyphos to analyze some data. Is everybody back?"

"Haven't seen Abernethy and Caveman yet, but the rest of the crew is here."

"Good." Rooster grabbed a steaming mug of coffee from the bar that I swear wasn't there a second ago. "Let's head to the Reliquary. We need to get started."

"Nae, Jackie," grunted an unmistakable Scottish brogue-laden voice. Turning to find the hulking frame of Big A suddenly standing there, he handed Rooster a crumpled piece of paper. "I need ye lads to check into something first."

"Is this for real?" Rooster asked, studying the document.

"Aye. Bring yer wee ice skates. And hurry."

"Perfect," I muttered.

Apparently, my long couple days just got a bit longer.

4

"Never understood the appeal of recreational ice skating," Rooster said, somewhat academically, as we pulled to a halt under a group of barren trees wrapped with white Christmas lights on the north side of the Boston Common.

A light snow drifted from the night sky as we overlooked the crowded skating rink on Frog Pond, quaintly illuminated by the twilight of the surrounding city. The post-holiday Friday night crowd happily zipped across the ice while doing their very best to avoid smashing into one other at high rates of speed. Some successful. Others, not so much.

"What the hell is there to understand?" I grumbled. "It's friggin ice skating. It's fun."

Hearing Rooster scoff under his breath in response, I had the sneaking suspicion that I'd just opened the door for some random story from my arcane colleague's sordid past that I really wasn't in the mood for.

"Fun," he grunted. "Flopping around on a half-frozen canal in the Netherlands with animal bones strapped to your feet with rope was so incredibly *not* fun. It was a horrible necessity. And in retrospect, the most ridiculous freaking thing—"

"The Netherlands?" I cut him off mid-rant. "When the hell did you do that?"

"Early twelfth century. It was the only way to get around back then once everything froze. We can thank the Dutch for that technological marvel. I mean, of all the dumbass things, right?"

"Animal bones. And rope, eh?"

"Yeppers. Ridiculous. Unfortunately, I didn't invent metal skates until a hundred years later. Took me a while to get the design right. There was something about the ambient temperature of the ice and the molecular composition of the blade that really screwed with the aerodynamic profile. I mean, the science was pretty basic, but given the tools I had to work with at the time and—"

"When am I gonna friggin learn," I muttered, as he fluidly transitioned to geek mode and continued to bloviate while throwing his hands around in the air.

Although he didn't look a day older than twenty-five, my ginger buddy had evidently been around a little while longer. I'd yet to figure out exactly how old he was, but at this point I was starting to suspect he might be pushing 'Old Testament' status.

"Hey, Brian Boitano," I cut in. "Can we get back to business here? We're on the clock, remember?"

"Did you just call me Brian Boitano?"

"I did."

"Not funny."

"It was pretty damn funny."

"No. No, it wasn't." His eyes formed a piercing squint and flashed an unnatural fiery red, indicating he clearly didn't appreciate my snide commentary.

I smirked anyway. "Let's agree to disagree."

Aside from being a centuries old technological mastermind, Rooster was a particularly rare type of nephilim called a liderc, and hence, had a bit of an angry alter ego.

And by *angry alter ego*, I mean he's been known to morph into an infernal fifteen-foot, scaly red hulk with talons the size of lawn mower blades. As such, I'd been trying not piss him off too much.

Snapping back into mission mode and muttering something under his breath, he pulled the otherworldly computer phone gadget from the pocket of his bomber jacket.

"So, what exactly did Big A want us to check out here?" I asked.

His eyes shifted back to their normal blue as his fingers feverishly danced across the screen of his wonder phone. "That piece of paper he handed me was a copy of a tweet that posted a few minutes ago."

"That one of those fritter things?"

"Twitter."

So, the fact that I'd literally dropped off the face of the Earth in 1998 and didn't resurface for fourteen years had me playing catch up on a few of the technological advancements I'd missed out on. For example, it was clear that the entire concept of a mobile phone had taken a radical shift during my involuntary hiatus from the land of the living.

While fourteen years ago I would've used one to actually make a phone call, it seemed their new purpose was to type stuff, take stupid-ass pictures of oneself, and then post said stupid-ass pictures on these 'social media' websites.

I wasn't sure why society had become fascinated with the notion of broadcasting every mundane aspect of their lives on the internet followed by 'LMAO,' but I did stumble across a couple of dancing pet videos that were pretty epic.

So, at the very least I had that going for me.

"Right," I muttered. "So, what was the treat about?"

"Tweet."

"Whatever. Just friggin tell me what we're doing here before I feel compelled to punch you in the face."

"Well," he said, handing the phone to me, "Seems that some dude using the handle @LadiesManLance411 took this video standing right here. Roughly nine minutes ago."

"Damn. Looks like the *ladies' man* has an affinity for large breasted women. Wow. No way those things are real, right? I mean, just look at them—"

"Not that," he grumbled, snatching the phone from my hand and manipulating the image with his fingers. "What do you see moving through the trees?"

Focusing on the clip, I picked up the distinct silhouette of two unnaturally large figures moving with great haste through the woodline surrounding Frog Pond.

Although they weren't in the video for more than a few frames, it was unmistakable. Anakim — the man-eating giants of legend and lore.

The bastard offspring of Heaven.

They were here.

I clenched my fists. "This was taken nine minutes ago?"

"Yes. Yes, it was."

"Which direction were they moving?"

"From the angle of the video, it looks like north. Maybe northwest." He turned and gazed into the darkness of the surrounding trees.

"Toward Beacon Hill?"

"Yeppers. The State House is right through that clump of trees."

"The State House...you don't think—"

And it was right about then that things took an interesting turn.

As if on cue, a rather horrific series of explosions ripped through the night like claps of thunder, causing the ground to literally quake beneath our feet. Subsequently, a barrage of impossibly large chunks of flaming brick wall filled the horizon like a surreal fireworks display.

"I think we found them," Rooster muttered.

As the familiar statue of J.F.K., which should've been proudly displayed on the State House lawn, hurtled through the night sky like a pissed off comet and blasted a sizable hole in the frozen ground to our immediate right, I grumbled, "That's just wrong."

"Seriously wrong."

"I think we should go say hi."

His eyes flashed a brilliant red. "Be rude not to."

Willing the cloak into being, it elegantly manifested in a spectral flash of white luminescence and billowed about my shoulders.

The Deacon's cloak — my gift and my curse.

The ever-present source of my abilities.

The wrath of God incarnate.

A divine means to an end.

Its otherworldly power coursed through my body like an electric current as my lips curled into a dark smile. Feeling the mental switch flip to the on position, I pulled in a long, deliberate breath.

Cleared my mind.

Focused my thoughts.

Found the Balance — the perfect balance between wrath and clarity.

As the unfathomable power welled up in the deep recess of my soul and the expected sensation of calmative awareness washed over me, I grumbled, "Game on."

Rooster nodded. "What's the plan?"

"Shoot'em in the knees. Cut their heads off." The ethereal gauntlets of indestructible, argent metal manifested on my forearms and fluidly encased my fisted hands. "Slap high fives. Call it a day."

He ripped off his leather bomber jacket to reveal the literal arsenal of guns, knives, swords, and other random shit strapped to his torso. "Try and keep up this time."

As his skin turned an unnatural red to match the color of his eyes, he drew both semi-automatic pistols from the dueling shoulder holsters hanging under his stringy arms and plunged headlong into the darkness of the trees.

"Keep up ... my ass," I muttered, pulling the hood of the cloak over my head and willing the spatha into being. Feeling the presence of the scabbard on my back, I drew the otherworldly gladiator sword in a blur of motion and took position on his flank.

As we made a determined beeline toward the giant beasties apparently ripping apart a historic corner of my favorite city, I had the unequivocal feeling that my long night was just getting started.

5

MOVING WITH UNNATURAL SPEED, we traversed the north quadrant of the Common in a matter of seconds. Emerging from the shadows of the park onto Beacon Street, directly opposite the State House lawn, I pulled to an abrupt halt as the awaiting vision of unadulterated destruction and fiery apocalypse was almost too much to wrap my head around.

The street itself was littered with burning sections of granite and brick, while the poor bastards that happened to be driving by at the time of the explosion crawled out of their mangled vehicles in various stages of disfigurement. The snow tufted; seven acres of pristine landscaping was a smoldering fallout zone like something you'd expect after a carpet bombing. And the grandiose state capitol building itself was nothing more than a steaming pile of rubble with the signature twenty-three karat gold dome lying haphazardly atop.

How exactly such a feat of mind-blowing demolition was accomplished in a matter of seconds was inconceivable.

As I stood momentarily speechless, people poured from the surrounding buildings like droves of frightened animals creating a horrid cacophony of shouts and screams. The blaring of sirens rang through the winter night as the streets quickly filled with primal panic.

"Fuck me," Rooster gasped. "How in the hell—"

"I've got movement!" I barked, picking up the flash of an oversized figure darting through the shadows of the smoky chaos as my amplified fight reflex kicked in. "Bad guys — eleven o'clock. You got eyes on?"

When he didn't acknowledge me, I turned to find him frozen like a peculiar statue, catatonically staring into oblivion.

"John!" I yelled, grabbing his shoulder, wondering what the hell was wrong with him. "We need to move."

"He can't hear you, Dean," said a voice that sent a harrowing chill down my spine as everything became unnaturally quiet like somebody hit a universal mute button. "You are too late. It has begun."

"Azazel," I grumbled, as the cloak flared out like a wild animal in reaction to the fallen angel evidently standing behind me.

Slowly turning around, I realized Rooster wasn't the only one in mannequin mode. It seemed every person within eyesight was also frozen in time as they all stood motionless against the catastrophic panorama.

Everyone, that is, besides the impossibly good looking, six-foot-seven asshole with celebrity grade hair, a pristine nice suit, and impossibly white teeth gleaming from behind a smug-ass grin. Although his crimson, snake-like eyes were utterly soulless, they danced with triumph as he condescendingly glared at me.

"You son of a bitch," I growled.

"Son of *Heaven*," he corrected, straightening his jacket. "Albeit more prodigal than not."

Ironically, everybody operated under the premise that Lucifer was the worst angel in all human history. While I won't dispute the fact that he's a total dick and definitely not a friendly, there's another fallen angel that made old Lew look like a friggin Boy Scout. His name is Azazel. And I was staring right at him.

Kind of like the Kevin Bacon of the supernatural world, you could literally trace every heinous act of war and bloodshed, throughout all of human history, straight back to his demented ass. So, take my word for it — he's a real douchebag. Azazel that is. Kevin Bacon, without saying, is a goddamn saint. Everybody knows that.

"Let them go," I barked, standing face-to-face with my adversary.

Waves of wrathful anger pulsed through my being as the cloak rippled anxiously on my shoulders. A subtle layer of infernal white flame formed around the gauntlets covering my hands and slowly crept along the blade of my sword as I readied to swing it through his neck with extreme prejudice.

"Should you choose to behave," he said, in sycophantic British dialect, "I will release my hold upon these *good people* in a few short moments. Conversely, if you decide to make matters disagreeable, I will take great pleasure in removing their spines with a mere flick of my hand. Now, kindly lower your blade. Or, do you prefer the route of unpleasantry?"

I really hate this friggin guy — angel — whatever.

Figuring I didn't have much choice at the moment in light of his human shield tactic, I sheathed the sword and glared at him.

"Much better." His grin was wolfish. "It seems that given the proper motivation, even the *great* Dean Robinson can be taught a lesson in civility."

"What do you want, dickhead?"

"For you to listen." He coldly gazed over my shoulder at the ruinous, flaming carnage that used to be the Massachusetts State House. "As you will soon come to understand, this is but one small example of that which has transpired across the globe. Within this very moment, all the *great* and *powerful* regimes of mankind have been reduced to ash. Their leaders slain and their petulant symbols of authority razed to the very ground of which they reigned supreme."

"Bullshit," I scoffed. "I don't believe you."

"You will." A smug tone rung heavy in his words. "From this day forth, *Father's* precious creation will suffer without bound. This is but the beginning. A demonstration of my intent, shall we say. Within the ensuing *seven* days, the world will watch in horror as my legions systematically pluck every remaining semblance of *civilization* from their feeble grasp. The perceived delusion of *world order* will very shortly cease to exist."

"Sounds ambitious. But we both know it's not going to work."

"And why is that?"

"Well, aside from the fact that your hair-brained schemes never seem to pan out, there's the small matter of us ending your sorry ass."

"The mighty *Deacons*?" he said, dripping of sarcasm. "I think not, Dean. Given your depleted ranks, I hardly think the dark soldiers of Heaven are in a position to offer any serious form of resistance. And even if you were, I'm afraid you'll continue to find yourselves hopelessly behind the *power curve*, shall we say. You of all people should appreciate that."

Upon his taunting words, a vision of the macabre 'collection' of enslaved Deacons flashed through my thoughts. The Machiavellian war of attrition recently waged by Azazel and his clandestine, traitorous angel ally resulted in the capture of nearly half of my forty-nine cloaked brothers. Bound in holy flame and tucked away like prisoners of war, they were being kept alive in some form of jacked-up stasis while an arcane extraction process sucked the mantles of divine Wrath from the very fiber of their being for the express purpose of being wielded against us.

While Azazel and his traitorous angel cohort still remained a few mantles short of their stolen divine power source quota, the Balance between light and dark was quickly swaying in his favor. And by consequence, we weren't exactly combat ready at the moment. But he sure as hell was.

I felt my face tighten into a deep scowl. "That won't stop us from fighting, and you damn well know it."

Apparently getting a real kick out of that, he broke into laughter. "I'm counting on it! For that is your noble purpose. And in the *noblest* of fashion, you and what remain of your misguided brethren will crush the Earth in the wake of battle as you clash with my forces. Or better yet, perhaps you plan to *smother* it with Judgment fire as you did with my shadow realm. Either scenario yields the same result — mankind will return to the darkness. There is but one alternative to avoid this certain and most unfortunate conclusion."

"You're going to surrender now?"

"Hardly," he said, brushing off my snide commentary with a feigning smirk. "You're going to see to it that the gates of Tartarus are opened and my brothers are liberated from their most unwarranted persecution."

"Right," I scoffed. "Let the Watchers roam free after six thousand years in the divine slammer. And then what? You guys move to Maui and open a bed and breakfast? Have you been friggin drinking?"

"Listen to me carefully, you insolent child!" His crimson eyes flashed with fury and his calm demeanor gave way to visible rage. "Before the great dog rises above the peak of Saphon, my brothers are to be set free. In turn, I solemnly vow to withdraw my legions from this wretched realm and never again plague the race of man. Ignore my demands, and I trust you understand the consequence. My terms are absolute. You are to carry this message to your masters — the *archangels*. And I suggest you make haste, as the sands of time have already begun to fall."

And just like that, he was gone in a powerful whoosh of air accompanied by the flutter of unseen, massive wings.

Almost like somebody unpaused the movie, the clamor of the surrounding mayhem instantly returned and the frozen gaggle of city goers snapped back into their previous acts of screaming panic.

"Where are they?" Rooster yelled, picking up where he left off a few minutes earlier, evidently looking for the anakim.

"Gone." The severity of Azazel's words hit me like a ton of bricks.

"Wait, what?" He lowered his pistols. "But you just said—"

"*Deacon Robinson and Cleric O'Dargan, the archdeacon requests your immediate presence in the Reliquary*," boomed the disembodied voice of Skyphos as an otherworldly portal manifested to our immediate front, awash in blue light.

"Let's go." A distinct lump formed in my throat as I walked toward the doorway. "I think we may have a bigger problem to deal with."

"Bigger than this? Where?"

Taking one last look at the raging nightmare laid out before us, I muttered, "Everywhere else."

6

CROSSING the threshold of the ethereal gateway, Rooster and I left Boston behind for the moment and stepped foot into the Reliquary.

But instead of the usual calm precision I'd come to expect from the Guild's otherworldly war room and communications center, the massive medieval rotunda was a frenetic hive of disorganized bustle. A distinct vibe of trepidation seemed to hang in the air like everyone was collectively dumbfounded. My stomach instantly churned, and I had the unequivocal feeling that the proverbial shit had hit a really big fan.

"Goddamn it," I muttered under my breath, reflecting on Azazel's smug warning of global catastrophe. "He wasn't bluffing."

"Who wasn't bluffing?" Rooster asked, pulling up alongside me, still clueless as to the widespread nature of recent events. "Holy shit. What the hell's going on here?"

All the throneView screens, lining each and every available inch of wall space throughout the vast candlelit rotunda, flittered with various and assorted video feeds depicting leveled buildings and mangled people.

An unfiltered tirade of hysterical reports rang out from the virtual, translucent displays hovering in midair over the countless work stations, while the clerics and acolytes manning them feverishly yelled into old fashioned telephones trying to make sense of what was going on. And in the center of the room, the ginormous screen depicting the virtual tactical map of the United States was lit up like a surreal Christmas tree as red concentric circles pulsed ominously over every state.

"Up here, lads," grunted the archdeacon from his usual perch on the command bridge, which inexplicably hovered thirty feet above the cobblestone floor.

Racing up the spiral staircase, we reached the floating platform in a matter of seconds to find Tango, Coop, and Stoner excitedly barking orders at various clerics through live teleLink feeds while simultaneously updating the map.

Adjacent the oversized wooden desk in the center, Big A, Caveman, and Crockett intently studied another video feed on the main throneView screen. And despite the rampant chaos, Duncan sat casually in the leather captain's chair, lapping coffee from a steaming mug. As he nonchalantly waved a hoof at me, I made the mental note to figure out why the miniature pig always seemed to get the damn chair. Figuring that could wait until later, I took up a post next to Big A.

"What are we looking at?" Rooster asked, evidently trying to decipher the harrowing images of smoking ruin flashing across the display.

"That's the White House, brosephius," replied Caveman, looking exceptionally disturbed despite his imposing mansquatch façade.

"Or what's left of it," Crockett added.

"The White House?" Rooster blurted out. "They blew up the freaking White House, too?"

"Aye," Big A grumbled. "Along with every state capitol building in the United States."

"Add the Pentagon to the list," Tango said, joining the conversation.

"And the Kremlin," Coop added, taking post aside Tango. "Reports are coming in from all over the dagum globe. Westminster Palace in London, the Reichstag Building in Berlin—"

"Goddamn it!" Rooster snapped, as his eyes flashed an unnatural red. "Would somebody please tell me what the freaking hell is going on?"

As if waiting for that very question, the disembodied voice of Skyphos boomed, "*At precisely 7:33 P.M. Eastern Standard Time, a simultaneous attack was conducted on a global scale.*"

"And the targets?" I asked, fearing I already knew the answer.

"I am still collating data, but it appears the target list is inclusive of high-ranking government and military officials, their associated decision-making bodies, and places of administration. It also seems anakim were sighted at each location shortly before the attacks commenced."

"The world is leaderless," I said. "It's Azazel's opening move."

"And how is it that you know that, lad?" asked Abernethy, raising an eyebrow.

"Because he told me."

"He told you?" Rooster said. "When?"

"About five minutes ago."

"Five minutes ago," he muttered, quickly putting two and two together. "He was at the State House, wasn't he? Which means I was time whammied. Goddamn it."

"What else did he tell ye?" Abernethy asked, ignoring Rooster's apparent displeasure at being stuck in mannequin mode by our least favorite fallen angel.

As I took the next few minutes and recounted Azazel's latest maniacal scheme to the group, everyone stood silent with a collective look of disbelief strewn across their faces.

"So basically," Tango said, "The archangels either open the gates of Tartarus and let the fallen Watchers out or Azazel spends the next seven days systematically returning Earth to the Stone Age."

"Yeah," I grumbled. "That about sums it up."

"Dagummit," muttered Coop, which I thought to be a rather tame expletive given the situation.

"Not good, homies," Caveman added, which prompted Duncan to momentarily stop slurping coffee and let out a guttural piggly growl in agreement.

"All right, lads," Abernethy muttered. "Let's take stock of what we know."

"How much time do we have, brohemoth?" Caveman asked.

"Not sure," I replied. "Azazel said the gates of Tartarus are to be opened before 'the great dog rises over the peaks of Saphon.' Failure to comply results in the next iteration of anakim running around the globe breaking shit — which I'm assuming will be slightly more devastating than the last."

"The peaks of Saphon?" Coop muttered. "What the hell's that supposed to mean?"

"It's Azazel being cute," Rooster said, waving a hand in the air and pulling up a virtual map of the Middle East. "Saphon is the highest point on the summit of Mt. Hermon where the Watchers illicitly defected to Earth in the early days of mankind — where they fell from grace. It sits between modern day Syria and Lebanon.

"Cursed ground," Stoner grunted, shaking his head. "All kinds of bad mojo."

Spitting some tobacco juice into his coffee cup, Coop said, "What the hell's some mangy mutt climbing up a dagum mountain have to do with anything?"

"I do not believe Azazel is referring to an actual canine, Cleric Rayfield," Skyphos replied. *"I believe he is referring to the Dog Star better known as Sirius. According to human perception, it is the brightest star in the night sky based on its intrinsic luminosity and close proximity to Earth."*

Rooster rubbed his forehead. "So, the question is, when will the star rise over Saphon?"

"According to my calculations, Sirius will be in perfect celestial alignment with Mt. Hermon this Saturday at exactly 8:00 PM."

"Saturday?" Caveman, asked. "As in tomorrow?"

"Friggin perfect," I grumbled. "So, Giantgeddon kicks into high gear in roughly twenty-four hours. At least we're not dealing with a completely unrealistic time table...again."

Rooster's eyes glowed a fiery red. "That'd be more than enough damn time...if we had any inkling of how the hell Azazel's got the juice to pull off a worldwide — simultaneous — freaking — assault right under our collective noses! I mean, seriously, it was only last week when Dean nuked his entire base of operations in that goddamned shadow realm *including* what should have been every freaking anakim in his unnaturally bred arsenal. Where the hell did these other ones come from? And where the hell is he hiding them *now?*"

"Wherever it is," Big A replied, "It's being shielded by a powerful being."

"Yeppers. Which lends some pretty credible evidence to the theory that he's got a traitor in Heaven working for him. So, the topic du jour is simple, who the hell is it?"

"An archangel," declared a commanding voice from behind us. "But I do not believe he's in the employ of Azazel. The relationship is most certainly the opposite."

"Stephen," I said, spinning around to find our deaconly superior standing on the command bridge in his signature black suit, looking exceptionally stoic despite the dire situation. Although I had no idea how he continued to show up completely unnoticed during pivotal situations, I was nonetheless highly impressed by his ability to make an entrance.

"An archangel," Rooster muttered as his eyes returned to their normal blue and he faced the alpha Deacon. "Wait, what?"

"Bloody hell," Big A added with a furrowed brow. "Are you certain, Stephen?"

"I am," he replied, crossing the platform to join our huddle. "It is the only logical conclusion, I'm afraid."

"To what point or purpose?" Abernethy argued. "Why would one of the archangels want to open Tartarus and free the Watchers? It was them that put the wee scunners there in the first place."

"The clue was in Azazel's demands." Stephen turned his attention toward me. "What specifically did he say he would do if his fallen brothers were released from their bonds, Dean?"

"He said he'd withdraw his legions from this realm and never again plague mankind."

"Then where the hell's he planning on going?" asked Stoner. "Maui?"

"No," I said, starting to piece the puzzle together. "Heaven."

"Son of a bitch," Rooster muttered. "He's going to use the Watchers as a freaking assault force to storm the gates."

"Nae," Big A said. "The fallen blighters were banished by the Father himself. Their return would result in nothing less than—"

"An angel war," Stephen cut in. "I believe that, and that alone, is the endgame of our traitorous seraph."

"That's one hell of an endgame," Tango grumbled.

"Durn skippy," muttered Coop.

"That's seriously bad news, brosephs," Caveman added, accompanied by yet another piggly growl from Duncan.

"I don't get it," Rooster said, visibly frustrated. "Why would a member of the seraphic court want to instigate an angelic civil war? What's the point?"

"I'm afraid his motives are as much of a mystery as his identity," Stephen conjectured. "The only certainty in this equation is his intention, and our duty to stop him before Earth and the Heavens alike are destroyed in the wake of battle."

"So, all we have to do is stop a *renegade archangel* who's working with a *demented fallen angel* who are collectively holding mankind ransom for the express purpose of freeing *another two hundred* — highly pissed off — *fallen angels* from their eternal bondage. Okay, guys. I got nothing. Any ideas?"

"I have one," I replied.

"Why do I get the feeling I'm not going to like this idea?" he grumbled.

"There's only one play here," I said, turning to Stephen. "Azazel made me his damn emissary. I need to deliver his terms."

"To the seraphic court?" Rooster scoffed. "Ah, that's probably *the worst* thing you could possibly do right now. Did we not just establish that Azazel is actually *working for* one of the archangels?"

"And if I don't go, the jig's up. The traitor will know we're onto him, and it's game over."

"What's your plan, lad?" Big A asked.

"I go see the God Squad and figure out which one of their halo-wearing asses is the barkangel. Then we out his sorry ass before Azazel can launch his next wave of destruction. Piece of cake."

Tango shrugged. "Barkangel?"

"The bad archangel," I said. "Thought it had a nice ring to it. Kind of rolls off the tongue."

"Barkangel." Coop chuckled, despite himself.

Caveman just shook his head. "That's terrible, bro."

"I kinda like it," Crockett muttered.

As the rest of the group contemplated my impromptu moniker for the heavenly traitor with mixed reaction, Tango said, "That's, ah, not a good plan."

"It's a piece of piss," Abernethy agreed. "A daft gambit at best."

"Perhaps," Stephen countered. "But at the moment, it remains our only course of action."

"Then its settled," I said, "Where exactly do the archangels live anyway?"

"Paradise City," Rooster replied, evidently not so pleased with the turn of events.

"Paradise City?"

"Yeah, it's what we call Tenth Heaven, the Powers and Dominions of Fire and Light. Generally speaking, it's not a place you go without good reason. In fact, I can't think of any good reason to go there. Ever."

"The grass ain't green and the girls ain't pretty," grumbled Stoner. "Good luck, Robinson. You're gonna need it. We're all counting on you. I need a drink."

"For the time being," Stephen said, "I suggest the rest of you keep searching for Azazel's new base of operations." Addressing Abernethy directly, he added, "And kindly inform the other archdeacons to follow suit."

Exchanging nods, they gripped hands. "Aye. Consider it done. I take it yer making a trip up *north* then?"

"I won't be long. Gabriel is expecting me."

"Well, you be wary in yer travels, mate. Keep a keen eye."

"I always do, old friend."

Turning to face the group, a mighty scowl stretched across Abernethy's bearded face. "All right, laddies, off yer arses and back to work. Let's smoke the bastarts out of their hidey holes. Double our efforts. We've got twenty-three good hours to find the wee scunners and give 'em a proper skelping. Mr. Crockett, yer our best tracker. Do yer thing."

"I'm on it, boss," the enigmatic outdoorsman replied, leaping from the Command Bridge like a supernatural Tarzan and zipping out of the Reliquary in a blur of motion.

"Dean, a word please," Stephen said, as he walked toward the arcane portal that subtly manifested at the far end of the command bridge.

Moving out of earshot from the rest of the group, I muttered, "So, couldn't help but notice that you neglected to tell the crew about a couple rather significant details regarding the severity of our current situation."

"Such as," he replied, knowing damn well what I was talking about.

"Well, for starters, maybe that the twenty-four Deacons they all think are *dead* are actually sitting like mushrooms in Azazel's private dungeon while his miscreant archangel boss sucks the Wrath out of them with a divine straw."

"Are you referring to the *barkangel*?"

"Exactly."

"Well, for the moment, that knowledge is our burden to bear. There will soon be a time when those details become relevant to disclose with the others. But that time is not now."

"It'll sure as shit be relevant when the barkangel figures out how to wield the Wrath and turns into Evil Über Deacon. Then we'll have some 'splaining to do."

"I'm not sure the moniker of *Evil Über Deacon* is entirely accurate for the traitorous seraph," he dryly replied, clearly unimpressed with my nicknaming proficiency.

"No? Then what would you call a celestial being juiced up with the divine power of twenty-five Deacons who's hell bent on storming the gates of Heaven with bad intentions?"

After a long pause, he said, "He would be a god, Dean."

"A god?"

"Any being laden with that much of God's Wrath — God's power — would be, by definition, a god himself. And one we could not hope to defeat alone."

"A god," I muttered, with a distinct lump in my throat as the weight of his statement hit me like a ton of bricks.

"However, fortunately for us, the so called *barkangel* will not possess the requisite divine power to become the *Evil Über Deacon* until he adds you or I to his 'collection.' Which, if I'm not mistaken, makes it more than incumbent upon the two of us to ensure that does not happen."

"Fair enough," I replied, figuring there wasn't much else to say. Although I was still pissed that we were keeping the team in the dark about the grander scheme, I trusted Stephen's judgment. "So, what's the plan from here?"

"I will prepare the way and send for you."

"You're going to Paradise City?"

"No," he replied. "I'm afraid one does not simply walk into Tenth

Heaven. I must first consult Gabriel and request an audience with the seraphic court."

"Can you trust him — Gabriel?"

"He is perhaps the only one we can trust. Rest assured, Dean, Gabriel is not the traitor."

"You mean the barkangel."

"I'd prefer not to use that term — ever again, actually."

"And it appears Evil Über Deacon is out, too."

"I should hope so."

"That's unfortunate."

"I will return as quickly as possible. Wait for me here."

"Roger that, sir."

"Dean," he said in a manner that sent a harrowing chill down my spine. "The stakes have never been higher. Ready yourself for that which follows. We cannot fail."

He then simply stepped through the otherworldly portal and melted from sight.

"Awesome," I muttered, thinking things were a hell of a lot simpler when all we had to do was fight giants.

Thinking that was a damn good idea, I made my way through the bustle of the Command Bridge and started down the spiral staircase.

"And where the blazes are ye going, Deannie?" Abernethy grunted.

"Dreghorn. I'm feeling the unequivocal need to punch something."

7

Locked eye-to-eye with the fifteen-foot, muscle-clad behemoth standing opposite me, I tightened the grip on my spatha as a fine layer of white fire formed on my gauntlets and slowly crept down the blade of the otherworldly sword.

Although the anakim was doing his very best to take his generally menacing motif to a new level, the fact he was wearing a jacked-up wife beater tee and spandex shorts in lieu of the usual body armor made me chuckle. "Nice outfit, asshole," I grumbled. "If you're going for Vin Diesel meets Richard Simmons, you nailed it."

Not getting much of a response besides a guttural growl accompanied by the waving of his oversized battle axe, I figured he must've missed the reference. Which is honestly a damn shame because it was probably one of my better one-liners.

Getting ready to lay the smackdown on his malignant, jazzercising ass, I felt the cloak ripple about my shoulders and instantly felt the presence of yet another unnatural miscreant stirring behind me.

My mouth curled into a dark grin as I willed the otherworldly shotgun into being. "Awww. Did you bring a friend? I didn't realize this was a double date. Now it's just awkward."

Instantly feeling the leather scabbard-like holster manifest on my back, I ripped the semi-divine 1887 Winchester free and spun to my rear to find the second anakim mere inches from running me through with a ginormous spear.

As my amplified fight reflexes kicked in and the calmative awareness washed over me like a warm ray of sunshine, I sidestepped the attack. Casually sticking my foot out and tripping the big dope as he careened past me with the speed of a bullet train, I watched as he plummeted to the stone floor in a pathetic heap.

About to pop a judgment fire-bolstered cap in his sorry ass, the cloak rippled again, and I instinctively swung my head just in time to avoid the big-ass battle axe hurtling toward me for the express purpose of lopping my face off.

"Now that's just rude," I said, turning my attention back to the Body By Jake wannabe, and pointing the business end of my shotgun at his massive frame.

As a blast of pure white flame flashed from both barrels and subsequently blew a basketball-sized hole through his oversized pectorals, he simply melted from existence. Spandex and all. To be fair, I was probably doing him a favor. He really didn't have the legs to pull off that outfit.

Checking in on Ginormous Miscreant Number Two, who was still flopping around on his back in the near vicinity, I holstered the shotgun and sheathed the sword. Reaching down and grabbing his flagpole-sized spear, I got a modest running start and plunged it straight through the bastard's rib cage. As he let out a rather disturbing primal scream in protest, I finished off the maneuver by driving the medieval skewer a solid foot into the ground, effectively pinning him there for the foreseeable future.

And as I stood there for a long moment admiring my handiwork, the onslaught of a splitting headache hit me like a force of nature.

Typical.

Feeling like my head was about to pop under an unimaginable force, I squeezed my eyes shut and grabbed my forehead with both hands. After an excruciating couple seconds, the pain subsided, and I coaxed my eyes open to find an unfamiliar scene laid out before me.

No longer in the Dreghorn, I seemed to be standing on a rocky ledge jutting out from what appeared to be the near top of a massive, snow-laden mountain in the center of an endless, desolate valley filled with nothing but obscure conglomerations of ice sheets and oversized cave-like bunkers. Although cast in a spectral twilight, the unmistakable movement of giant figures skulking around hundreds of bonfires strewn throughout the barren landscape made it pretty clear I was staring at anakim central.

And, of course, perched on the very edge of the cliff adjacent a blazing torch, my pal Azazel proudly overlooked his legion of oversized miscreants while smugly puffing on a cigar. Looking exceptionally happy with himself, he turned to his right as another figure fluidly manifested in the looming darkness.

"You have done well, brother," the clandestine newcomer announced.

Easily a head taller than Azazel and clad in a brilliant while cloak, his face was carefully concealed inside a leather praetorian helmet and an almost tangible aura of pure white light silhouetted his powerful frame.

It was the aura of an archangel. A friggin bad one.

"Why, thank you, my lord," Azazel replied, reaching into his suit pocket and handing him a cigar.

Callously tossing it on the frozen ground, the barkangel replied, "Celebration, *however*, is far from warranted in this early hour."

"I respectfully disagree, my lord. The wheels of progress have been set in motion. Within a day's time you will not only wield the needed complement of *Father's* Wrath, but command my legions of anakim *and* the fallen Watchers. The realms of Heaven will quake upon your approach."

"Do not underestimate the cunning nature of our opposition, Azazel."

"The seraphic court?"

"Among *others*."

"Others? Surely you are not referring to the *Deacons*, my lord. They are powerless to stop us now. You've said so yourself."

"There has been an interesting wrinkle in our calculations, I'm afraid. An ironic twist that I regrettably did not anticipate."

"I do not understand."

"Your understanding is not required."

"Then how am I to assist?"

"I will see to the resolution of this annoyance. *Personally*."

"And what of me?"

"When your *celebration* is concluded, ready your Maradim and proceed with the plan as discussed. I will join you at the gates of Tartarus when the time is upon us to free your brothers. Until then, remain vigilant. Have I made myself clear?"

"Abundantly, my lord."

Wondering what in the hell I'd just witnessed, the echoing sound of a faint yet familiar voice calling out from somewhere in the deep corner of my mind caused the surreal vision to blur. "Please tell me the phrase *stick around* isn't about to come out of your mouth."

"What?" I grumbled, instantly snapping back to reality to find Rooster and Erin standing alongside me in the Dreghorn.

Glancing downward at the impaled giant flailing around like a harpooned whale by my feet, he said, "You know, *stick* around?"

"Don't quit your day job," I muttered.

"You okay?"

"I'm fine."

"You sure? You look like you just saw a ghost."

"Not a ghost. An asshole. Actually, it was two assholes."

"Come again?"

"Never mind."

"That was quite a performance," Erin said, evidently commenting on my anakim slug fest.

"You saw that, eh?"

"The whole thing. Smack talking and all. I always knew you could fight but *damn*. That was—"

"Unnatural. I know."

"I was going to say awesome."

"Awesome is better. Let's go with that. Now, not that I'm not happy to see you two, but what the hell are you doing here?"

"Well, for starters, you've been here for hours," Rooster said. "It's like four in the morning."

"It's Saturday morning?" I scoffed. "Son of a bitch. I must've lost track of time."

"You sure you're okay?"

"I already told you, I'm fine. Just needed to blow off some steam before my trip to Paradise City, which is evidently not in paradise nor an actual city. Whooping up on giants is surprisingly therapeutic."

"While you're at it, I'd also recommend spending a little more time on your one liner material. Just saying."

"Piss off. Is Stephen back?"

"No. No word yet." Rooster's face flashed with frustration. "And the clock's ticking. T-minus seventeen hours and counting."

"Don't worry," I muttered. "He'll be here soon."

"Hope you're right."

"Of course I'm friggin right. This is Stephen we're talking about. So, what else is going on?"

"Nothing good."

"Meaning?"

"For starters, it's basically widespread global panic fueled by every flavor of conspiracy theory blasting twenty-four-seven across all media outlets known to man. Seems that everyone's trying to wrap their heads around how the entire world's leadership was decimated in a single attack carried out by giant men."

"What's the prevailing theory?"

"Well, depends on the media source, but it's kind of a running stalemate between ecoterrorists, aliens, mutated super soldiers, and your run of the mill 'end of days' scenario."

"Christ," I grumbled.

"Yeppers. It's a general dystopian shitshow, and steadily devolving by the minute. What's left of the world's military is trying to enforce martial law, and there's even rumors of 'robotic soldiers' popping up in random places."

"Robotic soldiers, eh? You wouldn't have anything to do with that, would you?"

"Me? No. I haven't built a robot since the late seventies. Shut it down after it developed a British accent and started making better beer than me. It's actually a funny story."

"And one I'm not interested in. Any progress on locating Azazel's new hideout?"

He sighed. "Not as of yet. The entire Guild is mobilized — all seven realms. We're sweeping the Earth with everything we got."

"Well, thanks for that more than depressing report," I said, unsheathing the spatha. "Now, if you two don't mind, I'm going to get back to taking out my frustration on simulated oversized miscreants until Stephen shows up."

Erin cleared her throat and glared at me. "In the event you've forgotten, Mariel said you would train me on the various species of nephilim."

"It's kind of a bad time, Doc."

"Tough shit. I'm not giving you any opportunity to go off and get yourself killed *again* before I get any useful information out of you."

"Ouch."

"*And* I can't help if I don't know what I'm up against."

"Help? Look, I know you're tough as nails but—"

"Do you want me to kick your ass in front of Rooster?" she said, bowing up to me with all of her five-foot-two petite frame.

Comically looking down at the top of her head, which barely reached my pecs, I couldn't help but chuckle. "No?"

She grinned. "Then let's do this."

"Okay. But don't say I didn't warn you."

"Sweet," Rooster chimed in. "Nepher 101?"

"Evidently so," I grumbled, jumping backward as my skewered gigantic buddy swatted at my feet, reminding me he was still there. "First we need to get rid of Moby Dickhead."

"Allow me," Rooster said, glancing upward. "Please end the simulation, sweetie."

"*Combat simulation concluded, Cleric O'Dargan,*" the disembodied voice of Skyphos responded as the anakim instantly vanished in a flash of brilliant light. "*And please refrain from calling me Sweetie.*"

"Who the hell said that?" Erin asked.

"*I said that, Doctor Kelly,*" the voice boomed from the ether.

"Doc, meet Skyphos," I muttered. "She's our eye in the sky, so to speak. I'll explain later."

Skeptically nodding, Erin turned her attention to Rooster. "So, that giant was one of the battle simulation things you were telling me about on the way here."

He nodded. "Although *simulation* is a bit of a misnomer. Leveraging some Skyphos tech that powers the arena, we're able to create fully autonomous physical constructs of each and every class of nepher that's ever laid a cursed foot on God's green Earth. Closest thing you can get to the real thing without actually having to fight the real thing."

"That's freaking cool."

"Right up until one of the bastards hits you in the mouth," I grumbled. "Then it's not so cool."

Ignoring my commentary, Erin gazed in awe around the vast, white-stoned structure completely devoid of people. "And this place, it sure as hell looks like the Coliseum but something tells me we're not in Rome."

"No. No, we're not," Rooster replied. "Technically, we're somewhere on the far northern border of the Seventh Realm of Third Heaven."

When Erin had absolutely nothing to offer in response but a blank stare, Rooster added, "We call it the Dreghorn. It's where we train and occasionally drink ... excessively. It may not be in Rome, but it is a full-scale replica of the actual Coliseum. As it appeared in the—"

"Second century, I'm guessing," she said, studying the mind-blowing architecture.

Rooster smiled ear to ear. "I knew I liked her."

"Yeah, well," I grumbled, "Don't like her too much. I may get whiny."

Erin shrugged. "Whiny?"

"Yeah, never mind. Back to Nepher 101. You sure you're ready for this?"

"I spent three years in Bosnia, another fourteen fending off drunk Bostonians, and I'm now standing with my undead boyfriend in a fake Coliseum somewhere in Third Heaven. Not sure much else could surprise me at this point."

"Boyfriend? When did that happen?"

"Really?" she said, in a manner that made me instantly regret asking.

"Right," I muttered, making the mental note that regardless of the fact I could slay unnatural beasties without breaking a sweat, I evidently still lacked the ability to coherently converse with women. "Let's get started. But first, you'll need a weapon. Or several."

"Got that covered," Rooster said, unslinging the olive drab duffel bag from his shoulder and placing it on the ground.

"Thanks, but I'm good." Erin pulled back her black leather jacket to reveal a shoulder holster strapped over her rather delightfully tight, royal blue tee shirt. "Brought my own."

"Damn, Doc," I chuckled, eyeballing the apparent short-barreled .44 Magnum. "Does Dirty Harry know you stole his hand cannon?"

"Not sure," she shot back. "Does Darth Vader know you stole his cape?"

"It's a cloak."

Giving my combination of arcane black cloak, white RoosterBragh tee, faded Levi's, and scuffed up jungle boots a curious once over, she said, "You know you're like a pair of tights away from being a low budget comic book character, right?"

"Thanks for that. Now, if we can kindly move off the topic of my wardrobe and get back to—"

"Wardrobe?" She scoffed. "It looks like you raided Rambo's dirty laundry then mugged a Jedi knight." As Rooster heartily chuckled in the backdrop, she added, "And when's the last time you had a haircut?"

"What the hell's wrong with my hair?"

"And this would be him being whiny," Rooster said.

"Whiny," Erin nodded. "Got it."

"I'm gonna punch both of you," I muttered. "Really friggin hard."

Erin's face curled into a shit-eating grin. "Back to Nepher 101?"

"Please. First thing you need to do is get rid of that six-shooter. It's useless."

"Like hell. This thing will stop an elephant dead in its tracks."

"Maybe so. But we're not hunting elephants. You've entered a world where weapons of man won't do shit beside piss somebody or *something* off."

"Is that a fact?" she said, cocking the hammer and pointing the Magnum at me. "So, this bullet won't have any effect on you?"

I shook my head. "Nope. Go ahead. Try it."

As her mouth curled into a mischievous grin, she then proceeded to squeeze off a round and blast me square in the damn chest. And although the bullet slammed into the cloak and harmlessly disintegrated, the complete and utter shock factor of being shot at point blank range caused me to topple backwards and awkwardly fall on my ass.

Scampering back to my feet, I muttered, "See, told ya."

"Very, *very* impressive," she said.

And there was just something about the way she said it that made me feel like I'd just lost a gazillion cool points.

Typical.

8

"Gotta admit," Doc said, holstering her hand cannon, "I was a bit skeptical about you being bulletproof."

"Wait," I muttered, "You were?"

"Totally."

"And yet you still shot me?"

"I did."

And when she offered nothing further besides a content smirk, I shrugged. "Moving on then. Rooster?"

"Yeppers," he said, grinning ear to ear as he fished through his duffel bag. "Understanding that Erin seems to be more proficient with handguns versus rifles and figuring the need for concealment and stopping power was more of a priority than stand-off distance, I've put together the following ensemble."

"How exactly do you know that about me?" Erin asked.

"They have files," I replied. "Very — detailed — files."

"That's awkward."

"You have no idea."

"And the first offering," Rooster said, trying to move the conversation along, "is a pair of semi-automatic Heckler & Koch USP Compacts with twelve round magazines of .45 caliber, barzel-tipped rounds. I've also taken the liberty of decking them out with some snazzy tac lights."

"Barzel-tipped rounds?" Erin asked, as Rooster slammed home a magazine and handed her one of the pistolas.

"Barzel is the metal of Heaven," I said. "Created in the angelic forges and pretty much the only thing that makes a divine being say 'ow.' So please think twice before shooting me with one of these, eh?"

"Behave yourself, and we shouldn't have an issue," she replied, eagerly grabbing the sleek gat and balancing it in her hand. "It's got a good weight to it. I've never seen a tac light like that before, though. Looks like something out of an old *Star Trek* episode."

"That's a little something new I've been working on in my lab," Rooster boasted. "You'll find that anakim have a sensitivity to bright light, so this little puppy allows you to hit them with a focused ray of spectral radiation and temporarily blind the bastards. All in all, it emits a beam equivalent to roughly a million lumen per square foot."

I chuckled. "Is that a lot?"

"Ah, yeah. It's basically like staring at the sun — if it was an inch from your face."

"Does it friggin work?"

"Of course it works. I mean, it should. Initial test results were very favorable."

"Sweet," Erin said, as I made the mental note to not be standing anywhere in the general vicinity when she tried it out. "How do I turn it on?"

"The pistol grip acts as a pressure switch that's perfectly calibrated to your hand strength and contour. All you have to do is squeeze it a little tighter and voilà...Rooster Ray."

"Rooster Ray," I muttered. "Good grief."

"Excellent," Erin said, ignoring my snideness. "What else you got for me?"

Handing her the other H&K accompanied by a slick looking dual shoulder harness, he reached into his bag o' tricks like a little demented Rooster Claus on Christmas morning.

"Okay, so aside from fire power, you're gonna need some cutlery. Bullets will slow nephers down, but the only way to truly end them is to cut their heads off. Standard issue is a barzel sword, but I figured something like *this* would be more your style."

Pulling what looked like a serrated machete from a black sheath, he handed it to Doc with a shit-eating grin on his face.

"Oh, hell yeah," she said upon accepting the oversized steak knife and flicking it around like a seasoned zombie killer.

"That's disturbing on many levels, Doc," I muttered, taking a healthy step backward to avoid being eviscerated. "Where the hell'd you learn to do that?"

Giving me a 'shut the hell up' glare, she turned to Rooster. "Anything else?"

"One more," he said, more than pleased that his handiwork was being appreciated. "Check this out." He then proceeded to hand Erin a pistol belt laden with several small cylindrical containers held securely in Velcro pouches.

"Is that mace?" I asked.

"Kind of," he replied. "But much, much cooler."

"Here we go," I grumbled, figuring I'd just opened the door for a bloviation opportunity.

"By combining some fringe elements of epigenetics, molecular biology, and elemental alchemy, I created a nasty little anti-nepher serum that I concentrated and weaponized using a high velocity aerosol delivery system."

"Let me guess," I said, taking another step or two backward. "Rooster Spray?"

"Come on, man. That's weak. It's called Nepheralyzer."

"Because that's so much better."

"What does it do?" Erin asked, pulling one of the canisters from the belt.

"Well, as the name so cleverly implies, it temporarily paralyzes any and all type of nephilim on contact. At least that's the theory."

"And how exactly does it do that?" I asked, more than a bit skeptical. "In friggin layman's terms."

"Simply stated, it essentially alters their hybrid physiology for a solid couple minutes by ossifying muscular tissue and fusing it to their skeletal structure."

"More layman. Less terms."

"It turns muscle into bone," Erin muttered, thumping me on the back of the head.

"Holy shit."

"On that note," Rooster added, "I'm pretty sure the Nepheralyzer also results in complete loss of any and all bodily functions. Just spray the bastards in the face and let it work its magic."

"That's brilliant," Erin said. "Awesome!"

"Wow," I grumbled. "You really outdid yourself this time, buddy. Can't wait to see that one in action. Maybe we should give it a try. You up for a live field test?"

As his eyes flashed red for a second, I decided we should probably just get back to business and proceed with the next phase of Erin's indoctrination process.

But, for the record, the thought of watching Rooster projectile shite himself while trying his damnedest to chase me around the Dreghorn with his muscles fused together was really hard to pass up. Really, really hard.

"All right, now that you've turned Doc into the Charlie's Angels version of Chuck Norris with a side of Batman, let's start with the basics. Nephilim are nothing more than hybrid beings originating from the breeding of fallen angels and—"

"Yep, got it," Erin said. "Aside from the giants, most of the them appear perfectly human until they transform or '*neph out*' — blah, blah, yada, yada. Can we get to that part and forgo the rest of the history lesson?"

"I'm really liking her," Rooster said smiling.

"Don't encourage this behavior," I grumbled. "It's intolerable."

Erin cleared her throat. "Anytime now."

"All right. Let's skip the tell and get right to the show."

"About damn time," she said, taking off her leather jacket and donning the various and assorted implements of arcane combat.

"Get ready for an up close and personal introduction to a few of the more terrifying things that go bump in the night," Rooster said.

"Who should we bring out first?" I asked.

"Let's start with an anakim, a draugr, a lychaon, and a varangian."

"What was that?" Erin asked.

My mouth curled into a dark grin. "A giant, a pseudo vampire, a big-ass wolf guy, and a bear monster...thingy."

Right on cue, four daunting figures emerged from the shadows of the towering arena wall roughly a hundred yards to our immediate front.

Ominously grunting at us, they rolled their heads back on their shoulders while shooting us a series of glares that would make the average man piss himself.

"Oh, my," Erin said, taking note as our new friends charged at us with unnatural speed while morphing into a macabre variety of otherworldly beasties.

"Oh, friggin my," I confirmed, pulling my shotgun from its holster and willing the argent metal gauntlets into being around my hands.

"Which one is which?"

"It really doesn't matter, Doc. Just start shooting. And watch where you're pointing that Rooster mace."

"Nepheralyzer," Rooster corrected.

Whatever.

9

"So, that could have gone better," I grumbled, seated at my usual stool at the Quartermaster wearing a pair of sunglasses. With my eyesight nothing more than a blurry haze, I unsuccessfully groped for the frosty beer that I knew was somewhere on the bar in front of me.

"I totally had that situation under control," Erin chirped from the seat next to me, sliding the mug closer to my hands.

"Is that you, Doc? Sounds like you, but something about getting blasted in the face with 1.21 gigawatts of spectral radiation has my eyesight a bit on the dull side."

"Well, maybe next time you'll stay out of my line of fire. You're damn lucky I only hit you with the Rooster Ray and not a bullet."

Laying it on thick, I muttered, "Would you be so kind as to spare some change for a poor, blind, semi-divine super soldier?"

"Knock it off. Quit acting like such a puss. Could have been worse."

"I second that," Rooster said, hobbling past us with both hands on his ass and smelling exceptionally foul. "I'd much rather have been blinded than nepheralyzed."

"But on the bright side," I said, trying my damnedest to hold back a smirk, "that stuff really works, man. I mean, when Doc squirted that anakim in the face with the nepher mace, you were nowhere in the general vicinity and it still smoked you like a cheap cigar."

He groaned. "Yes. Yes, it did. I'm going to take a shower now. A long shower."

"I'm really sorry about that, John," Erin said, forcing an awkward smile.

"Not your fault," he replied, still wincing from the aftereffects of being inadvertently doused with his own arcane bio weapon. "It seems the Nepheralyzer serum has a slightly wider potency radius than I anticipated. Either that, or I over pressurized the canisters and the jet nozzles need calibrating."

"That must've hurt like hell," I said, reveling in the moment. "I, *unfortunately*, missed the whole show due to having my eyeballs fried by Doc's tac light, but it sounded pretty gruesome. One of these days you'll have to tell me how it felt to have every muscle in your body turn to bone as your bowels instantaneously blew out."

"I'm really hating you right now," he muttered.

"Will you shut up already?" Erin grunted, elbowing me in the ribs.

"Right," I snickered. "Go get a nice hot shower, buddy. I'd recommend extra soap."

"If you say another word to him, I swear I'll shoot you."

Still chuckling to myself, the aftereffects of the Rooster Ray wore off and my vision snapped back into full focus just in time to see my enigmatic ginger colleague flipping me off as he waddled through a door behind the bar.

"Back to the topic of the Dreghorn," Erin said, grabbing her beer and taking a healthy slug. "You didn't need to step in. I totally had that situation under control."

"In all seriousness, you did good, Doc. I always knew you could shoot, but where the hell did you learn to move like that?"

"A solid decade of spending my free time with the Boston P.D. S.W.A.T., not to mention a few fringe paramilitary organizations I visited here and there."

"Are you being serious?"

"Hell yeah, I'm being serious."

"Why in the hell did you do that?"

"Really? After bearing witness to the unholy freakshow in that church fourteen years ago, how could I not come to the conclusion that extreme self-defense skills were a bit of a priority in the event I ever ran into another cannibalistic hulk? I mean, it's not like I had you around anymore."

"Fair enough," I muttered. Her words cut like a knife, and my mind flashed back to the Bosnian village of Brezovo Polje where this whole shit-show started in that fateful church.

More importantly, I now realized I wasn't the only one who had entered a new phase of existence that night. In her own way, Erin had done the same damn thing. The real cosmic irony with this whole dealio was that as abruptly as our paths diverged fourteen years ago, they'd once again united. To what point or purpose was yet to be revealed.

Making the mental note that perhaps there was a bit of credibility to Mariel's whole destiny concept after all, I decided to move on before I started likening things to gefilte fish.

"Well, whoever you trained with did you justice. And you can still shoot with the best of them."

"Seriously, though, Dean, I didn't need your help. I can take care of myself quite well nowadays."

"Duly noted. I'd like to say it won't happen again, but since we're like officially dating and all—"

"I will seriously punch you in the face if you finish that sentence."

"Gotcha."

"So, you don't think I'm combat ready, do you?" she asked with a marked edge.

"Here's to hoping we never have to find out," I replied, clinking my mug against hers and taking a gulp.

"And if we do?"

"Let's just say I wouldn't mind having you and those pistolas watching my back. That is, of course, if you stay behind me ... and give me ample warning before using those light saber things."

"I believe you're referring to the Rooster Ray."

"I'm not calling it that. It's a stupid friggin name. But, speaking of the

Rooster, whenever he regains positive control of his sphincter, you need to get him to fit you out with some body armor. Nothing tacky though."

"Deal," she said, taking a sip of beer while gazing around the completely empty Quartermaster. "So, everyone is out hunting for Azazel and his cronies?"

"Yep."

"Are thousands of eighteen-foot, semi-clothed giant men with bad teeth seriously *that* difficult to track down?"

"You'd be surprised," I grumbled. "And unfortunately, anakim aren't the only beasties in Azazel's employ."

"Rooster told me a little bit about his army. He called it the Maradim."

"Not so much an army. More of a militant organization of miscreant nephilim. In addition to the rogue gothen he recruits as monster muscle, there's an entire global network of sleeper cells tactically situated in every aspect of society. Bankers, lawyers, industry leaders, political figures, etc."

"So, they just blend right into day-to-day life until they're activated?"

"Or they do something that catches our attention."

"And then what?"

"Then we pay their sorry ass a visit of the not so friendly persuasion."

"Sounds a lot like the Army."

"It does." I chuckled. "To be fair, I've only really been at this for a couple weeks. The concept of time doesn't exactly work the same between Earth and Heaven. And I sort of lost a decade and a half after getting my ass handed to me in Bosnia. Long story."

"Heard about that. You know you slept through two Red Sox World Series championships, right?"

"Yes." I grunted. "I'm fully aware. Really appreciate you mentioning it, though."

She chuckled. "Anyway, Rooster said he visited you every day for fourteen years while you were getting your mojo back."

"That's not creepy at all."

"I thought it was pretty sweet, actually."

"I'm going with creepy."

"You would."

Leaning over the bar and refilling our mugs, she said, "So, what's this I'm hearing about you going to see the archangels? Is that for real?"

"Yep."

"As in, *the* archangels? Michael, Gabriel, Raphael, and Uriel?"

"There's actually seven of them."

"Who are the other ones?"

"Remiel, Raguel, and Saraqael. But, as I understand it, they're sort of lackeys to the big four. Together, they make up the seraphic court."

"So, you're going to see them despite the fact that everybody thinks one of them is actually the traitor working with Azazel?"

"That's the plan."

"That doesn't sound like a very good plan."

"It's quite possibly the worst plan ever. But it's all we've got at the moment."

"When are you leaving?"

"Soon as Stephen comes back to fetch me — which I thought would've happened already, to be honest. What friggin time is it anyway?"

"A quarter to six."

"Shit. Twelve hours left to sort this shitshow out."

"Where did Stephen go?"

"To set up the meet-and-greet with Gabriel and the God Squad. Evidently showing up to Tenth Heaven unannounced is frowned upon in the Establishment. Although—"

The flutter of massive wings accompanied by the unsettling feeling we were no longer alone caused me to instantly stop talking. Spinning around on my stool, I was more than surprised to find three blonde, statuesque male modes donning a surreal assortment of glinting plated armor, white linen tunics, and ginormous He-Man swords staring back at me.

"Dean Robinson," said one of the life-size Masters of the Universe action figures, with a peculiar accent and distinct air of superiority.

"Hey, guys," I replied, taking particular note of their otherworldly blue eyes, chiseled faces, and pure white auras. "Nice outfits. If you're looking for Skeletor, he doesn't work here anymore."

"You are to come with us," said the mysterious angel, clearly not appreciating my sarcasm.

I rose to my feet. "And who the hell are you?"

"I am Remiel," he replied, clearly annoyed that I had the gall to ask. "These are my brothers Raguel and Saraqael."

"The lackeys," Erin whispered to me.

"That's awkward," I grumbled back.

"You are to come with us," the archangel repeated, ignoring our side-bar. "The seraphic court is assembled and awaiting your arrival."

As the sphincter triplets stood like mannequins boring holes through my skull with their piercing, cold gazes, I said, "Although I'm flattered by the VIP escort, I was expecting to make the trip with Stephen. So, I'll just wait for him."

"I thought I smelled yer foul stench," Big A barked, appearing unnoticed from behind our visitors. "What business do ye have here, Remiel?"

"The bidding of Gabriel. Which is no concern of yours, Abernethy."

"Forgive me if I'm more than keen to disagree," Big A grumbled, placing himself squarely between me and the trio of armored seraphs like he was about to throw down on their angel asses.

"I see time has done nothing to improve your temperament." Remiel said, with a distinct edge. "You remain the petulant templar of centuries past."

"Aye. And ye remain the same skelpit arse with a wee halo and a swalt heid."

"What did he say?" Erin asked me in a hushed tone, evidently not yet able to decipher Big A's brogue.

"Spitballing here," I whispered back, "But pretty sure he just called Remiel an asshole with a little dick and a fat head."

"That's amazing."

"Abernethy's got a real way with words."

"You'd be wise to mind your tongue, mortal," Remiel muttered. "Or perhaps our next encounter will not end on such pleasant terms."

The Scotsman roared in laughter. "And what makes ye think this wee visit's gonna end *pleasantly*?"

"*Because*, despite your acrimony, you are of no consequence to me. My brothers and I are here on Gabriel's orders to retrieve the Seventh of Seven."

"Here to collect Dean, are ye? To what point or purpose?"

"If I'm not mistaken, to address the small matter of a common enemy that threatens the very survival of the precious *humans* you've so diligently protected all these many centuries. Be that as it may, I personally find the entire situation rather amusing and unworthy of our intervention. Nonetheless, orders must be followed."

"Amusing," Big A scoffed. "Reveling in the suffering of mankind has always put a smile on yer face."

"*Mankind* is a putrid sewer of fallibility — unworthy in all regards of all the greatness bestowed upon *it*. Humans are nothing more than an insipid race of animals more than deserving of any and all affliction that befalls them."

"Aye, and I presume the *affliction* at the hand of a fallen Watcher that's been conveniently slipping through the fingers of the *mighty* archangels for a few millennia is just a wee coincidence, is it?"

"If you're insinuating that my brothers and I are responsible for Azazel and his continued blasphemy," Remiel said, with a dark grin, "you are entirely more deluded than I had originally believed."

"Then I'm sure you'll be keen to enlighten me as to how a daft scunner like Azazel has made a career out of wiping his arse with the covenants of Heaven."

"I would pose the same question to you."

"Would you now?" Big A scoffed. "Was it not yerself that imprisoned him for all eternity all those many years ago?"

"It was Raphael and I. Yes."

"Well, don't mind if I point out that you did a shit job then. Either that or you let him escape."

"While I will agree," Remiel fired back, "that Azazel's ability to shed his eternal bonds was undoubtedly orchestrated by a divine traitor, the more plausible suspect is that of mortal origins — like perhaps *you* and your league of cloaked *abominations*."

"Ah, excuse me, fellas," I said, butting into the conversation. "Pretty clear that you guys won't be exchanging Christmas cards anytime soon, but we're burning daylight here. How about we focus on the actual bad guys?"

"Aye," Big A muttered, evidently putting his detestation of Remiel aside for the moment. Without another word, he slowly backed away and stood next to me.

"So, Stephen's with the seraphic court?" I asked, looking squarely at Remiel and somewhat shocked nobody tried to run a sword through me or blast me with judgment fire.

"He is." His cold gaze turned from Abernethy to me.

"And you're going to take me there?"

"I have orders to retrieve you."

"Ok, then let's go, Remdawg. Ready when you are."

As Remiel raised a blonde eyebrow as if trying to figure out if I just insulted him or not, Big A grabbed my shoulder and pulled me aside. "Yer not going anywhere with this daft lot."

"Not sure we have a choice here, boss. The clock's ticking."

"Remiel cannot be bloody trusted. For all we know, he's the traitor and yer gonna get sacked before ye even get to Paradise City."

"Stephen trusts Gabriel, and these guys are acting on his direct orders. Angels have to follow orders, right?"

"Aye," he grumbled. "And they cannot lie. But that doesn't mean they're telling the bloody truth either."

"We stick to the plan. It's the only way."

Shaking his head in protest, he muttered, "You watch yer arse, Dean-nie. These are powerful beings. Nae to be trifled with."

"Weren't you just about to fight all three of them?"

"Aye, but I'm Scottish."

Not really sure what to say to that, I shrugged and locked gazes with Erin. "Promise me you'll stay at the Quartermaster until we sort this out."

"Promise," she said, looking more than a bit skeptical about the situation.

"Don't worry," I assured her. "I hear Tenth Heaven is nice this time of year. Walk in the park."

Willing the cloak into being, it instantly manifested on my shoulders in a spectral flash as I turned to the angel posse. "Are we doing this or what?"

"Follow me," Remiel said, as he and his strong, silent-type brosephs stepped through the otherworldly gateway that appeared behind them.

"I'll be back," I said, with my very best Schwarzenegger impression as I winked at Doc.

"Good grief," I heard her grumble as I stepped through the door and melted from sight.

Followed by a faint yet definitive, "Bloody hell."

10

THE NOTION of Heaven is undoubtedly the most appealing concept in mortal life. A utopian, metaphorical realm of bliss and transcendence where the good folks are rewarded with an eternity of peace. A literal paradise that's devoid of pain and bathed in light. Generally speaking, a perpetual happy place allowing for worthy souls to recognize the true meaning of consummate fulfillment.

Most folks think there's only one Heaven, but in all actuality, there are ten. Each unique. Each with a distinct purpose. Now, granted, while I was no stranger to the realms of Third Heaven, I couldn't help but feel that I hadn't seen the good stuff yet. And despite the warnings about what a shithole Paradise City was, I was more than a bit excited to see where the archangels let their wings down in Tenth Heaven.

I mean, seriously, how friggin bad could it be? If there are ten levels of Heaven, logically that would mean the tenth level is like the penthouse.

The penthouse is always good.

It's a universal constant. Like beer.

There is no bad beer.

There is just beer.

And beer is good.

At any rate, stepping out of the otherworldly portal as it snapped shut behind me, I eagerly surveyed my surroundings and was more than a bit disappointed. Typical.

A desolate, never-ending panorama of dark, sandy foothills covered in scrub brush and man-sized saguaro cactus stretched out in every direction as far as the eye could see. A blood-red sun peaked above the horizon, and a gentle, cool breeze swept steadily across the landscape.

I turned to find the celestial version of the three amigos cautiously surrounding me like shrewd predators sizing up their prey. "Is it just me or does Tenth Heaven look a lot like Arizona in the winter?"

As they formed a semicircle around me and commenced to bore holes through my skull with their piercing gazes, I muttered, "Ah, I get it. This isn't Tenth Heaven, is it? We're still on Earth. And you've evidently brought me to the desert to kill me. How terribly cliché of you."

In perfect unison, Raguel and Saraqael methodically drew their massive swords and took a collective step in my direction. Holding my ground, I willed the otherworldly shotgun into being and instantly felt the presence of the leather scabbard-like holster as it fluidly manifested on my back.

"Lower your blades, brothers," Remiel said to his cohorts, as a macabre pair of brass knuckles featuring sizable spikes formed on his fisted hands in a spectral flash. Glaring at me with a truly wicked grin, he added, "The pleasure of ending this petulant animal is mine."

"Petulant animal?" I protested, making the mental note that I really should've listened to Abernethy and passed up on this trip all together. "That's a bit harsh, eh?"

Without any further words, the not-so-dynamic duo lowered their Conan-quality broadswords and turned toward Remiel, somewhat confused.

"The Seventh of Seven possesses great power, Remiel," one of the two said, carrying on the conversation like I wasn't even there. "It will take our collective resolve to end him. We must heed the warning of the seraphic court. He is a threat not to be trivialized."

Remiel scoffed. "The seraphic court overestimates the abilities of this *Deacon*, Saraqael. He is no more of a threat to us than a speck of dust is to the sun. We are the Father's *true* chosen sons. His perceived *power* cannot harm us."

"Ah, you guys know I can hear you, right?" I grumbled, waving a hand at the triumvirate. "I'm right here, fellas."

"Then what do you intend for him, brother?" the last of the trio, whom I assumed to be Raguel, asked.

"Pain," Remiel replied. "Gabriel believes this *treasonous* filth is concealing the location of the Vessel. That knowledge is more than vital to our cause if we are to put an end to Azazel's blasphemy and secure the borders of Heaven."

"You plan to interrogate him," Saraqael said, seemingly very pleased by this turn of events.

Remiel nodded. "Before drawing his final breath, Dean Robinson will gladly reveal the information he harbors or suffer like none have suffered before him in all the many wretched days of mankind. Then, and only then, will I grant him the *mercy* of death."

Saraqael sheathed his sword. "You've always had a particular talent for such brutal acts of necessity."

"Indeed," added Raguel, grinning a dark grin. "Do you require our assistance, brother?"

"No. Both of you should return to Tenth Heaven at once. Gather the seraphic court. Advise them that our quarry has been detained. Tell them I will join you shortly with the information we so desperately require — with the head of the Seventh of Seven on the end of my blade."

"As you wish," the two replied in a creepy single voice, as they simply vanished from sight in a whooshing sound of massive, unseen wings.

If I had any previous doubt as to the absolute stone-cold nature of archangels, it was so totally gone after bearing witness to that more than absurd conversation. Ready to make Remiel eat every word he just uttered, I ripped the Winchester free of its holster, cocked the lever, and pointed both barrels straight at the pretty face of my apparent executioner.

"We have precious little time," he said, in a surprisingly civil tone as his demeanor instantly changed and his brass knuckles melted from existence. "I mean you no harm, Dean Robinson."

"Wait, what?"

Closing his eyes and bowing his head, he then proceeded to murmur a few words in Enochian. Completing the incantation, he simply waved a hand in the air, and a shimmering aura of translucent primal energy manifested and snapped into place around us, forming a sizable dome. "This veil will shield us," he said.

"Shield us from what?"

"My brothers. It will not be long before they realize I've betrayed them and return. This will hold them at bay long enough for you to flee."

"So, let me get this straight. After that speech you just gave the sphincter twins, I'm supposed to believe you're a good guy?"

"You have many enemies, Dean Robinson, but I am not one of them."

"Well, that's interesting," I said. "Because friends don't typically bring friends to the desert with the intent to cut their friggin heads off."

"That rhetoric was a mere charade. My intentions are just. You must believe me."

"Believe you? Seriously? You've already lied to me. Twice."

"Angels do not lie," he replied, humbly.

"At the Quartermaster, you told me that you were taking me to seraphic court to meet Stephen. And unless there's a portal to Tenth Heaven lurking in a tumbleweed somewhere around here, that was complete and utter bullshit."

"I told you that Stephen was with the seraphic court and my brothers and I were sent to retrieve you at the command of Gabriel. Both of which are true. You simply insinuated the rest."

"Right. So, when you said you were sent to retrieve me, I should have also insinuated that you were going to take me to the middle of nowhere and string me up for vulture chow."

"My actions were regrettable yet necessary. A means to an end," he said, scanning the area outside the protective veil like he was expecting someone to show up at any moment. "Please, we have precious little time remaining. There are dark forces at work. It is imperative you listen to me."

Making the mental note that perhaps Remiel might actually be on the level and *not* the world class asshat that he was previously making himself out to be, I said, "Explain that statement."

"Do you not see? The seraphic court sent my brothers and I to execute you."

"Yeah, I kind of gathered that. Why?"

"Because you are a traitor in league with Azazel and his Maradim. Just as Stephen is. The seraphic court has condemned you both upon Gabriel's express recommendation. You are an enemy of Heaven. Marked for eternal damnation in the Lake of Fire."

"Gabriel's condemned us?" I muttered, struggling to follow this more than unexpected plot twist. "I don't understand. That doesn't make any sense." I lowered my shotgun. "Stephen is no traitor."

"Nor are you. I am fully aware of that. Something is wrong. Terribly wrong."

"Then what the hell's going on? Is Gabriel the barkangel?"

"The what?" he asked, shooting me a curious look.

"The bad archangel," I grumbled, making the mental note that perhaps that nickname might actually suck. "The traitor."

"We are no longer alone." His face flashed with anxiety as he drew his sword. "Listen to me, Dean Robinson, you must safeguard the Vessel. Keep it hidden. It cannot be found by Azazel or the seraphic court. Nor anyone else for that matter."

"Wait, the what?"

"The Vessel. It is the key to unlocking the gates of Tartarus. Do you understand?"

"Ah, no? The Vessel? What Vessel?"

And it was right about then when things took yet another unexpected turn. One of the several ginormous saguaro cacti inside the perimeter of Remiel's protective veil swung open like a set of saloon doors, and out stepped some jackass in a weathered, raw hide trench coat complemented by a crumpled faux cowboy hat and really nice Oakleys.

"You are late," Remiel said with a sharp edge.

"Suck it," replied the mysterious spaghetti western commando.

Without so much as another word, the apocalyptic cowboy then proceeded to blast the archangel squarely in the chest with what looked like a sawed off M79 grenade launcher. Didn't see that coming.

As the round exploded in a brilliant flash of purple-white flame, poor ole Remdawg careened backward and slammed into the wall of his arcane dome before plopping on the desert floor in a limp, fiery heap.

"Holy flame incendiary grenades," the Wyatt Earp wannabe chuckled with a badly chewed cigar clenched tightly in his teeth. "It doesn't really hurt the douchebags. Just puts 'em out of commission for a couple minutes."

Throwing open his jacket, he then slid the hand cannon into a holster strapped to his leg with braided strips of leather. Taking a moment to admire his handiwork, he lowered his sunglasses and took a closer look at Remiel, who was clearly unconscious and blazing away like a crate of fireworks sprayed with purple napalm. Chuckling a little more, he said, "Been wanting to do that for five hundred years. Felt good."

In a blur of motion, I trained the business end of my shotgun on the newcomer. Although he had the appearance of your average dude in his late-thirties, the swirling aura of muted colors forming a harrowing silhouette around his large frame indicated something to the contrary. Although I couldn't tell what he actually was, he certainly wasn't human.

Quickly taking in his lurking six-foot-three frame of broad shoulders and hardened yet somewhat jovial face hidden well within a scraggly ginger biker beard, I barked, "Who the hell are you?"

"Name's MacCawill," he said, plucking the stogie from his mouth and dropping it to the ground. "Roy MacCawill."

"What the hell are you doing hiding in a cactus?"

"I wasn't hiding. I was hunting."

"Hunting what?"

"You, dipshit."

"How'd you know I'd be here?"

"My employer gave me specific instructions. Said I'd find you right here. Right now."

"Employer?"

"You can put that pea shooter down, big mancho. This is a rescue mission. I'm under contract to save your sorry ass."

"Save me? From him?" I pointed at Remiel. "He was trying to help me, you friggin moron."

"Not from him, ace," he said, gazing behind me. "From them."

As the cloak rippled anxiously about my shoulders, I spun around to find Saraquel, Raguel, and half a dozen other heavily armored seraphs shooting me dirty looks from just outside the dome. With wings spread and swords drawn, it was fairly apparent they had figured out they'd been duped and were back in town for some serious smiting. Not good.

"Oh, them," I muttered, facing my new friend. "But why the hell'd you shoot Remiel?"

He shrugged. "Because he's an asshole."

"Well, he was actually starting to grow on me before you went all *Terminator 2* on him."

"We need to go," he said, pushing his glasses back up on his nose as he stepped toward the cactus escape hatch. "This veil won't keep the halos out for much longer. This way."

"Don't think so, bud. Stepping through portals with strangers of questionable character and peculiar wardrobes is exactly how I got myself into this mess in the first place. Thanks, but I'll pass. See ya 'round. And, ah, nice jacket."

"It's a duster, slick."

"Whatever."

Waving a halfhearted goodbye to the obscure cattle rustler, I focused my will on the Quartermaster and took three bold steps.

Now typically, that little arcane maneuver will instantly transport me just about anywhere I want to go given that I can picture the location clearly in my mind. But, as I still found myself standing in the very same spot after trying it a couple times, I came to a rather unsettling realization. I would either have to bite the bullet and go with this MacCawill jackass or turn and face the onslaught of pissed off angels seconds away from smashing their way through the rapidly deteriorating protective veil.

"Your little trick didn't work, did it?" He snickered.

"No. Not so much."

"That's why they picked this place. It's cursed ground. Damn near impossible to port in and out of."

"And I assume since you got in, you can get out."

"Wouldn't be much of a rescue mission if I couldn't, now would it?"

"Fair point."

"You ready to follow me now, chieftain?"

"Do I have a choice?"

"Well," he replied, looking over my shoulder at the celestial lynch mob, "you could always stick around and try to make nice with the fly boys. Good luck with that."

"Let's friggin go then," I grumbled. "You try anything, I'll shoot your ass six ways to Sunday. We clear?"

"Sure thing, budro. Whatever you say."

"Keep your hands where I can see them. Who the hell knows what else you've got stashed in that Inspector Gadget coat."

"I already told you, douche wagon, it's a duster."

"It's ridiculous."

"That coming from the guy in the cape."

"Cloak."

"Whatever."

Reluctantly following Roy MacCawill and his smartass mouth through the same cacti that he entered stage left from a few minutes earlier, I looked back and casually flipped off the posse of winged dickheads just before we melted from sight.

Sometimes it's the little things that put a smile on my face.

11

It is often said that desperate times call for desperate measures. While I'm not sure what literary genius coined that particular sage adage, I had the distinct feeling that the scenario of following a complete stranger, dressed up like an extra from *Tombstone*, through a dimensional portal hidden in a cactus for the express purpose of escaping a collection of hostile celestial beings was not at the top of his mind when he wrote it.

Nonetheless, as with most great sayings, it applied rather nicely to my current set of circumstances. Being labeled as a heavenly traitor, and subsequently marked for death by the God Squad was not part of the plan.

Then, of course, there was the small matter of Stephen, who I could only assume was at the mercy of the real traitor by now, and destined to join the collection of enslaved Deacons in Azazel's clandestine prison.

The more I thought about it, the more likely it seemed that was exactly what the friggin barkangel was talking to Azazel about when I voyeured in on their little mountaintop fireside chat.

And if that was the case, aside from the alpha Deacon being out of commission, the barkangel now had everything he needed to ascend to Evil Über Deacon status. Which ultimately meant that in addition to man eating giants, the world was about to be introduced to a malevolent god in the near future.

Bad had not become worse. It skipped worse and went straight to 'holy friggin shit.' And I had the unequivocal feeling it was just the beginning of a maelstrom-quality downward spiral.

"You good, slick?" asked my new buddy, as we fluidly transitioned into a curious, dark space waiting for us on the other end of his cactus escape hatch.

Unfortunately, I couldn't see much of anything beyond a few feet in front of me because the only light in the mysterious location was being provided by a peculiar lamp shaped like a voluptuous woman's leg perched on a small table. Interestingly, the unmistakable stench of stale beer, cigars, and bacon lingered in the dank, heavy air.

"Dean," I grumbled.

"Come again?" He pulled off his Oakleys and stuffed them in his coat.

"Not slick, or big mancho, or chieftain, or ace, or budro, or douche wagon, or any other dumbass thing you feel like calling me. My name is Dean."

"I know your name, hondo. Be right back. Need to make sure none of your halo'd BFFs followed us. Don't go anywhere."

"Hold on a damn second," I protested as he simply took a step toward the light and vanished midstride. "Or just ignore me and evaporate into thin air. That's fine, too. Friggin jackass."

Although I had no idea who the hell this MacCawill character actually was or who he supposedly worked for, I was a bit grateful that he helped me give the archangels the momentary slip. That being said, it was high time to ditch his sorry ass and get the hell out of Dodge. Or wherever I was at the moment.

I needed to get back to the QM. Bringing the team up to speed on current events was more than critical. There was little doubt in my mind that they'd already heard the fantastic news about me and Stephen being elevated to Heaven's Most Wanted status by now. There was also little doubt in my mind they believed any bit of that bullshit story.

And although my epic mission to Paradise City to sniff out the barkangel turned out to be an epic misadventure to the Arizona desert to sniff some cacti, Remiel did give me an interesting piece of intelligence before catching MacCawill's grenade in the chest.

The Vessel. The Vessel was the key to opening the gates of Tartarus.

And more importantly, it seemed to be hidden.

Of course, there was the small matter that I had no earthly idea what in the hell *the Vessel* actually was, but that was more information than I had a few hours ago. Information I needed to get back to the team.

The Azazel apocalypse clock was rapidly ticking away and the situation was now a bit more complicated to put it ever so mildly.

To that end, I again focused my thoughts on the Quartermaster and took three bold steps. Fully expecting to instantly port myself out of MacCawill's hidey hole, I was more than disappointed when absolutely nothing happened. Trying it a few more times with the same result, I muttered, "Son of a bitch."

"Sorry, chiefy," MacCawill remarked, silently reappearing right in front of me. "That's not gonna work here either."

"Why the hell not?"

"This place has more wards than Chins in a Chinese phonebook. Aside from keeping me well off the radar, they also ensure nothing gets in and nothing gets out. So, chillax. You're safer here for the moment anyway."

"Look, bud," I muttered, casually holstering my shotgun as I willed the gauntlets into being and grinned as they covered my hands and forearms in unbreakable, ashen hellstone, "Appreciate your help in the desert, but there's some serious shit going down, and I need to leave. Now. So, you can either drop your wards and let me zip out of here like a gentleman, *or* I'm going to beat you like a trench-coated punching bag until that scraggly beard falls off your face."

"No, no, and yes." Clearly unimpressed by my not-so-veiled threat, he just stood there grinning.

"What the hell's that supposed to mean?"

"No, you're not leaving. No, I'm not dropping my wards. And yes, I'd be happy to whoop your cape-wearing ass and stick you in the corner if you give me anymore shit."

I grinned back. "I already told you. It's a friggin cloak."

And then I sunk all my weight into a devastating right hook that ripped through the air in a blur of motion and connected my stone-covered fist squarely with his jaw. As his head whipped around from the blunt impact, causing his stupid ass Stetson to sail into the darkness, I dropped a left cross straight into his midsection that instantly doubled him over in a state of wincing pain. Lowering an elbow into his back for good measure, the poor bastard plummeted to the floor with a groaning thud that echoed rather nicely throughout the room.

"I'm getting too old for this shit," he grunted, sprawled out at my feet like a sack of potatoes.

"Do I keep going or you ready to let me out of here, *ace*?"

Slowly pushing himself off the ground in an attempt to shake off the shellacking he just took, he muttered, "Fifteen minutes."

"Come again?"

"In fifteen minutes, I'm supposed to bring you to my employer."

"What, so he can try to kill me next?"

"No, dipshit. If he wanted you dead, he would have let the halos end your ass. He wants to talk to you. He has the information you need."

"And then what?"

"You're free to go on about your epic quest to save the world and shit."

"Who the hell is this guy?"

"Someone with the balls to stand against the archangels. Which, at the very least, makes him an enemy of your enemy. For the time being anyway."

"What's his friggin name?"

"Can't tell you that. Part of the deal. But rest assured, he's evidently looking out for your best interests."

"I can look after my own interests."

"Well, dumbass," he said, back on his feet and trying to snap his jawbone back into place, "seeing as you've been marked for death by the seraphic court, I'd disagree. You've got a price on your head big enough to buy a couple continents. Soon as you pop back on the grid, every big nasty between here and the damn outer realms of Hell will be on you like stink on shit. And that's if the halos don't find you first. Or worse. The chance to off a Deacon *and* get paid for it? Trust me, mancho, that's going bring some scary powerful sons of bitches — and their freaking moms — gunning for your ass. Believe it."

"How the hell do you know that?"

"Because I'm a bounty hunter, moron."

"A bounty hunter," I muttered, thinking I should probably start hitting him some more just because.

"Here's the deal, slick. My job was to get you out of that desert before you got halo-jacked. If by some small margin of luck I succeeded, my employer instructed me to bring you to him. That's it."

"And Remiel?"

"Don't ask me why, but he's working with us. As such, he gave up the exact location where they were taking you. That's how I knew where to tether that portal. Said I'd have a two-minute window for the extraction before his butt buddies came back and made things interesting."

"Remiel said something about a vessel before you decided to turn him into a purple flame ball. What do you know about that?"

"Nothing. In my line of work, it doesn't pay to ask a lot of questions."

"So, what's in this for you, bounty hunter?"

"Well, aside from my life-long aspiration of making Remiel look like a little bitch, there's also the small matter of a not-so-small fortune. So, there you go. Way I see it, you can keep punching me until you get tired, or we can have a beer then go see my boss so you can get some answers. And I can get paid. What's it gonna be, ace?"

Not entirely convinced that MacCawill was the most trustworthy of sorts, it seemed I didn't have much of a choice but to play along. If half of what he said was true, I couldn't risk going back to the Quartermaster.

Not yet.

I was on my own until I figured out what the hell was actually going on. And to do that, it seemed I needed to talk to MacCawill's mysterious employer.

"All right," I reluctantly grumbled.

"We good?"

"We're good."

"Almost." Nodding, he extending his hand to evidently seal our newly formed partnership of necessity.

And wouldn't you know that as soon as I grabbed his right hand and gave it a firm shake, that son of a bitch belted me in the face with a stiff left hook. Should've seen that coming. Typical.

As the force of the crushing blow literally lifted me off my feet and slammed me into the wall next to his creepy stripper lamp, I made the mental note that there was a bit more to Roy MacCawill than met the eye.

"Now we're good." A shit-eating grin curled across his face as he produced a fresh cigar from his coat. "Make yourself at home. My casa is your casa. Welcome to the Man Cave."

Spitting out a healthy wad of blood, I muttered, "Thanks, asshole."

Retrieving his cowboy hat from the floor, he yelled, "Hey, Zig, can we get some light in here please? And how about bringing our visitor a beer before he gets violent again."

"But of course, sir," a subservient male voice replied from the darkness with a detectable British accent. "A visitor? How exciting! We never have visitors!"

Staggering back to my feet while wondering who the hell said that, an antique brass lantern fastened to the wall on my immediate left flickered to life, and a warm, orange glow began to slowly overtake the darkness. As my eyes started to adjust, another lantern further down the wall followed suit. Then another. And another.

"Damn," I muttered, willing the cloak and gauntlets into retreat. "Went a bit literal on the whole man cave concept, eh?"

Although furnished rather poshly with exquisite leather furniture, I found myself standing in an obscure alcove within an actual cave. Stepping into the main cavern, I was somewhat stunned to realize that it didn't appear to be naturally formed. Instead, it was expertly hewn out of solid rock into a perfectly rectangular shape.

And judging by the fact that there were no visible entrances or exits, I also assumed it was carved from the inside out. Exactly how such a feat was possible remained a mystery.

"Yep," he chuckled. "It's ghetto fabulous. Chicks dig it. Well, I'm sure they would if I ever brought any chicks here."

"What is this place?"

"One of my safe houses." He strolled toward a stunning, dark wooden bar on the far wall. Biting the end off his cigar, he lit it with a wooden match and took a hefty puff.

Taking a curious glance around, I couldn't help but be impressed. It was roughly the size of a three-car garage with an arched ceiling looming a few feet above my head. The chiseled walls were inlaid with intricate carvings of sigils, glyphs, and Enochian script that literally ran from floor to ceiling throughout the entire cavity. The floor was a stunning pattern of alternating rich wooden panels of various sizes and shapes that inexplicably melded together perfectly.

To the right of the bar, which boasted five or so taps of what appeared to be delectable craft beer, was a collection of buzzing computers and gaming consoles complemented by a flickering arrangement of huge flat panel screens forming a cockpit around an oversized leather bean bag. Rounding out the obscure dwelling was a gun rack displaying enough firepower to conduct a frontal assault on the gates of Hell.

"Not bad," I muttered. "Is this cave some kind of a shadow realm?"

"Hell no. Shadow realms draw too much attention from the halos. This place is on Earth. A solid three hundred feet underground."

"Under what ground?"

"Off the coast of Nova Scotia. Ever heard of Oak Island?"

"No."

"Never mind then."

And before I was able to delve further into the topic, a peculiar whirring and clicking sound caught my attention. Turning to my left, I was more than a bit surprised to see a metal beer keg with robotic arms and a seventies vintage TV set for a head speeding toward me on miniature tank treads.

Pulling to a gradual, and rather squeaky, halt before running over my foot, the kegbot proceeded to methodically raise its metallic arm and hand me a chilled mug of beer.

"Here you are, Deacon Robinson," it said, as a pair of digital eyes and a mouth appeared on the TV. "Welcome to our humble abode. Cheers!"

"Ah, thanks," I replied, carefully accepting the beverage.

"You're quite welcome, sir! May your taste buds be tantalized by the first batch of the Great Creator's latest brewing triumph — the Triple Bastard."

"Triple Bastard?" I chuckled.

"That's correct, sir," the almost laughable mechanized man servant responded. "It's a perfectly balanced Belgian style triple ale inspired by the Great Creator's heroic efforts in Brussels some three centuries ago. Yielding a delightfully sweet flavor of chocolate malt, the Triple Bastard will dazzle your palate with a full-bodied, hoppy taste accompanied by an intense fruity aroma of bananas. I do hope you enjoy it. I certainly would, but unfortunately, I have no taste buds, you see. How terribly unfortunate. Perhaps one day the Great Creator will see fit to grace me with some. Oh, to dream."

If a robot could sigh, it sure as shit did before quickly pivoting and rolling, at breakneck speed, toward the gun rack as I turned to MacCawill. "You have a brew bot."

"That's Ziggy," he said, pouring himself a beer from one of the taps. "He runs the joint. And it's a long story."

"He calls you the Great Creator?"

"I created him. What else would he call me?"

"Dickhead. Moron. Douche wagon. Asshat. Dumbass. Smart ass. Did I say dickhead already?"

Saying nothing, he blew a rather impressive smoke ring at me.

Pulling up a stool next to him at the bar, I said, "So, what now?"

Raising his mug, he proceeded to drain his beer in one gulp. "We've got a couple minutes to kill, which means I'm having another beer. Or ten. Tangling with archangels makes me thirsty."

"That's the first smart thing you've said since I met you." Taking a healthy pull of the Triple Bastard, I almost had an out of body experience as the frothy, amber goodness slid down my throat.

"Son of a bitch," I said, quickly taking another gulp. "You may be a dickhead, but you make one hell of a good beer. This stuff would give RoosterBragh a run for its money."

"RoosterBragh?" he scoffed. "Is that what O'Dargan is calling his piss water nowadays?"

"You know Rooster?"

"Yeah, I know him."

And seeming as that was all he had to offer on the topic, I figured it was best left alone. He didn't appear to be a Rooster fan. Interesting. "So, this employer of yours, where are we meeting him?"

"Atlanta."

"Why Atlanta?"

"He likes Georgia. I don't get it."

"Pardon the interruption, sir," said Ziggy the kegbot as he zipped toward MacCawill holding what looked like a severed human hand. "I believe you've broken your hand... again."

"Really? I didn't notice," MacCawill muttered, holding up his left arm to find his hand all but limp with a visible array of broken fingers. "Sure as shit did. Good catch, Zig."

"But of course, sir. I believe it happened when you ever so gracefully sucker punched our guest earlier. I've taken the liberty to fetch you a replacement from the morgue. Please be careful with this one, as our supplies are becoming disturbingly scant. Perhaps if you'd refrain from hitting people with such great frequency?"

Glaring at the brewbot, he snatched the gruesome 'spare' body part and tossed it on the bar. "I didn't sucker punch anybody."

"Of course you didn't, sir."

"And if I did, it's because he had it coming."

"Right you are, sir. He certainly did. I only regret that the Great Creator did not sucker punch Deacon Robinson harder. Or several more times for that matter."

Rolling behind the bar, I heard Ziggy mumble, "Always hitting and shooting people. It's no wonder we never have any guests..."

As MacCawill grunted something of a snide nature under his breath, I said, "Did he say morgue? Why the hell do you guys have a morgue? And is that a hand? Like, a real hand?"

Completely ignoring my question, MacCawill then proceeded to take off his rawhide duster and rip the left sleeve off the black, long sleeve Beastie Boys tee shirt he was wearing underneath. And unfortunately, what I saw next caused me to jump up from my stool and take a step or two backward.

Although his left arm looked and moved just like a rather muscular, normal arm, it was not an arm. Or maybe it was? But instead of flesh, it was made of metal.

A shiny, argent metal with no visible joints or seams like you'd expect on something of a mechanical nature. To say it was creepy as all hell does not begin to do it justice.

Making the mental note that I now understood why his left hook had the force of a freight train behind it, I said, "Ah, MacCawill, what the frig is that?"

He lightly tapped his shiny forearm in a couple places until his broken hand literally popped free at the wrist and plopped on the wooden floor with a horrid thud. "Haven't you ever seen a barzel-infused biological limb before?"

"No, Roy. I haven't."

"Clearly you've never been to the realms of Fourth Heaven. Smelting accidents are pretty commonplace in the angelic forges."

Carefully holding the replacement hand to his shiny stump of a forearm, he muttered something under his breath in Enochian, and it attached itself like an arcane magnet. Instantly becoming animated, MacCawill clenched it into a fist and wiggled his fingers a bit to make sure everything worked the way it was supposed to.

"Good as new. I'm gonna miss the other one, though. This one's a little smaller. Whatever. It'll work."

"Do I even want to know what the hell just happened there?"

"That depends. You know anything about necromancy?

"Ah, no."

"What about cadaveric allografts?"

"No."

"Then probably not," he said, putting his duster back on and producing a fresh cigar. "It's time to get this party started. We need to make a quick stop before heading to the rendezvous point. You ready to blow this pop stand?"

"Emphatically."

"Hey, Zig," he called out. "We're leaving. No crazy parties. And quit trolling those seedy internet dating sites. You do know that all those lingerie models you're chatting up are really fat guys with man tits sitting around in their tighty-whities eating microwave nachos, right? Goddamn disgusting."

"I was not aware of that, sir. Rest assured that I will take greater care in the management of my online social interactions. Perhaps if the Great Creator would devote his superior intellect to building me an autonomous cybernetic companion in lieu of making, and subsequently consuming, copious amounts of beer, I would not be relegated to conversing with overweight humans with poor hygiene habits."

"Whatever."

"Yes, of course, sir," the brewbot muttered in defeat as he spun around to face me. “Farewell, Deacon Robinson. It was an absolute pleasure to meet you. Please do visit us again!”

“Thanks, Ziggy. Keep it real. Or cybernetic. Or whatever?”

Yep. That was super awkward.

Chalking up yet another strange and unusual experience that I sincerely hoped to ne’er repeat in all the remaining days of my supernatural existence, I followed the more than peculiar character that was Roy MacCawill through the interdimensional portal that manifested adjacent the bar. It was time to get some answers.

Or at least that’s what the plan was. And we all know how well my plans were panning out as of late.

12

"We won't be here long," MacCawill grumbled, as we emerged from the otherworldly gateway into yet another one of his peculiar abodes. "Don't touch any of my shit."

"This another safe house?" I asked, taking in the eclectic collection of handcrafted wicker furniture and old-world artifacts carefully placed throughout an intricate array of ornate shelving that lined the walls of the odd, oblong structure.

Lit only by the morning sun peeking through the curtains on the small windows, it looked suspiciously like an outdated mobile home that Roy's great, great grammy left him in her will.

"More of a cache site. Been stashing goodies here for the better part of sixty years."

"That would explain why it looks like an antique thrift shop stuffed into the back of an RV."

"Blasphemy," he scoffed, opening a large armoire on the far end of the dwelling. "RVs are for pussies. *This* is an Airstream, slick. A 1936 Clipper to be precise. One of only four hundred of these babies ever made. Picked it up after World War II."

Making the mental note that MacCawill was a few years older than he looked, I muttered, "Airstream, eh? Pretty sure that still makes it an RV."

"Is a Lamborghini a freaking *car*? Is a Rolex a freaking *watch*? Is the *USS* freaking *Enterprise* just a goddamned *spaceship*?"

"Yes."

"No. No, mancho. They're not. They're engineering marvels of precision artistry. So, trust me when I tell you that an Airstream is by no goddamn stretch of the imagination *just* an RV."

Adding 'motorhome snob' to the growing list of MacCawill's eccentricities, I pulled back one of the off-white farmhouse curtains to take a peek outside. And wouldn't you know, we were surrounded by several rows of similar sausage-shaped, aluminum vehicles parked under carports that were artfully woven into a thickly wooded campsite.

"And the fact your Winnebago is sitting squarely in the middle of an RV park?"

"Airstream park," he corrected, still buried in the oversized cabinet. "A very private, highly exclusive *Airstream* park.

"And they let your sorry ass in here?"

"I own the place, douche wagon. And should you refer to the Clipper as a Winnebago again, I will hurt you."

"Relax, Cousin Eddie. Why did we come here?"

"For this," he said, producing an obscure piece of jewelry from the drawer he was diligently rooting through. Tossing it to me, he added, "My employer was adamant that you have it. Put it around your neck."

Snatching it from the air, my hand jerked backward as a powerful surge of unnatural energy pulsed through my entire body like a jolt of electricity.

Although the mysterious object seemed nothing more than a large, tarnished locket of some sort, as I rubbed the dust away with my finger, I found myself mesmerized by what lay beneath.

It was an amulet. An exquisite, almost too-perfect-for-words, amulet. Set flawlessly within a circle of expertly forged metal interwoven with overlapping patterns of Enochian glyphs, a brilliant bluish-white gemstone radiated an ethereal, spectral glow from its center. Inexplicably, it seemed to oscillate in and out of existence as I intently stared at it.

"Better if you don't look at that thing too long," MacCawill said, chuckling at my reaction to the befuddling object. "Trust me on that one, ace."

"What the hell is it?"

"The Talisman of Armaros. Picked it up on a job a few years ago."

"Armaros, eh?"

"He was a Dominion class angel that went rogue. As the story goes, he had an especially gifted knack for enchantments and bullshit like that. Made this nifty blingage to shield himself from the all-seeing-eye of the Heavens after he told the God Squad to suck it and defected to Earth."

"How'd you get a hold of it?"

"Long story. But the short version is that after a few centuries, the halos finally got tired of looking for him and put a bounty on his head. Rather chunky one as I recall."

"And you found him?"

"Of course I found him, slick. It's what I do. Tracked that sorry son of a bitch to a high rolling strip club in Montreal. New Year's Eve. 1983. Let's just say that little lap dance didn't have the happy ending he was expecting that night."

"What'd you do?"

"Dropped a Holy Flame hand grenade down his banana hammock. Poor bastard squealed like a pig for a solid twenty minutes. Served him right."

"I don't even know what to say to that, Roy."

"Anyway, after bagging and tagging his ass, I snagged the talisman. Told the halos it was destroyed in the skirmish. Figured it would come in handy one day."

"And why the hell don't you use it?"

"Come on, ace. I don't need some pimped out hood ornament to hide from the Heavens."

"Right," I muttered, again wondering just who the hell Roy MacCawill was.

"You, on the other hand, are a different story, chiefy. The fact you've been touched by the left hand of the great God himself makes you stick out like a blazing beacon on a pitch-black night. The wards on the trailer are keeping you veiled for the moment, but as soon as you walk out of here, you're going to bring a shit pot of unwanted attention our way. And then our little clandestine road trip becomes a hell of a lot more interesting."

"And this thing will keep me off the supernatural radar."

"Yep."

"How does it work?"

"Just hang it around your neck."

"That's it? There's no dumbass chant to recite or anything?"

"That's right, almost forgot about the prayer." He lowered his head and clasped his hands together. "Oh, great and powerful blingful trinket of Armaros the Dickless, I beckon thee to hide this jackass Deacon from all the many legions of unnatural sons of bitches trying to kill his really dumb, cape-wearing ass. Amen. Okay, that should do it."

"Do I need to start punching you again?"

"Whatever. Put your freaking necklace on and let's get moving."

"Fine," I grumbled, hanging the amulet around my neck and tucking it safely under my tee shirt. "What's next?"

"I deliver you to my employer. Then I get paid. Then I spend the better part of the next month making bad decisions with women of questionable morality that appreciate the value of disposable cash."

"Thanks for a mental picture I'll never erase from my memory banks."

"My pleasure."

"How do we get to the rendezvous point?"

"I set up a portal nearby. It'll take us straight there. Easy peasy."

"Where?"

"There's a public shower in the middle of the campsite. Couple hundred meters from here. Portal's in the third shitter from the right."

"You tethered a dimensional gateway to a shitter in a friggin trailer park," I grumbled. "Awesome."

"Relax, mancho. It's not like anybody's in there snapping a yambo."

"Doing what?"

"You know, honking out a dirt snake. Forcing the duck to quack. Filling the pond with brown trout. Dropping wolf bait. Crimping off a length. Baking a hot icicle. Making some trouser chili. Pinching the chimp. Burying the elf."

"Are you talking about taking a shit?"

"What the hell else would I be talking about?"

When it was pretty clear I had absolutely nothing to offer in response to his barrage of ass innuendo, MacCawill said, "This place closed down for the winter two months ago. There's not another soul for a solid ten-mile radius. A short walk in the park, and we'll be out of here before you can say 'shitter's full.' Now, let's go. I'm never late."

"If you say so." I willed the cloak into being as it manifested in a spectral flash and billowed about my shoulders. Calling for the spatha, I instantly felt the presence of the scabbard on my back.

"Quit acting so damn jumpy, slick. I've taken great precaution over the years to ensure this little cache site is well-hidden from any and all otherworldly voyeurs," he said, opening the door to the peculiar abode and stepping into the chill morning air. "Staying off the grid is one of my specialties."

Leaving the shelter of the highfalutin recreation vehicle behind, I stepped outside and got my first good look at the densely-wooded campsite. And damn, it was pretty sweet.

Dominated by an impressive collection of majestic hardwood trees, it sat on a ridgeline overlooking a plush valley of evergreens. Countless Airstream trailers, secured for winter storage, were tucked neatly in small clearings connected by a series of well-worn trails. And in the center of Roy's Red Neck Trailer Park Emporium sat a large log cabin, where I assumed the aforementioned interdimensional shitter resided.

"You own this whole place, eh?"

Casually strolling toward the cabin, he pulled a fresh cigar from his coat. "Yeah, I bought the land about a hundred and twenty years ago."

Studying the rolling mountain range in the distance, I asked, "Where exactly are we?"

"Smoky Mountains. East of Johnson City, Tennessee. Passed through here with the Union Army. Burnside marched us for twenty-five straight hours all the way down this ridgeline to beat the Confederates to Campbell Station. Pissed rain on us the entire way. Pure misery."

"Ambrose Burnside? The Civil War general?"

"Yeah, long story. At any rate, I came back thirty years later. Bought this plot and the couple hundred acres surrounding it. The whole damn area was nothing more than a meadow back then. Planted this entire forest myself."

"Why?"

"I like trees."

"No, jackass. Why did you buy the land? What's so special about it?"

Lighting his cigar with a match, he matter-of-factly said, "Needed a spot to set up my moonshining operation during Prohibition."

Not really sure how to respond, I just grunted.

"And, of course, there's the small fact that I realized this piece of ground sits in a supernatural rift. Only one I've ever found in all of North America."

"What exactly does that mean?"

"It means it's hidden in plain sight. Veiled from the Heavens and any other type of Being armed with the Sight. The perfect spot to lie low for a guy in my line of work."

"And then you turned it into a trailer park?"

"Why wouldn't I? It's the perfect cover. To anyone concerned, it's just another *Airstream* park sitting squarely in the middle of nowhere. Humans come and go and nobody's the wiser."

"You have any security measures in place?"

"No need for it," he muttered, as we pulled up to within a few feet of the log cabin. "There'll be a goddamned Pizza Hut on the freaking moon before anybody finds me here. Trust me, ace. I know what the hell I'm doing."

And no sooner did he complete that very statement did an athletically built, thirty-something dude saunter from the shadows of a large oak tree to our immediate right.

Although not incredibly tall, he had the frame of an NFL linebacker marked by powerful shoulders angled into a thick, chiseled neck and blocky head. Wearing designer skinny jeans, peculiar leather booties that went up to his knees, and a ridiculous fur coat like you'd expect on a Viking, the curious stranger had a more than satisfying smile plastered across his rugged face.

Surprisingly, the aura radiating from his stocky silhouette was even more bizarre than his wardrobe. It basically looked like an ethereal, raging dust storm of dark energy that perpetually enveloped itself.

"Still smoking those cheap cigars," the suave newcomer said with smooth bravado as he casually removed his wayfarer sunglasses and propped them on top of his expertly manicured mane of thick, jet black hair. "How are ya, buddy?"

"So, on the moon," I said to MacCawill, "is it fair to assume that a large pepperoni will come with a side of oxygen? Or do you think that'll cost extra?"

"Kruger," he muttered at the newcomer, ignoring my snide commentary. "You look well."

"You seem surprised."

"You should be dead."

"And why would you think that?"

"Because I killed you."

"Apparently not."

"I'll be sure and try harder next time."

"That a boy!"

"What do you want?"

"What do I want?" He chuckled, taking a bold step in our direction. "Come on, buddy. Did you really think you could cash in on the bounty of a millennium without me? We're partners, remember?"

"We *were* partners. Until you double crossed me. And cut my arm off. And left me for dead."

"Did not."

"Did so."

"Lies, slander, and denigration. Erroneous on all counts."

"Cut the shit, Cyrus. What the hell do you want?"

"The Deacon, Roy. I want the Deacon."

"You can't have him."

"Let's agree to disagree, buddy."

Then, with a dismissive flick of his hand, the smooth-talking stranger lifted MacCawill off his feet with an unseen force and launched him backward at breakneck speed.

Covering a couple hundred feet in the blink of an eye, my trench-coated pal uncontrollably slammed broadside into his prized Airstream, creating a rather impressive, gaping hole in the aluminum carcass. Without slowing down in the least, he then hurtled like a six-foot-three projectile into the darkness of the forest until he faded from sight.

Rather pleased with his handiwork, MacCawill's estranged partner smiled at me. "Roy and I are old friends. Go way back."

"You just launched him into a friggin motor home."

"It's a complicated relationship."

"Who the hell are you?"

"I'm Cyrus Kruger," he said, like I should know already.

"Cyrus Kruger?" I chuckled. "Seriously?"

"So, you've heard of me."

"Nope. Just think that name's a little too cute to be real. Got a suspiciously premeditated 'mid-level henchman with delusions of grandeur' ring to it. You look more like a George. Or a Ralph. Maybe a Hank."

"That's funny," he said, nodding his approval. "I heard you were funny."

"So, you know who I am."

"I do," he replied, with a wolfish grin. "*Captain* Dean Robinson. Soldier. Deacon. Mutinous conspirator. Heavenly outlaw. Fugitive on the run from the seraphic court."

"You're another bounty hunter, I take it."

"More of a mercenary, actually. Unlike Roy, I'm not as selective with regard to my clientele. I tend to gravitate toward those with the biggest pocketbooks."

"Like the God Squad."

"Not that I'm a big fan of the halos, but unfortunately for you, my friend, they've put a bounty of unmatched proportion on your head."

"I bet you say that to all the fellas."

"That's great." He chuckled. "You really are a funny bastard."

"Right," I muttered, thinking Kruger was definitely a few sammiches shy of a picnic.

"So, don't suppose you're going to let me take you to Tenth Heaven without pitching a fit, will you?"

"I wouldn't let you take me anywhere, pal. You're not my type. That leggings and fuzzy coat combination is a little too BeeGees with a twist of Liberace for my taste."

Getting a real kick out of that one, he stood there laughing for an awkward couple seconds. "Okay, seriously, last chance, Deano. You sure I can't talk you into surrendering? Make things a lot easier all around."

"Pretty sure, Hank."

"Figured as much. Well, good talk. Genuinely enjoyed it."

"Is this the part where we start fighting?"

"No." He snickered. "This is the part where I shoot you with Holy Flame and then cart your comatose'd corpus to Gabriel. I usually tell people it doesn't hurt, but that's total bullshit. It hurts like hell. Oh, and just so you know, it's nothing personal."

And then the rotten bastard pulled an old-fashioned flint lock pistol from his stupid-ass coat and blasted me in the chest with a fiery purple orb. As the Holy Flame musket ball slammed into the cloak and promptly fizzled out like a firecracker tossed into a pool of water, a dark smile curled across my face.

"Bummer," he said, as his happy-go-lucky façade faded.

I shrugged. "That didn't work out the way you planned it, eh?"

"No. Not at all."

"Sorry to disappoint," I said, closing the distance between us and willing the gauntlets into being. As they manifested in the form of unbreakable, ashen hellstone, I clenched my hands into tight fists. "Is it my turn now?"

And as that was really more of a rhetorical question, I focused all my supernatural strength and punched that smug son of a bitch right in the mouth.

Although I was fully expecting to knock him into next week with the crushing force of the blow, I was more than a bit surprised when my stone-covered hand plowed a hole straight through his face and his head subsequently exploded in a violent poof of reddish-brown dust.

And before I knew what the hell was happening, the rest of his body instantly turned to the same earthy material and simply crumbled to the forest floor in a macabre pile.

Hearing something behind me, I turned to find MacCawill stomping his way through the campsite.

"You okay?" I asked.

"Where is he?"

Willing the gauntlets into retreat, I pointed at the dust pile. "If I had to guess, knock knock knocking on Heaven's door."

"Shit," he grumbled, unholstering his grenade launcher. Cracking open the breech, he loaded a fresh round and scanned the forest anxiously.

"What are you looking for?"

"Kruger, you idiot."

"He's gone, Roy. We chatted. He shot me. I punched him. He turned into a pile of dirt. I think he's dead."

"Don't give yourself that much credit, slick." MacCawill grunted, carefully maneuvering toward the log cabin while pulling a bullwhip that would make Indiana Jones proud from somewhere in the bowels of his rawhide trench coat. "He's not dead."

"Ah, he's a pile of dirt."

"Trust me. That wasn't him. It was a golem. Kruger's still here."

"What the hell are you talking about?"

"He's an adamite — a terramorph."

"A what?"

"A terramorph. A class of nephilim that can perpetually regenerate the physical construct of their body from organic matter. Especially dirt. They can also create golems — identical clones of themselves that share a hive mind."

"So?"

"So? We're in the middle of the freaking woods, genius. Surrounded by nothing but miles and miles of organic matter."

"Come on, man." I scoffed. "As you saying that jackass can turn himself into an army of dirt twins? Bullshit."

"I'll admit, whipping up an entire army might be a stretch," Kruger said, emerging from the front door of the log cabin wearing the same absurd outfit. "But a *legion*, on the other hand, I can do that with my eyes closed. Let's dance, bitches."

Raising both his hands high in the air, the forest floor instantly erupted into a swirling landscape of unnatural, man-sized funnel clouds that voraciously pulled the surrounding dirt, shrubbery, and anything else in the near vicinity into whirring columns. And before I knew what the hell was happening, the endless sea of mini-tornados produced an endless horde of pissed off Krugers. And they were all smiling at me. Wickedly.

"Fuck," MacCawill grumbled. "Now you've done it."

"Me? He's your goddamn friend."

"It's a complicated relationship."

"If we survive this, I'm so gonna bury you with an elf."

"Whatever."

13

Admittedly, my career choices have put me in some rather precarious situations over the years. Case in point, during my mortal existence I chose the path of a soldier — a U.S. Army Ranger. As such, exchanging bullets with professional bad guys was fairly common practice. It was part of the job. An occupational hazard. Came with the territory. Hell, throughout the course of my ten years in uniform, I'd cheated death more times than should've been possible for a human being. That's just how it was.

Okay.

Fine.

And then, when death finally caught up with me, I put on the cloak and came to the arcane realization there was a whole new level of bad guy out there. Lurking just beyond the mortal veil were disgruntled fallen angels, 'roided-out giants, heavenly half-bred beasties, blah blah, yada, yada, and so on and so forth.

Yep.

Got it.

But let's get real for a quick second. To find myself literally surrounded by an otherworldly mercenary that possessed the ability to spontaneously create his own goddamned clone army out of friggin dirt? Come on. That's some serious bullshit.

You know I'm right.

At any rate, as MacCawill and I stood shoulder to shoulder amidst the unnatural mob of Kruger lookalikes, I couldn't help but think that I should've been a dentist. Or an IT guy. Or a misunderstood novelist. Damn the bad luck.

As the cloak rippled anxiously about my shoulders, indicating some serious shit was about to go down, I willed the shotgun into being and instantly felt the presence of the scabbard-like holster on my back. Calling for the gauntlets, they manifested in a spectral flash and perfectly encased my fisted hands and forearms in argent metal. Game on.

"Stand down, Cyrus!" MacCawill yelled, pointing his grenade launcher into the hostile crowd poised to pounce on us with bad intentions. "Robinson's coming with me. And that's that."

Evidently the Krugers thought that to be rather humorous because the entire forest erupted into hearty laughter.

"You never were much of a diplomat," replied the Kruger clone standing to our immediate front.

"But I'll tell you what," said another one on our left. "Since we're pals, I'll cut you a deal. You help me bag and tag the Deacon, and we'll split the bounty. Just like the good ole days. Whaddaya say?"

MacCawill shook his head. "Look, dipshit, there's more at stake here than a goddamn paycheck. You don't understand what's going on."

As the Kruger mob began to close in, yet another one said, "Nor do I care. And neither should you. It's business. I told you a long time ago that your conscience would be the end of you."

"It probably will. But not today."

"Come on, Roy. It's *two* of you against *five hundred* of me. You can't possibly think you're walking away from this."

"He's right," I piped in, ripping the semi-divine Winchester free of its sheath. "We can't fight five hundred of them. Him. Whatever." Then I pointed the shotgun at the nearest Kruger and blew a sizzling hole through his chest. "But four hundred and ninety-nine seems manageable."

"We finally agree on something," MacCawill muttered, as he followed suit and unloaded the holy grenade launcher of Antioch into a gaggle of Krugers, while simultaneously reducing another one to dust with a mighty lash of his bull whip.

Momentarily dumbfounded by the brazen maneuver, the doppelgänger brigade took a collective step backward in apparent confusion. Unfortunately, that only lasted for a second or two before they got really pissed.

And, much to my chagrin, the situation deteriorated pretty quickly from that point forward. Typical.

In a violent display of brute force and ignorance, the Krugers then descended on us like a Mongolian horde in fur coats and skinny jeans. As the unnatural band of miscreant mercenaries slammed into us like a tidal wave, we were instantly blown backward and clear across the campsite.

Amidst the chaos, the shotgun flew from my hand as a blinding barrage of clenched fists relentlessly pummeled my face and torso. Making the mental note that things weren't exactly going to plan, I instantly realized what it felt like to be a punching bag.

And for the record, it was not pleasant.

In a rather feeble attempt to beat back the perpetual onslaught, I managed to land a couple Ivan Drago-quality haymakers just before being completely overrun by the rabid mob of assailants literally launching themselves at us from all angles. Unable to stand my ground any longer, I lost my footing and toppled into MacCawill.

And judging from the cacophony of grunts, yelps, and winces emanating from my apocalyptic cowboy partner, it was fairly apparent he wasn't doing much better than I was.

"You okay?"

"I'm getting tea-bagged by three Krugers, so pretty fucking not okay," he grunted, as we collapsed under the crushing weight of the dogpile and slunk to the ground in a rather pathetic, two-man heap. "If you plan on doing some Deacon shit, now would be a swell time."

"Yeah, I got this," I muttered, thinking he was probably right and it was high time to quit acting like a cloaked piñata. "Standby."

Momentarily ignoring our absurd set of circumstances, I slowly pulled in a long, deliberate breath.

Cleared my mind.

Focused my thoughts.

Found the Balance — the perfect balance between wrath and clarity.

As the unfathomable power welled up in the deep recess of my soul and the expected sensation of calmative awareness washed over me, the blaring sound of an iconic guitar lick filled the forest.

Wait. What?

"Fucking theme music?" MacCawill barked. "Please tell me you can do better than that."

"Guns 'n' Roses?" A wide smile formed on my battered face. "Stoner."

And it was right about then when things took an interesting turn.

In uncanny, perfect rhythm to "Welcome to the Jungle," a deluge of barzel-tipped arrows and bluish-white energy balls slammed into the herd of Krugers with sniper-like precision until MacCawill and I were able to free ourselves from the dirt clone manwich.

As the golems systematically exploded in turbulent poofs of reddish-brown dust around us, I stood up just in time to see a familiar canary yellow 1963 Volkswagen van cutting a wide swath through the Kruger-filled campsite like a bulldozer. Better yet was the vision of Stoner and Coop peppering the battlefield with arcane projectiles as they shuffled across the roof in a synchronized Axl Rose snake dance.

Disturbing?

Perhaps.

Incredibly awesome?

You bet your sweet ass.

"Friends of yours?" MacCawill asked, throwing a couple stray Krugers off him and getting to his feet.

"Yep," I replied, willing the shotgun into my hand and very thankful that neither Stoner nor Coop were wearing pleather pants.

"Unconventional," he muttered, clenching a fresh stogie between his teeth and casually flogging a group of dirt clones with several cracks of his whip. "But I like their style."

Tearing through the campsite with reckless abandon, the Magic Bus traversed the network of trails with Dukes of Hazzard precision as the Kruger army frantically scurried about the woods like frenzied varmints getting smoked out of their burrow. It was priceless.

In classic A-Team fashion, the unlikely assault vehicle pulled a hard right and roared toward me and MacCawill, only to power slide to a dramatic stop right before running us over. Before I had the chance to shit myself or go blind, the passenger door flew open and Rooster, Caveman, and Tango sprung out with a rather impressive collection of brawny weapons at the ready.

"Happy to see us?" Rooster said, taking my left flank and spraying a healthy burst of bullets into the fracas with a tricked-out AK-47 assault rifle.

"Don't flatter yourself," I replied. "That happens to be a shotgun in my pocket."

"Awkward," Tango muttered, flashing past me in a cloud of whitish-green smoke while dismembering countless Kruger clones with a blinding torrent of kukri knife strikes.

Pulling up on my right flank in sweat pants and a grey hoodie while forcefully swinging his oversized battle axe into the midsection of a charging assailant, Caveman said, "Dizam, bromando. Looks like you made some new friends."

"You know me, Mick. I'm nothing if not popular."

"Yeah, man. Being on Heaven's Most Wanted list will do that. Hey, do you really have a shotgun in your pocket?"

As I momentarily contemplated whether or not to answer that, Coop launched himself from the roof of the Magic Bus like a redneck ninja and effortlessly landed with cat-like dexterity right in front of me.

Grinning, he spit a healthy wad of tobacco on the ground. "Hey, hoss, you mind ducking for a quick sec?"

"Ah, sure."

And then he simply drew back on his otherworldly long bow and sunk a trio of arrows into the respective heads of three bad guys perched in a nearby tree ready to pounce on me.

"Dagum, I'm good," he said, appreciating his handiwork.

"That's what she said." I grinned back. "Where's Crockett?"

"Grand Canyon. Tracking a lead on the anakim hideout."

"Speaking of tracking, how did you guys find me anyway?"

"They didn't," Erin Kelly said, casually emerging from behind the van while dropping Krugers from an easy hundred yards out with alternating shots from dueling H&K pistols. "I did."

"Doc?" I scoffed. "What the hell are you doing here?" Spinning around, I glared at Rooster. "Why did you bring Erin here?"

"Ah, for the record, she brought us," he said. "Who do you think was driving?"

"What?" I spun back toward Doc. "Why aren't you at the Quartermaster?"

Still squeezing off rounds, she said, "The better question is why are you in a Tennessee trailer park getting your ass kicked by the buff, grown-up version of the Backstreet Boys?"

"Long story," I grumbled, cocking the shotgun lever and sending a couple judgment fire blasts into the quickly retreating mass of dirt soldiers.

"Okay, and how is it that all these guys look the same?"

"Because they're not a *they* — they're a *he*," MacCawill announced, joining our impromptu battle position with grenade launcher at the ready. "His name's Cyrus Kruger. He's a terramorph. And a mercenary working for the halos. And an asshat of epic proportion."

"Guys, meet Roy. Roy, meet the crew. And the Doc."

"MacCawill," Rooster muttered, as his eyes flashed a blazing red.

"O'Dargan," Roy coldly responded in turn.

"You still have my robot?"

"You still pissing in a bottle and telling people it's beer?"

"What the hell are you doing here?"

"He's with me," I said, jumping in before they started slugging each other. "He's helping."

"Wait, freaking what?" Rooster blurted. "You're working with *him*?"

"I'll explain later," I said, pointing across the campsite. "But right now, me and MacCawill need to get to that log cabin."

"What the hell for?" Rooster raised a ginger eyebrow.

"Because there's a shitter I need to visit."

"Not a great time to be burying the elf," Stoner barked, from his perch atop the yellow magical mystery machine.

As I momentarily contemplated why I was the only one who didn't seem to know what that term meant, I said, "The shitter's a portal."

"A portal? Where the hell are you going?"

"To get some friggin answers."

"Ah, y'all," Coop interjected, gazing across the campsite. "The party ain't over. I'm thinking now would be a nifty time to make like a tree and get out of here."

And although it first appeared that Kruger and his merry band of derelict dirt doppelgängers were cutting their losses and exiting stage left, it seemed that wasn't exactly the case. For, as the surviving members of the decimated clone battalion huddled on the far end of the campsite surrounding the log cabin, the rest of the woods erupted in a swirling mass of man-sized funnel clouds.

"Fuck," both MacCawill and I muttered in unison.

"Ah, guys," Erin said, slamming new magazines into her pistolas. "What the hell is happening?"

"Nothing good," Rooster grumbled.

And before I had the opportunity to drop another series of heartfelt expletives, the cyclone barrage dispersed to reveal a new and improved batch of Krugers. Lots and lots and lots of Krugers. Like, the entire goddamned woods were filled with the bastards.

More disturbingly, it seemed there was no way in hell I was fighting my way through them to reach the aforementioned interdimensional toilet stall.

As I pondered that for a second, the swarm of bad guys conglomerated into a massive horde and began to charge at us like it was it was a goddamn scene out of *Braveheart.*

"So, that just happened," Tango muttered, fluidly morphing from smoky haze back to his signature pastel look. "What now?"

Grabbing Erin and tossing her in the van head first, I said, "You guys need to get out of here. Now!"

"Everybody in the bus," Stoner declared with commanding authority as he executed a wizardly combat roll off the roof and slid into the driver's seat. "Fucking pronto, ladies!"

"Get in," Rooster said, glaring at me.

"I'll make my way from here."

Pointing at the incoming stampede, Stoner barked, "Get in, Robinson. Unless you plan on growing some fucking wings, there's no way in hell you're getting through that shitshow. I'll get you and the Outlaw Josey Wales where you need to be."

Shrugging his shoulders, MacCawill looked at me. "Axl's got a point, mancho."

"Fine. Let's go."

As everyone except for Caveman hastily crammed into the cargo bay, Stoner coaxed the engine to life and spun the yellow mirth mobile around to face the rapidly approaching incursion force. "You coming, Mick?" he grunted.

"Nah, I've got my own ride," Caveman replied, holding his fingers to his mouth and letting out a hellaciously loud whistle. "Lil' D! Time to go to work. It's rhino time, buddy."

"Rhino time?" Erin asked.

Rooster grinned. "Rhino time."

"Is that a code or something?"

"No. It's a pig. Or something."

Right on cue, the ground began to quake and a haunting series of guttural snorts rang out from the depths of the woods behind us. The windows of the Magic Bus rattled to the point of shattering as the relentless pounding of large hooves steadily increased to a feverous pace. Spinning around and looking out the window, I couldn't help but smile as the great white war pig streaked past the van with the speed of a locomotive moving at full tilt. Roughly the size of a pickup truck, the ivory white beast, covered in rhinoceros-like armor plating, was on a determined collision course with the Kruger militia.

Ripping off his hoodie to reveal a furry, muscle-clad chest, Caveman nephed out and fluidly transitioned from a mellow humanish mansquatch into a predatory, and much hairier, canine-hybrid über warrior. Effortlessly jumping on Duncan's meaty back like a skilled rodeo rider, he gallantly raised his oversized battle axe high in the air and let out a blood-curdling howl while somehow still showcasing his razor-sharp teeth.

It was terrifying.

And amazing.

And very well-choreographed.

As Lil' D lowered his meaty head and positioned his jagged, elephant-sized tusks just above the forest floor, the obscure duo busted through the center of the enemy formation like the parting of the Red Sea. Eviscerating

Kruger clones like a hot knife passing through butter, the rabid hog o' war and his furry jockey continued to barrel through the charging mob until they simply disappeared in a mammoth cloud of reddish-brown dust, leaving a wide path behind them.

Seeing our opportunity, Rooster yelled, "Punch it!"

Stoner replied by slamming the Magic Bus into gear and going from zero to sixty in about half a second. Making the mental note to ask him what the hell he had under the hood at some point down the road, I grabbed onto my seat for dear life.

MacCawill, on the other hand, made the mistake of grabbing onto to Erin, which earned him a stiff shot to the dangly bits, compliments of Doc's elbow. Haha.

"Hands to yourself, Young Guns," she barked, pushing his big ass toward Tango.

Crossing the few hundred yards in no time at all, Stoner literally stood on the brakes as we nearly careened into the log cabin. Throwing open the side door of the van, I jumped out and immediately waylaid a few bad guys waiting for us at the entrance with my metal fists of fury.

"Thanks for the lift," MacCawill forced out, delicately cradling his twig and berries as he slowly exited the van and staggered through the front door of the cabin. "We should do this again. But let's not."

"I'll be in touch," I said, nodding at the crew. "Thanks for saving my ass. Now, get the hell out of here."

"I'm coming with you," Erin said.

"No. You're not. And unfortunately, you can't go back to the Quartermaster either. The seraphic court will know you helped me. You're fugitives now. All of you."

"No worries, hoss," Coop chimed in. "I've got a place we can lie low for a spell. Ain't nobody going to find us at the Farm."

"Is it off the grid?"

"Hid better than a tick in a steer's ass."

"Is that a good thing?"

"Depends on whether you're the tick or the steer, I reckon."

"Right," I muttered, trying to clear yet another Cooperism from my mind.

"You don't need to do this alone," Rooster interjected, with a sharp edge.

"I don't intend to. But first, we need information."

"What's your plan?"

"I'm going to see a man about a horse. You guys need to disappear. I'll contact you in a few hours and we'll plot our next move."

"Make it snappy," Stoner barked, glancing at his watch. "Less than twelve hours and counting until the shit starts flying again."

"Be careful," Rooster added. "We're in unchartered waters."

"Don't do anything stupid, Dean," Erin said with a hard gaze.

Glancing at the mammoth albino hog rampaging through the surrounding forest while mangling aluminum motor homes and obliterating otherworldly beings conjured from dirt, I muttered, "I'm thinking the bar's set pretty low at this point, Doc."

14

In the ranking of things I never envisioned myself doing, squeezing into a trailer park shittery with a guy in a rawhide duster, with both hands wrapped around his smooth criminals, was definitely up there. While arguably not quite as outlandish as the thought of skinny dipping with laser-beam retrofitted mako sharks, it was close.

"So, not that I'm not enjoying being crammed in a crapper with a dude that's fondling himself, but I'm seriously not enjoying being crammed in a crapper with a dude that's fondling himself. You plan on firing up the portal anytime soon?"

"Need a minute," MacCawill winced.

"Hurry up. We've got shit to do. And that wasn't toilet humor."

"Well, if your girlfriend hadn't seen fit to drop an atomic elbow on my nethers—"

"I thought you had balls of steel. Or is that just your arm?"

"Fuck off," he grumbled.

"And for the record, Doc isn't my girlfriend. It's complicated."

"Who is she then?"

"No one really. Combat medic. Cardiothoracic surgeon. Pint-sized badass. Jaw dropping minx. Red Sox fan. Good with pets. And she pours a mean black and tan."

"She's totally your girlfriend."

"Don't make me whiny, Roy. You wouldn't like me when I'm whiny."

"Whatever," he said, removing his hands from his pants, evidently satisfied that Elephantiasis of the nuts wasn't in his near future. "Let's get out of here before your not-girlfriend comes back."

"Oh, is it time to leave? I didn't realize your solo afternoon delight was finished. It's not like I'm in a big fucking rush or anything."

Grumbling something of an unpleasant nature under his breath, he murmured a few words in Enochian and then flushed the toilet three times. As the swirling water produced a brilliant flash of white radiance, we instantly transitioned from one shitter stall to yet another one. A much, much smaller one. Typical.

And judging from the surrounding clamor of disgruntled voices set to a horrific soundtrack of labored grunts, rapidly flushing toilets, and intermittent running water, I suspected we were in a rather bustling public restroom. A suspicion that was quickly confirmed as my nostrils were mercilessly assaulted by an unfortunate potpourri of greasy fast-food ass interlaced with tropical fruit air freshener and a lingering hint of piss.

Awesome.

"Anytime you feel like letting us out of here would be really great," MacCawill said, hunched over the toilet and pinned like a contortionist against the back wall.

"Right," I grumbled, awkwardly rotating around in the claustrophobic space until I faced the door. "Standby."

"And lose the cape before anybody sees you."

"That won't be a problem. Nobody sees me."

Fumbling around for a second or two, I felt the latch disengage, causing the door to swing open. No longer pinned in place like a sardine, I rather clumsily staggered out of the stall, slipped on some toilet paper, and executed a perfect face plant onto the grimy restroom floor.

As if that wasn't bad enough, shortly after I got a face full of gummy restroom tile, I got manwiched by two hundred and fifty pounds of arcane bounty hunter.

"Friggin oaf," I grunted, pushing MacCawill off me and scrambling to my feet.

"Lose — the — cape," he insisted as we both stood upright to find a host of seriously disturbed looks from the long line of dudes waiting their turn on the porcelain throne.

"They're all looking at me. Why can they see me?"

"Because you're wearing the talisman, douche wagon. Lose the goddamn cape."

"Well, this is awkward," I chuckled, willing the cloak, gauntlets, and arsenal of unnatural weaponry into retreat as I waved at everyone. "Ah, hey, fellas. I wouldn't go in there for a few more minutes. Pond's filled with brown trout if you know what I'm saying. My buddy here had Mexican for lunch. Might want to light a match or something."

"Let's go, slick," MacCawill said, pushing his way through the crowd while pulling his Stetson down over his face. "We're late."

Reluctantly following him, I exchanged a few uneasy pleasantries with the collection of gawking patrons, and we quickly emerged from the bathroom to find ourselves in a bustling corridor of frenzied people.

Quickly assessing the scene, I said, "Is this an airport?"

He nodded. "The world's busiest. Hartsfield-Jackson International in Atlanta. Terminal V. Home of Variant Airlines. Rendezvous point is at Gate 13. Hopefully my employer is still there."

Now, granted, airports are generally a shitshow in their best of hours, but this — this was a whole new level of insanity. Glancing up and down the massive terminal, bathed in obnoxious fluorescent light, it had the distinct appearance of a full-on third-world refugee camp that had run out of food and water weeks earlier. Every gate was absolutely overflowing with gaggles of people in varying stages of shock, despair, and rage.

All the TV screens hanging from the ceiling were flittering with news reports featuring images of smoking carnage and global ruination accompanied by the latest accounts of 'giant man' sightings and doomsday scenarios. And an incessant, almost deafening barrage of undecipherable announcements rang from the loud speakers in various languages, causing people to frantically race to new gate assignments or just completely lose their shit and start screaming.

Conversely, other folks didn't seem to care anymore and were simply sprawled out on chairs, suitcases, and makeshift camp sites strewn about every inch of available floor space.

And worst of all, it was hot. Like ninety-eight degrees hot. Like the damn heat was purposely blaring on full tilt just to add a bit more misery to the mix.

"This isn't an airport," I said. "It's a circle of hell."

"I imagine that's the intent."

"What the frig happened here?"

"Whole place has been on lockdown since the attacks last night. Nobody can get in or out, which evidently happens when the entire world goes on terror alert. Variant Air is the only airline still flying."

I shrugged. "How is that?"

MacCawill grinned. "You'll understand when you meet my employer."

Continuing to wade through the terminal, we reached Gate 13 only to find a sizable, hostile crowd formed around an unusually content, uniformed gate agent perched behind an oversized pedestal desk. Proudly displayed on the wall behind him was an obnoxiously large logo depicting an inverted red triangle and the tagline 'Variant Air. Fly the Winds of Change. Where Every Soul Counts.' Looking down upon the masses, he sat like a content king addressing his suffering court of plebeians.

"There he is," MacCawill said, pointing at the would-be airport potentate.

"Who?"

"My employer."

"The friggin gate agent?"

"Yep. Let's go."

Making the mental note that a low level, power tripping airport employee was probably about the last person I was expecting MacCawill's clandestine bossman to be, I nonetheless wove my way through the mob of incited travelers to get closer.

And as soon as I got a good look at him, it all made sense.

Perfect sense.

"Lucifer," I grumbled. "You work for Lucifer."

Didn't see that coming.

Dressed in a fire engine red blazer, crisp white shirt, and loosely knotted black tie, the roguishly handsome, George Clooneyesque fallen angel ran a hand through his slicked-back, silver-speckled hair and adjusted his Buddy Holly spectacles as he happily looked upon a ranting, highly pissed off customer.

With charming eloquence, I heard him say, "Kindly rest assured, good sir, that we at Variant Air are doing everything *humanly* possible to guarantee your seat on the *very* next flight to Los Angeles. In the interim, may I suggest you find yourself a nice, quiet place to properly mull over those fleeting thoughts of self-immolation racing through your deluded subconscious at the moment."

"Excuse me?" the befuddled traveler indignantly barked.

Lucifer smiled. "I believe you know what I'm referring to. There's a good fellow. Go forth and wallow. Here, take this spork. And please be sure to complete an online survey. Every tormented soul *counts* at Variant Air."

As the poor bastard defeatedly turned to leave, Lucifer gave him a dismissive pat on the head and proudly announced, "Next *valued* customer please."

"Nice outfit," I grumbled, approaching the desk as I took notice of his white plastic nametag, "Lew."

"Ah, the good Master Robinson," he replied, with a creepy, wide smile in his signature smarmy dialect. "A sight for sore eyes in this darkest of hours. I was beginning to think Mr. MacCawill had failed in his appointed task."

"Sorry," MacCawill muttered. "There was a slight complication retrieving the talisman."

"I take it you were successful?"

"Of course."

"You have done well, Roy. You always do. Consider our debt settled and your fee paid in full."

"Pleasure doing business with you. And don't call me again — like, ever. Seriously."

"I certainly will not," Lucifer replied, with a wink and a nod.

"Whatever," MacCawill grumbled. Turning to me, he simply nodded. "Good luck, mancho. You'll need it. See ya around. But probably not."

"Wait," I said. "That's it? Where the hell are you going?"

He shrugged. "To settle a score with an old friend." Then he simply faded into the gaggle of people and melted from sight.

"Too bad," I muttered. "That jackass was actually starting to grow on me."

Lucifer sighed. "Parting is such sweet sorrow. But fear not, Dean. I don't believe you've seen the last of Roy MacCawill."

"And why's that?"

"For it's only the second act. His part, as is yours, is far from played out."

I couldn't help but shake my head. "So, what the hell am I doing here, Lewis? Didn't think I'd be seeing you again so soon. Or ever."

"You say that with such disdain. Have I not *saved* your life for the second time in as many weeks?"

"Yeah, you're a real Boy Scout. And for the record, you can't really *save* my life. I'm already dead. So, what do you want?"

"What I have always wanted. The Balance restored. The world of man returned to a more favorable environment for the transacting of my ever-so-important business matters."

"Like talking people out of their souls and damning them to Hell?"

"You have your business. I have mine. In the end, we all do that which is intended by the *great* God. To think otherwise is simply irresponsible. Isn't that right, Erin Kelly?"

"What?" I scoffed, spinning around to find the Doc and Rooster pushing their way through the surrounding multitude.

"Who the hell are you?" Erin said with a distinct edge as she pushed past me and approached the desk. "And how do you know my name?"

"Don't be so modest, poppet," Lucifer replied, with a seductive grin. "Such striking beauty laced with delectable, boiling ferocity. How could I not?" Turning his attention to Rooster, he said, "Eóin, what a lovely surprise! You look well, my son. Very well."

"Hello, Father," Rooster replied. His faced lacked any hint of emotion.

Father?

Wait.

What the frig just happened?

15

"FATHER?" I scoffed, looking at Rooster with my jaw squarely on the floor. "Him? Lew? Friggin Lucifer is your dad?"

I think he was about to defend himself when Doc came to the very unfortunate realization that she was standing face-to-face with—

"Lucifer?" She gasped, and her face drained of color.

"At your service, my sultry vixen," Lew replied, seemingly captivated by Erin.

"Lucifer. As in Satan?"

"Guilty as charged."

"And you're manning the ticket counter — at an airport — in Georgia?"

"I'll have you know that I do some of my best work in airports. Marvelous places. The caged anxiety. The looming desperation. The voracious hostility. Airports, my dear poppet, bring out the absolute *worst* attributes of human nature. I enjoy them so much, I bought an airline."

She shook her head. "You're saying that Variant Air is literally owned by the Devil."

"Indeed. And the return on my investment has been simply immeasurable. You'd be surprised how quickly someone will quite literally sell their soul for *additional* leg room and a complimentary vodka tonic."

"That's repulsive."

"That's business, dearie, and Variant Air is a veritable goldmine. Although, I must admit, it's still centuries behind my financial services division. I'm kind of the only name in consumer credit these days. Sort of a big deal."

"You're actually him," Erin muttered. "You're Lucifer."

He grinned. "Please, Miss Kelly, call me Lew. All my friends do. Isn't that right, Dean?"

"Friends?" she barked, glaring at me.

"Not friends." I backpedaled a step or two. "More of fleeting acquaintances. It's actually a funny story—"

"Shut up," she snapped, spinning toward Rooster. "And *you* — you're *his* son?"

"One of many," Rooster retorted. "And very estranged. Also a funny story?"

"You guys officially suck. Both of you." She turned her icy stare back on Lucifer. "Quit ogling me, jagoff."

"So feisty," he quipped. "Simply adorable. I just *love* you."

"Bite me."

"Is that an invitation, my plucky strumpet?"

Stepping between them, I muttered, "Keep your pitchfork in your pants before you make me whiny, Lewis."

"Yes, of course," he chuckled. "Business before frivolity."

"What business is he talking about, Dean?" Rooster asked. "What exactly are you doing here with *him*?"

"Your pops hired MacCawill to save me from the archangel death squad. He supposedly has information. Information we need to set things right."

"And you believe him? *Him*?"

"Come now, Eóin," Lucifer chided, "You should be relieved that I have taken an interest in these matters."

"Relieved." Rooster scoffed. "My ass."

"Do you not trust me, son?"

"I haven't *trusted* you for two thousand years, *Father*."

"If you're referring to that bit of fun in Ireland—"

"Bit of fun? You sent me into a village to barter for food only to find a mob of pissed off druids waiting to jump me."

After a smug chuckle, Lew said, "As I told you then, it was merely an exercise in character building. A longstanding family tradition."

"Ah, they burned me at the stake. When that didn't work, they buried me alive. Then they dug me up and threw me off a cliff. And then buried me again."

"So?"

"I was six."

"And a better man for it, Eóin."

"You're an asshole. And nobody calls me Eóin anymore. It's John. Or Rooster."

"*Rooster*? How farcical."

"For Christ's sake," I butted in. "Why don't you guys exchange email addresses or something. We have more important shit to talk about."

"We certainly do." Lew smirked. "Where shall we begin?"

"How about with who the friggin traitor is?"

"I would have thought that rather obvious at this point."

"Meaning?"

"Master Robinson." His voice dripped of condescension. "Who is the architect of your near demise at the hands of his winged minions? Was it not Gabriel himself that gave the order to *end* you in that cursed desert?"

"That doesn't make him the traitor."

"Yet it gives you a certain insight into his motives, yes?"

"Something else has to be going on. Gabriel's the only archangel Stephen trusted. I can't believe he turned on us."

"And yet, he did."

"Doesn't feel right."

"Your *feelings* betray you, Dean. Gabriel is an archangel. He's not driven by emotion. He's driven by a deluded vision of divine grandeur and new world order. He *is* the traitor. And the sooner you come to terms with that unfortunate realization, the better off you'll be. If you doubt me, why not ask your precious Stephen?"

"I can't."

"And what's preventing you?"

"He's kind of off the grid at the moment."

"How peculiar. And what was the *greatest* of Heaven's dark soldiers doing when he so abruptly *vanished*?"

Although I didn't exactly trust Lew, I couldn't exactly refute the evidence. "He was going to meet Gabriel."

"An uncanny coincidence?"

"Maybe."

"Don't be so callow." Lew scoffed. "It was nothing less than a masterfully orchestrated ambush. And your instincts tell you the same despite your *feelings*."

"But why?" Erin said. "Why would the left hand of God betray Heaven?"

"The answer lies in your question, poppet. Gabriel is a loyal solider who's carried out the dirty bidding of our Father since the beginning of time itself. Slaughtering and butchering through the millennia without question or hesitation. His hands stained red with the blood of angels that dare oppose the tenets of Heaven. Rumor has it brother Gabriel has simply become weary of it. Subsequently, he believes a change in management is well overdue."

"And Azazel's part in this?"

"A willing lieutenant. His zeal to exact revenge on mankind over the years has proven a worthy distraction. That is precisely why Gabriel freed him from his eternal bonds in the depths of Dudael."

"A distraction?" I grumbled. "Distraction for what?"

"For brother Gabriel to take control of the chess board, of course. To patiently and strategically move his pawns into position."

"What pawns?"

"Those angels tired of the status quo. Those ready to *rise up* in the name of revolution. All that remains to ignite this malicious coup de gras is a single spark."

"The Watchers," Rooster muttered.

"Indeed," Lucifer confirmed. "The greatest collection of fallen angels condemned to eternal damnation for crimes against humanity."

"And what about him being outed as a traitor?"

"And that, my dear Eóin, is perhaps his greatest triumph. That dubious honor has already been laid upon the brow of another party. Perhaps you know them? A pair of humans resurrected from the great beyond and bestowed with the power of God's Wrath. To all those concerned in the matter, Heaven was *betrayed* by the very humans Father saw fit to wield his divine power in defense of the Earth."

"That's total bullshit," I grumbled.

"Yes, but perception is reality, Dean."

"So, this whole thing about Azazel making me his emissary to deliver terms to the seraphic court was a setup. Gabriel knew we'd take the bait. We played right into his hands."

"Precisely. And if not for the information shared with me by Remiel resulting in the timely intervention of Mr. MacCawill, you'd presently share your master's fate, or perhaps far worse."

"*Remiel*?" Rooster scoffed. "You two are working together? How is that exactly?"

"He had become suspicious of Gabriel's intentions as of late and quite certain the seraphic court had become compromised."

"And he allied himself with you?"

"Politics create strange bedfellows, Eóin. I merely presented a partnership of convenience. Someone outside the walls of Heaven with a vested interest in maintaining the status quo."

Fixated on Lucifer, I said, "How do we put a stop to this bullshit?"

"With grace and artistry. Gabriel is playing chess. To defeat him, you must remove the most powerful piece from the board."

"This isn't a game," Erin grumbled.

"Why yes, poppet, it most certainly is. We could play another game if you like. Just the two of us."

Restraining Doc from kneeing Lew in the ballsac, I said, "Before catching a grenade in the chest, Remiel said something about a vessel. Said it was the key to unlocking the gates of Tartarus. Is that the piece you're talking about?"

"Top marks, Dean," Lew replied. "But he wasn't speaking of *a* vessel. He was speaking of *the* Vessel."

Connecting the dots, Erin said, "The Ark of the Covenant."

I shot her a 'how the hell do you know that' look, and she simply shrugged her shoulders. "What? I went to Catholic school."

"The Ark," Rooster muttered. "Of course."

Lucifer nodded. “And without it, Gabriel cannot open Tartarus and release the Watchers. An unforeseen glitch in his calculations.”

Rooster shook his head. “But the Ark is in the possession of the seraphic court. Everybody knows they snagged it from the Templars centuries ago and locked it away somewhere in the vaults of Tenth Heaven.”

“They did. Or so they thought.”

“Wait, what? Please tell me you didn’t steal the Ark of the freaking Covenant?”

“I swear I didn’t steal the Ark of the Covenant.”

“Son of a bitch. You totally stole the Ark of the freaking Covenant. You asshole.”

“Of course, I did, Eóin. Absolute power such as that — in the hands of human beings, no less? I think not. Terribly, terribly bad for business.”

“How did you do it?”

“Well, after witnessing the destruction of Jericho, I paid a visit to the Philistine encampment and replaced the actual Ark with a strikingly authentic forgery of my own making. It was quite elegant. And quite harmless.”

“And then?” Erin asked.

Lew winked at her. “And then, poppet, I hid it away from the world. That is, of course, after spending a rather memorable evening with an absolutely charming Canaanite priestess. Very limber, as I recall.”

“So,” Rooster said, “if the seraphic court is looking for it, they must realize that the one they have is a fake.”

“Indeed,” Lew replied. “And from what I understand, they’re turning over Heaven and Earth to locate the genuine article.”

“But, if you stole it, then it’s beyond Gabriel’s reach, right?”

“I’m afraid the tale is a bit more complicated, son.”

“Shocker,” Erin grumbled. “Here we go.”

Ignoring her snide commentary, Lew said, “To truly put an end to Gabriel’s treachery, the Ark must be destroyed.”

“Okay. Then destroy it,” Rooster said.

“Sadly, I cannot. Although constructed by humans, the Ark embodies the hand of God himself.” Fixing his smug stare on me, he added, “And therefore can only be unmade by the hand of God. Or those touched by it, as it were."

"Fine," I grunted. "I'll nuke the friggin thing. Where is it?"

"Ah, and there's the final rub."

"What rub, Lewis?"

"With great disdain, I must confess that it's no longer under my purview."

"Freaking seriously?" Rooster scoffed. "What happened?"

Lucifer cleared his throat. "*She* has it."

"She?"

"Yes, Eóin. She."

"*She*, she? No way."

"Unfortunately, yes way."

"Well, shit. That really blows."

"Who the hell are you two talking about?" I asked.

"My mother," Rooster said, as his eyes flashed a blazing red. "We're talking about my mother."

"And that's bad?"

"It ain't good." He turned to Lew. "Please tell me you didn't lose it in the divorce."

"I swear I didn't lose it in the divorce."

"Son of a bitch. You totally lost it in the divorce. You asshole."

"I had no choice, Eóin. Your *mother* was quite adamant. Either I hand over the Ark or bequeath her my rightful claim to the entire kingdom of Hell. The *entire* kingdom, mind you. There was no middle ground to be struck. You know how unreasonable she can be."

"And what makes you think she's going to give it to me?"

"Come now, son. You were always her favorite. Do you not remember how she used to dress you up like a delightful little—"

"Yep, got it," Rooster blurted. "I'll figure something out."

Making the mental note that I'd really like to know what Rooster's mom used to dress him up as, I fixated on Lucifer. "So, you're saying to find the Ark, we need to pay a visit to your ex-wife because she handed you your ass in divorce court."

"I'm afraid that is accurate."

"That's beyond absurd."

"Be that as it may, your path is clear, Dean. To put an end to this madness, you must locate the Ark and bathe it in Judgment fire before it falls into the hands of the seraphic court. A more than trivial task for a creature of your combative prowess and particular skill set."

"Yeah, piece of cake."

"Very well, it's sorted. Now, off you go. Make haste. Time is not an ally in these matters, as you are well aware. If the archangels retrieve it before you, all is lost. If you'll excuse me, children, I must now bid you good day. I have work to do."

"Where can I find her?" Rooster coldly asked.

"Manhattan is her usual haunt this time of year," Lucifer replied, as he hopped down from his pedestal desk, straightened his gaudy red blazer and hailed a nearby airport golf cart making its way through the terminal.

As droves of disgruntled people leapt out of the way upon the approach of the indoor assault vehicle, he added, "Remember, when you find the Vessel — do not open it under any circumstances. Destroy it. Without its power at his disposal, Gabriel will have no remaining course of action."

"And then what?" I asked.

"*Checkmate*, Master Robinson. You can expose brother Gabriel for the treacherous malcontent he truly is and clear your good name in the process. And then, we can all go on about our proper course of business, yes?"

Issuing us a cliched two finger salute, Lew then hopped into the driver's seat of the golf cart and sped off while playfully tossing mini-bottles of booze and bags of airplane snackage into the surrounding hordes of strung-out travelers.

"Eat, drink, and be merry, my pets!" he yelled as people dropped whatever they were doing and frantically scampered to retrieve the items. Much to his delight, the somewhat civilized crowd instantly devolved into a frenzied mob of bloody fisticuffs.

"What a dick," Erin grumbled.

"We'll deal with him later," I said turning to Rooster. "First things first. Where can we find mommy dearest?"

"Corner of Fifth Avenue and East 89th Street," he replied.

"A street corner in New York City?"

"Yeppers."
"Ah, is she like a hooker or something?"
"No. But she'll probably be naked."
"Oh, good."
And I thought this was going to be awkward.

16

"All right," I grumbled as we left the pandemonium of Gate 13 behind and began to maneuver through the bowels of the fallout zone-like terminal. "Before we get too far down this road, I assume you took precautions to make sure you and Doc aren't being tracked."

"Please," Rooster scoffed, checking the time on his peculiar antique pocket watch. "Is this amateur hour? Erin and I are warded with some of my best 'off the books' Rooster tech. Not even the all-seeing gaze of Skyphos can find us."

"Rooster tech, eh?"

"I wasn't always the fine, upstanding cleric you see standing before you."

"And this gadgetry of yours actually works?"

"Of course it freaking works. We're as good as ghosts. Question is, how the hell are you staying off the radar?"

Digging around in my shirt, I pulled out the amulet MacCawill had given me earlier.

"Wait, what the shit?" Rooster blurted. "How did you get your hands on the Talisman of Armaros? I heard it was destroyed when the seraphic court put the kibosh on his sorry ass back in the eighties. He had some

Hugh Hefner wannabe thing going on in Montreal. Horny bastard. Liked speedos a little too much."

"MacCawill had it," I said, trying to forget about that speedo comment. "It was stashed at his trailer park."

"MacCawill." Rooster's eyes flashed red. "That shady son of a bitch. Can't believe—"

"So that explains what you were doing in Tennessee," Erin said, thankfully diffusing the impending Rooster rant before it went thermonuclear.

"It does," I muttered. "But it doesn't explain how you found me there. And it sure as shit begs the question of how you found me here."

She grinned, smugly. "I already told you. It's my job to keep you out of trouble."

"You're not going to tell me, are you?"

"Nope."

I turned to Rooster. "What about the rest of the team? They good?"

He nodded. "Everyone's holed up at Coop's farm. They'll be safe there until it's go-time. Or until Stoner loses his shit from being stuck in close quarters with three other guys on high protein diets ... and Duncan. Actually, we shouldn't leave them there for much longer now that I think about it."

"How about Abernethy? Does he know you're with me?"

"Yes. Yes, he does."

"And he's good with it?"

"Grouchy as hell, but good. He's toeing the party line with the seraphic court until we get the proof we need to move on the traitor. Until then, we're on our own."

"What about Skyphos? Can we count on her to help?"

"No. But on the bright side, she sort of agreed to not actively hunt us."

"Is that good?"

"Could be worse."

"Could definitely be worse," Erin said. "At least we're not basing our entire plan on advice from freaking Satan."

I could almost feel the tension as they both glared at me for an awkward moment. "Look, I don't like it any more than you guys do. And just so we're clear, despite Lew and his celestial gossip column bullshit, I'm still not convinced that Gabriel's the traitor."

"I'm sensing a 'but' here."

"*But* that jackass makes a good point. If the Ark is truly the key to opening Tartarus, which seems to be the general consensus, we need to find it. And we need to find it before the archangels, Lucifer, or anyone else. It's our only move."

Erin shrugged. "Well, it's definitely better than your plan to go to Tenth Heaven by yourself and take on the *barkangel.*"

"Thanks, Doc. Really appreciate that."

"This plan is only *mostly* stupid."

"Exactly. Which is precisely why it's going to work. Rooster?"

"What the hell," he said, pulling to a halt outside a locked janitor's closet in an unusually quiet spot amidst the surrounding backdrop of airport calamity. "I haven't done anything stupid in the past few hours — ish."

"All right, then let's go see your naked mom." And that sounded so much better in my head.

"Yeah, about that, there's a few things you should know before we go and casually ask my mother to just hand over her most prized possession so we can turn around and blow it up."

Rather delicately, Erin asked, "Who exactly is she, John?"

"Her name is Lilith."

"She's a nepher?" I asked.

"No. No, she's not."

"Angel?"

"Ah, no."

"Demon?"

"No."

"Giant mutated alien ecoterrorist?"

"Really?"

"She's human," Doc said, like I was a total dumbass. "Lucifer's an angel and John's Nephilim, which means his mother has to be human."

"Right," I grumbled. "That was my next guess."

"What I can't figure out is how old she is."

"She's, ah, pretty old," Rooster said.

"Like, how old?" I asked, making the mental note that she may not have any right being naked on a street corner after all.

"Like, beginning of time *old*."

"Beginning of time? Like Adam and Eve?"

"Sort of."

"And?" I waited for the punchline.

"Well, despite what mainstream religion would have you believe, Eve was not the first woman created by God. The *first* woman was my mother, Lilith. She was created from the same dust as Adam."

"Chickenman say what?"

"It's true."

"And why is she not mentioned in the Bible?"

"Basically because she wasn't down with the whole 'women are supposed to be submissive' thing. Adam was created from dirt. She was created from dirt — they were equals. Subsequently, she told Adam to suck it, and ditched his sorry ass."

"And then what?"

"Then, she kind of went batshit crazy and shacked up with Lucifer for the next few millennia. They got married, did the honeymoon thing, and then proceeded to crank out a legion or two of Satan spawn heavenly half-breed nephers."

"Lidercs."

"Yeppers. The very first of the nephilim."

"Goddamn," I grumbled. "That creation story sucks."

"Yes. Yes, it does. Fast forwarding a bit, God opted for a divine take two. Enter Eve. Not exactly a fairy tale ending there either *but* much less with the trailer park drama. And evidently, *Adam and Eve* seemed to have a better ring to it than *Adam and Lil.* So, there you go."

"What happened with her and Lew?"

He shrugged. "Never did get the whole story. Always figured it had to do with my father's legendary philanderous exploits with any creature in possession of a pair of tits and the ability to walk upright."

"Think I just threw up a little."

"Welcome to my world. So, who's pumped to meet my mom?"

"I think we should go right now before we change our minds," Erin offered.

"Seriously," I chimed in. "When's the last time you saw her?"

"It's only been a few hundred years," Rooster said. "I'm about due for a visit."

"All right," I grumbled. "Let's go. How do we get out of here? And I'm really hoping it doesn't involve another shitter."

"Shitter." He scoffed. "Do I look like Roy *freaking* MacCawill?"

"Not at all. He's much taller. Broader shoulders. And has a metal arm." As Rooster's eyes flashed a blazing red for a split second, and he grumbled something of an unpleasant nature under his breath, I made the mental note to lay off the MacCawill jabs. "Just kidding, buddy. You actually look a lot like MacCawill... minus all the cool stuff."

After that one, of course.

He rolled his eyes. "Are you finished?"

"Yep."

"Good," he muttered, stepping toward the janitor closet. "Stand back. I'm about to Rooster tech the shit of this door. Since we can't dial up Skyphos and have her zip us down a portal, we'll have to go old school."

Digging around in the pockets of his signature leather bomber jacket, a smug grin curled across his face as he whipped out a pad of bright yellow sticky notes.

I sighed. "Oh good, you brought sticky notes. We're saved. Awesome."

Completely ignoring me, he produced a vintage, red fountain pen from another pocket and began to scribble an indecipherable string of sigils and glyphs on the first note before forcefully ripping it free of the pad and holding it triumphantly in the air.

"Okay, all set," he declared. "It's closing in on noon. We need to haul ass. You guys ready?"

"Ready for what?" I asked.

"To get out of here."

"Is the sticky note going to help with that?"

"It's not a sticky note. It's Rooster tech."

"And does it do anything else besides remind us to pick up a gallon of milk?"

"You tell me," he said, forcefully planting the Roosterized sticky note on the door and murmuring a few words in Enochian. And before I had the opportunity to offer a witty comeback, the door to the janitor closet morphed into a swirling radiance of spectral blue light indicating the presence of an otherworldly portal.

My face curled into a shit-eating grin. "Rooster tech, eh?"

"Yeppers. That, my skeptical friend, will take us straight to Lilith."

"Damn, that's a pretty impressive sticky note."

"Yes. Yes, it is."

"Okay, boys," Doc grunted, "are we doing this or what?"

"Ladies first," Rooster said, offering her a cliched bow.

She shook her head. "Just so you know, you two are a total pain in the ass." Then she stepped through the portal and melted from sight.

Figuring Doc probably had a pretty valid point, I followed her through the arcane gateway that Rooster nonchalantly conjured from a mundane office accoutrement and couldn't shake the feeling that things were beginning to look up.

Or, conversely, the shit was about to go down.

Either way, I think I was more concerned about seeing Rooster's mom naked.

Seriously, that's just awkward.

17

"I THINK you got the coordinates wrong," I grumbled as we quickly emerged from the otherworldly sticky pad portal into the vast foyer of some highfalutin, futuristic looking museum. "We might be in Manhattan, but this sure as shit ain't a street corner."

"We're in the right place," Rooster said, making his way to the directory in the middle of the majestic lobby of towering, scaffolded walls set against a stunning backdrop of polished granite floors, metal catwalks, and pristine white accents. "Be right back."

I was about to tell him to hurry up when some hipster in a slick sport coat, super nice khakis, and sassy wing tips inadvertently barreled into me and dropped a stack of pamphlets on the floor. "Pardon me, sir," he gasped, trying to wrap his head around how I essentially materialized out of thin air right in front of him as the disapproval of my sullied jeans, tee shirt, and jungle boot motif was pretty apparent on his face. "I didn't see you there."

"Don't worry about it, handsome. Not your fault."

As he stood there gawking at me in silence, I grinned. "You work here?"

"Ah, yes, I do. I'm a docent," he said, extending his hand. "My name is Charles."

"Dean. Nice to meet you, Chuck."

"It's Charles, actually."

"Got it, Chaz. Quite the place you got here."

"Yes, it is," he grumbled, clearly not appreciating being Chaz'd. "And thank you for coming out today to support the museum's 'Stand Against Terror.' I know it can't be easy given the current status of things. I'm afraid we're all in a bit of shock after what's transpired."

"Stand against terror," Erin cut in. "Is that why the museum's open? I would've thought it would be closed in a time like this."

Sighing, he handed Doc a pamphlet. "It's times like these when people need places like this the most. Despite what's happening outside these hallowed walls, our precious collections and exhibits will continue to remain open to the public in hopes of reminding people of better times."

"So, let me get this straight." I chuckled. "The world is literally going to shit, and you guys are *fighting back* by keeping your museum open?"

"So, I take it you're not here to 'Stand Against Terror?'"

"Actually," I chuckled again, taking note of the irony, "I guess we kind of are."

"That's great!" He perked up and handed me a pamphlet. "If you'd like to make a donation, please feel free to stop by our reception desk—"

"Don't push it, Chachi."

Awkwardly nodding, he retrieved his scattered belongings from the floor and scurried off into the surrounding crowd of folks coming and going in a noticeable haze.

Glaring at me, Erin said, "Was that really necessary?"

"What?"

"Being a total dick to *Charles*. He's just trying to do his job."

"Exactly. He's a friggin moron. Why the hell *Chuck* and the rest of these people are acting like it's a normal Saturday afternoon is beyond me."

"And what would you like them to do? Throw their hands up in defeat? Riot in the streets?"

"Hell, I don't know. Just feels wrong."

"This isn't their fight. It's ours."

"It's mine."

"Regardless — *we* need to finish it."

"We'll see about that," I muttered, as my eyes drifted upward and took in the mind-blowing architecture that was actually more reminiscent of an intergalactic hippodrome than a museum.

The eclectic, space-age edifice boasted several stories of accordion-like floors that wrapped around the lobby and jutted several hundred feet in the air. As a series of peculiar glass elevators, artfully nestled into the tiered floor configuration smoothly ushered patrons up and down the breathtaking construct, I started to wonder if we were still on Earth.

"Do you seriously not know where we are?" Erin asked, in a manner that made me realize I probably should.

"Of course I know where we are."

"You don't have a freaking clue, do you?"

"No. Not so much."

After a pronounced sigh, she said, "How many weekends did you spend in New York City when you were at West Point?"

"Hell, I don't know. A lot."

"And you really don't know what's on the corner of Fifth Avenue and East 89th Street?"

I shrugged. "I could probably name every dive bar in Greenwich Village if that's any consolation."

"We're at the Guggenheim, you dope," she grumbled. "As in, *the* Guggenheim. It's kind of a famous landmark. You know, like the Statue of Liberty."

"Is that in New York City, too?"

"Let's go," Rooster said, rejoining us. "Lilith is on the fourth floor."

"She works here?" Erin asked, as we quickly moved toward the elevator.

"No. It's more of a residency."

"Wait, are you saying she *lives* here?"

"Sort of," he muttered, as the elevator door conveniently opened upon our approach and we hopped in. "Hard to explain. It's easier to just show you."

"Great," Erin grumbled. "So, what's the plan?"

"Well, the first step will be getting her attention — which is sometimes a bit more challenging than not."

"That doesn't make any sense, but okay. And then?"

"*Then*, I'm going to tell her the truth about what's going on and appeal to her good nature."

"Good nature, eh?" I cut in. "I thought you said she was batshit crazy."

"Easy there. That's my mother you're talking about."

"Who apparently stormed out of the Garden of Eden and eloped with Lucifer."

"Is it too late to make a case that I was adopted?"

Luckily, we didn't have to answer that question, as a rather pleasant dinging sound accompanied by the sliding open of the elevator doors indicated we'd reached our destination.

Stepping out onto a catwalk, we maneuvered through an excited crowd of eclectic, artisan-type folks snapping pictures with their phones while casually trading the latest rumors and hearsay about the global 'giant man' catastrophe. Still baffled as to why they felt compelled to visit an art museum at a time like this, I figured to each his own and followed Rooster around the rotunda to a slick-looking alcove which housed a gallery of sizable paintings.

Approaching the portrait of a rather stunning woman hung prominently on a perfect white wall and dead center of the other works, he stopped and slid his hands into the pockets of his bomber jacket. After fishing around for a few seconds, he produced one of those analog cooking timers from the bowels of his coat, wound it a few times, and carefully placed it on the floor.

"Before you ask," he muttered as Erin and I pulled up alongside him. "That's not an egg timer. It's Rooster tech." When we offered him nothing in response but a pair of blank stares, he added, "It's a warding device. Makes everyone in the near vicinity instantly want to go somewhere else."

"By turning their muscle into bone and making them machine gun shit themselves?" I asked.

"By sending out a mild, yet highly suggestive, feeling of dread, compliments of some nifty magus mojo."

"And why do we need that?" Erin asked.

He grinned. "Trust me. It'll be better for all parties involved if nobody's around when my mother makes an appearance. Her entrances are usually a bit traumatic. She's kind of a diva. Actually, she's more like the original diva."

"Uh huh," Doc muttered as the surrounding patrons abruptly stopped whatever they were doing and un-assed the immediate area with great haste.

Quickly finding ourselves completely alone in the cozy gallery, Rooster let out a deep breath and focused all of his attention on the incredibly life-like portrait of the nubile enchantress hanging on the wall before us. "Always did like Collier's work," he said.

"Who's Collier?" I asked.

"The Honorable John Collier," Doc replied, reading a blurb from a fancy pewter plaque hanging on the wall. "Amongst other things, he was a rather famous eighteenth century English artist. This is evidently a collection of some of his more renowned pieces."

"That's really swell," I grumbled, taking a closer look at the risqué painting Rooster was ogling. "Not that I don't enjoy really big pictures of scantily clad women, but I thought we were here to find—"

"Lilith," Erin murmured, motioning at the name plate under the portrait.

Gazing at the portrait again, I was instantly mesmerized by the haunting depiction of a pale, yet voluptuous nude femme fatale standing seductively deep within a dark woodland.

With a face of dominating beauty, her head was erotically tilted to the side, allowing her ravishing red hair to flow down her back and clear past her thighs. Showing absolutely no attempt at modesty, her arms alluringly cradled her torso, allowing a rather brazen display of her impressive bare breasts. In fact, the only thing preventing her from being butt-ass naked, was the ginormous snake appropriately, or totally not appropriately, positioned around her waist and curled around her legs. With her eyes closed and the ever-so-faint glimmer of a sultry smile on her pursed lips, she nestled the sizable head of the serpent under her chin.

Actually, the longer I looked at it, the more disturbing the whole thing became.

"Ah, Rooster," I managed to force out after an impossibly long thirty seconds. "Why did you bring us here to stare at an oil painting centerfold of your mom?"

"Actually, Dean," Erin grumbled, "I think you're the only one staring."

"Am not."

"And that's not drool on your scruffy chin either, is it?"

"I have allergies."

"Quiet," Rooster grunted, "I'm trying to get her attention."

"*Her*?" Erin asked, befuddled. "That's just a painting, John."

"I think she'd disagree with you," he replied, as the young seductress in the portrait opened her eyes and looked straight at us.

"Holy fuck," I blurted out, taking a step backward and doing everything within my power not to will the cloak into being.

Straightening her head and carefully releasing the big ass snake to happily slither along the forest floor of the painting, the now stark-naked Old Testament exhibitionist smiled cunningly and casually stepped out of the portrait and into real life.

So, just to be clear, she literally stepped out of the portrait, leaving behind a noticeable void on the canvas in the shape of her silhouette, and was standing right in front of us as large as life. And, of course, she was naked.

In the buff.

In the raw.

Topless.

Bottomless.

Full friggin monty.

Wearing nothing but a smile.

Rooster's mom.

Nakie!

18

Letting out an eccentric yet highly spirited, "My darling, Eóin! My dearest baby boy! How I've missed you," Rooster's mom then proceeded to wrap herself around him in a creepy, full body hug. The exceptionally uncomfortable part was that she looked easily five years younger than him.

Making the mental note that I was going to need some serious, serious therapy when this was over, I turned to Doc. "Damn, did not see that coming."

"Wipe the drool off your face. You're embarrassing yourself."

"Right, sorry."

"Hello, Mother," Rooster mumbled, trying his best to wrestle free of the maternal mixed martial arts leg lock maneuver. "Sorry it's been so long since my last visit. Work's been crazy. You know how Abernethy is."

"Unfortunately, I do not," she said in an alluring, nasally tone that was something in between Michelle Pfeiffer's Catwoman, Marilyn Monroe, and any one of the Spice Girls. "Not from lack of trying either, darling. Such a rugged, *beastly* man. That kilt — simply *delicious*."

"Okay, thanks for that," Rooster cut in, looking like he was about to blow chunks. "And now we're switching topics ... You, ah, maybe want to put some clothes on?"

"And why would I do such a thing, dearest?"

"Because I want you to meet some friends of mine. And it'd be really awesome if you weren't completely freaking naked."

"*Friends?*" She purred, turning her vampish gaze on me and Doc. "Yum."

"No, no, no," he blurted out. "Not yum."

"Are they not *those* kinds of friends, darling?"

"No. No, they're not."

"Double drat." She pouted. "You disappoint, Eóin. Such a terrible tease."

"Gross," Erin muttered.

"Ugh," I added for good measure.

"Okay, we're *so* starting this conversation over," Rooster grumbled in exasperation. "Mother, this is Dean Robinson and—"

"Erin Anne Kelly," Lilith said, intently gazing at Doc like she was looking straight into her soul.

"You know me?" Erin asked, completely taken aback.

"Fearless determination wrapped in untamed beauty," the beguiling femme playfully replied as a silken, shoulder-cut dress of pure white gracefully manifested over her pale body. "Your very existence gives me *credence*."

When Doc offered nothing in response but an icy stare, Lilith said, "More to the point, child, I know what you're meant to do."

"I don't understand."

"You walk in the shadow of a certainty *destiny*, or so you've been told. Am I right?"

"My purpose. You know what it is."

"I do," Lilith replied, keenly studying Erin like a fortune teller. "But you do not. Not yet."

"Mariel told me—"

"What you needed to hear. Nothing more. And much, *much* less. For that's what *angels* do. Incessant race of *meddlesome,* pompous dissidents. *Gag* me."

"Okay," Erin muttered, "You totally lost me there."

"Worry not, child," she somberly replied, placing a hand on Doc's forehead in an obscure motherly fashion, almost like she felt compassion for her. "Your will is strong. Stronger than that of any *angel* and certainly that of any *man*. You will soon understand all that you must." Instantly switching back to batshit crazy mode, a deviously wide smile curled across Lilith's flawless face. "Yay! You've *so* much to look forward to. How exciting!"

"Ah, what the hell was that about?" I grunted.

Shifting her acute stare to me, her smile morphed into a flirtatious grin as her pristine blue eyes danced with an intoxicating fiery madness. "Wouldn't you like to know?" she teased, tapping a finger on my nose. "But you can't."

"Why the hell not?"

"*Because*, lover, such a *precious* secret is not for me to tell. My *lips* are sealed, *Dean Robinson*, Seventh Deacon of the Seventh Line. Unless, of course, you would like to *un-seal* them?"

"Gonna pass, Lil," I muttered, making the mental note that Lucifer's ex was definitely a couple twists short of a slinky. "You, ah, don't mind if I call you Lil, do you?"

"*You* may call me whatever you wish," she quipped, circling me like a praying mantis while running her hands through her lavish ginger mane. Momentarily mesmerized by her overbearing, unnatural wiles, I found myself strangely at a loss for words. "I know about *you,* Dean Robinson," she continued, holding me hostage with her vexing gaze.

"Ah, you do?"

"Such terrible trouble you've caused for the seraphic court," she playfully scolded. "So wonderfully *naughty*."

"Look, I don't know what you think you know, but—"

"Oh shush, lovie. I haven't seen the Heavens worked into this much of a tizzy for millennia. You and that interminable do-gooder, *Stephen,* have caused quite the *fuss* with your *mutiny*."

"Mutiny?" I grunted. "That's total bullshit."

"Oh, simmer down, *Captain*," she replied, like I was a total buzzkill. "Do you not think me wise enough to see what's unfolding? I'm well aware of where your *loyalties* lie."

"Wait, you do?"

"Of course, silly boy. More pressing, however, I must admit that I'm simply *tickled* you finally got around to paying me a *visit*. I understand you're quite *popular* these days."

"Come again?"

"Don't be shy, Dean. I'm in possession of what you *need,*" she said, smacking her lips. "Aren't I?"

"Ah, what?" I grumbled, completely caught off guard by what I hoped wasn't a double entendre from Rooster's mom. But I was pretty sure it was.

"You know why we're here," Erin said, thankfully placing herself between me and the physical embodiment of original sin.

Lilith winked at her. "I do, child. I've been expecting you. *All* of you."

"Wait, what?" Rooster chimed in. "You know? You know we're here about the Vessel?"

"Why else would you be here, dearest? To pay homage to your beloved mother who pines for you, moment by *painful* passing moment, throughout countless centuries?"

"Ah, maybe?"

"Sadly, I think not, Eóin."

"Ouch," I muttered.

"Okay," Rooster cringed, "I may have deserved that. Missed a few Mother's Days over the years."

"No matter, dearest," Lilith said, stroking Rooster's cheek, "You'll always be my absolute *fabbest* fave despite your prodigal nature. Your brothers, much to my dismay, are all their *father's* sons. But you, *you* have always been mommy's little boy."

"Well," I muttered, making the mental note to reuse the living shit out of 'fabbest fave' in every future conversation I ever have with Rooster, "This was fun. A really special and incredibly strange family moment. And now that it's friggin over, can we start talking about the part where you give us the Ark? Please tell me it's not somewhere in that picture with the snake. I hate snakes."

"Give you the Vessel?" Lil scoffed amongst a sultry laugh, "You misunderstand me, lovie. I have no intentions of *giving* you anything. Unless, of course, we've transitioned from business to *pleasure*. In which case, I'd be happy to—"

"No, no, no," Rooster cut in. "We're still proceeding with the business end of things here. Wait, that came out wrong. What I meant was—"

"You want to make a deal," Erin said, fixated on Lilith and thankfully shutting Rooster up.

"Something for something," she replied. "Anything less, my dears, would be charity. And there's no enterprise in charity. Is there, darlings?"

"Time for you to appeal to her good nature, fabbest fave," I grumbled at Rooster, who responded with a quick flip of his middle finger.

"What are your terms, Mother?"

"Eóin, shame on you, dearest," she chided. "Please tell me you didn't come to ask for that which is mine without compensation in hand?"

"Ah, I totally didn't come to ask for that which is yours without compensation in hand."

"For Christ's sake," I muttered, having had enough. "We don't have time for this bullshit. What do you want, Lil? Money? Subscription to the friggin jelly of the month club? A nice two-bedroom condo painted into your portrait? What?"

"Your negotiating skills seriously blow," Erin grumbled.

"Interesting," Lilith said with a truly wicked grin, "Am I to understand you are willingly entering into negotiations with me, Dean Robinson?"

"You're goddamn right I am."

"No, he's not." Rooster said. "I am."

"No, you're not," I grunted. "I am."

"You don't understand—"

"Will you shut the hell up already? I know what I'm doing."

Reaching into her sultry gown, Lilith produced a small dagger etched with some curious Enochian script, which was somehow unnaturally concealed in her voluptuous bodice. Holding out her right hand, she proceeded to open a sizable gash on her palm.

"Give me your hand," she ordered, as her eyes lit up and started a slow transition from pristine blue to fiery red. Offering my right hand in response, she ran the dagger across my palm and tightly gripped it in her own.

"Dean Robinson," she said, squeezing with otherworldly force as her eyes glowed a harrowing, blazing red and a spectral silhouette of arcane energy framed her body. "My terms are simple. As blood is given and blood is received, so shall be the nature of our binding pact. I solemnly swear to furnish you with that which you desire. And, in turn, you shall do the same for me. Should either party renege on this arrangement, their very *soul* do they forfeit to the other. Do we have an accord?"

As blood literally gushed from our locked palms and trickled onto the surrounding floor, I locked gazes with her. "You're goddamn right we do."

Releasing her death grip, her eyes flashed back to normal as she callously wiped her bloody mitt across the torso of her immaculate white dress.

"Very well," she said as her mouth curled into a triumphant grin. "Now that the formalities are concluded, shall we discuss *payment*?"

And there was just something about the way she said it that made me instantly realize I'd just made a mistake.

A really friggin big one.

19

"AH, MOTHER," Rooster said, like a real momma's boy.

"Yes, dearest?" Lilith replied, with the gaiety of an apex predator that just swallowed her prey whole.

"You mind if I have a moment with Dean and Erin? Just need a minute. Quick chat. Guy stuff. I mean, guy stuff and Erin stuff."

"But of course," she purred. "Go right ahead."

Pulling me aside, Rooster said, "Are you out of your goddamned mind?"

"Seriously, Dean," Doc added. "What the hell were you thinking?"

"What?" I shot back, glaring at them.

"*What*?" Rooster scoffed. "Do you have any freaking idea what you've just done?"

"I got us the Ark. Plain and simple."

"At what cost?" Erin asked.

"Oh, I'm sorry, Doc. Did I miss something? Or, was it not pretty fucking crystal clear that Rooster's whack job of a mom, no offense, wasn't going to simply give it to us with a goddamn bow on top."

Rooster shook his head. "You should have let me make the deal."

"Not a chance. I don't need that on my conscience."

"You don't get it. This is echelons above your pay grade. You ever negotiate with a supernatural being that's as old as time itself? No? Oh, I didn't freaking think so. My mother is literally a force of nature. You have no idea what she's capable of."

"Well, I guess we're about to find out," Erin said, coldly.

"Yes, we are," I chimed in. "Unless there's any more guy stuff to talk about."

"You might not have any *guy stuff* left when she's done with you," Rooster muttered, under his breath.

Hoping like hell that wasn't the case, I grumbled, "We good here?"

"Look," he said, with the utmost of sincerity, "whatever you do, be *very* literal in your terms. Okay? Like *very* specific. If you do anything less, she'll eat you alive. Don't assume anything."

"Literal. Got it."

"*Very* specific."

"Yep."

"Like making a wish to a genie in a bottle."

"Will you friggin stop already?"

"Are you darlings finished with your little *confab*?" Lil said, still smiling like she won the damn lottery.

"All set," I muttered. "Let's do this."

"Yay! Let's!"

"I hope you know what you're doing," Erin said, clearly not happy with the way this was playing out.

"Relax, Doc. I got this."

"So, lovie," Lil said, with a distinct air of legality, "what is it that you *desire* from me?"

"You know what I want," I replied. "The Ark of the Covenant. Also known as the Vessel."

"You *want* the Ark of the Covenant," Lilith confirmed.

Watching Rooster cringe, I added, "Ah, more *specifically*, I want the Ark of the Covenant, formerly in the possession of Lucifer, that you may or may not have procured with extreme prejudice during the most unfortunate marital warfare campaign you waged against your dirtbag, fallen angel ex-hubby."

"Very well," she nodded. "I agree to your terms of wanting the Vessel as you have so described."

"You do?"

"I do," she said, matter-of-factly. "And in return, you will agree to perform a single favor for me. A favor whose nature will be disclosed at the time of its necessity."

"A favor."

"A teeny, tiny *favor.*"

"What kind of favor?"

"That is for me to decide. When I decide it."

"And I can't refuse this *favor,* whenever the hell you ask for it."

"Of course you can, lovie. But, let me remind you that in accordance with the terms of our pact, you'll have to willingly forfeit your *soul* in recompense."

"Always good to have options," I muttered, feeling sympathy for the Devil for actually being married to this crazy bitch. And for the record, that was totally a Rolling Stones reference.

She grinned. "So, do we have an accord, Dean Robinson?"

I nodded. "We have an accord."

"Yay!" She clapped her hands together and twirled around like a child on Christmas morning. Doing this for several seconds, as we all stood there and awkwardly watched, she finally stopped and gave Rooster another full body hug. "It was just wonderful to see you, Eóin. Please do visit again, dearest." Spinning toward me and Doc, she added, "The very best of luck to you, darlings. And, Dean, I'll be in *touch* sooner than not. Toodles!"

As she began to elegantly waltz toward her portrait, I said, "Aren't you forgetting something? What about the Ark?"

"What about it?"

"You just agreed to give it to me."

Stopping in mid-stride, she turned around. "I did no such thing, lovie. We agreed that you *wanted* the Ark of the Covenant. Do you not still *want* it?"

"Of course I goddamn want it."

"You see? My end of the bargain is upheld. Now, if you'll excuse me—"

"Oh, hell no," I grunted. Glancing at Rooster, I shrugged my shoulders. "Sorry about this, buddy."

"Wait, what?" he protested to no avail as I willed the cloak into being and it elegantly manifested in a spectral flash of white luminescence. Billowing about my shoulders, its otherworldly power coursed through my body like an electric current as my lips curled into a dark smile. Feeling the mental switch flip to the on position, I called for the shotgun and instantly felt the presence of the leather, scabbard-like holster on my back.

Ripping the semi-divine 1887 Winchester free, I trained both barrels on Lil's bodacious tatas. "We just entered hostile negotiations."

"My, *my*," she purred, rolling her head back on her shoulders and creepily soaking in the arcane power emanating from the cloak. "Is it just me or did it suddenly get *hot* in here?"

"Cut the shit, crazypants. In less than seven hours, the goddamn barkangel and his demented main minion, Azazel, are going to rain down an unholy fucking shitstorm on mankind."

"What, pray tell, is a *barkangel*?"

"The bad archangel," both Rooster and Erin unenthusiastically mumbled in unison.

"Be that as it may," Lil continued without further commentary on my moniker for the Heavenly traitor, "I don't see what any of *that* has to do with little old *moi*."

"It's like this," I muttered, taking a bold step toward the wicked whack job witch of the oil painting. "We need the Ark to stop the barkangel. You have the friggin Ark. And despite your bullshit cutesy pie play on words, you and I just made a deal for it. A deal you're gonna deliver on. Right goddamn now."

"Or what, Dean Robinson? What will you do?"

Focusing my will for a quick second, I cocked the shotgun lever and grinned as the both barrels glowed with Judgment fire and the cloak rippled like a caged animal in a brazen show of force.

"You make a *compelling* argument," Lilith jested, looking like she was enjoying the moment as her eyes glowed a harrowing, fiery red. "But I remain *unwilling* to alter the terms of our arrangement. A *deal* is a deal."

"Please, Mother," Rooster pleaded. "Be reasonable."

"*Reasonable*? And why should I do such a thing, dearest?"

"Because if you choose not to help us," Erin said with the utmost of sincerity, "you'll be helping the seraphic court by default."

"It's that simple," I added. "Us or them. Which side are you on?"

"Neither," she said, as her eyes flashed back to their normal intoxicating blue. "But, call me *curious*, what are your intentions for the Vessel should it come into your possession?"

Figuring things couldn't get much worse at this point, I grunted, "To turn it into a pile of splinters so the gates of Tartarus can never be opened."

"You mean to *destroy* it?" Lilith gasped as Rooster cringed for the second time in as many minutes. And then things took an interesting turn. As Rooster tried his best to smooth over the situation, Lilith's face curled into a beaming smile. Fixing me with a truly wicked gaze, she said, "Do you *promise* to do so?"

"Ah, what?" I replied, completely caught off guard.

"Do you promise to destroy that *wretched* trinket should I provide its whereabouts?"

Still trying to wrap my head around what the hell just happened, I sheathed the shotgun. "Hell yes, I promise."

"Very well. I may be *inclined* to help you after all."

"Wait, what?" Rooster scoffed. "You are? Ah, why?"

"That's simple, dearest. I absolutely *loathe* your father. And for some deluded reason, *he* cherished that miserable *object* above all else. I simply reveled in *ripping* it from his grasp. My intentions were to reduce it to ash myself, but I've found *Father's* earthbound treasure chest annoyingly impervious to my power. Or any *other* power for that matter. But perhaps that of a *Deacon* would finally rid me of that haunting reminder of him. What a *delicious* thought!"

"Right," I grumbled, thinking that I probably shouldn't ruin all the fun and tell her that Lew also wants us to nuke the friggin thing. "So, does that mean you'll give it to us now?"

"Well, truth be told, lovie, I haven't had the Vessel for nearly four decades."

"What do you mean you don't have it? You said—"

"I *never* said it was in my possession. You simply assumed it was. In all actuality, I bartered it away to a charming young time phantom who owed me a favor. But I can tell you where it is. Or more appropriately, *when* it is."

"Wait." Rooster scoffed. "You made a deal for something you don't even have? That is so freaking typical..."

"I am what I am, dearest. You honestly should have seen that coming."

"Okay, I give up," I muttered, making the mental note to never ever ... *ever* try to negotiate with Rooster's mom again. "Where is it, Lil?

"October 21st," she said. "1975."

"I'm sorry, what?"

"A day in time," Rooster said, somewhat rhetorically. "Clever."

"I couldn't have it fall back into the hands of your *father* now, could I, dearest? Unable to destroy it, I took precaution to ensure it was tucked away in the absolute last place he'd ever look."

"A day in *time*?" Erin said, trying to wrap her head around the concept. "What the hell does that even mean?"

"And what the frig is a time *phantom*?" I asked, more than lost with the obscure turn of events. "Is that some kind of opera shit?"

"No. No, it's not," Rooster said. "I'll explain later." He shifted his full attention to Lilith. "Who is he? Who's the time phantom?"

"An absolutely *strapping* young beau named Richard Ronkowski."

"So, you just gave him the freaking Ark of the Covenant?"

"Of course not, Eóin. We struck a very favorable deal for which I was duly compensated. Time and time and *yummy* time again."

"And thank you for another visual I'll never get out of my head," he grumbled. "So, assuming we can even get to October 21st, *1975* — where can we find this Ronkowski guy?"

"No telling, dearest. For that one single day in history, the globe is his playground. He could literally be anywhere."

"How the hell are we supposed to find him then?"

"That's the point, silly. No one is *supposed* to find him. Not even me. It was a contingency of our agreement."

"Okay, just so I'm clear," Rooster muttered, shaking his head in frustration. "You're saying that to find the Ark, we have to travel back *thirty-eight years* to a single day in history and then track down some random temporal jumper, who could be anywhere on the entire freaking planet, before that single day expires."

"Exactly!"

"Ah, Mother, that's freaking impossible. Is this seriously your idea of helping us?"

"Oh, don't be such a sour puss. I'm sure you'll think of something. You've always been so *resourceful*. Besides, finding him will be the very least of your challenges."

"There's more? For reals?"

"Just another minor detail, dearest. In accordance with our *terms,* should Mr. Ronkowski lose possession of the Vessel, he will forfeit his soul to me. So, needless to say, he'll be less than inclined to part with it."

"But you *are* going to help us with that part, right?"

After a prolonged giggle, Lil said, "And renege on my side of the pact? I think not, dearest."

"Are you friggin serious?" I grumbled.

"Tell you what, lovie," she playfully winked, "I'll *think* about it."

"Great. Thanks, Mom," Rooster muttered. "That's amazing. Like beyond words. Really special."

"You're *most* welcome. Is there anything else I can do to *help*?"

"No. No, there isn't, Mother. In your usual fashion, you've done more than enough."

"Yay! And please do let me know how you make out. I just adore happy endings."

"Was I adopted?"

Ignoring Rooster's snide question, Lilith evidently decided it was time to go and simply said, "Toodles!" while blowing us a series of big, wet kisses. And, of course, as she happily danced back toward her arcane portrait, her blood-riddled, silken dress melted from existence, leaving her, once again, butt ass nakie.

Nakie!

Casually turning and offering me a quick wink, she snapped her fingers and was inexplicably sucked back into the painting only to resume the sultry pose we had found her in moments earlier.

"Ah, guys," I grumbled, completely befuddled by the last thirty seconds, "What in the literal fuck was that about?"

"Which part?" Erin asked, looking like she wanted to punch somebody.

"All of it?"

"Well," she replied, "I might have missed a few details here and there amidst the psychotically eccentric babble, *but* it sounded like Lilith actually *had* the Ark of the Covenant at some point, but then *traded* it for sexual favors to a guy who *lives* in a single day in 1975. *And*, we evidently have to go *back in time* to find *him* before we can ultimately find *it*."

"That's what I thought I heard, too. But that can't be right because it's totally friggin insane. Isn't it?"

"Ah, which part?"

"All of it," Rooster muttered, whipping out his arcane pad of sticky notes and fountain pen. "But that doesn't mean it can't be done. We need to go."

"Where are we going, Marty McFly?" I scoffed. "Back in time?"

"It's not like I have a freaking DeLorean with a flux capacitor just sitting around in some random workshop," he said like I was a total dumbass. "We can't just up and go back in time."

"I'm strangely relieved to hear you say that."

"Time travel requires planning. And resources. And bubble gum. Lots and lots of bubble gum. I need to make a few phone calls. Come on, guys, we've got work to do."

Without so much as another word, he determinedly stepped through the sticky pad portal that manifested on the wall next to Lil's portrait and vanished.

As Erin and I stood there for an awkward moment or two blankly staring at each other, she finally said, "That was a joke, right? He's not serious."

I shrugged. "Not sure, Doc, but, if there is a DeLorean with a flux capacitor on the other end of that sticky note, I'm *so* riding shotgun."

20

WITH DOC ON MY HEELS, we emerged from the ass-end of yet another ethereal gateway to a snowy vision of Rooster fumbling around with a large wooden door to a rustic A-frame cabin situated in the center of a small cluster of white-dusted pine trees.

Taking a closer look as I quickly established my bearings, the dilapidated structure appeared to be inexplicably positioned on the literal crest of a big ass mountain in a much, much *bigger ass* mountain range.

Absolutely stunned by the sheer grandeur of the majestic landscape, Erin muttered, "Holy shit," as we both gazed in complete awe at the vast panorama of snowcapped peaks forming a mind-blowing three-hundred-and-sixty-degree perimeter around us. The afternoon sun was creeping toward the horizon line, and the dark blue sky provided an ominous reminder that Saturday night was closing in on us. And we were running out of time.

"Where are we?" I asked, snapping out of the momentary daze as a gust of frigid air belted me in the face and I instantly became conscious of the subfreezing temperature.

"Montana," Rooster muttered, clearly frustrated that he couldn't seem to get the door open, "Tobacco Root Mountains in the northern Rockies."

"Rockies, eh?"

"What exactly are we doing here?" Erin asked as she zipped up her black leather jacket in an attempt to hold the arctic wind and drifting snow at bay.

"I have some commo equipment stashed inside," Rooster said. "If it still works, we can radio the team and hopefully connect a couple dots."

I shook my head. "So, this shit box of a cabin isn't a time machine?"

"Nope. It's one of my old safehouses. And for the record, if I was going to make a time machine, I wouldn't make it out of a shit box cabin. I'd trick out a phone booth. Straight up Bill and Ted style."

"*Excellent Adventure* or *Bogus Journey*?"

"Please." He scoffed. "*Excellent Adventure* ... *Bogus Journey* was total crap."

"How old is this joint?" Erin asked, not appreciating the movie banter.

"Couple hundred years. Me and Caveman built it back in the early-1800s during the Gold Rush. I call it The Crow Nest."

"The *Crow* Nest, eh?" I muttered.

"Yeppers. It's a *Rooster* mountain fortress ... and roosters *crow,* ergo it's the *Crow* Nest. Get it?"

"Yeah, I get it. Came up with that all your own, did ya?"

"I can't take all the credit. Caveman helped. Good, right?"

"Amazing. Exceptionally clever with a detectable hint of dumbass," I muttered, thinking they should have let Duncan name the joint.

I mean, hell, that could have yielded some absolute jewels like The Pocket Pig Mountain Top Emporium, Lil' D's Highland Hog Haberdashery, or Duncan's Yellow Snow Swine Chalet. Could've been epic.

"Mountain fortress?" Doc said, clearly unimpressed by the place *and* the name. "Looks more like an abandoned crack house."

"Yeah, she's seen better days for sure. I haven't been here since the early eighties. And evidently, I can't remember how to disable the locking wards I set up on the damn door. In retrospect, think I may have gotten a little too cute with the cryptogram."

"That doesn't sound like you at all," I grunted, feeling like my face was about to fall off from a combination of the sub-zero temperature and the persistent pelting of the icy wind gusts.

Figuring a well-placed application of brute force and ignorance would more than do the trick, I willed the gauntlets into being and instantly felt them cover my hands and forearms in argent, glinting metal.

"I've never seen a lock like that before," Erin commented through chattering teeth as she studied the medieval looking security mechanism for a few seconds.

"It's a wheel cipher," Rooster said, quickly slipping into bloviation mode. "It's probably coded with a Fibonacci sequence or some variation thereof. That was my go-to for years. Back in the day, I used to pride myself on constructing all manner of unbreakable mystical security measures—"

Not really in the mood to hear how that story ended, I sunk all my supernatural strength into a crushing right cross and dropped my metal fist squarely into his centuries-old arcane gadget. As it promptly shattered into a gazillion pieces and the door swung open, Rooster grumbled, "I hate you."

I grinned. "You're welcome."

Entering the minuscule backwoods shack to find it furnished by nothing but a dust-covered, metal-framed bunkbed and a series of Cheryl Tiegs posters thumbtacked to the slanted walls, Rooster murmured a few words in Enochian, and a mammoth fire roared to life in the modest hearth on the back wall.

"That's more like it," he said, closing the door and latching it from the inside. "Now we can get to work. You guys hungry?"

"I'm starving," Erin replied, scurrying to the hearth while rubbing her hands together in an attempt to avoid certain frostbite.

"You have food?" I asked, glancing around the absolutely barren, single room shanty. "In *here?*"

"Oh, ye of little faith," Rooster grumbled, reaching down and tapping three times on a crooked board directly under the poster-sized cover of the February, 1983 *Sports Illustrated* Swim Suit Edition displaying 'Sizzling Cheryl' beating the heat in Jamaica.

And before I had the chance to dispel a witty comeback, the wooden floor retracted into itself to reveal a set of mammoth stone steps leading to a sizable sub level. "I keep the good stuff down below," he said, with a cheesy smirk.

"That's what she said," I muttered, traversing the stairs into the Crow

Nest's secret lair. As several torches sputtered to life upon the snapping of Rooster's fingers, the dark room was bathed in flickering orange light, and as much as I hated to admit it...it was pretty sweet.

Much like MacCawill's clandestine Man Cave, the Crow Nest basement seemed to be impossibly cut directly into the surrounding mountain. About double the size of the shit box shanty looming above, the rock-walled bunker featured a small, yet impressive array of kitchen equipment and a couple 1960s vintage La-Z-Boy chairs positioned around a big ass old school TV set complete with rabbit ears. Most impressively, set in the far corner were some seriously dated, military spec radio equipment and what appeared to be a Commodore 64 personal computer with a floppy drive and dot matrix printer, infused with some goofy looking Rooster tech.

In fact, the only thing really missing from the place was—

"Beer?" Rooster asked, opening the fridge and pulling out a couple silver cans adorned with the signature RoosterBragh logo.

"Does a bear shit in the woods?" I said, as my mouth started to water.

Doc smiled. "I'll take two."

Throwing us a couple cold ones while firing up a modest kiln and sliding in some frozen pizzas, Rooster said, "Seems like we'll have to make do with pizza. Caveman must've cleaned out the rest of the chow. Either that or he's been sneaking chicks in here *again*. On that note, you guys might not want to sit on the chairs. No telling what those stains are."

Trying to erase that mental image from my memory banks, I happily cracked open the frosty beverage and inhaled its twelve ounces of liquid nirvana in about two seconds flat.

"Did you even taste that?" Erin chuckled.

"I don't need to taste it. I already know it's good. Is there any more?"

Tossing me another one while plopping down on a metal stool next to his dusty array of eighties electronics, Rooster powered up his archaic computer and began to methodically turn the various and assorted knobs lining the base console of the radio.

"Hello, gorgeous," he mumbled, running his hands all over the equipment like it was his girlfriend. "Daddy's home."

"Yep. Could've gone for the rest of my afterlife without hearing that," I grumbled, draining my second beer. "Whenever you finish tuning up your digitals over there, you think we could have a little group discussion about what exactly you and Lil were rambling on about in her museum penthouse?"

Taking a healthy gulp of RoosterBragh, Erin said, "Like starting with — are we *seriously* contemplating going back in time to find the Ark of the Covenant? And if so, how exactly are we planning to go back in *freaking time* to find the Ark of the Covenant?"

Rooster spun around on his stool to face us. "I should probably explain a few things, huh?"

"You think?" Erin scoffed.

Grabbing yet another beer from the fridge, I muttered, "And for Christ's sake, give us the short version."

"Short version," he said, "I can do that."

"Pretty sure you can't. But go ahead and try."

"Okay. So, time doesn't exactly work the way everyone thinks."

"How so?" Erin asked, finishing her beer and crushing the can with the heel of her boot before cracking open another one. And if that ain't dead sexy, I don't know what is.

Rooster grinned. "It's all about perception. What do you guys know about string theory?"

"I know a lot about string cheese," I said. "Stringy. Chewy. Salty. Friggin delicious."

Glaring at me, Erin shook her head. "Are you talking about physics, John? Black holes and condensed matter? Things like that?"

"Exactly!" Rooster said, with a shit-eating grin, "And yet, not at all."

"Here comes the long version," I muttered, as my enigmatic ginger colleague slipped into bloviation mode *again*. "Do we have enough beer to endure this?"

"Time itself," he continued, ignoring my snide commentary, "is *not* linear. It's concurrent. It only *seems* linear because otherwise the human mind couldn't conceive the difference between order and chaos."

Erin nodded. "So you're saying that Einstein was right? There's no difference between the present, past, and future?"

"That's exactly what I'm saying. All *time* exists simultaneously."

"That's ridiculous," I grumbled.

"Is it?" Rooster said, like a smug college professor. "I'll give you an example. Sunlight."

"What about it?"

"Sunlight travels through *space,* and by the time we *see* it on Earth, it's already eight minutes old."

"So?"

"So, we're literally seeing eight minutes into the *past* every time we look at sunlight. *But* if we perceive sunlight as instantaneous, we could literally see any point in time."

"Meaning?"

"*Meaning,* that if time and space are linked, or more specifically, they're the *same* thing, then why can't people with the ability to perceive reality differently just place themselves in another place *or* another time as they see fit?"

"Because, people can't perceive reality differently," Doc said, catching onto the plot. "But I'm guessing angels can."

"Yes. Yes, they can. Angels *and* a very rare species of nephilim. The tempus phasmatis. Also known as—"

"Time phantoms."

"Yeppers. Time phantoms, or temporal jumpers as they're also known, can, *quite literally,* move at will through the space time continuum. Or, in the case of Richard Ronkowski, choose to stay in a single day or even a single moment."

"But wouldn't they be continuously rewriting history?"

"And that's the real magic in the paradox. By virtue of their very nature, they exist everywhere *and* they exist nowhere. They can't *impact* the timeline as they move through it because everything is *happening* in a single simultaneous moment. Awesome, right?"

"Not awesome," I grumbled.

"But it makes sense, doesn't it?"

"Not so much," Erin muttered.

"So," I said, trying to wrap my head around Rooster's magical mystery tour mashup of *Doctor Who,* Stephen Hawking, and every episode of *Quantum Leap,* "In order for us to get back to Ronkowski and snatch the Ark from his sorry ass, we need our own time phantom to take us there."

Rooster nodded. "Exactly."

"Damn. So, no DeLorean, eh?"

"No DeLorean."

"That blows."

"So, what next?" Doc asked, clearly not as upset about the lack of a DeLorean in this time travel equation as I was.

Spinning around on his stool and turning his attention back to his array of dust-covered electronic gadgetry, Rooster said, "Time to find us a tempus phasmatis."

"How do we do that?" I asked.

"I've got a plan."

"Which is?"

"I'm going to fire up RoosterRadio and call Big A."

"And then?"

"I'm going to ask him to find us a time phantom using the nepher scanner in the Reliquary."

"And then?"

"*Then,* we go and find the time phantom, press-gang his ass into joining our crew, and make him take us back to 1975."

"Does that make us time pirates?" Erin asked.

"Pirates or no pirates," I muttered, about at my wits end, "that plan needs some serious work."

"I haven't gotten to the best part yet," he continued, undeterred. "*Before* we do all that, we choke down some pizza and have another beer."

"Although, it may be just the kind of outside the box thinking that we need at the moment."

"We're out of beer," Erin sadly announced.

"Or not."

21

"Gray Fox, Gray Fox — This is Red Squirrel. Over."

As the monochrome screen to Rooster's archaic Commodore 64 flickered to life, he methodically spun a few dials on the adjacent radio base station and depressed the transmit button on the World War II vintage microphone.

"Gray Fox, Gray Fox," he repeated. "This is Red Squirrel. Do you copy, Gray Fox? Over."

And before I had the opportunity to offer snide commentary on his prolific set of call signs, a distorted image began to form on the oversized VGA monitor accompanied by an unmistakable, brogue-laden voice barking at us through the metal speaker.

"Aye, Wee Squirrel. This is Gray and Foxy. You copy me, do you? Over the hill, yeah? Bloody hell, is this thing on?"

"What the frig did he just say?" I chuckled.

"Big A's never really grasped the whole concept of proper radio etiquette," Rooster muttered, shaking his head. "Roger that, Gray *Fox*. This is *Red* Squirrel. Copy you loud and clear. Is the line secure?"

"Aye, Jackie," Abernethy responded, as his black and white image came into full focus to reveal the burly Scotsman in all his bearded glory. "It's secure. How are you, laddie?"

"We're doing okay, boss. Not dead...yet. How're things on your end?"

"Aside from the occasional archangel crawling up me arse, things are no different than when you left, which is the primary problem. Is that Deannie and the wee lass I see with ye?"

"It's us, sir," I answered.

"Bloody hell. Ye look like shite, lad."

"Thanks?"

"Nonetheless, I'm happy to see you. Thought fer sure you'd be gutted like a wee fish by now. Half of the Heavenly Realms are on the lookout fer you. The whole lot of you."

"Really? Haven't noticed. What about Stephen? Have you heard from him?"

"Nae. Not a peep. Was hoping you would have some news on the matter."

"Negative."

"We're running out of time, lad. Less than four hours until Azazel's deadline."

"What about the anakim. Any leads?"

He shook his head. "Crockett thought he'd found something in Arizona but nothing definitive yet."

"Arizona, eh?"

"Aye, he followed a pack of beasties to the Grand Canyon, but they pulled a wee vanishing act. He's posted there with a team of clerics in the event they show themselves again. Aside from that, we're shite out of luck."

"Hence the reason for my call," Rooster said. "I think we have a way to expose the traitor."

"About bloody time. What is it, Jackie?"

"It's kind of a long story. But we need your help to find a temporal jumper."

"A phantom? What fer?"

"If I told you, you wouldn't believe me."

"Right," Abernethy grumbled, figuring he was better off not knowing. "Let's see if we can track one down then."

Fumbling around with his phone-sized computer thingamajig for a second or two, Big A ran his mammoth fingers across the screen. "Bad news," he said. "Not picking up any signatures on the scanner. Seems they may have all fled the present and made fer greener pastures in other time periods. Given the current state of affairs, you can hardly blame 'em."

"Fuck," I muttered, which was immediately echoed by Rooster and Doc in ominous unison.

"Just a wee second," Big A murmured, focusing intently on his gadget, "I may just have one after all. He's trying to ward himself but thankfully doing a piss poor job of it. His identity is coming up as... Bloody hell, Jackie, it's Owen Trask."

"Wait, what?" Rooster said, elated. "That's great!"

"*Great*? Did you not hear me, lad? I said it's Owen bloody Trask."

"I heard you. Where is he?"

"Can't be sure. His signature's weak. He's somewhere in North America, but that's the best I can do. Trask is a tricky blighter, Jackie. He'll be a needle in a haystack if he's even that. And not to mention yer sordid history with him."

"That's okay. I've got an idea."

"I'd be keen to know what it is."

"Trust me, boss. You really don't."

"Aye. You best get on with it then. You lot be wary. Watch yer arses."

"Do the same. I'll be in touch."

As Big A's chiseled face began to fade from the screen, he said, "And Deannie, whatever it is yer planning on doing, do me a wee favor, and hurry the hell up!"

"Roger that, boss," I grumbled, despite the fact I really had no earthly idea what it was we were doing yet.

"So," Erin cut in, "what now?"

"You want the good news or the bad news?" Rooster said, spinning the radio dial to a different frequency and banging some keys on the old ass keyboard.

"The good news," I muttered. "Please."

"Well, as the fates would have it, Owen *Octavius* Trask, or Double OT as he's better known in most circles, is one of Coop's old drinking buddies. Back in fourteenth century England those two were thick as thieves. Mainly because they were *actual* thieves."

"Coop? Was a friggin thief?"

"Yeah, long story. He went by a different name back then. Dude was a straight up arrow-slinging outlaw. Wasn't too popular with King Richard. Stole from the rich to pay the poor. Blah, blah, yada, yada. Instead of his usual crimson, he used to wear—"

"Don't say it," I grumbled, making the mental note that if Cooper Rayfield actually spurred the legend of Robin Hood, I didn't want to know. Mainly because I didn't want to start picturing him in tights. Goddamn it, I just did.

"So," Doc said, moving the conversation along, "you think Cooper will know where this Owen guy is?"

"Yes. Yes, I do," Rooster said.

"Then what's the bad news?" I grumbled.

"You want the first part or the second part?"

When I offered him nothing in response besides an icy stare, he said, "Gotcha. So, firstly, Owen and I had a bit of a *minor* disagreement a few years back, and he most likely won't be all that excited to see me."

"Minor disagreement, eh?"

"Wasn't a big deal. Just a difference of opinions ... during a rather heated game of backgammon."

"Backgammon? Were you drinking?"

"Maybe."

"And I'm assuming there was a woman involved."

"Perhaps."

"You didn't happen to go all big, red, and scaly on his ass did you?"

"It was an accident."

"Son of a bitch," I grumbled. "What the hell happened?"

"Wasn't my fault," he said, looking rather sheepish, "Okay. Maybe it was a *little* my fault, but Double OT was being a total dick. First off, he was hitting on my girlfriend the entire freaking day, and *then* he had the audacity to try and steal my damn horse and skip town."

"Your *horse*?" Doc scoffed. "When was this, John?"

"Late Middle Ages. Big A had me in northern France trying to infiltrate a cell of rogue gothen posing as knights in the employ of the Duchess of Burgundy. I bumped into Owen at a tavern in Cambray. He evidently took a gig working for Charles V as a merc in the French Army."

"Is he making this up?" Erin asked me.

"Trust me, Doc, you can't make this kind of shit up." I turned to Rooster. "So, this Owen dude — he was a friggin mercenary?"

"Yeppers. Double OT bounced around the ages fighting in just about every major war in human history. He was kind of the ultimate soldier of fortune for a solid millennium. Total badass."

"Did he work with the Guild?"

"Sometimes. If the price was right. Had more than a few run-ins with us as well."

"So, what happened with you two at the tavern?"

"Well, one thing led to another, and the next thing I knew, we sort of ended up in the middle of town jousting each other. Anywho, I was kicking his ass until he time phased his lance through my armor and impaled me like a metal-encased shish kebab. That, unfortunately, made me angry."

"And I'm guessing the situation degraded pretty quickly from there."

"Yes. Yes, it did. Went full on liderc in front of an entire town."

"What does that mean exactly?" Doc asked, trying her damnedest to follow the plot.

I sighed. "Well, basically it means that our friend Rooster here lost his shit and transformed from his stringy, jovial ginger self into a nightmarishly buff, red, scaly behemoth with talons the size of machetes and a really gross toothy beak thing for a mouth."

"Aha," she muttered, in a manner that indicated she wished she hadn't asked. "And what happened next?"

"*Well*," Rooster continued, "after I beat Owen to a bloody pulp, he managed to time jump himself out of there. Unfortunately, that was the last I saw of him. And he may or may not have sworn to kill me in a very descriptive and unnatural manner *if* he ever saw me again."

"Christ," I muttered. "We're screwed. Did you say there was a second part to this bad news?"

"Yeah. From what I've heard, Owen turned a new leaf at some point over the past few centuries. He evidently traded his militant ways for a more peaceful existence. Considers himself to be some sort of a time hippie, rock and roll demigod nowadays."

"So, you don't think he'll help us?" Doc asked. "Even with the future of mankind at stake?"

"Dunno. Views himself as neutral. Doesn't care about the light or the dark anymore. He just sort of — is."

Clenching my hands into fists, I grumbled, "Then we'll be persuasive."

"He's a quirky dude. It'll be tricky. Double OT's not likely to be talked into anything he doesn't want to do. And not to mention, if you piss off a time phantom, he might just jump your sorry ass to the beginning of time itself, or to the bottom of the Pacific Ocean in 1942, or worse — New Jersey."

I grinned. "So, we'll be very friggin persuasive. He and Coop are still buds, right?"

"That's what I'm hoping," he replied, spinning around on his stool and fumbling with the radio. "Let's find out."

Punching the 'Enter' key on the blocky keyboard, Rooster turned the dial to the proper frequency and depressed the button on the microphone.

"Lost Sheep, Lost Sheep — this is Red Squirrel, over. Do you copy, Lost Sheep?"

After a few excruciatingly long couple seconds of static, the radio crackled to life with the voice of a familiar country boy. "Howdy, howdy, Red and Squirrely. This here's Crazy Cooper coming at ya. Dagummit, is this thing on? Y'all hear me?"

Within seconds, a vision of the maroon hoodie-wearing, wiry bowman manifested on the monochrome screen. Sitting in front of what appeared to be a ping pong table in a designer log cabin, Coop ran his fingers through his scraggly ginger goatee in eager anticipation of our message.

"Roger, *Lost Sheep*. This is *Red Squirrel*. We *read* you loud and clear, over."

"Roger dodger, good buddy. I got my ears on. How're y'all?"

Shaking his head, Rooster muttered, "I'm *so* reviewing our radio procedures with everyone when this is over." After a prolonged sigh, he pressed the transmit button again. "We're okay, Coop. How's things with you and the boys?"

"We're all right. Getting a little antsy, though. And about tired of Duncan whooping us in ping pong."

Erin blanched. "Duncan plays ping pong?"

As a little white ball slammed into the side of Coop's head followed by a giggly snort from somewhere in the background, I said, "And he's evidently pretty good at it."

"Y'all got any good news?" Coop asked, glaring offscreen at what I presumed to be the minuscule table tennis marauder.

"We're not sure yet."

"Damn, hoss. You look like death on a cracker."

"So I've heard," I replied, making the mental note I evidently needed to clean myself up a bit.

"We need a favor," Rooster said.

"Name it, pard," Coop replied, spitting a healthy wad of chew into a Styrofoam cup.

"You still tight with Owen Trask?"

"Double OT? Sure am. Caught his new show a few weeks back before all this nonsense started."

"His show?"

"Yessir. He's been doing some kind of one-man-band rock opera bit down in Tallahassee. Some sort of a death metal rendition of the Jimi Hendrix Experience with a Neil Diamond slant. And there's this Mary Poppins thing where he floats around on an umbrella and spits on folks."

"That sounds friggin awful," I muttered.

"It was crazier than a sack of ferrets. But I really enjoyed it...after a bottle of bourbon. Or six."

"Tallahassee," Rooster muttered, evidently not impressed by the thought of a metal mashup of "Sweet Caroline" and "Voodoo Chile."

"Yeah buddy. He's been held up at the MidKnight Jayde for the past few weeks."

"Is he still playing there?"

"I reckon so. Why you asking? You ain't fixin' to slap him silly again, are you? You know he's still madder than a wet hen about that whole thing in France."

"We need him to take us back to 1975 so we can, ah, find the Ark of the Covenant...and summarily destroy it."

Coop's faced went blank. "Y'all been drinking?"

Completely ignoring the comment, Rooster said, "Can you meet us at the MidKnight Jayde in twenty minutes?"

"Ah, sure thing."

"See you soon. Watch your back."

"Ain't my back I'm worried about, pard. Y'all be careful."

As the redneck archer's face faded from the screen, Rooster hit the power button on his array of radio equipment and stowed the microphone.

"So, Tallahassee, eh?" I muttered.

"Yeppers," he replied, getting up from his stool and shuffling toward the kiln to check on his pizza while pulling out his peculiar pad of sticky notes.

"Where are we meeting Cooper?" Erin asked, adjusting her shoulder holster to ensure her pistolas were neatly concealed under her jacket.

"The MidKnight Jayde Karma Café."

"What exactly is a *karma* café?"

"It's, ah, sort of a supernatural gathering place run by a couple vexens named Willa Knightly and Harlan Jayde. Place has been around for as long as I can remember ... and that's saying something."

"Gathering place, eh?" I muttered. "You mean like a coffee shop?"

"They serve coffee," Rooster said, in a manner that made me think they served a hell of a lot more than that.

"And what's a vexen?" Erin asked.

"Vexens are a kind of an elemental magi. But instead of being wise *men,* they're women. Usually delectable blondes with mesmerizing blue eyes and large—"

"So, they're witches," I interjected before Rooster's balls wound up on the wrong end of Doc's kneecap.

"Well, sort of, but not really. In simple terms, they're like a magus but they have the ability to freely manipulate the four elements — fire, water, earth, and air. And they can do *other* stuff."

"Like what?"

"Pray you never find out, my friend. And word to the wise, should you refer to one of them as a *witch* while in their presence, you'll most likely lose the ability to pee while standing upright for the rest of your unnatural afterlife."

As I contemplated that for a second or two, Rooster meandered toward the kiln and proudly announced, "Sweet! Looks like the pizza's—"

Unfortunately, my enigmatic ginger colleague never finished that sentence because he was distracted by the distinct sound of heavy footsteps emanating from above.

"Somebody's here," Doc muttered, just above a whisper.

Fixated on the wide-open trapdoor separating the cabin from the Crow Nest secret lair, we locked gazes and instinctively drew our respective weapons. With enough fire power trained on the top of the stairs to take out an entire platoon of hostile insurgents, we waited with perfect patience to give our mysterious party crasher a proper welcome.

And as fate would have it, what came through the trapdoor was neither a person nor an unnatural beastie. It was a small, pineapple-shaped object that methodically tumbled down the chiseled, stone steps until it reached the floor and rolled to an ominous halt between us.

Somewhat perplexed by the unexpected turn of events, Rooster gawked at the peculiar object now resting on the edge of his boot. "What the hell? Is that a—"

"Grenade!" I yelled, willing the cloak into being.

Grabbing Doc by the waist and spinning her out of the immediate blast radius, I dropped to a knee and shielded her with my body in anticipation of the imminent blast.

So, to quickly recap current events:

It seemed we weren't having any pizza.

Which sucked.

And although we'd caught a break and tracked down a time hippie to jump us back to 1975, we were regrettably about to be sent to a rocky grave instead.

Which really sucked.

And, of course, we were out of beer.

There were no words for that disappointment.

Grenade, anyone?

22

As the confined space filled with the telltale odor of stale gun powder, and the fuse of the old school fragmentary grenade violently hissed away like the wick on a firecracker, I waited with clenched teeth for the ensuing deafening explosion of searing shrapnel and splintered mayhem.

And although I was pretty sure it was going to hurt like hell, I was also pretty sure that literally being at ground zero of a detonating frag wouldn't do all that much damage to me. Or Rooster for that matter.

Doc, on the other hand, was a different story. As such, I made damn sure she was fully concealed by the cloak as I wrapped my arms around her as tightly as I possibly could.

Fully prepared for a truly horrific explosion, I was more than a bit surprised to instead hear a soft fizzle followed by a distinct popping sound indicating that the fuse burned out before igniting the primer. And, as I knew from experience with old-ass munitions, the olive drab orb was instantly rendered to nothing more than a nostalgic pineapple-shaped paperweight.

"Dagnabbit!" a male voice bellowed from the cabin above us in a raspy, gruff tone. "Goldurn fuse cap! Dangit all." Regaining his composure, our mysterious assailant huffed a few times and cleared his throat.

"All right, listen here, you sumbitches. I want hands in the air. Ain't no need to make this any worse on yourselves. Y'all hear me?"

Releasing my death grip on Erin, I rose to my feet to find Rooster curled into the fetal position next to his pizza oven. Upon hearing the cartoon character-like voice of the man upstairs, he jumped to his feet and shook his head in disbelief. "No freaking way. Tuck? Tuck Corbin? Is that you?"

"You're dagburn right it's me, you infernal jaybird. I finally got you right where I want you. Now, I'm a' coming down there on the count of ten. And you best not try any of that funny stuff now, boy. I'm taking you in."

"John," Erin asked, trying to figure out what the hell was happening, "Why is Foghorn Leghorn trying to kill you?"

"Seriously," I grumbled, "You know this friggin guy?"

"Yes. Yes, I do," he said, drawing his pair of signature Glock pistolas from somewhere deep in the bowels of his bomber jacket as he cautiously maneuvered toward the trapdoor.

"Well, who the hell is he?"

"One of twelve members of an ancient society of liderc hunters. And trust me, we do *not* want him down here."

"Can't you just sticky pad portal us out of here?"

"Not so much," he muttered, "The Crow Nest wards are airtight. We need to get outside before I can open a portal."

I nodded. "All right. I'll get rid of him. Cover me."

As Doc instinctively slid her H&Ks from the dueling holsters on her shoulder harness and assumed the ready position, I boldly placed myself at the bottom on the stone steps.

Clearing my throat, I said, "Attention, asshole in the cabin."

"You ain't O'Dargan," he grunted in response, still concealed somewhere in the shadows at the top of the stairs. "Identify yourself."

"This is Dean Robinson."

"The wayward Deacon. Yeah, I know who you are, boy. Lucky for you, I ain't got no interest on the bounty you're carrying on your goldurn head."

"Oh, good. That's such a relief," I grumbled, with a slight hint of sarcasm. "Now, listen up, jackass, I'm heavily armed, out of beer, and really fucking pissed. You drop another frag down here, and I swear to

God, I'll stick it so far up your ass you'll be coughing up gun powder for a month."

"Just who do you think you're a talking to, boy?"

"Gomer Pyle?"

"Lookie here, Robinson," he said, indignant, "*this* is Tecumseh Corbin. And I'm operating on official business, boy. Got me a writ signed by Gabriel himself for one John James Jehoshaphat O'Dargan, a.k.a. *the* Rooster. A writ, mind you, that gives me full authority to deport that jackleg of a liderc back to the deepest, darkest corner of Hell."

"Sorry, pal," I muttered, trying my damnedest to get a look at him to no avail. "That ain't happening."

"So, it's gonna be like that, eh? Well, boy, seems we got ourselves a problem."

"Seems we do."

"Lucky for you, problem solving is my specialty."

But as *Tecumseh* was a complete and utter hayseed, he said it like 'spesh-she-ali-tee.'

"That's your specialty? Seems like cartoon voiceovers would be more up your alley."

"Don't sass me, boy. Listen here, this can go one of two ways. The first of which is you let me down there all gentlemanlike and we come to terms on the execution of my official business matter."

"And the second?"

"I push the button on my fancy little device here and let the archangels know where you're holed up."

"And remind me again why I just don't shoot your sorry ass and call it a day."

"You could try," he snickered, "but not before I bring half of Tenth Heaven to your dagburn doorstep. After I send the signal, a legion of halos will be here in about three seconds. Maybe four if they stop for coffee. I hear halos got a real hankering for coffee."

"Aha. That's actually a pretty good reason."

"Hoo doggie! We got ourselves a *genuine* standoff here, Robinson. Your move, boy."

"Goddamn it," I muttered, trading glances with Doc and Rooster. "Give us a minute, would ya?"

"Take your time, boy. Been waiting two thousand, five hundred, and sixty-one years to bring O'Dargan to justice. Another minute won't kill me, I suppose. I do have me some supper plans, so kindly don't take too dagburn long, though."

Huddling with the crew, I said, "Friggin Foghorn seems to have us by the short hairs. What now?"

"Let him down here," Rooster grumbled. "I think I can reason with him."

"*Reason*? With him?" Erin scoffed. "He dropped a grenade on us. And he talks like Jed Clampett. I vote for shooting his ass."

"This guy's been hunting me my entire freaking life. We're practically family. Maybe I can talk some sense into him."

"I'd kinda like to shoot him, too," I muttered. "Just saying."

"Wouldn't do any good besides piss him off."

"Why the hell not?"

"He can't be killed. I've tried. More times than I can remember."

"Is he nephilim?"

"No. No, he's not."

"Angel?"

"No. Nor is he a demon *or* a mutated alien ecoterrorist. He's a Sumerian Knight."

"Sumerian?" Doc said. "Like from *Sumer*? As is in Mesopotamia?"

"Yeppers."

"As in the civilization that lived like three thousand years ago?"

"More like five to six thousand years ago."

"So, he's human?" I said.

"I think?" When it was pretty clear both Doc and I were clearly not following the plot, Rooster said, "Okay, back in the early days, after Lucifer and Lilith started cranking out little lidercs, they thought it would be funny to let them loose on mankind for a while. Kind of like a demented field trip."

"That doesn't sound like them at all," Erin muttered.

"As such," Rooster continued, "My brothers and I pretty much wreaked unfettered havoc on the Earth for a solid few centuries. Right up until the Sumerian nations had enough of our shit and formed an unholy band of assassins to take care of business. Known only as the Knights of

Uruk, they were a collection of ruthless warrior types from across the ancient lands charged with one hallowed purpose — to hunt lidercs and deport them to Hell with extreme prejudice."

"How the hell did they do that?" I asked.

"That's the thing. Nobody really knew how they did it. Rumor had it that the Knights were imbued with a dark power from the Sumerian goddess of war, Inanna, who granted them near immortality and superhuman abilities. Some said they were actually *gods* themselves."

"That doesn't make any friggin sense."

"Regardless of what actually happened, it worked. Over the years, they got every last liderc except for a handful that went into hiding."

"Including you."

He nodded. "Including me."

"Okay," Doc grumbled. "So, Howdy Doody up there is an immortal assassin spawn from the literal architects of human civilization. Got it, I guess. But, why the hell does he talk like he just walked out of a scene in *Blazing Saddles*?"

"Well, after Stephen recruited me to join the Guild, old Tuck couldn't hunt me anymore. And since I was the last liderc topside, he really had nothing to do. *So*, he kind of retired. Last I heard, he settled down in sixteenth century Kansas and became a federal Marshall. I suspect he got a little too carried away with the Old West thing."

"Christ." I grunted, making the mental note that I really wished we weren't out of beer. "We let him down here. You talk to him. If you can't *reason* with him, we pop the bastard and get the hell out of Dodge."

"What if he uses that tracking device to tip off the seraphic court?"

"I've got a plan."

"A plan?"

"More of an idea, actually."

"You sure about this?"

"No. But, there's no more time to dick around. We need to get out of here and meet that time hippie guy in Tallahassee. And I can't believe those words just came out of my mouth."

"Me neither," Doc muttered, chambering a round in both pistols and removing the safeties. "Let's do this."

Looking up at the trapdoor, I yelled, "All right, you win. Get your ass down here, Jethro. Nice and slow."

Corbin chuckled. "Had a feeling you'd come to your senses, boy. Y'all stand down. Here I come."

Not really sure what a millennia-old Sumerian Knight would look like, I was more than a bit surprised when the figure that emerged from the shadows, and casually strolled down the steps like he owned the joint, looked more like somebody's kindly gramps than a merciless immortal assassin.

Sporting pleated khakis and a stylish green sweater vest, the meticulously groomed silver-haired aristocrat was a little less than average height, and had a noticeable middle-aged pooch hanging over the waist of his trousers.

In fact, except for the peculiar ceramic body armor that covered his torso and the impressive array of eclectic weaponry strapped around his waist, he looked like he should've been lounging at a hifalutin gentlemen's club sipping brandy from a snifter and smoking a pipe.

"Do all Sumerian *Knights* dress like extras from *Caddyshack*?" I asked.

"I'm retired," he grumbled, clearly not appreciating the comment.

Holding nothing in his hands except a blinking device, which I assumed was his aforementioned angel beacon, he reached the bottom of the steps to find the business end of Erin's H&Ks trained squarely on his head.

He smiled. "Ain't no need for those six-shooters, girlie. Besides, ain't nobody ever tell you that sticking a gun in someone's face was unladylike?"

Returning his smile, Doc responded by pointing both pistols at his ballsac instead. "Is that better?"

Figuring he wasn't going to win that battle, he gave Erin a dismissive glare and turned his full attention on Rooster. "Long time, Johnny. I told you I'd be there when you fell from grace. Ain't no hiding behind the Guild anymore. You're on the wrong side of the line, boy."

"Good to see you too, Tuck," Rooster said, holstering his Glocks. "Retirement looks, ah, good on you?"

Corbin sucked in his gut. "I ain't gone soft, boy. You best believe I'm as good now as I ever was."

"Well, if it's any consolation, you don't look a day over four thousand five hundred and fifty-two."

"All right, all right, quit trying to butter me up."

"How'd you find me anyway?"

"When word came over the wire about your bounty, I had a feeling you'd show up here sooner or later."

"But how'd you even know about this place?"

"Please," he scoffed. "You ain't got no secrets from me, boy."

"Have I mentioned how much I've missed our little chats."

"Yeah, I bet you did. You ready to face what you got coming?"

"About that, we've known each other for a long time, right?"

"Since before the days of Methuselah, I reckon."

"And have I ever lied to you?"

"Can't say you ever have."

"Then before we proceed, I need you to hear me out about something. For old time's sake."

"All right, you jaybird, I'm listening. But make it quick. Already made it known that I got supper plans. The missus gets all ornery when I'm late for supper."

Picking his words carefully, Rooster said, "What if I told you that the seraphic court was compromised and one of the archangels is a traitor. A *traitor* who's conspiring with Azazel."

"I'd say you're all hopped up on that fire water you call beer. You ain't been hitting the sauce again, have you, boy?"

"No. He hasn't," I chimed in. "Mainly because we don't have any."

Ignoring my commentary, Rooster said, "Tuck, I'm telling the truth. They're trying to open the gates of Tartarus and free the Watchers to start a civil war in Heaven. And they're using mankind as the ransom."

"And I suppose now you're about to tell me that I should let you go because you and your compatriots here have been wrongfully accused of the charges made claim against you, and you're actually trying to expose this heavenly traitor and set things right."

"That's right. But how—"

"How'd I know?" A wolfish grin stretched across the hayseed assassin's face. "Simple, boy, because that's exactly what they said you'd say."

And it was right about then when shit went south. Real quick like.

In an utter blur of motion, the obscure elder statesman reached into his bizarre breast plate and produced two daggers that he effortlessly flung across the room and straight into Rooster's kneecaps. As my enigmatic ginger colleague let out a primal scream, and instantly dropped to the floor in a state of excruciating pain, Doc's pistolas barked to life as she opened fire at the suave old timer while fluidly drifting to her left to seek cover behind one of the barcaloungers in the center of the bunker.

Already moving toward our unwelcome guest, I closed the distance between us with unnatural speed as a turbo jolt of arcane adrenaline rocketed through my body. Literally within inches of the bastard, the argent metal gauntlets took form over my hands as I willed the spatha into being.

Ripping the otherworldly sword from its sheath in a spectral flash, I swung it with all my supernatural strength at that dirty son of a bitch's right hand only to lop it clean off at the wrist. As his severed mitt plummeted toward the floor, I snatched it in midair and proceeded to pry his precious angel beacon from its spasming fingers.

"Dagnabbit!" he yelled, clutching his bloody stump and gawking at me like I just took his lunch money. "What the Sam hell'd you do that for? That was my good hand!"

"Oh, sorry about that," I grumbled, slapping him a couple times with his disembodied meat hook. "You want it back?"

"I'll have your head for that, boy!"

Admiring his nifty seraph summoning device, which was no larger than a ballpoint pen and still emanating a constant pulse of spectral blue light, I grinned at him. "This thing actually work?"

"Course it works, b—"

I'm pretty sure he was about to call me *boy* again when I punched him squarely in the grill with my metal fist. Hurtling across the room like a sack of potatoes, our good friend Tecumseh then slammed into the back wall of the bunker and slid unconscious to the floor. Figuring he'd be visiting la-la land for the foreseeable future, I tossed the angel beacon on the floor and crushed it with my boot.

"Was *that* your plan?" Erin asked, getting back to her feet and holstering her pistols.

"More or less. You okay?"

"I'm good."

"Rooster?"

Yanking the daggers from both of his kneecaps with his eyes blazing a fiery red, he grunted, "Never better. But I gotta ask, did your *plan* involve me getting shivved by Corbin?"

"No. It didn't."

"I'm pleasantly surprised to hear you say that."

"I was expecting him to shoot you."

"Wait, what?"

"Either way, I figured you'd be fine. For the most part. More importantly, though, it would give me and Doc a window of opportunity to get that device out of his hand and keep us all from being angel fodder. Worked like a charm."

"Is that supposed to make me feel better?"

"Did it?"

"No."

"Ah, guys," Erin said, staring at the soon-to-be Sumerian Knight version of Captain Hook. "He's waking up."

"Time to go," Rooster said, moving toward the stairs with great haste. "We've got a rock opera to crash."

"Sure you don't want to stick around for another few minutes?"

"Wait, was that a knife joke?"

"Maybe?"

"Really?"

Evidently, it was too soon for knife jokes.

But that doesn't make them any less funny.

23

"Never thought I'd be this happy to see Tallahassee again," Rooster muttered as the latest sticky pad portal snapped shut behind us and he unzipped his bomber jacket.

Standing in the twilight of a rather pleasantly warm winter evening, we found ourselves on a street corner adjacent an ornate traffic circle located squarely in the middle of an ominously desolate, yet artfully quaint, downtown block.

Shrouded in darkness, the surrounding locale was lined with an impressive array of upscale brew pubs, trendy bars, eclectic eateries, and designer coffee shops, which were all seemingly vacated in a hurry. A big hurry.

In fact, lit only by a few random street lamps, the entire area seemed utterly devoid of life in every direction, and had a distinct zombie apocalypse feel complete with blinking red traffic lights, police tape, and sidewalks haphazardly strewn with trash.

Erin scanned our new surroundings. "What happened the last time you were here?"

Rooster shook his head. "Botched mission of epic proportion."

"What kind of mission?"

"Well, I kinda got drunk and crashed a sorority party. Woke up the next morning in a dumpster. And my pants may have been hanging from a flag pole."

Trying to erase that particular mental image from my mind, I willed the cloak into retreat and was more than pleased that my face wasn't about to fall off from howling winds or blistering snow. Giving my grimy, blood-spattered RoosterBragh tee a quick glance, I also made the mental note to track down a change of clothes at some point in the near future.

"So, that's Florida State University," I muttered, gazing across the street at a ginormous football stadium on the outskirts of a deserted conglomeration of abandoned academic buildings, dorms, and apartments.

Rooster nodded. "Yeppers. This is the heart of the CollegeTown district. Downtown is a couple miles up the hill to our northeast."

Looking into the evening sky, I saw a hovering cloud of thick smoke in the near distance. "Let me guess, that's where the state capital building is."

"Or was." His brow furrowed. "Right up until last night. This was pretty much ground zero for the Florida chapter of the anakim demolition party."

"That would explain why it's a ghost town," I grumbled, envisioning what should have been a hopping Saturday night scene of twenty- and thirty-somethings darting in and out of the various drinking and eating establishments.

Taking note of the old school vinyl record made into an analog clock hanging in the window of the retro music store behind us, Rooster said, "Yeah, well, it's going to be a lot worse tomorrow if we don't get moving. It's almost six o'clock. We're two hours away from the next phase of Azazel's global shitshow."

"So, let's quit dicking around."

More than ready to get the show on the road, Erin said, "Where's this karma cafe joint?"

"If memory serves, the MidKnight Jayde is a couple blocks due north of here," Rooster answered. "Coop's probably wondering what the hell happened to us."

After a quick jaunt up Gaines Street, in which Doc and I were forced to endure Rooster's seedy recollection of crashing various and assorted '90s sorority parties, we hooked a hard right onto Macomb Street into what appeared to be a vacant lot. Scanning the darkness for a quick sec, he said, "Yep. This is the place."

"What place?" I asked, squinting to see nothing but a large concrete slab on the far side of a disheveled dirt parking lot, overrun by a small jungle of fledging saplings and oversized weeds.

"The MidKnight Jayde."

"Where?"

"Right in front of us."

"There's nothing right in front of us besides an overgrown goddamn parking lot."

Looking exceptionally pleased with himself, my jackass ginger colleague uttered a few words in Enochian, and the night air over the concrete slab began to shimmer like somebody dropped a pebble into a pool of perfectly still water.

Then, almost as if a pair of invisible curtains were slowly opening, a blurry vision began to steadily come into focus as Doc and I stood there wondering what the hell was happening.

"Prepare to be amazed," Rooster said, evidently expecting the MidKnight Jayde in all its karma cafe glory to materialize in front of us.

Needless to say, he was more than disappointed when we instead found ourselves staring at a breathtakingly adorable teenage girl casually seated on a fold-out chair with her head buried in a Stephen King novel. A warm light, emanating from nowhere discernible, inexplicably illuminated the general area surrounding her as she flipped pages without acknowledging our presence in the least.

No more than fifteen or sixteen years old, the teenage beauty queen of bronze skin and deep brown eyes was sporting a black Bob Marley tank top — that showed way too much of her six pack abs than I bet her father appreciated — accompanied by designer cut-off jean shorts and a pair of different colored Chuck Taylor high tops.

"Who's that?" Erin asked, under her breath.

"I've no idea," Rooster said, trying to figure out what was going on. "That, ah, wasn't supposed to happen."

Still ignoring us, the urban outfitted fashionista simply continued to read her book at a feverish pace while running a hand through her blondish auburn hair, which was highlighted with obscure streaks of dazzling colors that seemed to randomly fade in and out of existence. And as she did that, I was drawn to perhaps the most peculiar aspect of the mysterious youngster's motif — the intricate arrangement of ethereal tattoos that mystifyingly glided up and down her chiseled arms.

In what appeared to be a masterfully drawn rendition of the solar system inked with an artful Celtic flare, the string of nine planets and blazing sun seemed to be alive on her skin as they floated up one arm, over her shoulders and down the other in perfect sync.

It was mesmerizing.

"Are we in the right friggin place?" I asked Rooster.

"Absolutely. At least, I think so. Granted, it's been a while since I've been here. Actually, maybe we aren't."

"Well, should we ask her?" Doc impatiently offered.

"Good idea," I muttered, clearing my throat and taking a cautious step toward the kiddo. "Ah, hi?"

"Sup, dude," the stylish teenybopper replied with complete disinterest, still fixated on her book.

"What're you reading, kid?"

"Who you calling 'kid,' old man?"

"Old man?" I scoffed. "So, first off, *princess*, I'm not old—"

"Yeah, you are. Totally on the wrong side of thirty. And you kind of have that old man smell."

"That's just hurtful."

"The truth hurts, dude."

"What's your name, kid?"

"Mack."

"Mack. Like Mackenzie?"

"Nah. Mack. Like the truck."

"Okay look, ah, Mack," Rooster impatiently cut in. "We're looking for the MidKnight Jayde."

"Congratulations," she said, still flipping pages like we weren't there. "You found it."

"Ah, okay, cool. But, we kinda need to go inside."

"Go ahead."

"And how do we do that?"

"To *go* in, you just have to *get* in."

"Okay and *how* do we do that?"

"If you don't know, I can't help you. Sorry, dude."

"But, it's *really* important we get inside," Rooster said, trying his best to keep calm.

"Really not my problem, dude."

"So, you're not going to help us?"

"Nah."

"Why not?"

"House rules."

"House rules?" I chuckled. "What are you like the friggin bouncer or something?"

"No, old dude, not *like* the bouncer. I *am* the bouncer."

"Quit calling me old, kid. And aren't you a little young to be a bouncer?"

"Nah."

"And since when is there a *bouncer* at the MidKnight Jayde?" Rooster asked, now totally perplexed by the steady dose of teenage logic.

"Since now, dude. Have you not been paying attention to current events? The world's a dangerous place."

"Ah, yeah, I know. That's why we're here."

"Figured as much."

"Wait, what? You know why we're here?"

"Yep. My brother told me."

"How does he know?"

"He knows stuff."

"So, if you knew we were coming. You must know who we are."

"Course I do."

"And you still won't let us in?"

"Already told you, dude, you can go in whenever you want. You just have to *get* in."

About at his wits' end, Rooster's eyes flashed a blazing red as he started to pace back and forth.

As Doc and I exchanged befuddled glances confirming that neither one of us had a clue as to what to do next, the bushes on the periphery of the parking lot began to rustle, and a bare-chested beefcake came stumbling out holding an empty bottle of Jack Daniels.

Training her gaze on the newcomer, Mack closed her book and placed it on the ground at the feet of her chair. As her flawless face curled into a dark smile, she cracked her knuckles a few times and rolled her head back on her neck like she was ready to throw down on his big ass.

Although she was barely five feet tall *and* a friggin teenybopper, there was something about the look in her eyes that made me think she could probably do it.

"Open the door and let me in, Mackie," the drunken party crasher bellowed in a ridiculous Australian accent as he stomped across the parking lot. "I said open it! Now, you ankle biter!"

Easily six-foot-four and full of muscle, I grabbed his shoulder and yanked him backward. "Back off, Vegemite Sandwich. Leave the kid—"

"Relax, old dude," Mack said, calmly stepping between me and the plastered Aussie. "I got this."

"Yeah," the 'roided out Crocodile Dundee wannabe quipped. "*Relax*, ya dill wanker."

"Go home, Ned," Mack said, locking gazes with the mouthy meatstick literally three times her size. "You can come back tomorrow."

"Bugger off, Mackie. I need a drink."

"You've had enough to drink."

"Not yet I haven't. Open the damn door already."

"Nah."

"Why you *cheeky* little—"

And before the dumb bastard had the opportunity to complete his slurred statement, Mack's eyes turned a harrowing yellow, and her entire body, including her face, was overtaken by a sparkling sheen and she was instantly covered by a body suit of diamond plating.

Then, in what seemed like a single motion barely perceptible to the human eye, she forcefully threw a flying knee squarely into the jackass from down under's smooth criminals while simultaneously driving a devastating uppercut into his jaw.

"Damn," I muttered, watching as the big dope collapsed to the asphalt with a horrendous thud. "Mack. Like the truck."

"Holy shit," Erin said, smiling ear to ear.

With the excitement over quicker than it started, Mack's uncanny armor casually melted from existence, and she happily resumed her post on the foldout chair. Shooting us a satisfied grin while retrieving her paperback, she said, "Did you guys have any more questions?"

Erin smiled. "Just one. Can we please enter the MidKnight Jayde?"

And much to our astonishment, Mack said, "Sure."

"Wait, what?" Rooster scoffed. "Just like that?"

"Yep."

"But, why?"

"She said please. *And* she's not creepy. Gingers creep me out. Sorry, dude."

As I made the mental note that the kid had good taste, I watched in certain astonishment as a sizable wooden door began to manifest on the empty concrete slab. And within a quick second, the rest of the obscure dome-shaped building followed suit.

Winking at us like she knew something we didn't, she said, "Behave yourselves in there. And good luck."

"Sure thing, kid," I muttered. "Keep it real."

"Nobody says that anymore, dude."

"I do."

"That's because you're old." Then she buried her face in her novel and promptly proceeded to ignore us again.

"Nice kid," I grumbled, as we made our way across the parking lot.

"Why did she wish us luck?" Doc asked.

"Probably because the MidKnight Jayde isn't exactly your run-of-the-mill watering hole," Rooster said. "It's got a bit of a reputation."

"I thought you said it was a coffee shop."

"I said they *served* coffee."

"I'm not following."

"It'll be fine. Nothing to worry about."

Wondering what that was all about, I muttered, "What the hell kind of place is this anyway?"

And as soon as we reached the front door, and I got my first good look at the building, I think I answered my own question.

24

"TOTALLY NOT A COFFEE SHOP," Erin said, taking in the massive dome-shaped corrugated metal structure covered completely in intricate, slithering patterns of neon otherworldly graffiti and riddled with what appeared to be bullet holes, claw marks, and blood spatter.

"More of a supernatural roadhouse," Rooster muttered, removing his Rambo-worthy hunting knife from its sheath and concealing it in the sleeve of his bomber jacket. "But their cinnamon bourbon lattes are the stuff of legend."

"Really?"

"No. Not really."

Standing before the ginormous wooden door that looked suspiciously like it was ripped from a medieval castle, my eyes drifted to a hand-carved sign tacked haphazardly to one of the mighty panels. Amidst a very interesting array of sigils and glyphs that blazed bright with hissing white flame was etched 'The MidKnight Jayde. Karma, Whiskey, and Everything Ever After. All are Welcome and Welcomed are None. Shoes and Shirts Optional. Enter at your Own Peril.'

The best part of it was that the word '*Peril*' was crossed out, and the word '*Perdition*' was scratched above it.

"Catchy slogan," I grumbled. "Friendly with a touch of horror movie.

Something tells me that even Swayze himself wouldn't step foot in this joint."

Rooster chuckled. "Not when he was alive anyway."

"Alive? Hold the friggin phone. Are you telling me Patrick Swayze is *dead*? Seriously? When the hell did that happen?"

"Four or five years ago. Pancreatic cancer."

"Well, that just friggin blows. Not only do the Red Sox win two World Series during my fourteen-year dirt nap — Patrick friggin Swayze kicks the bucket. Why the hell didn't somebody tell me this?"

Doc snickered. "I didn't realize you were such a big fan."

"For real? Darry. Bodhi. Dalton. Johnny friggin Castle. Please. Best roles ever played."

"You've seen *Dirty Dancing*?"

"Once."

"Once, huh?"

"Okay, maybe twice. Definitely not more than six times."

"I really could've gone the rest of my life without knowing that," she said, as she wrapped her hand around the doorknob, which was actually a shrunken skull, and threw the mammoth door open like she owned the joint. "Try not to let anyone put you in the corner, okay, baby?"

"Let's do this," Rooster said, thankfully moving off the topic. "Keep a low profile in there. Try not to draw any attention to yourself. And most importantly, let me do the talking. They know me here."

"But if they know you, aren't we running the risk of somebody calling in the fly boys?"

"Or more friggin bounty hunters?" I added.

"Nope," he said, as we crossed the threshold into the otherworldly roadhouse. "The MidKnight Jayde is neutral ground."

"Meaning?"

"It's a safe zone with Vegas rules. What happens here, stays here. Period."

And as my eyes adjusted to the more than obscure scene laid out before me, I about shite myself.

It was ridiculous.

Even by my standards.

Which should really give you pause.

At any rate, much like the Quartermaster, the interior of the MidKnight Jayde was a gazillion times bigger than what it appeared to be from the outside. And it was absolutely crammed full of people. Some looked human. Others, not so much.

Perhaps the most peculiar aspect of the surreal venue was the fact that since all the available floor space was maxed out, droves of sloshed patrons were literally standing on the surrounding walls and ceiling like the friggin law of gravity was on hiatus.

"Ah, guys," Doc muttered, evidently as perplexed as I was at the mind-boggling feat. "People are standing on the ceiling."

"You'll get used to it," Rooster said, like it was no big thing.

Lit by an armada of floating orbs composed of a subtle neon flame that systematically circled the ridiculous warehouse-like structure, the place was loud enough to make your friggin ear drums bleed. And despite the cacophonous booms of crowd noise, a mind-blowing, live rendition of "Back in Black" dominated the airwaves like a force of nature.

Looking for the source of the music, it appeared the hard rock serenade originated from a twenty-something blond bombshell wearing a Vince Neil straw cowboy hat, stylishly torn jeans tucked into snakeskin boots, and a vintage Bon Jovi tee shirt purposely cut into a low hanging tank top.

And despite the fact that the dreamlike scene was already beyond epic, the floating ensemble of spectral guitars and drums that surrounded the mystical musician while somehow playing themselves in perfect unison with the melody somehow took it to the next level.

"Holy shit," I muttered, fixated on the stage. "Who the hell is that?"

"That's Harlan Jayde," Rooster said.

"One of the witches—"

"Vexens," he interjected.

"Right. Vexens," I concurred, making the mental note that I very much valued the ability to pee while standing up. "Where the hell's Cooper? We need to find this time hippie dude."

"Follow me," Rooster said, making his way toward the massive pentagram-shaped bar strategically positioned in the middle of the warehouse floor.

Scoring some semi-open real estate at the peculiar bar, which looked like it was made from the monoliths of Stonehenge, Rooster hailed the bartender while Doc and I basically stood there gawking at the collection of unnatural patrons rocking out to the infectious beat that relentlessly pulsed through the air like waves of electricity.

As I contemplated the fact that literally every friggin species of nepher seemed to be intertwined throughout the bizarre crowd, a seven-foot conglomeration of fur, fangs, and claws slammed into me. Profusely apologizing, he then slapped me on the shoulder and happily faded into the crowd like a furry Ricky Martin.

"You'll find most folks that come here aren't looking for trouble," said an unusually young bartender, in a surprisingly deep voice. "But those that are — usually find it."

Wearing a classic white and black ringer tee that accentuated his rather impressive biceps, the suavely handsome teenager boasted a thick mane of dirty blond surfer hair, intense blue eyes, and a pair of old school Colt revolvers slung low around his waist like something out of a John Wayne movie.

And there was just something about his aura that indicated he wasn't prone to taking shit from anyone or anything.

"Take this clown for example," he said, nodding at a mammoth bull-necked bald dude with an intricate Celtic cross tattooed across his grizzled face who was forcefully pushing his way through the crowd like a bulldozer.

Pulling up alongside us, the jackass barked, "More whiskey, junior. Make it snappy."

To which the witty bartender just smiled and pulled his six shooters like Billy the Kid only to tauntingly place them on the bar.

"That supposed to scare me?" The man mountain chortled.

The bartender grinned. "Nope. It's supposed to distract you."

"From what?"

And before I knew what was happening, the youngster's shadow jumped off the floor and formed an eight-foot, wraithlike silhouette that loomed over him like a spectral attack dog waiting for the command to pounce.

"From this," he said, with a content smirk, as the shadow creature proceeded to reach across the bar and wrap a ghostly hand around the belligerent bastard's meaty throat. Lifting his big ass a few feet in the air and shaking him like a rag doll for a solid couple seconds, it then effortlessly slammed him to the floor before melting from existence in a blur of motion.

As the big dope scampered to his feet and began to sprint toward the door with a look of pure horror plastered across his face, Rooster said, "Guys, meet Jesse Jameson. Jess, meet—"

"Erin Kelly and Dean Robinson," he cut in. "I know."

"Let me guess, you're Mack's brother," Erin said, as Jesse grabbed his pistolas, twirled them like a seasoned gun fighter, and slid them into their holsters.

"Yep."

"Nice moves, kid," I said, offering him a fist bump.

"Thanks," he replied, totally leaving me hanging. "But seriously, nobody fist bumps anymore."

"I do."

"That's because you're old."

"High five?"

"That's so nineties."

"That's hurtful, kid."

"Let's not make a big thing of it."

"And, for the record, I'm not friggin old."

"You're totally on the wrong side of thirty. Own it."

"Did your sister tell you to say that?"

"So." He grinned, moving off the topic as he studied me with an intent gaze. "You're really him, eh? The *Seventh Deacon* of the *Seventh line*."

"I am."

"Wow. Okay, weird."

"What's weird?"

"Well, you're pretty buff and all, but from all the stories I've heard, I seriously thought you'd be taller. Like ... much taller."

Jumping into the conversation, Rooster said, "Maybe you can help us, Jess. We're looking for—"

"Cooper Rayfield. Yeah, I know. My aunt will be here any second to take you guys to him."

"Your aunt?" I asked. "Is she the other —"

"Vexen," Doc said, before I said the 'W' word.

Jesse nodded. "My Aunt Willa and Miss Harlan run the joint."

I nodded back. "Well, how about a drink while we wait? Dying of thirst over here."

"Sure thing. Would you like a smoothie? Perhaps something with a heavy dose of fiber?"

"Fiber? Wait, was that an old guy joke?" As the smug youngster offered nothing but a mischievous chuckle in response, I grumbled, "Nevermind. Beer, please. Several of them."

"Sorry, dude. We don't do beer."

"Perfect. What do you *do*?"

As he pointed to a chalkboard hovering above the bar, I couldn't help but smile as I read the words, "Whiskey. Coffee. Both."

"And unless you're feeling brave," he smirked, "I'd stay away from the coffee if you know what I'm saying."

"Whiskey then. Three of them."

"Good call. Be right back."

"Nice kid," Rooster said, thoroughly appreciating the browbeating I was being handed by the juvenile wisenheimer.

And before I had the opportunity to make a snide remark about having a stern talk with his parents at some point down the road, a very energetic female voice called out, in an old school New England accent. "Rooster! How are ya?"

Spinning around just in time to see another blonde bombshell emerge from a crackling cloud of blue smoke that curiously manifested directly behind us, I made the mental note that these vexens were no joke.

Looking a hell of a lot like Harlan Jayde, what I presumed to be the aforementioned Willa Knightly was easily a head taller than her witchy counterpart, and clad in a flowing black sundress replete with several layers of primal necklaces that boasted distinct patterns of arcane runes. Young and vivacious, her skin seemed to radiate a warm, placid glow and her platinum blonde hair flowed about her striking features like a steady stream of unseen wind was mildly caressing her entire body.

Appearing quite jovial in nature, her blazing blue eyes seemed to be filled with brewing thunderstorms that emitted tiny bolts of lightning and sparkled with a palpable intensity.

"Give me a hug, you!" she declared, wrapping her petite yet powerful arms around Rooster but turning her attention to me and Doc. "Is this who I think it is?"

"Yes. Yes, it is. Willa, I'd like to introduce—"

"Dean Robinson and Erin Kelly," she said, giving us both a healthy hug.

After an awkward embrace, I said, "Nice, ah, to meet you."

"Machu Picchu? Wonderful place. Are you going there?"

"I'm sorry, what?"

"Rooster doesn't have a big butt! To be honest, it's actually kind of flat."

"I didn't say that."

"Rat! Where?"

"What the hell are you talking about?"

"Sorry! I didn't mean to shout."

"Okay, seriously, are you screwing with me?"

"You'd like some peppermint tea? Or, do you really have to pee?"

"Auntie," Jesse yelled, returning with three snifters of whiskey as he tapped on his ear.

"Oh! Right!" Willa replied, rubbing one of the runes hanging from her necklace.

As a small, but noticeable ring of sparkling energy formed around both her ears, she said, "Can you hear me now?"

"I could hear you the whole friggin time," I grumbled. "Can you hear me?"

"Yep. Sorry! My hearing hasn't been the same since the trials. So much for my weekend getaway in Salem!"

"Salem, eh?" I muttered, making the mental note that even though Willa barely looked old enough to legally drink, she must've had a rough go during the Salem witch trials, which, for the record, happened like three hundred years ago.

"If you'll follow me, I'll take you to Cooper. And I understand you're in a hurry. So, let's go, you three!"

Slamming all three drinks in about two seconds flat, I nodded at Jesse the wisecracking wonder boy barkeep before following Willa through the unnatural crowd, toward a secluded alcove in the back of the thumping warehouse. Pulling up to a smaller, more private setting laid out like a cozy diner decorated with an impressive series of eighties cult movie posters and vintage arcade games, we found Coop sipping from a stout bottle of booze while he methodically sharpened his arrows.

With a bright smile, Willa said, "Okay, guys, here he is. If there's anything I can do to help, please don't hesitate to ask."

"Thank you, Willa," Doc said.

"No problem!"

"Yeah, thanks," I muttered.

"A *tank*? Why do you need a tank?"

"Not a tank. Ah, hell, never mind."

"Okay," she grinned. "Hugs!"

After another round of spirited hugs, Willa, again, bid us farewell and vanished in a breathtaking cloud of bluish-white smoke that appeared and summarily disappeared in the literal blink of an eye.

"Damn, it's good to see y'all," said the redneck archer, taking a healthy gulp of dark whiskey. "What took so dagum long?"

"I'll explain later," Rooster grumbled. "Where's Double OT?"

Nodding at a badly rusted metal door next to the Ms. Pac-Man machine at the far end of the alcove, Coop said, "In his lair."

"His lair?" I asked, taking note of the handwritten sign hanging from the doorknob that read 'Lair of the NecroLord — DO NOT ENTER — Except if you're bringing me booze ... in which case, get your silly ass in here. I am the egg man. I am the walrus. Sham on.'

"NecroLord?" Rooster scoffed.

"That's what Owen's calling himself nowadays," replied a female voice marked by a proper southern drawl.

Turning to find none other than Harlan Jayde, I instinctively backpedaled a few steps as the unadulterated primal power emanating from her tiny persona hit me like a tidal wave.

"Whassup, Jaydie girl?" Coop said, with a heavy application of good ol' boy charm.

"Don't you *Jaydie* girl me, Cooper Rayfield. You know I hate it when you call me that."

"Come on now, little darling, if I had feelings, they'd be hurt."

Holding out her palm and conjuring a swirling maelstrom of blue lightning, she jested, "Cooper Rayfield, you call me 'little darling' again and your feelings won't be the only thing that gets hurt tonight. Is that my bourbon you're drinking?"

"Maybe," Coop sheepishly replied, handing her the bottle.

Taking a healthy swig, she turned her attention to me and Doc as her face curled into a warm smile. Capping the bottle and tossing it to me, she said, "If y'all are going to see Owen, you'd better take this."

"Why's that?" I asked.

"Because he's drunker than Cooter Brown on a Sioux City Saturday night, and won't take kindly to be disturbed."

"What the hell's he doing in there that's so important?"

"If I had to guess, he's probably playing with himself."

"Excuse me?"

Without so much as another word, she vanished in a whisk of unnatural smoke accompanied by an impressive clap of thunder.

"Ah, Coop," I grumbled, making the mental note that Harlan seriously knew how to make an exit. "What did she mean by that?"

"Come on, y'all," Coop replied like it all made perfect sense. "If Owen's playing with himself again, we sure as hell don't want to miss it."

And then he simply opened the peculiar metal door to the NecroLord's lair and eagerly disappeared into the darkness.

Convinced I was missing something in translation, I turned to Rooster with a blank stare.

He smirked. "Nobody plays with themselves like Double OT."

And for the first time in a long time, I found myself profoundly at a loss for words.

25

"Ah, guys," I protested, as Doc and I followed Rooster and Coop down the dark labyrinth of concrete steps toward the sound of blaring music somewhere in the near distance, "Shouldn't we, like, knock or something?"

"Nossir," Coop said, disturbingly more than okay with the notion of busting in on some dude who was evidently smack in the middle of a hot date with Rosie Palmer. "We don't want to interrupt him. Sounds like he's still going strong."

Turning to Doc to make sure I wasn't the only one that thought this was more than a bit ludicrous, she just shrugged her shoulders. "Don't look at me. They're your friends."

Fortunately, as we reached the bottom of the stairs and I got a good look at what the hell was going on in NecroLord's *lair*, it all made sense.

Sort of.

Actually, it really didn't.

But, to be fair, that's nothing new.

Not sure why I bother trying to figure this shit out anymore.

At any rate, in the dead center of a white, octagonal room decorated with nothing but black curtains and a staggering collection of empty whiskey bottles, stood three guys amidst a towering forest of ginormous amplifiers. Feverishly shredding a heavy metal version of "Purple Haze," they seemed oblivious to our presence as their vintage array of guitars unnaturally rang out like an anarchist's symphony in uncanny, perfect tempo.

And oddly, each of them appeared to be subtly flickering in and out of existence faster than my eyes could perceive what the hell was actually happening.

And more oddly, they all looked the same.

Exactly the same.

Almost like it wasn't three guys.

It was one guy.

"*Playing* with himself," I grumbled.

"Pretty dagum impressive, ain't it?" Coop said, stuffing a wad of tobacco in his cheek.

"I'm just glad his pants aren't around his ankles."

"What'd you say, hoss?"

"Never mind. How the hell is he doing that?"

"With a lot of concentration," Rooster said, busting out his air guitar and playing along with Owen, who was still fully engrossed in *playing* with himself.

Awkward?

Doc shook her head in disbelief. "That's incredible. Can he clone himself like that Kruger jackass or something?"

"No. No, he can't. But what he can do is time phase between the past and the future in such infinitesimal increments that it *appears* there's three of him in the present."

"Perfect," she muttered, clearly regretting she asked. "Because having the ability to play three different guitars in perfect harmony while straddling the space-time continuum in either direction makes so much more sense than being able to clone yourself."

"I don't much care how he does it," Coop chimed in, "I just dagum love watching Owen play with him—"

"Coop," I grunted, "you really need to stop saying that, man."

"Seriously, Cooper," Doc added.

Shaking off the disturbing double entendre for the moment, I focused my attention on the enigma that was Owen Octavius Trask — A.K.A. the time hopping Ayatollah of Rock 'n' Rolla, who evidently still had no earthly idea we were standing there.

Easily six feet tall and built like Brad Pitt with a certain Matthew McConaughey flair, the otherworldly mercenary-turned-arcane-guitar-hero was sporting an obnoxious tie-dyed tee shirt ornately airbrushed with a gigantic fluffy kitten shooting laser beams from its adorable mega paws at a crowd of screaming people.

And I think I might've actually given him a pass on the shirt if the rest of his outfit didn't consist of a baggy pair of Spider Man boxer shorts, froufrou cowboy boots bedazzled with hundreds of multicolored rhinestones, and goofy oversized Elvis glasses.

But it did.

Not looking a day older than thirty, the peculiar time phantom happily jammed with reckless abandon as his majestic mane of dark brown, shoulder-length hair epically flipped and tossed about his shoulders like that Fabio guy from the nineties commercials. Matching his flowing locks was a thick, artfully sculpted beard that melded into a grungy culmination of hairy tentacles proudly protruding from his chin.

And if all that wasn't enough, every inch of skin on both his arms was covered in intricately inked tattoos of snaking Japanese dragons that formed surreal sleeves extending to the very tips of his fingers.

"Should we, ah, say something?" I asked, getting the distinct impression that given the opportunity, Double OT would continue playing *guitar* with himself for the foreseeable future.

"Before we actually get his attention," Doc said, "how do you guys intend to convince *NecroLord* to join our cause?"

Rooster grinned. "Well, Owen's an unorthodox kind of dude, so I sort of have an unorthodox kind of plan."

"Unorthodox, eh?" I muttered. "Care to elaborate?"

"Trust me, you probably don't want to hear it. But you'll know it's working if everything looks like it's completely gone to shit. And when that happens, just go with it."

"Right. Okay, so does anyone else have a slightly better plan?" When both Coop and Erin just shrugged their shoulders, I grumbled, "Then we're evidently going with Rooster's plan of letting everything go to complete shit. Friggin perfect. How do we get the time hippie to stop, ah, playing with himself?"

And I can't believe I just said that.

Putting his fingers in the corners of his mouth, Coop then proceeded to let out perhaps the loudest goddamn whistle I'd ever friggin heard.

Which unfortunately scared the living shit out of Owen, causing him to immediately stop playing and look up like he was being mugged. With his concentration broken, his past and future incarnations melted from existence and two of the three guitars he was playing crashed to the floor in a horrid thud, accompanied by screeching amplifier static.

"Ah, howdy, cuz," Coop muttered, staring at the now trashed Fender Stratocaster and Gibson Les Paul strewn about Owen's feet in various and assorted pieces.

"Cooper Trooper?" he yelled, in a highly animated, raspy voice featuring a noticeable twang. "Hashtag — what the frak'n flip, bro? I mean like holy shit on rye. You can't be creeping all up in a brother's *lair* like that. Didn't you see my sign? Damn, man. This is *not* coolio, son. You feeling me, brah?"

Coop shrugged. "My bad. We were just—"

"Ha! LOL!" Double OT screamed, ripping his glasses off and tossing them across the room as he started to pace like he was having an inspired epiphany. "Okay. I see what's happening here. *This* ain't real. I'm having another drunkadelic halluncinatory interlude. You're not Cooper Trooper. *You're* just a figmentation of my imagination. Whiskey!"

"It's me, Owen. I'm really here."

"Hells no you ain't."

"Yessir, I am."

"That's a big negatory, morning glory. Wanna know how I know? *Do ya*?"

"Ah, sure?"

"Because, *faux* Cooper Trooper, the *real* Cooper Trooper would never, *ever, ever, ever,* sneak Rooster *flipping* O'Dickhole into my sanctimonious sanctuary of peace, harmony, and zendebrah. *Ergo,* my fake bald brother from an imaginary baby mama, *you* are not real. *Hence,* I need another drink — or several. Boom! Ha! Cat!"

"I'm sorry, cuz, but we're really here. And we need your help."

Covering his ears, Owen blurted out, "Blahdyblahdablah. Blahbaganda and *blah*sphemy!"

"Owen—"

"No, sir! I'm gonna close my eyes and count to three. And *then* — you, Johnny Roosterballs, the brooding buffola in the ratty jeans, *and* the brunette Hottie McHotterson will be long gone. Actually, I hope she's still here, *but* the rest of you imaginary fools need to be outtie five thousand. Feel me? Good! One — Two — Three!" And when he opened his eyes to find all four of us awkwardly waving at him, he yelled, "You're still here!"

"Yes. Yes, we are," Rooster said, taking a step toward the befuddled time hippie. "And we need your help. It's important."

"Wait, are you telling me this is actually happening? You're really real? Like for reals?"

"Yeppers."

"Hmmmmm," he muttered, pondering the circumstances for a second or two. "Excuse me for uno momento. I'm suddenly finding myself in dire need of sage counsel."

And before I knew what the hell was happening, another version of him, which I could only assume was from nanoseconds into the future, shimmered into existence. Then he began talking to himself. Literally.

"Dude!" he said to himself, somewhat under his breath.

"*What up, broselfio?*" he answered.

"Why the flipping funk is Rooster O'Dargan in our lair?"

"*Tis' a curious conundrum. Maybe he's popping by to apologize to us for acting like a total douchepants in France.*"

"You think?"

"*Ha! No! He's here to kill us!*"

"Hashtag — holy jalapeño popper! That's what I thought, too."

"*We should kill him first.*"

"We should. But we don't do that sort of stuff anymore, remember? We're all zenful and shit."

"*We'll make an exception. He's a dick.*"

"He's a total dick."

"*Kill him!*"

"Hells yeah! How should we do it?"

"*With an umbrella.*"

"Why an umbrella?"

"*Because we don't have any bananas.*"

"Ha! Excellent point!"

"*Okay, good talk.*"

"Yeah, good talk. See you soon, brah. Hasta."

"*Word.*"

As future Owen faded from existence, present Owen turned to face us seemingly now ready for business.

"So," Rooster muttered, "you know we could hear you the whole time, right?"

"Is my first-person narrative happening out loud again?"

"Totally."

"Son of a bitch! Gilmore promised me he was fixing that in the last edit. That rat bastard!"

"Who?"

"Never mind, laments the dashingly suave hero ... Sigh."

"What the hell are you talking about?"

"Exposition. It's the best part of any story."

"Ah, okay, look, Owen—"

"NecroLord."

"Ah, okay, NecroLord, I don't want any trouble. I'm only here to ask you for your help."

"Ha! I knew it. You sick, *twisted* bastard. What kind of dude asks for another dude's help to kill the same flipping dude? That's some seriously jacked up jedi shit, bro. Well, it ain't working on me, son!"

Then *NecroLord* did something I think I might actually remember for the rest of my unnatural afterlife.

In a blur of motion, he grabbed an umbrella leaning against one of the speakers and proceeded to, somewhat comically, charge at Rooster like it was a scene straight out of a Monty Python movie. Screaming the entire time, he attempted to clumsily thrust the friggin umbrella straight through Rooster's chest like it was a goddamn spear. But, as it was not a spear, and he was piss drunk, all he ended up doing was poking Rooster in the chest hard enough to make the parasol of death flip open.

Completely undeterred by the failed assassination attempt, Owen continued to jab, bob, and weave while yelling, "That's right, bitchacho! *Feel* the pain. No mercy!"

As Rooster's eyes and skin flashed an unnatural red, he frustratingly grabbed the improvised lance and snapped it in half like a twig. "Damn it, man. Will you freaking knock it off already? We only came to talk. That's it."

"Lies! Lies! And, OMG — *more* lies! Wait! You serious, bro? You're not, like, here to kill me?"

"No! And, ah, I'm really sorry about that thing in France, okay? I was a total dick. We good?"

Spinning toward Coop, Owen said, "Is this legit, Cooper Trooper?"

"That's what I've been trying to tell you, cuz."

Suspiciously eyeballing me and Doc, he asked, "And what about Hottie Biscotti and monkey man over there?"

"They're with the Guild."

"The mother flipping *Guild*? For reals?"

"It's, okay, pard. They're friendlies. Trust me."

"Friendlies, eh?"

Handing him the bourbon Harlan gave me earlier, I said, "Here. Take a drink before you have a friggin aneurysm."

Happily snatching the bottle and uncorking it with his mouth, he muttered, "Now you're talking my language, whistlebritches."

Draining the contents in one fell swig, he stared at us for a long second or two as his eyes danced with rapid thought. Then the crazy bastard screamed, "Thai food!" before disappearing in a flickering shimmer of light accompanied by a distinctive yet subtle popping sound.

"Where the hell'd he go?" I scoffed, looking around to no avail. "And did he just call me whistlebritches?"

"I think he also referred to you as a 'brooding buffola' as well as 'monkey man,'" Rooster said. "Just in case you missed it."

"Thanks for pointing that out, 'Johnny Roosterballs.'"

"Owen does have a way with words, don't he?" Coop snickered.

"So, is he coming back?" Doc asked.

"Of course *he's* coming back, tootse," Double OT scoffed, flickering back into existence wearing a completely different outfit and holding a steaming plate of crispy noodles and pan-fried tofu, drenched in curry sauce. "*He* happens to live here. Sometimes anyway."

In lieu of his KittenZilla shirt and boxer short motif, he was now sporting an untucked black dress shirt that looked a few days overdue for a trip to the cleaners, ripped jeans, and some bright blue Vans with fat white laces. Sitting Indian style atop one of the mammoth amplifiers, he proceeded to voraciously shovel food into his mouth with a pair of chopsticks like he hadn't eaten anything for a month.

"Did he just call me tootse?" Doc grunted.

Rooster nodded. "And 'Hottie McHotterson,' and 'Hottie Biscotti.'"

"So," Double OT mumbled, with a mouth full of grub as he looked down on us from his impromptu perch, "now that we've established that I'm unfortunately *not* having another hallucinatory episode *and* you're not here to kill me, what the hell do y'all jokers want? Autographs? Signed NecroLord paraphernalia? Take a few NecroSelfies? Maybe trade some cat pics?" He grinned. "Cat pics are epic. I like cats."

"Look, Owen," I grumbled, having had about enough of this bullshit, "we need you to take us back to 1975 and track down some jackass named Ronkowski. It's very—"

"NecroLord," he mumbled, mid-bite.

"What?"

"You heard me, dickholio. My *name* is NecroLord. Dig?"

"Did he just call me 'dickholio'?" I grunted, looking at Rooster.

"Yes. Yes, he did."

Glaring at the time hippie, I barked, "All right, you friggin jack—"

"Be nice," Erin said. "We need his help, remember?"

"Right. Nice. I can be nice."

"You were saying something, dickholio?" Double OT quipped, as he tossed a couple pieces of tofu at me.

A dark grin curled across my face. "You know what, *Owen*, I think we got off on the wrong foot. Let's start over, shall we?"

Willing the cloak into being, it manifested in a spectral flash and billowed about my shoulders like a goddamned raging animal. And since I felt the compelling need to break some shit, I called for the gauntlets and clenched my fists as the unbreakable ashen hellstone instantly covered my hands and forearms.

"Allow me to introduce myself," I said, boldly stomping toward the towering eight-foot amplifier he was still using as a seat. "I'm Dean. And this is me being nice."

I then proceeded to pummel the big ass speaker like it was a friggin punching bag.

After all, you only get one chance to make a first impression.

26

"Damn, hoss." Coop chuckled, gazing at the comical vision of Double OT sprawled out on the floor amongst smoking bits and pieces of his broke-ass amplifier with Thai food remnants splattered across his face. "I do believe you kicked that speaker's ass."

Making no attempt to get up as he gazed at me through widened, blood-shot eyes, Owen simply muttered, "Does this mean you're not here for NecroSelfies?"

"Maybe later," I said, willing the cloak and gauntlets into retreat as I helped him to his wobbly feet. "First we need to talk business."

"Business!" he yelled, instantly perking up as he ripped off his food-stained dress shirt to reveal a yellow tee shirt boldly emblazoned with the catchphrase 'I Did It All for the Wookie.'

"Yes, business."

"Wait, what kind of *business* does a flipping Deacon want with me? This ain't about that toodling tata thingamadoodle back in Singapore is it? Cause that was *not* me, good sir. That was that deviant doucheball NecroLaird."

"Isn't that you?"

"LOL! I'm Necro*Lord*. But Necro*Laird* is my third cousin, twice removed. Total stalker. Drives around in a creeper van and everything.

Actually, I'm not even sure we're related. Although he does share my affinity for epic cat pics."

"Okay, whatever. I don't care what happened in Singapore."

"Hashtag — phew! Cause it was totally me! Just so you know."

"I don't friggin care."

"Sphincter says what?"

"What?"

"Ha! Dude, loved it! Made me snortle."

"That's it." I grunted, turning to the crew. "I want to punch him. Somebody else talk. Is there any bourbon left?"

Slinking toward Erin like Pepé Le Pew, Owen said, "Bonjour, mon amie. I do not believe you've had the dubious pleasure of making my acquaintance. Allow myself to introduce *myself*. I'm—"

"I know who you are," Doc grumbled. "I'm Erin."

"Erin, Erin, *bo*-berin. Banana-fana *fo*-ferin. Fee-fy-mo-merin. *Erin*!"

Doc shook her head. "And now I want to punch him."

"Look, Owen," Rooster cut in. "We seriously need your help. It's important. We need you to focus."

Grabbing a guitar and breaking into song as he flipped his hair like Paul McCartney, Double OT yelled, "*Help*! Johnny Rooster needs my ... *Help*! Not just any Rooster ... *Help*! You know he needs some—"

"Owen!"

"Sorry, John Boy, no can domundo, brah. I got a show tonight. *But* if y'all high rollers want to come back next month — or *never* — official office hours are between 3:00 and 3:15 every third Saturday *not* to include long weekends *or* shomer Shabbos. NecroLord don't roll on Shabbos. Dig?"

Turning to Coop, I muttered, "What the frig's wrong with this guy?"

He shrugged. "How much time you got, hoss?"

"Is he always like this?"

"Pretty much. Although, I will admit he's in rare form tonight. By the look of things, I think he may've actually drunk the MidKnight Jayde out of whiskey. Which ain't no small feat."

"Fuck it," Rooster grumbled, winking at us as he dug around in the pockets of his bomber jacket, "We don't have time for this shit. Time for Plan B."

Producing a pair of handcuffs etched with Enochian script, he then proceeded to slap one on his own wrist and the other on Double OT's.

"What the flipping frak, bro?" Owen protested to no avail as Rooster then whipped out a peculiar glass vile and doused the inebriated time phantom with a fluorescent yellow liquid.

As Owen instantly froze in place and his face went blank, I said, "Holy shit, did you hit him with the Rooster mace?"

"The Nepheralyzer? Hell no."

"Then what the hell is that crap?"

"That, my friend, is a concentrated dose of my special Rooster Sobrie-a-Tea."

"Tea?"

"Not just any tea. It's a pretty slick recipe I came up with after years and years of analyzing the molecular composition of—"

"Please stop," I grumbled, seriously not in the mood. "What does it do?"

Clearly disappointed he was robbed of yet another bloviation opportunity, he mumbled, "Adding a mere drop of it to a glass of water will render the drunkest of the drunk stone cold sober in a matter of minutes."

"And what happens if you empty the whole friggin bottle on somebody?"

Rooster pulled out his pocket watch and intently stared at it. "No clue. But I think we're about to find out. You guys might want to back up a few steps." And, as if on cue, Double OT snapped back to life looking like he just slammed a million shots of espresso laced with rocket fuel.

With his eyes literally popping out of his head and his body shaking like he was having an epileptic fit, the poor bastard then let out a blood-curdling scream that rang out at full volume for a solid five seconds before degrading to a half-hearted gurgle with the occasional burp thrown in for good measure.

Instantly appearing perfectly lucid with a noticeable green hue to his skin, he calmly asked, "Why am I handcuffed to Johnny Rooster?"

"You were tore up from the floor up, cuz," Coop said. "Rooster got you all sobered up."

"And *how* did he do that exactly?"

"With some Rooster tea, I reckon."

"Great ballsac of fire! He tea bagged me into sobriety! How drunk was I? Did anybody take pictures? Was it a brodak moment?"

"Wait, what?" Rooster scoffed. "Nobody freaking tea bagged anybody."

Skeptically, Owen asked, "You sure?"

"Yes. Yes, I am."

"Are there pics?"

"What? No!"

"Balderdash! I knew it! How can you be *sure* if nobody took pictures?"

"Can we get him drunk again?" I grumbled. "I think I like him better that way."

"I second that!" Double OT agreed. "And can someone *please* uncuff me from this tea bagging ginger ass monkey?"

Completely ignoring the *tea bagging ginger ass monkey* comment, Rooster said, "Sorry, Owen. First, we talk. Then I uncuff you. And, just so you know, these are hex cuffs that negate the abilities of anyone they bind."

"Yeah? So what?"

"So, you won't be able to time phase yourself out of here."

"*Hmmmmmm,* and you can't turn yourself all big, red, and fugly bugly either, eh?"

"No. No, I can't."

"Good to know. *So,* whatcha wanna talk about, doucheypants?"

"We need your help," I chimed in.

"What *kind* of help? You need some e-dating advice, brah? I can hook you up just like I did for Cooper Trooper."

"Ah, that never happened, y'all," Coop blurted out.

"We need help getting back to 1975," I grumbled, trying to erase the mental image of Coop's profile pic on an internet dating site.

"Hell yeah!" Owen yelled. "The seventies are my fave. Ha! Lemme guess, you wanna take the little hottie tottie with the *naughty* karate body over there to a vintage Stones concert. You sly dog! Old school Stones concerts are better than taking a bath in Jell-O. Feeling me?"

"I don't even know where to go with that, Owen."

"You ever take a bath in Jell-O, big man? It's life altering. Highly recommend it. Orange flavor is the best. Trust me."

Feeling like my head was about to implode from Double OT's unrelenting stream of anti-logic, I took a deep breath and tried like hell to eradicate the last thirty seconds from my memory banks. "Look, it's very goddamned important that we find a time phantom named Rick Ronkowski. He's supposedly hiding out on October 21st, 1975."

"Ronk? Shit, yeah. I know Ronk."

"Wait, what?" Rooster scoffed. "You do?"

"Yepperoonies. Everybody knows Ronk."

"When was the last time you saw him?"

"Time? Ha! I don't do time, mandingo. Time *does* me. Wait, that came out wrong. Or did it?"

Jumping into the conversation, Erin said, "Where was he, Owen? Where did you see Ronkowski last?"

"Bend over, and I'll show ya, tootse. Boom!"

As her face curled into an exceptionally evil grin, Doc then pulled one of her H&Ks from its holster, chambered a round, and jabbed the muzzle squarely in Owen's crotch.

"Sausage!" His squeal was a piercing falsetto.

"What?"

"Last time I saw Ronk, he was pushing his sausage cart around a city. And there was a game going on. It was a tournament or something."

"What kind of tournament?"

"Tennis!"

"Was it in 1975?"

"Hell, I dunno. Maybe?"

"Can you take us to him?"

"Can we continue this conversation without your gat jabbed all up in me groinage? Super pretty please with orange Jell-O on top?"

Holstering her man-sized pistol, Doc said, "Do us both a favor and hold the Jell-O."

"So, you'll help us?" Rooster chimed in.

"Depends on one *minor* condition," Double OT said, with a wolfish grin.

"Which is?"

"Somebody coming clean about what the hell you're *really* doing here?" And then, Owen Octavius Trask did another thing that I think I'll remember for the rest of my unnatural afterlife.

Before any of us had the first clue as to what the hell was happening, he simply flickered out of existence only to instantly reappear behind Rooster with a friggin samurai sword held to his throat tight enough to draw a fine layer of blood. With a big shit-eating grin on his face, he slid off the hex cuff, which up until recently was supposedly suppressing his abilities, and slapped it on Rooster's other hand.

"So," he said, with the cold demeanor of a seasoned assassin, "Cooper Rayfield strolls into NecroLord's Lair with Johnny O'Dargan, Dean Robinson, *and* Erin Kelly in tow. Not often I get a personal visit from Heaven's most wanted. That's right, kids. I know who you are. Question I can't wrap my head around is, what the hell are you up to?"

"Wait a friggin minute," I muttered. "You knew who we were the whole time?"

"Roger dodger, monkey man."

"And how'd you get out of the cuff?"

"Please." He scoffed. "Child's play."

"So that whole thing about you being piss drunk was a ploy?"

"Ha! No! I was totally lit. Seriously, I was like smashed out of my mind. For reals."

I shrugged, hoping this was all part of Rooster's plan of letting everything go to shit. "So, what now?"

"Simple, whistlebritches. You tell me what this is about and *maybe* I won't give Roosterballs an extra close shave."

"What happened to you being all zenful and shit?"

"Being *zen* don't equate to being a dumbass, *dumbass*."

"At least I'm not the dumbass who thinks that blade's going to do anything to Rooster besides really piss him off."

"Ha! Wrong! Thanks to the *fact* that Johnny's wearing his own kinky hex cuffs, his fugly alter ego can't come out and play. For the moment, he ain't nothing more than a stringy human. And trust me, monkey man, that means this here katana will snuff the Rooster faster than Oprah loses weight. Ain't that right, John Boy?"

As Rooster mumbled something indecipherable mainly because he had a friggin sword pressed to his adam's apple, Owen just stood there grinning. "It's *almost* like I meticulously manipulated this whole series of events to amazingly culminate in this diabolical, suspense-filled conclusion. Overly dramatic sound effect anyone? Bum, bum, *bummm*."

"Son of a bitch," I grumbled. "You planned all this?"

"Bingo! Guess the shoe's on the other foot now, eh? And by *shoe*, I mean *cuff*. Just so there's no *confusion* with my choice of metaphors. Feel me?"

"Wow," Doc muttered. "That's actually impressive."

"*Right*? That metaphor was killa. Nailed it!"

"I don't think she was talking about the metaphor, cuz," Coop said.

"Of course she wasn't! What was she talking about, Cooper Trooper?"

"Probably the fact that you backwoods snookered us."

"Oh, that! Epic, right?"

Trying my very best to ignore the fact that we'd been thoroughly outwitted by a sloshed, time hopping rock star with an affinity for cat tee shirts and Underoos, I muttered, "So, you want the truth about what we're doing here."

"Are you about to tell me that I can't handle the truth in a totally epic Jack Nicholson voice?"

"No."

"Total buzzkill. But tell me anyway."

"All right, here's the short story. One of the archangels is a traitor working with Azazel and his oversized cronies. Together, they're holding mankind ransom to force the seraphic court into opening the gates of Tartarus and free the fallen Watchers so they can launch some kind of angel mutiny. As such, we've got less than two hours to expose the traitor and put a stop to all the bullshit before the anakim army systematically lays waste to the Earth."

"Egads, man! That's an ambitious plot arc. Are you yankin' my wang?"

"No."

"Holy shit! This is intense. I'm on the edge of my seat here, monkey man. What's next? Sex, danger, interdimensional espionage, British accents, Germans with eye patches, creepy hairless cats? Pirates? Evil clown guys? More sex? More cats?"

"There's none of that."

"All right, I dig it. I'm disappointed, but I still dig it. *So*, what does finding Ronk have to do with all this?"

"We've got good reason to believe he's in possession of the key to exposing the traitor and ensuring the gates of Tartarus stay sealed. All we have to do is find him."

"And what exactly is this most fabled key?"

"It's, ah, the Ark of the Covenant."

"Great galloping gonads! For reals?"

"For reals."

"Well, spank my fanny and call me horsepucky."

"Ah, no?"

"Ha! *So*, tell me, how do you know Ronk has the God box?"

"Rooster's mom told us," Erin chimed in.

"And how does Johnny's mom know Ronk?"

"She was screwing him."

"I knew it! There *is* sex involved! Bum, bum, *bummmm*. Hold the phone. Johnny's mom? You talking about Lilith?"

"Yes."

Talking directly into Rooster's ear, Owen said, "*So*, I might've heard, through the grapevine, that she and your pops kind of broke things off a while back. Is she, like, dating anyone nowadays or—"

"Dude!" Rooster scoffed as the sword pressed into his throat. "Awkward?"

"Ha! Sorry, Johnny! Your mom has it all kinds of going *on* though, brah. Just saying."

"What's it gonna be, Owen?" I grumbled. "Will you help us or not?"

"So, lemme get this *straight*, you want me to abandon my comfylicious lifestyle of music and mamacitas to join your crew of militant outlaws so we can embark on an epicalarious Indiana Jones misadventure to save the world from certain demise by defeating a maniacally rogue *archangel*. Did I get that about right?"

"Pretty much. You in?"

"LOL! There's a better chance of Cooper Trooper waking up tomorrow morning looking like David Hasselhoff than *me* joining *your* seriously suicidal escapade into the nether regions of insanity!"

"That's hurtful, cuz," Coop mumbled under his breath.

"Okay, Owen. I guess we're done here," I said, willing the cloak into being and heading toward the door as I winked at Doc. "Real friggin shame. We really could've used a man of your unconventional talents."

"And superior intellect," she added, picking up on where I was going. "Not to mention the legendary fighting skills. And hair."

Double OT smirked. "Ah, okay. I see what y'all rascals are doing. But, it ain't working. Now, if you'd be so kind as to get the flipping frak out of my *lair*, I have very important *stuff* to tend to."

I shrugged. "Sorry for wasting your time and, ah, beating the shit out of your amp. Now, if you wouldn't mind letting Rooster go, we'll be on our way. It's time for Plan C."

"Plan C?"

"Was hoping it wasn't going to come to this, but we're out of options."

"And what's Plan C?"

"Nothing for you to worry about. We'll take it from here."

"Call me curious."

"Well, if the *greatest* time phantom in all of history is too busy to help us get back to 1975 and quite literally save the world, we're going to use Rooster's time machine to do it."

"What the shit biscuit? Did I hear that right? You're gonna put the fate of mankind in the hands of a flipping *time machine*? And one made by Roosterballs for that matter? Serious sauce? I mean, hellfire and Dalmatians, he probably slapped that piece of funk together with spare parts from his dang PlayStation and a broke-ass Rubik's cube. And, not to mention, *you* don't even know where Ronk is in 1975."

"Don't have much choice at this point. It's our only play. So, if you'll please remove your ninja sword from Rooster's throat, we need to get going. Clock's ticking. Bad guys to smite. World to save. You know the drill."

"All right," he muttered. "I'll help you."

"I'm sorry, what was that?"

"This ain't amateur hour, son. This is the big show. And nobody does the big show like NecroLord. You *need* my skillz, dig?"

"What about all the *stuff* you have to do?"

"*It* can wait until after I save the world."

"So, you're in."

"Ha! I'm *so* in! Can I kill Johnny now?"

"I'd really rather you didn't."

"Pretty please with orange Jell-O on top?"

"No. And hell no."

"Fine," he mumbled, sheathing the sword on his back in a blur of motion as Rooster stepped free and instantly turned harrowing red from head to toe.

With his eyes literally glowing like fiery orbs, he smiled at Double OT and broke out of the hex cuffs like they were made of paper.

"Wha? Wha? Whataboutwha?" Owen gasped. "But you said those cuffs were—"

"I lied," Rooster grunted.

"So, you could turn all red and fugly bugly the whole time?"

"Yeppers."

"Twisted! You counter snookered my snookery. That is *so* badass! It's *almost* like you meticulously manipulated this whole series of events to amazingly culminate in this diabolical, suspense-filled plot twist."

"Epic, right?"

"Bum, bum, *bummmm*. So, John Boy, I gotta know — did you seriously build a time machine?"

"No. No, I didn't."

"Shut your mouth! I got double dog counter-snookered to boot? Dude! Loved it!"

"Welcome to the team."

"LOL! Hey, guys, *so* now that I'm pretty much your de facto leader, I'm gonna need a cool uniform."

"You're not our leader," we all muttered in perfect unison.

Completely ignoring us, he said, "I'd like to suggest a nice blue spandex jumpsuit with an obnoxious, yet super sweet, yellow stripe down the middle. And I'll need a badge. Preferably a large, shiny one. Do we have a catchy slogan? Mascot? Secret handshake? How about a Facebook page? Speaking of, I totally need to update my status to 'In a relationship with Heavenly Fugitives.' Epic!"

"Does part of the plan involve putting duct tape over Owen's mouth?" Erin asked.

"It does now," I grumbled.

"Kool and the Gang! I love duct tape!"

And so began the next phase of the mission.

Unfortunately, shortly thereafter, we realized we didn't have any duct tape.

Bum, bum, *bummmm.*

27

"WHAT'S THE PLAN, HOSS?" Coop asked, as we all watched Double OT diligently sift through a heaping pile of guitar cases and other random shit scattered across the floor of his peculiar lair.

"Simple," I muttered. "Soon as *Necro*Dork is done with whatever the hell he's doing at the moment, me, Doc, and Rooster will blast to the past, find Ronkowski, and snatch the Ark from his sorry ass."

"And then?"

"And then it gets complicated."

"What do you need from me?"

"Stay here. If we pull this off, I'm guessing we'll be back before you know it."

"And if you're not?"

"Get to Abernethy. Tell him what's going on."

"Then what?"

"Then I have the sneaking suspicion you're gonna need a lot more arrows, my friend."

Breaking into the conversation, Erin said, "So, Owen, how do we do this, exactly?"

"Do what?" he replied, still fully engrossed in his search for God knows what. "Take a Jell-O bath?"

"No, jackass. Travel backward in time. How the hell do we travel backward in time and find Ronkowski?"

"Oh, that. Bummer!"

"*So*, how do we do it?"

"Ain't nothing to it but to do it, tootse."

Rapidly losing all semblance of patience, I grumbled, "What's your plan to find him?"

"*Plan*?"

"Yes, Owen. Your friggin plan."

"Well, Deano, firstly I need to locate my tools. *Then* I will reveal my *plan*."

"You don't have a plan, do you?"

"Ha! This situation calls for action, *not* plans. And, lucky for you, *action* happens to be my middle name. Comprende?"

"I thought Octavius was your middle name."

"Okay, you got me there. But seriously, I need to find my tools. Can't possibly do any precision time hopping without them. You know how it is. Or not. Anyway, I keep them in a trunk around here somewhere. Or at least I did. Hey, you don't mind if I call you Deano, do you, monkey man?"

When I offered him nothing in response besides an icy stare, he just smiled and continued rooting through the mound of junk while humming a Steely Dan song I couldn't quite place.

Jumping into the conversation before I got whiny-er, Rooster said, "The last time you saw Ronkowski, you said he was at a tournament. A tennis tournament?"

"Pretty sure."

"And he was in a city."

"Perhaps."

"What city?"

"A big one. Might've been a small one, actually. Or a medium-ish one."

"How about the country? You remember that?"

"Yes! Actually, not so much."

"Your uncanny attention to detail is truly astonishing."

"Word!"

"Anywho, you also said something about him pushing a cart around, right?"

Continuing to comb through his junkpile, Owen muttered, "The Sausage Rocket."

"Come again?"

"Ronk's cart. He calls it the Sausage Rocket."

"Are you saying that the guy sells sausage, cuz?" Coop asked. "You mean like actual sausage? Or, you talking about—"

"LOL! Get your flipping mind out of the gutter, Cooper Trooper. We happen to be in *mixed* company."

"So, he's like a street vendor." Doc chimed in before another unfortunate double entendre presented me with a mental image I really didn't have the stomach for.

"Exactruly, Erin Bo-Berin. *Ronk* and his fabled Sausage Rocket are the premier street dispensary of smoked kielbasa wrapped in toasty warm sourdough buns and drizzled with *sautéed* sauerkraut. It's so flipping good that folks instinctively flock like the salmon of Capistrano to wrap their watering mouths around Ronk's meats. It's a Polish thing."

And it happened anyway.

"Can we redirect this conversation," Rooster grunted. "Freaking please?"

"Sure thing, John Boy. Whatcha wanna talk about, doucheball?"

"Look, we have it on good authority that Ronkowski's somewhere on October 21st, 1975. So, in theory, we already know *when* he is. All we need to figure out is *where* he is. And, you *think* you saw him pushing a cart—"

"The Sausage Rocket."

"Yes, okay, the freaking Sausage Rocket. You think you saw him pushing the freaking Sausage Rocket at some tennis tournament in some random city. So, on the off chance that you're actually right, and *not* having a hallucinatory episode, we need to figure out what tournament he might've been peddling his wares at so we can figure out where he is — or, at least, was."

Coop shook his head. "This is making my brain hurt, y'all."

"Where the hell do they play tennis in October?" I asked.

"Hell if I know, monkey man. I always preferred baseball myself. All those girlies wearing miniskirts and grunting at each other when they smack the ball over the net. Epic!"

"That ain't baseball, cuz." Coop chuckled. "That's tennis."

"Ha! I always get those two confused. What's baseball then?"

"Wait a friggin minute," I muttered, as Double OT's anti-logic made some semblance of sense. "He not talking about a tennis tournament. He's talking about a friggin baseball tournament."

Erin nodded. "And there's only one baseball tournament played in late October. The World Series."

"Don't remember nothing about no *World Series*," Owen muttered. "But I do remember a certain lack of girlies in miniskirts whacking balls at each other. Which was super unfortunate. For reals."

"Holy shit," I barked, suddenly feeling more than vindicated for being a life-long Red Sox junkie. "Game 6!"

Somewhat startled by my apparent revelation, Coop asked, "What are you talking about, hoss?"

"October 21st, 1975 — perhaps the greatest — most epic — most awe-inspiring — most friggin amazing moment in baseball history — ever. Red Sox versus the Cincinnati Reds. Game 6 of the World friggin Series!"

"Wait, what?" Rooster said, as a lightbulb went off. "I remember that game. It was at Fenway Park."

"You bet your ginger ass it was. Bottom of the twelfth inning. Carlton Fisk hit a walk off homer to win the game and tie the goddamn series! Actually, what the hell am I talking about? It wasn't a mere walk off homer. It was a towering shot of majestic awesomeness that Fisk waved fair, with both friggin arms, as he ran down the first base line and—"

"And, unfortunately, the Red Sox were summarily defeated the very next day in Game 7 by a heartbreaking score of 4-3. You're missing the point. This means Owen was in *Boston*."

"Total buzzkill," I grumbled.

Turning to Double OT, Erin said, "So, it was Boston. You saw Ronkowski in Boston."

"I did? I mean, I *did*."

"You sure?"

"About what?"

"Do you think he's still there?"

"Hope so. I could really go for a kielbasa dog and some onion rings. You hear what I'm screaming? Starving!"

"Hiding the Ark in Boston actually makes a lot of sense," Rooster said, thinking out loud.

"Why's that?" Doc asked.

"Well, the city itself was built on a literal nexus point of the seven primary ley lines that run through the Earth. That's exactly why the Quartermaster is able to exist there."

"Ley lines?"

"Yeppers. The vectors of primal energy that literally bind the Earth together. They also link this realm with the various and assorted *other* realms that exist beyond the mortal veil."

"I see," Erin muttered, clearly regretting she asked.

"My point is that even if stashed on a single day in history, the amount of raw power generated by the Ark would make it impossible to truly hide. *But* if it was sitting on the intersection of a lay line or two, its energy signature would be virtually undetectable. I mean, shit, the more I think about it, Boston is the perfect place for Ronkowski to be."

"And what if he's not?"

"Let's worry about that when the time comes," I muttered, shifting focus to Owen. "Hey, *Doctor Who*, it's time to go. You ready to fire up the flux capacitor and get the show on the road?"

"Found it!" Double OT yelled, holding up a modest antique wooden trunk bound together with dilapidated leather straps.

"You don't seriously have a flux capacitor in there do you?"

"A what? Oh, wait, was that another cleverly placed pop culture reference that Gilmore slid into our ever-so-witty dialogue? That sly dog! Loved it."

"What the hell are you talking about? Who's this Gilmore jackass anyway?"

"Huh? Oh, he's no one of consequence, monkey man. Über fourth wall break! Boomsauce!"

Making the mental note to revisit that particular topic at a later time, I grumbled, "What's in the box, Owen?"

"Just a few things I'll need for the most epic of journeys we're about to embark on. Behold!"

Carefully placing the chest on the floor, he removed the straps from the rusted buckles and proudly opened it for all of us to see. And unfortunately, the smell emanating from the carcass of the thirty-pound, grey cat sprawled out inside made my nostrils about fall off.

"Aw, for Christ's sake, Owen. Is that a dead cat? What the hell, man?"

"Cat?" He scoffed, looking in the box. "Ha! There he is. Thought I'd lost him in Singapore. Had to leave in a bit of a *hurry*, after all. He must've got all liquored up and crawled in the trunk before I blew town. Probably been sleeping this whole time. Hey, buddy, time to wakie wakie."

"Dude," Rooster winced, holding his nose. "I don't know when you left Singapore, but that cat's been dead for like a year."

"Nah, he ain't dead. Probably just hung over, as usual."

"He smells like a rotting corpse," Erin forced out, pulling her shirt up over her mouth and nose.

"Shush your mouth! Asshole's a sensitive son of a bitch. You may offend his smooth jazz sensibilities. And, besides, he always smells like that."

"You named your cat Asshole?"

"What? Hell, no. I *named* him Rooster. Ha!" Poking the fat ass feline a few times, he said, "Wake up, Asshole. Rise and shine, you flipping fuzz bucket. Daddy's got work to do."

And much to our astonishment, the oversized furball snapped to life and let out a prolonged yawn. Promptly leaping out of the trunk and lazily meowing a few times as it dismissively glanced at the group of us with some really creepy yellow eyes, it then proceeded to waltz toward Rooster.

"Damn, cuz," Coop said, "That thing looks like a bowling ball with teeth. What the hell you been feeding it?"

Owen grinned. "Chihuahuas, mainly."

Squatting on Rooster's boot, Asshole then took an impressive piss before sauntering off into the darkness of the amplifier forest and disappearing.

"Think he likes you," Doc chuckled, as Rooster muttered something of a snide nature under his breath.

I turned my attention back on Owen. "Was there anything else besides your undead cat you needed out of the box?"

"Right! My tools." Reaching into his trunk and pulling out a series of peculiar objects, he laid them out on the floor and stared at them for a long couple seconds.

Studying the obscure accoutrements, Erin muttered, "An old ass compass, a piece of string, a tin of mints, and a man purse. Those are your tools?"

"Man purse? It's a satchel, whistlebritches. A very *manly* one at that."

"And what about the other crap?"

"This *crap*, my dear sassy pants, happens to be the highly sophisticated implements of temporal navigation that will undoubtedly lead us directly to Ronk."

"And how do these highly sophisticated implements work, exactly?"

"Well, to get back to a place that I've been before, I only need two things. A bearing and a memory. Dig?"

"So, now that we have narrowed down the location to Boston on October 21st, 1975, you're saying you can use your compass to guide us there?"

"Exactly!" Owen said, tying the string around the index finger on his left hand.

"And the string?"

"*And* my trusty string will drop us off in the exact moment I last saw Ronk."

"Because it helps you remember?"

"Much more better. It's a foci that actually *stores* all my memories. Right here. In this eensie weensie piece of string. Killa, right? Willa made it special for me with some coolio vexen mojo. Mainly because I could never remember how to get back to the MidKnight Jayde. And once when I did, I sorta ended up naked in the women's bathroom in 1942. Long story."

Erin shook her head. "And what about the mints?"

"For fresh breath. Would you like one? They're wintergreen."

"No."

"You sure? Didn't want to say anything, but you kinda need one."

"Piss off."

"Owen, we seriously need to go," I muttered.

"Almost ready, Deanbean," Double OT said, spinning the bezel rings on his peculiar compass into a specific configuration.

"So that's an actual temporal compass, eh?" Rooster asked, admiring the highly polished, bronze instrument artfully set in a rustic wooden frame completely covered with carefully engraved Enochian sigils. "Never seen one before."

"This here is the genuine article, John Boy."

"Is it accurate?"

"Accurate? Ha! In the hands of a skilled tempus phasmatis, this little baby will get you within nanoseconds of your intended destination. Every time. Guaranteed."

"And how about in your hands?"

"Results may vary. Terms and conditions apply."

"What the hell's that supposed to mean?" I barked.

Still madly twisting the bezel rings, he said, "Don't get your cloak all up in a wad, monkey man. Nothing to worry about. I'm all over this like stink on Johnny. As long as I get my calculations sorta right, we'll be better than money for nothing and chicks for free."

Wishing like hell Rooster had actually built a time machine, I muttered, "Why do I have the unequivocal feeling that we're seriously screwed?"

Completing his haphazard tinkering, Double OT then announced, "Alrighty, I think we're all set, boys and girlie. Boston, October 21st, 1775. Here we come."

"1975!" Rooster scoffed. "October 21st, 1975!"

"Exactly! That's what I said."

"No! No, it wasn't!"

"Really? Well, that's what I meant. You guys ready?"

"Good luck, y'all," Coop muttered, collecting his longbow and taking several steps back from the group. "See you soon?"

"Sooner than you know, Cooper Trooper. Everybody get in close. *Time* to get this party started. Cue the music!"

And, much to our chagrin, "Jive Talkin'" from the BeeGees began to inexplicably thunder from every speaker in NecroLord's lair as a marble-sized ball of swirling white radiance elegantly shimmered into existence above Owen's compass.

Watching in horror as the light ball began to spin at a mind-blowing pace while exponentially growing in size, Erin yelled, "What's happening?"

"Temporal vortex, baby!" Owen reached into his man purse and pulled out a few packs of bubble gum, which he tossed at us. "Here, this will help with the spatial acclimation. Chew it like you stole it!"

"What are we supposed to do?" I grunted, thinking there would have been a bit more preparation to friggin time travel than some jackass handing out Bubblicious.

As the ball of ethereal light fluidly morphed into a man-sized, gyrating cyclone and began to literally suck us in like a surreal vacuum cleaner, Owen shouted, "Easy peasy, Deano! Just unwrap a piece and pop it in your mouth."

"Not the gum, you friggin moron. The fucking time jump! What the hell are we supposed to do?"

"Just relax!" he screamed. "And don't stop believing! Hold on to the feeling!"

"Those aren't instructions, asshole! Those are fucking Journey lyrics!"

And before Rooster, Doc, or I could lodge another spirited protest, an ungodly screeching sound filled the room, and the friggin vortex voraciously swallowed us like a spectral whale.

Feeling like I'd been tossed into a goddamn washing machine in the middle of a turbo spin cycle, I was blinded by the waves of pulsing light as sensory overload kicked in with extreme prejudice. The brilliant light steadily transitioned to harrowing darkness, and despite my best efforts to focus on Doc and Rooster, I quickly drifted into the ether.

Right before everything faded to black, I couldn't help but wonder how much better this experience would've been if orchestrated by Christopher Lloyd and Michael J. Fox instead of Owen Octavius Trask.

Typical.

28

The clamor of slow-moving cars, beeping horns, and chattering voices gently coaxed me out of one hell of a trippy comatose state as an Aerosmith song I couldn't quite place softly played from somewhere in the general vicinity.

Feeling like I'd been roofied and stuffed in the trunk of a car after being relentlessly punched in the face by Mike Tyson, I struggled to open my eyes as my muddled mind fought to achieve a state of functioning consciousness.

Making the mental note that perhaps bubble gum played more of an important role to surviving time travel than I'd previously thought, it took all my effort to roll over and sit up.

"Hey, sleeping beauty," I heard a gruff voice bark at me as a boney finger persistently poked me in the chest. "Get your ass up."

"Where am I?" I sluggishly asked, opening my eyes yet unable to see anything but a blurry haze.

"You look like total shit." He chuckled, ignoring the question. "You get hit by a car or something?"

"Where am I?"

"You're on Westland Avenue, moron."

"Westland Ave. In Boston?"

"Of course, *in* Boston. Are you deaf or just stupid?"

The stranger's voice began to sound unfortunately familiar. "What did you say?"

"You heard me, schmendrick."

Schmendrick? Shit. I rubbed my eyes until a foggy vision of a frail man appeared standing over me. "Binkowicz? Is that you?"

"Of course it's me."

"Son of bitch," I grumbled, staggering to my feet, still summarily dazed and confused. "NecroDork must've screwed up the damn coordinates."

"What are you babbling about?"

"The friggin vortex. It brought us to Boston, but in the goddamn present."

"What?"

"It didn't work," I grunted, trying like hell to shake the cobwebs out of my head. "I'm not supposed to be here."

"Yeah, no shit. This is *my* spot."

"No, goddamn it, you don't get it. I'm supposed to be *here*. Just not *now*. It should be October 21st—"

Cutting me off mid-sentence, he grumbled, "Are you freaking high? It is October 21st, you schmendrick. Now get up and get outta here before I call the cops."

"Wait, what?" I muttered, as my vision snapped back into focus and I got a good look at Fred Binkowicz.

And then I about shite myself.

Although still cantankerous as hell, he was by no means the eighty-year-old crusty bastard I knew in 2012. He was—

"Young," I blurted out, pointing at him like an idiot. "You're — young!"

Dressed to the nines in some ridiculous green argyle v-neck cardigan and gold-colored polyester slacks, he suspiciously looked me over while taking a seat on a foldout chair positioned on the sidewalk right next to the friggin entrance to the Quartermaster.

"This some kind of joke?" He glared at me like I'd lost my mind. "Did O'Dargan put you up to this? Who the hell are you, anyway? And how do you know my name?"

And it was right about then when the realization of where I was hit me like a ton of bricks. I'm pretty sure Fred kept talking, but I didn't hear another word as I spun around to find a scene straight out of *Starksy & Hutch* meets *The Rockford Files* laid out around me.

"Holy — shit," I muttered under my breath, both shocked and elated. "It worked!"

Despite the fact that everything was strikingly familiar, it was markedly different. Case in point was the puke green Ford Granada parallel parking behind the shiny yellow AMC Pacer across the street. Both of which were brand new and looked like they had rolled straight off the showroom floor.

Continuing to scan the area, it seemed that the brownstone apartment buildings were generally where they stood thirty-seven years from now but everything else wasn't. The most glaring disparity was that in lieu of the franchise fast food joints and parking garages that lined the streets in the future, there was an eclectic combination of rundown bodegas, old school laundromats, seedy billiard joints, and adult film theaters.

And, of course, rounding out the surreal retro experience were the excited waves of pedestrian traffic moving up and down the sidewalk dressed like extras from the Brady Bunch, complete with crazy hairdos, sanctimonious sideburns, and all variations of bell bottom blues.

With Binkowicz suspiciously staring me down like I was a complete lunatic, I think I was about to say something else incredibly stupid when I caught a glimpse of Double OT strolling up the sidewalk trying to get my attention.

Decked out in a double-knit denim leisure suit complete with an oversized butterfly collar and snazzy high heeled boots, he motioned for me to shut the hell up as he slapped Binkowicz on the shoulder like they were old pals. "Funky Freddy B! What up, you prophetic pimping jive turkey?"

"Trask," Binkowicz muttered, evidently less than happy to see him. "What do you want, time freak?"

Sliding up next to me, Owen said, "I think you mean time *phantom*."

"No. I don't. What the hell are you doing here?"

"The seventies are my jam. I'm just blowing through like a *cool* breeze, dig?"

"Well, do us both a favor and blow somewhere else. Like maybe Nagasaki in 1945."

"Ha! That's really funny yet incredibly hurtful. Loved it! Anywho, I see you found my amigo."

Fred nodded at me. "You know this putz?"

"Hell yeah, I know him. This is my main man, Chappie. He's a roadie for my band. Been looking all over for him."

"Chappie?"

"Yessiree," Double OT smirked. "Chappie Chapperson."

"What the hell kind of name is that?"

"It's a family name. Lot of incest."

"He looks inbred all right."

"Don't you mind Chappie now, Fred. Despite the fact he drinks like a fish and is *clearly* not the smartest of folks, he's good people. Ain't no doubt he's dumber than a box of rocks, but he's harmless. Ain't that right, Chap?"

Biting my tongue with every fiber of my being, I just forced an awkward smile.

"Well, isn't that cute?" Binkowicz muttered. "And I suppose now that you found your moronic *boyfriend*, you'll be leaving. You know you're not exactly welcome around here."

"Serious sauce? Is Big A still mad about that—"

"Yes. He is."

"Right. And on *that* note, we'll be exiting stage left. Got a show to do anyway. Check you later, funkanator. And dig the pants. For reals. Brings out the premature wrinkles on your forehead. Hasta!"

Reaching into his godawful sweater vest and pulling out his signature pipe, Fred just scowled at us for a long second before sinking into his foldout chair.

As Owen and I left the younger, yet still incredibly disgruntled, version of Frederick Binkowicz behind and made our way across the street in the late afternoon sun, Owen muttered, "So *that* was a sticky wicket. Good thing I found you before you blew our cover, Chapster."

I shook my head. "Don't ever call me that again."

"But it's got such a nice ring to it. *Chappie* Chapperson. Chappie *Chapperson*. Chap*pie*—"

"Say it one more time, and I will knock your fucking teeth out."

"Ha! But seriously, Dean machine, you gotta be more careful. You ain't no tempus phasmatis."

"No shit. What's your point?"

"Well, for starters, hombre, you can't be chatting up the natives. *Especially* people you know in the future. Unlike *me*, everything *you* do in the past has the potential to ripple through time."

"So?"

"*So*? Time paradoxes ... alternate timelines ... spatial implosions. Anything of this ringing a bell?"

"No."

"Damn, son, thought you knew that."

"How would I possibly friggin know that, you asshole?"

"Maybe because we talked about it *ad nauseam* at the MidKnight Jayde. Der!"

"Was that before or after you threw packs of Juicy Fruit at us and started singing Journey's greatest hits?"

"All right, all right. So maybe I neglected to share a couple small details. Don't sweat it, monkey man. No harm, no foul. Fast Freddy B won't remember seeing you forty years from now. All good."

"Speaking of, why the hell did I wake up in front of the goddamn Quartermaster? What happened to Doc and Rooster?"

"*That,* my buff buddyboo, is a curious conundrum. The vortex dropped the rest of us off in that alley up ahead. You must've caught a rip current or something."

"Rip current? What the hell is that?"

"Damn if I know. Temporal navigation's more of an art than a science. On the upside, at least you made it here *intact* and your body wasn't subatomically peeled apart and scattered across unknown quadrants of the interspatial riff like teeny chunks of turkey jerky."

"Are you saying that was a friggin possibility?"

"Did we not talk about this?"

"I'm really not liking you right now, Owen," I muttered, making the mental note to punch him squarely in the face when this whole thing was over. "So, is this where you saw Ronkowski the last time?"

Looking at the piece of string carefully tied around his left pinky finger, he said, "Must be. Stringy Stringerson is never wrong. Ronk's gotta be close. Fenway's a couple blocks from here, right?"

"Yeah."

"*So*, he was probably pushing the Sausage Rocket to the tennis game when I ran into him last time."

"Baseball game," I grumbled as we approached a dark alley about halfway down Westland Avenue. It was tucked inconspicuously between the Shamrock TripleX Emporium and Tipsy's Budget Wine and Liquors, Your Friendly Neighborhood Packie.

Ducking into the cover of the backstreet, my nostrils were assaulted by the overpowering stench of urine and garbage as I was more than happy to see Rooster huddled next to a large dumpster.

Wrestling with the butterfly collar on a truly horrific mustard yellow belted sweater as he uncomfortably squirmed in a snazzy pair of white bell bottom corduroy slacks, his eyes flashed red as he grumbled, "Not a word about my outfit."

I chuckled under my breath. "What are you talking about? You look good. Sort of like a transvestite version of Robert Redford mixed with a less hairy Burt Reynolds."

"You're an asshole."

"Tell me something I don't know. Like, for example, where the hell's Doc?"

Boldly emerging from behind the dumpster while tucking her dueling shoulder holsters into a retro denim jean jacket complete with a white fluffy sherpa collar, she was dolled up in a flower print halter top tied into a bow and showing off enough midriff to induce spontaneous drooling in any red-blooded American male.

Completing the outfit with a pair of mesmerizing lowcut jeans held in place by a colorful tapestry belt and some sassy brown leather boots that looked like they belonged to Lynda Carter, she was the vision of a retro goddess to put it ever so mildly.

"Sweet baby Jesus," I muttered, making the mental note that the seventies looked a helluva lot better on Doc than it did on Rooster.

"Your turn," she smirked, tossing a peculiar aerosol can at me.

"What the hell's this? Deodorant? Look, I know I could probably use a shower, but—"

"Ha!" Double OT said. "It ain't deodorant, whistlebritches. Although you are a bit *funky* at the moment. And I'm not talking about the good funky. Like Funky Brewster. Definitely more like a funky bum muffin with a serious case of the funky booty syndrome. Comprizzle?"

Offering him nothing but an icy stare in response, he said, "Alrighty then, just give yourself a squirt of my Garb Gas, and we can get this show on the road."

"Did you just say Garb Gas?"

"Yeah, buddy. Think of it as a time traveler's urban camouflage. Made special by Willa and Harlan."

"And what does it do?"

"Duh! It's an enchantment that instantly transforms your attire to the *provincial* particulars of whatever time period you happen to find yourself in. Go on now, getchu some."

Figuring I didn't have much to lose, I gave myself a healthy application of the obscure mist and watched in somewhat disbelief as my sullied jeans, blood-stained white RoosterBragh tee shirt, and jungle boots morphed into a short-sleeved, powder blue jumpsuit complete with a hood and white sneakers.

"Twisted!" he yelled. "Nothing says party in the front like a stretch terry onesie. That's some serious polyester, monkey man. Sham on!"

"You gotta be kidding me with this shit." I scoffed. "I'm not fucking wearing this."

"Why not?" Rooster snorted, absolutely beaming at my absurd get up. "You look great. Only thing you're lacking is a pornstache and a hair helmet. Actually, you kind of have the hair helmet going on, so—"

"Change it back," I grumbled, glaring at Owen. "I want my other clothes. Right now."

"No candomundo, big man. It's a one-shot spell. But, don't worry, it'll wear off soon as we get back to the future."

"All right," Erin said, more than ready for business, "now that we all look ridiculous — some of us *so* much more than others — how do we find Ronkowski?"

"He's gotta be close," Double OT muttered, thinking out loud. "What would I have been doing in this part of town last time I was here? Hmmmmm."

"Well," Rooster grumbled, "seeing as though your freaking memory string dropped us off in between a smut shop and a liquor store, I'm gonna go way out on a limb and guess you were either getting drunk *or* watching a skin flick. Or both."

"That doesn't sound like me at all. *Hashtag* — it totally does! We should check out the smut shop first. My skintuition's tingling."

"Ugh," Erin muttered.

"Let's get moving," I said, as we began to make our way back toward the street with Owen on point. "When we find Ronkowski, let me handle it."

"Lilith said he's not going to give up the Ark without a fight. Remember?"

"I remember, Doc."

"So, what are you going to do?" Rooster asked, chambering a round in both Glocks before tucking them back into his pants.

I grinned. "I'm going to be nice."

"Nice, eh? And if that doesn't work?"

"Then I'm going to be really nice."

"Great," he grumbled. "Dean's plan is a Patrick Swayze quote from *Roadhouse*. This should go down without a hitch."

Ignoring his snide commentary, I turned to Owen. "Hey, NecroDope, what are we looking for? What does Ronkowski look like?"

Pulling to a halt at the very edge of the alley, he spun around to face us. "Well, he's a big feller. Strong as a motherfogrel. Biceps like bowling balls. Got some shaggy Mark Harmon hair. And, *most importantly*, he'll have the Sausage Rocket with him."

Rooster nodded. "So, we're looking for a big ass body builder guy pushing a big ass cart. That shouldn't be that hard to track down."

"Exactamundo, doucheball. Any more questions? Or can we actually go and *find* him now?"

"By all means, lead the way."

Impatiently mumbling something of a snide nature under his breath, Double OT stepped out of the alleyway only to be absolutely leveled by a rather elaborate stainless-steel food cart being pushed down the bustling sidewalk by one of the largest human beings I'd ever laid eyes on.

As Owen yelped in protest, the absurd mobile meat dispensary, decorated with airbrushed flames and cartoon pigs in astronaut suits, battered him with the force of a freight train before pulling to an abrupt halt.

"Think we found him." Doc snickered.

Happily watching as Double OT and his smartass mouth plummeted to the pavement in a pathetic flash of leisure suit and mussed hair, I couldn't help but think the whole situation played out rather nicely.

"That's a — big — fucking — dude," Rooster muttered, slapping me on the shoulder as we all stood there watching the antics unfold from the shadows of the alley. "You might have to be *extra* nice."

"Or drop a school bus on him," Erin added, studying the mighty physique of the time-hopping street vendor. "Make that an aircraft carrier. I can see why Lilith was into him, though. Just saying."

Awkward?

Yes.

That was awkward.

"What the fuck?" The twenty-something man mountain barked in a thick Massachusetts accent as he made his way to the front on the infamous Sausage Rocket, looking like he was geared up to pluck somebody's limbs off with his bare hands. "Watch where you're going, dumbass. I've got Polish sausage here. It's very delicate."

"Hi, Ronk." Double OT winced, sprawled out on the sidewalk as people continued to shuffle by, making a wide swath around him. "How you been, buddy?"

"Odie?" he replied, like they were long lost pals as a huge smile curled across his baby face. "Is that you?"

"What's left of me ... I think. Ha!"

"Pissah! Good to see ya, man. What are you doing here?"

"Oh, nothing. Just hanging loose — on the sidewalk — in the fetal position. I think my spleen's broke, actually. You?"

Ronkowski then proceeded to effortlessly lift Double OT off the ground with one arm and dust him off a bit. "Didn't mean to whack you with the Rocket like that."

"No trouble." Owen winced again. "I oddly enjoyed it. *So*, what's up with the hurrycane, amigo?"

"Yeah, sorry, man. I'm heading to Fenway. World Series, bro. Usually make a killing on the pregame crowd. Place'll be hopping in about two hours. Gotta get my lucky spot."

Taking note of Ronk's skintight 'Welcome to Ashbury Park, NJ' tee shirt, showing off his massive upper body, Double OT said, "What the flipping frak, bro? Don't tell me you're still listening to Springsteen."

"Get the fuck outta here. Of course I'm still jamming on the Boss. He's the fucking boss."

Owen sighed. "Springsteen makes me placid. Or is it flaccid?"

Chuckling for an awkward moment, Ronk flashed Double OT a somewhat curious glare. "Hey, seriously, good to see you and all, but what are you doing here? You got a show or something? Don't tell me you're playing at that joint in Chinatown again."

"I wish. They haven't invited me back since I stuffed fortune cookies down my pants until they starting popping out of my fly. I'm *here* on business."

"That a fact?" Ronk grinned. "What kind of business?"

"Oh, nothing really. Just trying to save the world and shit like that. Typical stuff."

As the peculiar duo continued their conversation, I turned to Doc and Rooster. "You guys stay out of sight. I got this."

"What are you planning on doing?" Rooster asked.

"What we came here to do — have a chat with sausage boy."

"By yourself?"

"Yep. We don't want to spook him. If he phases out of here, we'll never find him again."

Erin looked more than skeptical. "You sure about this?"

"I got this, Doc."

"All right," she grumbled, as they quietly retreated into the darkness of the alley and ducked behind the big ass dumpster.

Stepping onto the sidewalk, I boldly placed myself in front of Ronkowski. "Hi. You don't know me, but we need to talk. Right friggin now."

And, unfortunately, the situation degraded pretty quickly from that point forward.

Typical.

29

"You know this fucking guy, Odie?" Ronkowski chuckled, seriously getting a kick out of my powder blue onesie.

Double OT nodded. "Yepperoonies. This handsome son of a monkey's uncle is Dean Robinson — my *colleague*."

"Colleague, huh?" Ronk jested. "This have to do with all that saving the world and shit?"

"Ha! You know it. Pretty flipping coolio, right?"

Ronk broke into a hearty laugh. "Yeah, whatever, Odie. You're still one crazy bastard. That's for sure."

"This isn't a friggin joke," I grumbled, with the big man's oversized pectorals practically poking me in the face.

Smiling ear to ear, he nonchalantly slapped me on the back like we were drinking buddies. "Take it easy, jumpsuit. I'm just fucking around. Any friend of Odie is all right by me. Even if he dresses like one of the Jackson Five."

"Look, we need to talk."

"So, what's your deal, Robinson? You in Odie's band or something? Lemme guess, I bet you play a mean skin flute." To which he and Double OT burst into a spirited round of very friggin annoying laughter at my expense.

"Okay, asshole," I grunted, having taken more shit from Tweedle Dope and Tweedle Dickhead than I was willing to endure, "Listen to me very carefully. Some seriously bad shit is going to happen thirty-seven years from now."

"Bad shit happens all the time," Ronk said, still chortling.

"I'm talking like apocalypse bad."

"Yeah, so?"

"So, you're going to help me stop it."

"That a fact?"

"That's a fact."

"Okay, I'll bite. How am I gonna do that?"

"You've got something I need."

He grinned. "Like what? A set of balls?"

I grinned back. "No, asshole, the Ark of the Covenant."

And it was right about then when his jovial demeanor vanished as he abruptly stopped laughing and glared at me like I just punched him squarely in the nose. After a long second or two, he muttered, "Don't know what you're talking about."

"I think you do."

Evidently no longer interested in any further discussion on the topic, he simply turned to Double OT. "Hey, ah, good seeing ya, Odie, but I'm late. Gotta run."

And before either one of us had the chance to reply, the man mountain hastily resumed his position at the helm of his sausage yacht and began to push it down the sidewalk again.

Grabbing the mammoth cart, I said, "We're not finished."

"Walk away," he grumbled. "Please."

"Can't do that."

"This is going to end bad for you."

Standing my ground, I said, "If I don't get the Ark, it's going to end bad for everybody."

"I already told you. Don't know nothing about that."

"I know you have it."

"You don't know shit," Ronkowski barked, stepping out from behind the Sausage Rocket.

"You made a deal with Lilith. Keep the Ark hidden on a single day in history."

His eyes danced with rapid thought upon hearing the statement. "Who told you that?"

"She did."

"That crazy bitch," he muttered. "She also tell you about the fine print?"

"The part about if you lose the Ark, you lose your soul?"

"Yeah. So, unless she sent you here to void our agreement — you and me got nothing further to talk about."

"You're not listening to me, asshole. The future of mankind is on the line, and you're holding the key to setting things straight. We can do this the easy way or the hard way, but either way — you're giving me what I need."

Cracking his knuckles, his face broke out into a wolfish grin. "Your mouth shouldn't write checks your ass can't cash."

"Whoa, fellas, ease up on the throttle," Double OT cut in, trying to keep the peace. "We can work something out here, right? Let's talk it out over a couple kielbasa dogs. Extra mustard? Yes? No? Ah, how about some Jell-O then? I often find that Jell-O makes the even the tensest of situations blissfully palatable. For reals. Am I right? Guys? Group hug?"

When neither one of us offered a response, he muttered, "Okay, then. *Well*, if you guys are gonna start beat'n on each other, I'm gonna zen out for a bit at the Rocket. Starving!"

"Last chance," Ronk grumbled, looking like he was ready to snap me in half, "Walk away."

I shook my head. "I'm not leaving without the Ark."

His eyes flamed with intensity and bore holes through my skull. "You'll be leaving all right. Just in a few more pieces than when you got here. Sorry about this. Nothing personal."

And then, in a shimmering blur of motion, he proceeded to pick me up like a twig and hurl me into the alley with all his unnatural might. Making the mental note that I probably could've handled that situation *just* a little better, I soared through the air like a man-sized football and careened into the dumpster a solid fifty feet away.

Completely caving in the side of the oversized metal box as my body slammed into it with the force of a meteorite, I managed to pry myself loose and stumble to my feet only to find Doc and Rooster standing there shaking their heads.

"So," Rooster muttered, "everything proceeding as planned?"

"Fuck off."

As the super-sized pollack raced toward me with unnatural speed and bad intentions, Erin asked, "What the hell did you say to him?"

Brushing off the shellacking, I said, "I was just negotiating the terms of his cooperation."

"You think maybe we should help?"

"Nah. Wait here, this won't take but another minute. Two tops."

And then I willed the cloak into being. Elegantly manifesting in a spectral flash of white luminescence, it billowed about my shoulders as I felt the otherworldly power course through my body like an electric current. Feeling the mental switch flip to the on position, I pulled in a long, deliberate breath.

Cleared my mind.

Focused my thoughts.

Found the Balance — the perfect equilibrium between wrath and clarity.

Pulling to an abrupt halt at the sight of my cloak, Ronk scoffed, "Wait, you're a fucking Deacon?"

Figuring that didn't warrant a response, I called for the gauntlets. My mouth curled into a dark smile as the unbreakable ashen hellstone formed around my fisted hands. Then I focused all my supernatural strength and slugged the big bastard squarely in his six-pack abs.

Chunks of brick and mortar exploded into the dank air as the brute force of the blow sent him rocketing backward into the wall of one of the brownstones bordering the alley. As he doubled over in pain, I sunk all my weight into a heavy-handed uppercut that pretty much exploded his nose, followed by a left hook that connected squarely with his big ass chin. As a rather disgusting combination of blood and teeth sprayed from his mouth, Ronkowski then face-planted on the asphalt like the felling of a mighty tree.

Seemingly down for the count, I willed the gauntlets into retreat and rolled the big bastard over. Then I slapped him in the face a couple times until his eyes opened. "You ready to help me now?"

Smiling at me with a battered face and crimson-stained teeth, he said, "That depends."

"On what?"

"If you're still breathing after round two."

Then he flickered out of existence only to instantly reappear back on his feet standing directly opposite me. No longer smiling, he was completely healed and holding some kind of a metal staff with a really friggin big scimitar blade on the end of it.

As the cloak rippled anxiously about my shoulders, Ronk sprung toward me in a blur of motion while expertly swinging his rod of eviscerating death at my neck. Swapping out the stone gauntlets for argent metal, I managed to deflect the blade with my left fist just as he skillfully used the counter momentum to take my legs out with the staff. Tumbling backward, my back slammed onto the asphalt, and every ounce of air exited my lungs as I clumsily rolled to the side, just in time to dodge his boot from stomping my face in.

Making the mental note that perhaps my negotiating skills may indeed need some work, I flipped back to my feet and called for the spatha. Feeling the presence of the scabbard manifest on my back, I clutched the stout hilt of the otherworldly gladiator sword and ripped it free as a distinct hum of palpable energy pulsed through the alley. Not relenting in the least, a harrowing scowl formed on the face of my seriously disgruntled Polish sparring partner as he raised his staff in a strike position, fluidly advancing on me with the poise of a seasoned street fighter.

Fully prepared to parry his attack and shove that rod straight up his ass, I was more than disappointed when he shimmered out of existence mid-assault. Thinking that couldn't be good, the cloaked flared out like a caged animal, causing me to instinctively duck and spin around just in time to see his blade rip a menacing arc through the air in the exact spot my neck was a millisecond earlier.

Not giving him a chance to pull the backdoor maneuver again, I sheathed my sword, grabbed his staff with both hands and head butted that big fucker as hard as I could. As he grunted in protest, I then focused all my strength and snapped the rod in half while throat chopping his ass with my elbow.

Happily watching as the big bastard reeled backward, gasping for breath, I finished things off with a well-placed kick to the midsection that sent him hurtling headlong into the side of the dumpster.

As the enigmatic time traveling street vendor slumped unconsciously to the ground, Doc, Rooster, and I cautiously huddled around his limp body, hoping like hell he was actually done trying to decapitate me.

"So, I'm curious," Doc asked, "does the word '*negotiate*' translate to 'beat the ever-living shit out of somebody' in Deanspeak?"

"He started it," I grumbled.

Glaring at Ronkowski, Rooster asked, "So, you think he's ready to listen now?"

"Definitely. There's no way in hell that guy's got any fight left in him."

Unfortunately, it seemed that wasn't the case.

I was wrong.

He was now officially pissed.

Staggering to his feet in a fury-fueled 'roid rage, Ronk's mouth literally frothed with anger as he murmured something under his breath in Enochian. As a spectral haze of arcane energy sparked to life and framed his hulking silhouette, he picked up the four-thousand-pound dumpster like it was made of cardboard and held it over his head like he was going to throw it at me.

Actually, there was no *like* about it.

He was totally going to throw it at me.

Fortunately, it was right about then when things took an interesting turn.

For, as I stood there contemplating what in the hell to do next, a rather peculiar fellow in a perfectly cut sharkskin suit carrying a briefcase handcuffed to his left hand strolled into the middle of our unnatural slugfest. And although he wasn't exactly physically imposing, there was just something about him that exuded a serious 'I'm the Man' vibe.

Boldly placing himself squarely in front of Ronk, the highly pedigreed mystery man removed his quaint spectacles and said, "Am I to assume *you* are Richard Ronald Ronkowski?"

"Yeah," Ronk replied, clearly befuddled by the turn of events.

"Of course you are. My name's Stern. Attorney Zekaryah Stern. I represent the Law Offices of Stern and Pelchovitz. You may call me Zeke if you wish."

"Ah, okay."

"Now, if you'd kindly refrain from this hostile conduct for just one moment, we have an important matter of business to discuss." When Ronk, much like the rest of us, just stood there gawking at him, Zeke commandingly said, "Put — the — dumpster — down, Mr. Ronkowski. I happen to be on a strict time table. When our business is concluded, you may resume bludgeoning Dean Robinson, or vice-versa, to your collective heart's content. It matters not to me, I assure you."

Dropping the massive metal box like a sack of potatoes, Ronk snapped out of berserker mode. "What the hell do you want?"

"To deliver a message on behalf of my client," he replied matter-of-factly, producing a small key from the inside pocket of his jacket, and unlocking his snazzy briefcase.

Carefully cracking it open and removing what appeared to be a scroll of parchment, he methodically unrolled the peculiar document while deliberately clearing his throat. Placing his glasses on the very tip of his nose, he then began to read.

"My dearest Richard: In accordance with the tenets of our mutual agreement, you have dutifully protected the Vessel for a term of my satisfaction. As such, I summarily release you from any further responsibilities and offer you a termination of our contract should you wish to exercise it. Mr. Stern will present you with the details and see to all the arrangements. XOXO, Lilith. *P.S.* Call me!"

"Lilith?" Ronk scoffed. "Wait, she's letting me off the hook?"

"In a matter of sorts, yes," the practitioner of infernal law replied.

"But I don't get it. Why now?"

"An *explanation* was not provided with my instructions, Mr. Ronkowski."

"So, I'm free. Just like that?"

"It would appear so," he said, reaching into his suitcase and producing yet another parchment. "Here is your termination notice. I'm confident you'll find that everything's in good order."

"What's the catch?" Ronk muttered, eagerly inspecting the document.

"There is no *catch*. However, you will notice that this agreement is contingent upon one very specific condition. You are to surrender your stewardship of the Vessel to Dean Robinson, Seventh Deacon of the Seventh Line. That would presume, of course, that you choose not to squash him with a *dumpster* in another fit of unfettered vexation."

"Oh, that? I was just messing around. I actually like Robinson. We were just working a few things out. You know how it is."

"Yes, of course. Well, as pleasant as this has been, I must be on my way. If you'll be so kind as to make your mark, I trust you'll provide Deacon Robinson the whereabouts of the Vessel before enjoying your newfound liberation."

Ronk chuckled, happily accepting a quill from Zekaryah Stern and scratching his name in macabre red ink on the peculiar document. "I've been wanting to get rid of that freaking thing ever since she saddled me with it forty years ago. You have any idea what it's like to be stuck on a single day? In 1975 no less?"

Quickly inspecting the parchment before tucking it back into his briefcase, the uncanny attorney simply said, "Good day to you, Mr. Ronkowski." Then he just waltzed out of the alley like he owned the joint and melted from sight.

Making the mental note that it would've been really nice if Lil had sent her friggin lawyer along *before* Ronk and I started slugging each other, I turned my full attention on the big oaf euphorically standing there like he'd just won the lottery.

"Where's the Ark?" I asked.

"You know where I'm gonna go first, jumpsuit?" he muttered, like he didn't hear a thing I'd said. When I offered nothing in response, he grinned a shit-eating grin. "East Rutherford, New Jersey. August, 20th. Nineteen eighty-*fucking*-four. The greatest Bruce Springsteen concert — ever."

I grinned back. "That's really swell. Where's the friggin Ark?"

Smiling ear to ear, he then dug an ornate skeleton key out of the pocket of his jeans and tossed it at me.

"What the hell is this for?" I grunted, as Doc and Rooster pulled up on my flank.

"You'll figure it out."

Having completely lost my patience, I barked, "Where's the fucking Ark, Ronkowski?"

Again ignoring the question, he said, "Go get yourself a kielbasa dog. Oh, and be sure to try the sauerkraut. It's pissah."

And without another word, he simply flickered out of existence.

"Wait, what just happened?" Rooster asked.

"What about the Ark?" Erin scoffed, equally as perplexed.

I studied the bizarre key for a second or two. "Well, unless the most powerful biblical relic known to mankind is hidden somewhere in that moron's goddamned sausage cart, I think we just got hosed."

And as we stood there gawking at each other for a long second or two, Rooster said, "Wait, you don't think the most powerful biblical relic known to mankind is actually hidden somewhere in that moron's sausage cart, do you?"

"No way."

"Way?"

Busting out of the alley onto the teeming sidewalk only to find Owen sitting atop the super-sized mobile meat dispensary like a bell-bottomed Buddha, we all curiously huddled around the infamous Sausage Rocket.

"Dudes!" he yelled with chunks of food spraying from his mouth. "You guys have seriously gotta try one of these kielbasa dogs. Totally fabumendous! Hey, ah, where's Ronk?"

Completely ignoring him, I said, "That is one big ass cart. One might even say it's suspiciously big."

Doc nodded. "But is it big enough to hold the Ark?"

"Well," Rooster said, slipping into bloviation mode while mentally measuring the obscure pushcart, "according to the Bible, the Ark was two and a half cubits long by one and a half cubits tall and wide. So, I'd say it's more than big enough."

I shrugged. "What the frig is a cubit?"

He rolled his eyes like I was a complete dumbass. "An ancient unit of measurement based on the length of the forearm. It was all the rage back in the day."

"The length of a forearm, eh?"

"Yeppers. As measured from the tip of the middle finger to the bottom of the elbow. *But*, as you can well imagine, there was inherent variation from region to region based on certain demographic and physiological factors. For example, I remember this one time in ancient Rome when I accidentally used an Egyptian cubit while bartering for ..."

As my esteemed ginger colleague continued to explain, in excruciating detail, the innate distinction between a Roman cubit and an Egyptian cubit, I grunted, "For Christ's sake, John! How big is the goddamned Ark?"

Looking at me like I stole his lunch money, he said, "Roughly four feet long by two and a half feet tall."

Taking note of the easily eight-foot-long and four-foot-high, stainless steel sausage cart, I glared at Owen, who was still happily chomping away on a fistful of buns like he hadn't eaten in a year. "Hey, NecroDolt, where's Ronkowski keep the goddamn sauerkraut?"

"Hell yeah!" He yelled, flipping open a lid on one of the several bays lining the top of the Sausage Rocket. "Going straight for the cabbage. That's what I'm talking about, monkey man. Get some!"

Much to his dismay, Rooster, Doc, and I then proceeded to feverishly shovel heaps of pickled cabbage into his lap until the vat was completely empty.

And wouldn't you friggin know that discretely tucked in the far corner of the bay was a peculiar keyhole set in the dead center of an elegantly arranged series of Enochian sigils that glowed and hissed a brilliant white flame.

"Are those warding glyphs?" I asked Rooster.

He nodded. "Powerful ones. Like über powerful ones."

"You ever seen anything like that before?"

"Can't say that I have. Somebody would only go through the trouble of constructing something that intricate for one reason — to protect something of an invaluable nature."

"Try the key," Erin said, more than anxiously.

"Here goes nothing," I grumbled, inserting the peculiar skeleton key Ronk gave me a few minutes earlier into the arcane locking mechanism and giving it a careful twist.

"It's working," Rooster gasped as the flaming wards instantly fizzled out and the false bottom of the enigmatic food cart retracted to reveal two golden cherubim set atop an ornate gold-plated chest hidden deep within.

Looking like he was about to shit himself upon the realization that he was literally sitting on the Ark of the Covenant, Double OT murmured, "Hellfire and Dalmatians. Is that ... is that what I think it is?"

"Yes," Rooster said, totally mesmerized by the otherworldly artifact. "Yes, it is."

My face curled into a dark smile. "Game on."

Shit just got real.

30

As the latest time vortex returned us to the MidKnight Jayde just in time to catch a fleeting glimpse of our past selves getting sucked away in the first time vortex, I made the mental note I was going to need some serious therapy if we lived through the next few hours.

"Good luck, y'all," Coop muttered, as he stood there watching us leave. "See you soon?"

"Sooner than you know, Cooper Trooper," Double OT jested, laying atop of the Sausage Rocket like a sultry lingerie model and apparently pretty friggin happy to be back in his obscure lair. "How's that for some deja voodoo? Boom! Miss me?"

Summarily confused as to what in the hell just happened, Coop just stared at us for a long couple of seconds as our retro attire melted from existence, and we thankfully looked like we did before we left.

"We're back," I grumbled.

Coop repeatedly shook his head. "But, y'all just left."

"Evidently."

"And now you're back?"

"We just covered that, Coop."

Still trying to wrap his head around the uncanny phenomenon of watching us time hop to the past and subsequently return to the present within nanoseconds of each other, he just shrugged. "I'm more confused than a cow on astroturf."

"Join the friggin club."

Looking at me kind of funny, he reluctantly asked, "Ah, hoss, were you wearing a onesie a couple seconds ago?"

"What? Hell no. Your eyes were probably playing tricks on you. Must've been a temporal mirage or something. That's a thing, right?"

"It worked, Coop," Rooster said, thankfully changing the subject as he nodded at the oversized food cart. "We have the Ark."

"You serious, pard?"

"See for yourself."

As Owen jumped off the Sausage Rocket, allowing the redneck archer to get his first peek at the divine chest hidden within, Coop muttered, "Well, I'll be a slack-jawed mule deer strapped to the hood of a rusted-out turnip truck."

Brushing off the latest Coopersim, Doc said, "Now that we have it, what the hell do we do with it?"

"It's leverage," I replied, "We use it to draw out the barkangel."

"Leverage?" Rooster said, raising a ginger eyebrow, "What about destroying it so the gates of Tartarus stay sealed?"

"We will destroy it. Just not yet. It's our only bargaining chip."

Apparently not enthused with my answer, he pulled out his antique pocket watch. "It's quarter past six. We've got an hour and forty-five minutes until the doomsday clock expires and Azazel turns his anakim loose for a seven-day global binge fest. I assume you have a plan?"

"Of course he does," a sarcastic voice replied from behind us. We all spun around to find a familiar archangel standing there like he'd been listening to us the whole time. "And I'm sure it's laughably heroic and reeks of his signature altruistic flare. Unfortunately, I'm afraid none of you will see it come to fruition."

"Remiel?" I said, more than a bit surprised to see him.

"Remiel," Rooster muttered, as his eyes blazed a fiery red. "What are you doing here?"

He grinned at us. "Collecting the fruits of my labor, of course."

"What is he talking about?" Erin asked, clearly as confused as the rest of us.

As my mind raced to connect the dots, I glared at the smarmy archangel. "You son of a bitch. It's you. You set me up. You're the friggin—"

"The what, Dean Robinson? The *traitor*?" And then he simply waved his hand and pinned the entire group of us to the wall of NecroLord's lair with an unseen, bone crushing force. "I prefer the term liberator."

"I will end you for this," I forced out, trying to will the cloak into being to no avail as I found myself barely able to breathe under the indescribable weight of the unnatural force.

"I think not," he said. "But I must thank you for delivering the final piece of the puzzle I required to achieve my objectives. Without the Vessel, I'm not entirely sure what I would have done. Needless to say, I was more than disappointed to discover the seraphic vaults contained a well-conceived counterfeit, *and* Lucifer, of all beings, was in possession of the actual artifact. Then, of course, was the small matter of him surrendering it to that abomination, Lilith. I honestly can't thank you enough for retrieving it like a good little pet."

"But, how...how'd you find us?"

"Find you? You never left my sight, *Deacon*. Thanks to that wonderful trinket hanging around your neck, I've been monitoring your every move like a rat in a maze."

With my innards about to pop out of my mouth, I grumbled, "Goddamn MacCawill sold me out."

"Please," Remiel rolled his eyes. "Roy MacCawill lacks the conviction for such chicanery. For a bounty hunter, he possesses an annoyingly high sense of morality. As such, I took it upon myself to visit his *clandestine* cache site and place a hex on the amulet before you arrived. He was none the wiser."

"What about Lucifer?" I grunted, feeling like I was seconds from blacking out.

"The Morning Star? A simple pawn fueled by jealously and all too eager to believe that *Gabriel* was conspiring to overthrow the Heavens. I simply perpetuated Lucifer's delusions in anticipation that he'd send you to retrieve the Vessel. Which, of course, he did. And here we are."

"And Stephen?"

Looking me squarely in the eye, he feigned sympathy. "Sad, sad news,

Dean Robinson. Your precious mentor was summarily executed for his perceived treachery. By all accounts, he was struck down by the very hand of Gabriel himself."

And it was right about then when a blinding flash of pure white light erupted behind Remiel, and out stepped a cloaked figure like he owned the fucking joint.

"It would seem the rumors of my death have been greatly exaggerated," Stephen muttered as his cloak ferociously billowed about his shoulders like a raging spectral beast.

Without so much as another word, an ethereal gauntlet of hissing white flame manifested over his left hand as he swatted Remiel with a crushing backhand that sent him hurtling across the room like a rag doll. As the traitorous seraph violently collided with the far wall of Owen's head-banging romper room, Stephen recited a few words in Enochian, and a ring of Holy Flame flared to life, effectively trapping him there for the foreseeable future.

"Hell of an entrance," I grumbled, as Remiel's death grip faded, and my chest no longer felt like it was caving in on itself.

The faint trace of a smirk flashed across Stephen's face. "I had a feeling you'd appreciate it."

"Bet your ass I did." I grabbed his shoulder in complete and utter disbelief as the team slowly huddled around us. "Especially since I thought you were—"

"Dead? Apparently, that's merely a matter of perspective."

I grinned. "Fair enough. But how'd you get away from Gabriel?"

"Fortunately, I didn't have to," he said, as a whooshing sound of unseen massive wings filled the entire room and a statuesque figure, clad in surreal black armor, was just all of a sudden — there.

"Gabriel," I gasped, taking a step backward and willing the cloak into being as Doc, Rooster, Owen, and Coop looked like they were about to piss their pants at the sight of the left hand of God.

"Dean Robinson," he bellowed, as he glanced at the Ark and took a bold step in my direction, "you and your associates have done well. Very well. The seraphic court is in your debt."

"Wait, what?" Rooster blurted out.

"Wait, what?" I echoed, having absolutely no idea what just

happened.

Clearing his throat, Double OT stepped forward. "Ah, hey there, Mr. Gabriel, sir. How's it shaking, bro? Big fan ... in a really terrifyingly 'Please don't smite my silly ass kind of way.' Dig? *Anywho*, I'm NecroLord — *leader* of Deanbean's little gangapalooza here."

Not exactly sure what to make of the peculiar time phantom, Gabriel said, "I am well aware of who you are, Owen Trask."

"No shit? Wow. That's great! Wait, is it? Probably not, right? Never mind. I don't wanna know. Moving on, I just wanted to say that it was my esteemed pleasure to spearhead this here *mission*. I mean it's not every day you get the chance to save the world and shit, right? Am I right? Hell yeah! Ha? Okay, *well*, when you said the seraphic court was *'in our debt'* does that mean like free tickets to Aerosmith concerts and stuff? Maybe a couple back stage passes to groupie gropes—"

"Will you shut the hell up, cuz," Coop cut in, which prompted Owen to sheepishly offer a contrite bow to the archangel and slink toward the Sausage Rocket to presumably devour another dozen kielbasa dogs.

Figuring it was well past time to get some friggin answers, I willed the cloak into retreat and placed myself squarely in front of the archangel. "I take it we're no longer fugitives?"

Pensively scanning the group, he said, "No. You are not. In all actuality — you never were."

"Well, that's interesting, Gabe. Because it sure as shit felt that way."

"I'm afraid that was the intent, Dean Robinson."

Doing my damnedest to follow the plot, I muttered, "You're going to have to explain that."

"What Gabriel is saying," Stephen said, "is that the only way to draw out the traitor within the seraphic court was to lay the mantle of treason on another party. Hence the reason for my perceived incarceration and the bounty laid upon your head."

The gears started turning in my befuddled brain. "So, this whole thing — it was a trap."

He nodded. "A well-laid trap. And, regretfully, you were—"

"The bait," I grumbled putting two and two together. "You should've told me."

"That was not his decision to make," Gabriel said. "An unspeakable conspiracy had infected my ranks like a festering plague. I could not risk that information leaking to the actual traitor."

"You mean Remiel," I muttered.

"Yes," he replied, coldly gazing at his angelic brother's limp body trapped with the Holy Flame. "My most trusted lieutenant. The revelation of his betrayal was more than disappointing to say the very least."

"But why the hell didn't you snag him in the desert? You must've known he was the friggin barkangel at that point?"

As Gabriel's brow furrowed in puzzlement upon hearing my moniker for the divine traitor, Rooster said, "The bad archangel. A.K.A., the barkangel. A.K.A., the traitor."

Evidently less than impressed with the nickname, Gabriel said, "Unfortunately, Remiel managed to elude capture in the desert and subsequently fled beyond our Sight. It was then that I realized he would only again resurface to claim the one thing he required to fuel his revolution."

"The Ark," Rooster chimed in.

"That is correct, John," Stephen replied.

"And you knew we'd figure out a way to get it first," I muttered.

"I had faith that would be the case. Yes."

"But, what about Azazel?" Rooster asked. "We may've stopped Remiel from unleashing the Watchers on Heaven, but the anakim militia are still on schedule to lay wreckage to the Earth."

Gabriel shook his head. "No. They are not. As we speak, ten legions of my brothers are descending upon Azazel's stronghold and exorcising both him and his league of bastard offspring from existence."

"What?" I blurted, both shocked and elated. "How'd you find him?"

With a very uncharacteristic grin, the archangel simply replied, "You have your methods, Dean Robinson, and I have mine."

"So, it's over," Doc said. "We won?"

"It is over, Erin Kelly," he said, causing Double OT to stop scarfing down sausage dogs and yell, "We won! Ha! That's what I'm flipping talking about, bitches! Hash tag — Booyah! Can I get a *hell yeah*? Let me hear you guys say it. On three. Ready? One. Two. Three!"

When nobody offered a response, he halfheartedly muttered, "Go team?"

When nobody offered a response to that either, he defeatedly went back to eating.

"It's not over," I grumbled, gazing at the obscure food cart and the arcane object hidden within. "What about the Ark?"

"It must be secured within the vaults of Tenth Heaven," Gabriel replied. "Far from all who seek its power for discord and insurrection."

"Secured, eh? And how'd that work out the last time for you, Gabe? Oh, wait, maybe I should ask Lucifer because if I'm not mistaken, I believe he stole it right from under your nose a few thousand years before you even friggin knew he stole it."

As his eyes flashed a deep black, the archangel said, "Am I to understand you have a wiser course of action to offer, Deacon?"

"I have a more permanent solution in mind. Something to ensure it never ends up in the wrong hands again."

He sagely studied me for an excruciatingly long second or two. "Are you suggesting that the Vessel, an instrument imbued with the physical embodiment of God himself, be destroyed?"

"I'm suggesting that the only thing capable of opening the gates of Tartarus be removed from the equation. Once and for all."

"Interesting," he muttered under his breath like he was having a minor epiphany. "Regardless of the fact that I may be in agreement, such an act would be nothing less than blasphemy to the very highest of degrees. Even if warranted to secure the future of Heaven and Earth alike, no angel could possibly carry out nor condone such a task."

And as I stood there thinking what the hell to say next, Stephen casually strolled toward the Sausage Rocket and gazed inside. Clearing his throat, he said, "Although quite regrettable, it appears the Vessel has suffered irreparable damage during its recovery." Then he glanced at Double OT like a skilled lawyer leading a witness. "Would you not agree, Mr. Trask?"

"Damaged?" Owen scoffed, also peering into the massive food cart. "Hell flipping no, bossman. It's—"

"A friggin mess," I said, picking up on where Stephen was going as I elbowed Double OT in the ribs to shut him up. "Must've hit one of those time currents or something on the way back. Right, Owen?"

“Damaged, you say?” Gabriel asked. “That is highly unfortunate. Are you quite sure it cannot be salvaged?”

“I fear it is beyond mending,” Stephen replied in his signature stoic fashion.

“If the Vessel has been sullied, then it most certainly cannot be returned to the Heavens. However, even in a compromised state, its power is nothing to be trifled with. Perhaps you should transport the remnants to a *safe* location and properly *dispose* of them. For, as Dean Robinson so astutely noted, it would be more than irresponsible to allow any last splinter of the only instrument capable of opening the gates of Tartarus to fall into the wrong hands *again*.”

I grinned. “Wait, are you saying you want us to—"

"I trust you understand what must be done,” Gabriel said. And then he and the still comatose Remiel simply vanished in a powerful burst of air, accompanied by the whooshing sound of unseen massive wings.

“Ah, dudes,” Double OT said, trying to wrap his head around what was going on, “What the flip just happened?”

Rather matter-of-factly, Coop replied, “Well, cuz, it seems that by exploiting an apparent loophole in seraphic jurisprudence, Stephen just gave Gabriel a somewhat legit way to tell us to torch the Ark so this whole shitshow don't become a sequel.”

“Ha! Did you just say jurisprudence and shitshow in the same sentence, Cooper Trooper? Loved it!”

“Durn skippy.”

I turned to Stephen. "Gabe's starting to grow on me."

“And apparently you’re growing on him,” he replied.

“Seriously? How can you tell?”

“Mainly by the fact that he didn’t behead you for calling him Gabe ... twice.”

“Right,” I muttered, making the mental note to quit mouthing off to celestial über beings at some point down the road.

"So," Rooster said, as we all stood there looking at each other, “Seems like this is as much of a happy ending as we’re going to get. What the hell do we do now?"

“I don’t know about, y’all,” Coop said, resting his signature long bow on his shoulder, "but, now that we ain't criminals, I'm seeing a cold beer and a warm filly in my immediate future."

"Hells yeah!" Owen yelled. "I love horses. Can I come?"

As everyone shook their heads in unison, Stephen said, "Might I suggest that you all return to the Quartermaster. I'm sure Abernethy will be quite relieved to see you. Dean and I will join momentarily."

Nodding his head, Rooster smiled ear to ear. "That sounds like the first good plan I've heard in a week. Hey, Sweetie, can you hear me?"

"*Of course I can hear you, Cleric O'Dargan,*" instantly boomed the disembodied voice of Skyphos from the ether.

"Miss me?

"*No. I most certainly did not. And kindly refrain from calling me sweetie.*"

"Yeah, you missed me. Hey, be a doll and get us home, would ya?"

In response, an otherworldly portal fluidly manifested adjacent Double OT's amplifier forest, and the crew began to happily file through it.

Before Erin faded into the swirling radiance of spectral blue light, she turned to me. "Please be careful."

"Don't worry, Doc. Piece of cake. It's not like I'm going to some undisclosed location to nuke a divine relic with the power to melt my face off."

Oh, wait.

31

WITH A SOMEWHAT SKEPTICAL LOOK, Erin stepped through the arcane gateway as it snapped shut, leaving Stephen and me standing in momentary silence.

After a second or two, he said, "Let us finish this."

"Not yet," I grumbled. "What about the fallen Deacons? If Remiel's the damn barkangel, he knows where they're being kept. We can still save them."

"And we will. That information will be extracted from Remiel, and we will see to the release of our brothers. I promise you that, Dean. But first we must tend to the task at hand. It will take our collective power to grapple with the Ark."

I nodded. "Well, it's a damn good thing you showed up when you did. If Remiel added me to the collection, it would've been game over. He'd have the final piece he needed to become the—"

"Evil Über Deacon? I thought we agreed not to use that name."

"To be fair, I think you agreed. I'm still kind of partial to it. Rolls off the tongue. Snappy."

"Well, fortunately for both us, it is now officially a moot point."

I chuckled. "Guess it's time to pour some lighter fluid on the Ark of the

Covenant and set a match to the biggest bonfire in human history. And I can't believe those words just came out of my mouth."

"These are unusual times, indeed," he muttered, as a portal of swirling black smoke manifested with a casual wave of his left hand.

"So, where are we going?"

"A dark place. Somewhere far from both the Heavens and the Earth — where no human soul ever hopes to find themselves."

"Why do I get the feeling I'm not going to like this place?"

"Because your intuition serves you well."

"Hold on," I said, pointing at the portal. "Please tell me that's not a doorway to friggin Hell. Are we seriously going to Hell?"

"Yes. We are."

"Awesome," I muttered, making the mental note that I don't get paid enough for this shit as I willed the cloak into being. "Hopefully Lew's still screwing around at the airport. I've had enough of that smarmy bastard to last an afterlife, if you know what I'm saying."

And much to my chagrin, Lucifer emerged from the infernal gateway with a shit-eating grin stretched across his face and a wooden box of cigars in hand. "Why, Master Robinson, should I be flattered or insulted?"

Damn.

That was awkward.

Strolling past us and happily gazing upon the Ark still situated within the oversized food cart, he started to clap. "Well done, gentlemen. Well, well done."

"Lucifer," Stephen coldly muttered, as his cloak billowed and surged upon his shoulders. "What an unpleasant surprise."

Lew smirked. "Come now, Stephen, did you really think you could unlatch the proverbial fence to my backyard without my taking notice?"

"Apparently not," he grumbled, willing his broadsword into being as it manifested on his back in a spectral flash and reaching back to grasp the mighty hilt.

Dismissing the show of force, Lucifer said, "I assure you, my good man, there is no need for that."

"What are you doing here, Lew?" I grunted, willing the shotgun into being.

"Why I've simply come to offer my hearty congratulations on your successful endeavor. After all, I can't help but retain some small sliver of pride for aiding in the resolution of these most troubling matters. Would you not agree, Dean?"

"Yeah right," I muttered. "You were a huge help. Pinning Gabriel as the traitor and teaming up with Remiel — the actual traitor — to take him down. Goddamn brilliant. Nice work. Seems you got played, Lew."

"Yes, well, perhaps things were not exactly as they seemed. But such details are always the case in love as they are in war. Nonetheless, here the three of us stand together at the very threshold of victory! This grand tale could not have arrived at a more fitting end. So, I say again, well done, gentlemen."

Stephen drew his sword from its scabbard and rested it on his shoulder. "We have work to do. What is it that you want, Lucifer?"

"As I've told you both before, I simply *want* what I have always wanted. The Balance restored. Do you not understand?" When Stephen nor I offered anything in response besides a pair of scowls, he said, "I would've thought it rather obvious at this point. Very well then. Perhaps I should simply show you and be done with it."

And then, in a blinding torrent of spectral light, a brilliant white cloak manifested on Lucifer's shoulders and a nightmarish leather praetorian mask formed over his face.

As the unadulterated power pouring off of his aura slammed into me like a friggin tidal wave, my mind raced to catch up to what was happening.

Then, unfortunately, it hit me like a ton of bricks.

Remiel was not the goddamn barkangel.

Lucifer was.

Fuck.

In what felt like extreme slow motion, I watched as Stephen instinctively swung his sword at Lucifer's neck, only to have it batted away like a twig as Lew covered his fisted hands with argent metal gauntlets and effortlessly dropped Stephen to the floor with a crushing blow to the head.

Barely able to keep my feet, I reached back and ripped the semi-divine Winchester free of its holster and cocked the lever. Training it squarely on Lew's chest, I heard, as much as felt, him erupt into a harrowing, guttural laughter as he knocked it from my hands and clutched my throat in a vice grip. Lifting me off my feet with one arm, his eyes glowed a blazing crimson like orbs of hellfire, and a fine layer of hissing white flame crawled across his gauntlet toward my face.

My skin began to sizzle as the wrathful power of twenty-four Deacons visibly pulsed from his cloak, causing the surrounding air to literally boil.

"I was not *played*, Master Robinson," he said, as I focused all my supernatural strength on prying his hand from my throat to no avail. "For the game was never *just* about the Vessel. There was always a greater prize at stake."

"Me and Stephen," I forced out.

"The *alpha* and the *omega*. The first and last Deacons within the *mighty* lines of Seven. Of course, I only required one of your mantles to complete my ascension, but, as a matter of guilty pleasure, I simply had to have both. The real trick in the matter, you see, was constructing the proper scenario that would make you both ripe for the picking, shall we say. Hence, I fabricated a common enemy."

"Remiel."

"Albeit an incredible simpleton, that overzealous archangel did not disappoint. He's been doing my bidding for quite some time now without the slightest inclination of such. And here you both are — practically delivered to my very doorstep in a neat — little — package. Impressive, yes?"

"Fuck off," I managed to blurt out.

"I will miss our little chats," he quipped, tightening his grip. "But I'm afraid it's time for me to go. For I have a date, Dean. A very special date with a long-awaited *destiny*. As such, it's well past time for you and your fearless mentor to take your rightful places in my collection. Once I've harnessed your collective power and liberated the fallen Watchers, I will descend upon the Heavens like a vengeful wraith and rain down the fires of Judgment until there is not but ash beneath my feet."

"What about the Earth?"

"The Earth." He scoffed. "Why, the race of man will undergo the greatest *reformation* in all of its sordid history at the hand of Azazel and his anakim. The mere thought of it brings a tear to my eye."

"Good luck with that," I forced out amidst a labored chuckle. "Azazel's dead, you asshole."

"Is he? Perhaps you've not been paying attention. The more likely scenario is that the many legions of angels sent to end him are now residing in a special corner of Hell. For in his usual ignorant fashion, *Gabriel* unwittingly sent them into a very well-orchestrated ambush. In fact, as we have this enlightened conversation, Azazel is preparing to unleash his children on your precious humans. Exciting times, Master Robinson. Exciting indeed!"

Within seconds of blacking out, a horrendous crash rang through the air and the door to NecroLord's lair blew off its hinges to reveal a familiar apocalyptic cowboy holding a sawed-off M-79 grenade launcher. "Hey, fuck face," Roy MacCawill grunted, spitting a badly chewed cigar on the floor. "You know what else is exciting?"

And then he launched a Holy Flame incendiary grenade squarely into Lucifer's chest, causing him drop me like a sack of potatoes as slithering tendrils of purple fire encompassed his body, forcing him to stagger backward a step or two.

Still on his feet yet clearly feeling the effects of the Holy Flame, Lew locked eyes with me as I willed the shotgun into my hand and swung the muzzle at his face. Grabbing Stephen's unconscious body and tossing it on the Sausage Rocket, he said, "Until we meet again, Master Robinson."

And then he simply snapped his fingers and vanished with both Stephen and the Ark as the portal to Hell snapped shut and melted from existence.

"Goddamn it!" I barked, as MacCawill holstered his hand cannon and helped me to my feet.

"You okay, mancho?"

I ignored the question. "What the hell are you doing here?"

"Apparently saving your sorry ass for the second time in as many days. You're welcome, by the way."

Ripping the hexed Talisman of Amaros from around my neck and throwing it at him, I said, "Yeah, friggin thanks."

"Look, mancho, you know I didn't have anything to do with that, right? That son of a bitch Remiel broke into my trailer."

"I know. But you're still a dickhead."

It was right about then that a shimmering virtual screen flickered into existence and an image of Rooster came into perfect focus. With his face as white as a ghost, he said, "Something's wrong. You need to get back to the Quartermaster."

"Be right there," I grumbled.

As the teleLink dissolved in midair and a portal fluidly manifested in its place, MacCawill said, "You gonna tell me what the hell's going on here, slick?"

"Let's go. I need your help."

"For what?"

"To give the Devil his due."

32

Emerging from the gateway with Roy MacCawill on my heels, I was unfortunately less than surprised to find the Quartermaster in a state of complete and utter chaos.

Judging from the impressive collection of full pint glasses littered across the bar and surrounding tables, it seemed that whatever impromptu celebration was taking place quickly devolved into a panic-stricken call to action as every throneView screen lining the walls flittered with live news feeds of anakim packs laying waste to various and assorted locales across the globe.

Gaggles of clerics and acolytes loaded down with a wide array of impressive weaponry raced toward the various exits lining the walls of the otherworldly outpost as Abernethy, Rooster, and the rest of my arcane strike team stood amidst the madness barking orders at them.

"Christ," MacCawill muttered, pointing to a newscast blaring from the throneView screen on the wall directly above us. "You seeing this?"

"It's *not* a hoax!" shouted a haggard and disheveled reporter standing in the middle of a surreal backdrop of flaming carnage and frantic droves of screaming people. "I repeat — not a hoax! This is Rex Buckley bringing you the Cold Hard Truth live from Times Square. Giants! They're real! And they're here! And they're quite literally ripping the city apart! The police are urging residents to stay in the safety of their homes, but take it from me, people, there is no refuge from these — these — *things*! They're, they're barbaric. And — and — they're *eating* people. Get out of the city while you still can! Run! Hide! Shit — cut to commercial. It's coming toward us. No — no! Get back—"

Unfortunately, that seemed to be the inglorious end to the smarmy reporter's broadcasting career as an amped up anakim, frothing at the mouth, and clad in blood-spattered leather body armor, plucked Buckley's arms from his body like flower petals and began to feast on his still screaming carcass on live TV.

"Ouch." MacCawill snickered, evidently not much of a Cold Hard Truth fan. "Guess the Buck stopped there, eh?"

"Let's go," I muttered, wading through the quickly dwindling crowd to join Abernethy and the crew.

Pulling up alongside Rooster, who was feverishly swiping his fingers across the screen of his prized handheld computer gadget with Doc and Double OT intently watching, I asked, "How bad is it?"

Looking uncharacteristically somber, Owen said, "It ain't good, whistelebritches."

"I don't get it," Rooster barked, holding up the contraption to show me a map of the country covered in pulsating red concentric circles. "Look at this shit! The anakim — they're freaking everywhere."

"It gets worse," I grumbled.

"Worse? How could it possibly get any freaking worse?"

With the massive room now mostly vacant with exception of the usual suspects, Abernethy turned his attention toward me. "Deannie. Where's Stephen, lad?"

"He's not coming, boss."

"Not coming?" Caveman chimed in, as Coop, Tango, and Stoner joined the impromptu huddle at the bar. "What's the dealio, bromando?"

After a long pause, I said, "We were wrong."

"About what, Dean?" Erin asked. "What happened?"

"Remiel. He's not the traitor. He was a pawn."

"Wait, what?" Rooster said. "Then who is?"

"Lucifer," I muttered. "He's behind everything."

As everyone shared a look of complete befuddlement, Big A grunted. "Bloody hell."

Instantly turning a harrowing fiery red from head to foot, Rooster's eyes flashed with horrifying anger. "That son of a bitch. He freaking used us to get the Ark. I'm gonna kill him!"

"The Ark," Abernethy said, "Where's—"

"He took it," I replied, with a distinct pit in the bottom of my stomach. "And there's something else. He took Stephen, too."

"Took him?" Coop scoffed. "What do you mean, hoss?"

"Maybe he took him to dinner, Cooper Trooper," Double OT cut in. "They're probably grabbing fish tacos and a Fresca. *Brah*, I love me some fish tacos. Serious."

Ignoring Owen's commentary, Caveman said, "How could he take him? Lucifer's no match for Stephen."

"He is now," MacCawill replied. "Trust me."

"But, how?" Rooster asked, looking exceptionally pissed. "And freaking why?"

Figuring it was past time to read the team into the dirty little secret that up until now only Stephen and I had been privy to, I reluctantly said, "Look, there's something I haven't told you. Any of you. The twenty-four Deacons that were killed by Azazel and the Maradim over the past year — they aren't dead."

"They're not?" Tango protested, as a collective silence fell over the group. "Where the hell are they?"

I cleared my throat. "Azazel's keeping them alive in some subdued state of existence. They're bound in holy flame in a secret prison. Hidden from our Sight."

Clenching his weathered hands into tight fists, Abernethy grunted, "To what point or purpose?"

"To siphon off their power. Apparently, for Lucifer to wield as his own."

"Hold on, Robinson," Stoner barked. "Are you saying that asshole's stolen the power of twenty-four Deacons? That would make him a fucking—"

"God," I said, as everyone shook their heads in disbelief. "To complete the process, he needed one final mantle. Mine or—"

"Stephen's," Rooster grumbled. "And now he has it. That son of a bitch. This whole little game of his was never just about the Ark."

"No. It wasn't."

With a somewhat suspicious glare, Abernethy asked, "How is it that you know all this, Deannie?"

Feeling like an exceptional dick for not telling him earlier, I grumbled, "I've seen it."

"Seen it, have ya? How, lad?"

"Visions, I guess. Hard to explain. They're random. And when it happens it's almost like I'm really there — but I'm not."

"Aye," he nodded, like he understood the phenomenon I was describing. "These visions of yers, Azazel is always a part of them, yeah?"

"That's right."

"And Stephen was aware of this, was he?"

"He was."

"Freaking visions?" Rooster said, spinning to face me and clearly a bit miffed he was learning all of this for the first time. "And how long have you been seeing things?"

I shrugged. "Couple weeks now."

"And why the frik haven't you told us?"

"Look, I wanted to. But—"

"Something tells me Dean didn't have much of a choice in the matter," Big A said, bringing instant ease to the more than tense situation. "You need say nothing more, lad. You did what you thought proper. And that's all any of us can do."

Although he nodded in agreement, Rooster shot me a look that made it pretty clear we'd be rehashing this conversation later.

"So, we got like a serious shitshow on our hands," Caveman said, as Duncan scampered across the floor and took his usual post at his feet. "What's the plan?

Rooster shook his head. "Seeing as though Stephen's down for the count, my freaking father's hopped up on divine steroids with the Ark of the Covenant in his back pocket, and Azazel's jacked-up giants are running unchecked across the globe — there's only one thing we can do."

"We fight," I said, scanning the crew to find nothing but marked conviction in their eyes. "Lucifer hasn't won. Not yet."

"Aye," Abernethy agreed. "We beat the daft scunner at his own game. We take the fight to him."

"*So*, for those of us not paying attention," Double OT chimed in, "what game is Lucifer playing? Is it like backgammon or something? He doesn't look very athletic. More of a card shark than a baller. Just saying."

Shaking off the latest Owenism, I said, "His game is chess, and his final move is to open the gates of Tartarus. And if that happens it's friggin checkmate."

Erin nodded. "So, we'll get there first."

"And where is *there*?" Double OT asked. "Somewhere tropical, perhaps? Fruity drinks with teeny weeny umbrellas ... scantily clad womenfolk ... Tom Cruise and some displaced Irish guy with a fake accent?"

"Tartarus is a lost realm," Stoner said. "It's a forsaken cursed hole in the dimensional fabric that the archangel Uriel tossed the fallen Watchers into six thousand years ago. And then he tossed the fucking hole in after them. Nobody knows *where* it is. That's the point."

Big A scowled. "Aye. Mr. Stoner's right. So, how in the bloody hell do we find a place that doesn't exist?"

Starting to pace like he was having a minor epiphany, Rooster said, "It does exist. Just not the way we think it does. That's exactly why the Ark is the key."

"What are ye thinking, Jackie?"

He grinned. "Reverse astral physics. Tartarus may be lost, but it's still a realm. And a realm must be tethered to the Earth in order to exist. But, in this case, the realm is so far on the fringe of metaphysical reality that the tether is infinitesimal and therefore its location is virtually unknowable. It makes perfect sense. You guys get it?"

Caveman scratched his furry chin. "Yeah, not so much, brofessor."

"Seriously, pard," Coop added, stuffing a sizable wad of tobacco in his lip.

Undeterred, Rooster said, "The tether can't be found. So, to gain access to the realm, it must be literally pulled to a physical point on the Earth. And to do that would take power. Immense power. Intangible power."

"From the Ark," Abernethy nodded.

"Exactly."

Still not following the plot, I muttered, "And how is this helping us figure out where that's going to happen?"

"Because even if you had something capable of generating that much spectral radiation, you'd need a way to focus it. And there's only one way to do that."

"With massage oil," Double OT said, like he was the foremost expert on the subject. "A lot of it. And we'll need lingerie models to test it on. At least a couple hundred of them. I'll handle that part, guys. Happy to do it. I got really soft hands. Always have."

"Shut your suck hole, douche wagon," MacCawill grumbled, glaring at Owen. "O'Dargans's talking about an obelisk. Lucifer's gonna need a friggin obelisk to pull this off."

"Hmmmm. You sure, Roybot? Coulda sworn it was massage oil. I could give you a good rub down, too. Big fella like yourself could probably go for a nice—"

"Don't piss me off, Trask," MacCawill muttered, throwing open his raw hide duster to reveal an impressive array of oversized pistolas.

"An obelisk," Caveman said, somewhat rhetorically. "You mean like a pyramid?"

"Sort of like a pyramid," Rooster replied. "But taller and skinnier." When Caveman continued to gawk at him, he added, "Like the Washington Monument."

"Ah, right on."

"Although, the Washington Monument's not *truly* an obelisk. The real ones are monolithic."

"And you lost me again."

"They're monoliths — made from a single piece of stone. The Egyptian pharaohs built them at the entrance to all their temples back in the day. Everybody thought they were for decoration, but their actual purpose was to harness the power of the sun and punch holes into other realms, allowing the *gods* to have free reign of Egypt."

"Wait," Doc said, doing her damnedest to take all this in stride. "Are you saying the Egyptian gods are real?"

"Real? Yes. Gods? No. They're just ancient nephilim with eccentric wardrobes and funkily shaped heads. Most of them are actually pretty cool. Except for Horus, who's an incredible asshat. His real name's Joe."

"Ha!" Owen yelled. "I know Joe. He's badass. The ladies love him. Dude's a disco phenom."

"Do you have a goddamn off button?" Stoner barked.

"I used to, but it didn't survive the colonoscopy. Or was it the vasectomy? *Hmmmm.*"

With a furrowed brow, Big A said, "So, we're looking for an obelisk. Question is — which bloody one? There's gotta be at least—"

"*According to my calculations, archdeacon,*" the disembodied voice of Skyphos boomed, "*there are exactly thirty-two true obelisks currently standing across the globe. The majority lie within Egypt and Rome, with a smattering of others in Paris, London, Istanbul, Florence, Urbino, Catania, Wimborne, Arles, Caesarea, and New York. Additionally, I have identified another twenty obelisk-like structures, such as the Washington Monument, which are scattered across the United States, France, Italy, Argentina, Venezuela, Uruguay, Brazil, Germany, Sweden, and the U.K. Transferring the coordinates to each of you now.*"

"Fifty-two total," Rooster said. "We can probably narrow down the list to likely candidates based on size and proximity to lay lines—"

"Negative," Stoner grunted. "If Lucifer has the Ark, none of that shit's gonna matter a damn bit. Any of them are fair game."

"*Cleric Stoner is correct, Rooster,*" Skyphos announced. "*Given the sheer power generated by the Vessel, any obelisk or similar structure of at least thirty meters in height would suffice.*"

"Shit," I muttered. "So, we have to put eyes on all of them. And right friggin now."

"Aye," Abernethy confirmed, "Divide and conquer. Break into teams. Tango, you're with me, laddie. We'll take Egypt."

As Duncan let loose with a piggly growl, Caveman said, "Lil' D says we'll take Rome."

Nodding, Rooster said, "Me and Dean will take the U.S."

"I'm going with you," Erin added.

"No. You're not," I said. "You're staying here." And when she whipped out one of her man-sized gats and pointed it at my chest, I muttered, "Doc's coming with us."

Slinging his bow across his back, Coop said, "Me and Stoner got France, Germany, Sweden, and the U.K."

"And I'll take the rest of them," MacCawill announced, lighting the stogie clenched in his teeth with a stout match that he struck on his scruffy chin.

"Looks like I'm going with you, Royster," Owen said, resting his hand on MacCawill's shoulder. "When do we leave? Can we take a couple road sodas? And Slim Jims?"

"And I work alone," MacCawill grumbled, pushing Double OT's hand away as he blew a ring of smoke in his face. "And Slim Jims are for women."

"Let's go, NecroLord. You're with me," I said. "Hate to say it, but I'm kind of getting used to having you around."

"Ha! I knew it. Bromance!"

"And now I hate you again."

"All right," Big A said, scanning the group, "Listen carefully, you've all got one hour. This is strictly a wee reconnaissance effort, yeah? Stay out of sight. Ye find anything unusual and ye contact the rest of us so we can regroup. Nobody does anything daft. We're only going to get one shot at this, and we need not tip our hand."

"You going to call in backup, boss?" Rooster asked.

"Aye. I'll alert the archdeacons to the situation and make damn sure they ready their lads. We'll need every last one of them to stand against Lucifer when the time comes."

"Any news from Gabriel or the archangels?" I asked.

"*I have already sent a communication to the seraphic court, Deacon Robinson,*" Skyphos replied. "*Thus far, I have received no response, which is highly unusual. I fear something may be afoul.*"

"That ain't good," Coop muttered.

"We can't worry about that now," Abernethy said, willing his cloak into being as it violently manifested around his hulking frame. "Meet back here in an hour. Stay in communication. And be bloody careful."

As five portals flared to life around us, Rooster reached into the bowels of his bomber jacket and produced a handful of squishy marble-sized gadgets. Handing them out, he said, "Use these to stay in touch. Put it in your left ear. Tap it once to open the channel. Tap it twice to return to the Quartermaster."

With a steely eyed gaze, Abernethy said, "Is everyone ready?"

"Wait!" Owen yelled.

Not to be outdone by the Rooster tech, he reached into his manly satchel and pulled out yet another peculiar aerosol can. Vigorously shaking it, he then flickered in and out of existence while circling the group until we were all literally doused in a thick haze of yellow gas.

"What the fuck?" MacCawill barked, as the smoke cleared and we found ourselves all decked out in similar black fatigues and barzel-plated body armor.

With an extremely satisfied grin, Owen said, "Now we're ready, big bossman. Gotta look the part. Epic, right?"

Strangely pleased by his black kilt and metal breast plate ensemble, Big A grinned as well. "Aye, that'll do, Mr. Trask. Now let's get to it."

Exchanging nods as we all stepped through our respective portals to embark on easily the strangest recon mission I'd ever been a part of, I couldn't help but think that life was so much friggin easier when the bad guys were just disgruntled giants, pseudo werewolves, wannabe vampires, and evil bear monster thingies.

Typical.

33

"How much time we got left?" I grumbled, as we emerged from another arcane gateway to find ourselves standing in the dark shadows of a trashed building situated on a deserted street corner.

Rooster gave his antique pocket watch a quick glance and sighed. "Twenty-six minutes. Still no word from the rest of the crew, and we've got two more stops after this."

"We need to pick up the pace."

Peering out from our concealed position to take in the smoldering landscape, Double OT asked, "Where the flip are we now? Mordor?"

"We're in D.C.," Erin said, pointing at the looming silhouette of the Washington Monument jutting far into the night sky about a mile away. "That's the National Mall across the street."

"Or what's left of it," I muttered, as a stiff, winter breeze blew through the barren panorama.

Holding up a mangled sign he had retrieved from a pile of ash at his feet, Rooster said, "Welcome to the Smithsonian Castle."

"You think we're too late to get a tour, John Boy?" asked Owen as he gazed at the burned-out hulk of a building shrouded in an ominous twilight.

"Yes. Yes, I do."

Carefully scanning the surrounding darkness to find nothing but a desolate landscape highlighted with billowing smoke, ginormous piles of rubble, and burning embers, I muttered, "Place is a damn wasteland. Not a soul in sight."

"It's quiet," Doc murmured, barely above a whisper.

"Too quiet."

Peering through the collection of flaming dogwood trees lining the once majestic Jefferson Street, Rooster shook his head. "Lucifer's not here. We should move on to New York."

"What about the friggin monument?" I protested.

Clearly frustrated, he grunted, "This is a waste of time. Look around, what do you see?"

"A whole lot of flipping nothing," Double OT cut in, pulling his manly locks into a tight ponytail.

"Exactly," Rooster said, swiping his fingers across the screen of his nepher phone. "If Lucifer was here, there'd be a goddamned army of anakim surrounding this place. Trust me. This is a dead end. Just like the others."

Owen nodded. "Johnny's got a point, monkey man. Our next target's in Central Park. We need to get a move on with our groove on."

Not entirely convinced but also finding it hard to disagree given the look of things, I said, "All right. Let's bug out. Fire up the portal."

"Wait," Erin said, still fixated on the five-hundred-foot obelisk in the near distance. "Something's — off."

"I'm off my meds," Owen said. "Does that count?"

Ignoring him, she pointed down the street. "Look at the sky around the monument."

Following her gaze, I focused my Sight and was more than surprised when I picked up on a faint, yet definitive shimmer in the air like it was being turbo charged by an unseen, blazing heat source. Pointing toward the anomaly, I said, "Doc's onto something. You guys seeing that?"

Rooster squinted. "Son of a bitch. Is that a veil?"

"A friggin big one. Looks like it's covering the entire monument and at least a few hundred meters around it. I think we just found the right obelisk."

"I'm calling it in," he said, tapping his ear piece. "The target's in D.C. I say again — the target's in Washington, D.C. You guys read me?"

When none of the team replied, I tapped my ear piece. "Anyone copy that?"

After a brief hiss of static followed by an indecipherable voice, the line went completely dead like somebody pulled the proverbial plug.

"What happened?" Doc asked.

"Comm's are dead," Rooster barked in frustration, pulling the gadget from his ear and tinkering with it. "Skyphos, you read me? Come in, Skyphos. Sweetie, you there?" After several more failed attempts, he muttered, "We're cut off from Skyphos. Something's wrong."

And it was right about then when an obscure clatter originating from somewhere to our rear caused us to spin around just in time to see an unnaturally pale, hollow-cheeked street person emerge from the shadows pushing an empty grocery cart.

"Zombie!" Double OT screeched. "It's a mother flipping zombie!"

"He's not a friggin zombie, you asshole," I grumbled. "He's homeless."

"Zombies *are* homeless, whistlebritches. It's their signature characteristic. Everybody knows that!"

Barely able to keep himself upright, our unexpected visitor stopped dead in his tracks and just gawked at us with a blank stare. Carefully approaching the stranger, Doc asked, "Are you okay, sir? Can you speak?"

After a long couple seconds, he whispered, "Yes."

"Look, buddy," I said, pulling alongside Doc. "Looks like you had a rough night. We'll get you somewhere safe, okay?"

"There is no such place," he murmured, as his piercing, sunken eyes drifted from me to Rooster. "Not anymore."

Somewhat taken aback by the intensity of his stare, Rooster said, "What are you doing out here?"

"Waiting," he replied, after another prolonged pause.

"Waiting for what?"

"To deliver a message. A message ... for you, Eóin O'Dargan."

"Wait, how do you know my name?"

As we all stood there wondering what the hell was going on, our peculiar new friend ripped open his sullied shirt to reveal a gruesome series of Enochian symbols carved into his chest. Judging from the ominous shreds of ripped flesh and streaks of crimson running down his abdomen, it was apparently done with a jagged object.

With an emotionless expression on his weathered face, he produced a small dagger from somewhere within his disheveled clothing and proceeded to run the blade across his neck with unnatural strength.

Effectively cutting his own throat with surgical precision, he fell to his knees and grabbed Rooster's hand as he locked eyes with him. In something between a raspy murmur and a gurgling growl he said, "In nomine patris et ortum conquor. The Morning Star commands you. Bring death to his enemies."

And then he simply collapsed to the cold ground in an oozing puddle of his own blood.

"What just happened?" Doc blurted out, instinctively bending down to ensure he was beyond saving.

"He's dead," Rooster said, as his eyes flashed a blazing red and he began to involuntarily twinge. "And we have a problem."

At a complete loss, I asked, "What the frig was that about?"

Grabbing my shoulders and spinning me toward him, Rooster barked, "Listen to me very carefully. You need to get out of here. All of you. Now!"

"I'm not going anywhere," I said, as the force of his spasming fingers began to literally dig into my flesh. "Tell me what's happening. What the hell did he do to you?"

Struggling to speak, Rooster said, "In nomine patris et ortum conquor. It means rise and conquer in the name of your father. Spoken to a liderc with a blood sacrifice sets us on a path. A path of destruction ... slaughter—"

Overcome with excruciating pain, he dropped to his knees and buried his face in his hands as he let out a primal scream that made me backpedal a step or two.

"Tell me how to help you."

Still screaming, he said, "You can't help me! Don't you get it? He's commanded me to kill you. I won't be able to stop myself. Run. Now! Please—"

Watching in horror as he was overcome with uncontrollable convulsions and his entire body turned a deep, ghastly red, the reality of what was happening hit me like a ton of bricks.

Clearly freaked out by the turn of events, Doc barked, "Please tell me what's happening!"

"Angry Rooster is apparently coming out to play," I said. "And Lew's evidently sicced him on us."

"What? How?"

"Not sure that's relevant at the moment, Doc." I turned to Owen as calmly as possible. "Take Erin to the Quartermaster."

Intently watching Rooster grotesquely morph from man to hulking beast, causing his clothes to rip from his body, Double OT said, "Ain't gotta tell me twice. What about you?"

"I'm not leaving him. Not like this."

As the fully neph'd out Rooster slowly rose to his feet and turned to face us with a surreal, animal-like madness in his eyes, Doc's face went instantly blank. Turning pale white and reeling backward at the mind-blowing sight of our friend in his true form, she gasped, "John? Oh my God!"

"Trust me, girl," Owen muttered, "God ain't got nothing to do with that kind of fugly bugly."

In a nightmarish, gravelly voice that sent a bone-chilling pulse through my spine, the creature said, "My father bids you welcome to the final act."

And right on cue, the arcane veil surrounding the Washington Monument melted from existence to reveal a scene straight out of Dante's friggin Inferno.

The monument itself blazed like a hellish beacon set against the night sky, as tendrils of greenish flame writhed and lashed about the structure like spectral serpents trying to bore a hole into another dimension. And worse, a seemingly impenetrable skirmish line of giant figures, fortified with interwoven bastions of burned-out vehicles and towering piles of half-eaten human carcasses, strategically formed a menacing perimeter around the structure.

The cloak rippled on my shoulders, sending a jolt of divine power coursing through my system as Rooster loomed over us, frothing at the mouth. Willing the spatha into being, I felt the presence of the leather scabbard manifest on my back as I ripped the otherworldly sword free. Grabbing Owen, I barked, "Take Doc. Get out of here. Now!"

In an uncharacteristically serious tone, he said, "He's gonna kill you dead."

"No, he's not. I can bring him back."

"No," he coldly replied. "You can't. The Johnny you know is gone."

"Go," I muttered, stepping between him and Rooster.

Without another word spoken, he simply nodded before wrapping his arms around a still traumatized Erin and flickered out of existence.

"John, listen to me, you can fight this—"

Gazing down at me with bad intentions, the mind-warped beast snarled, "What makes you think I want to?"

"Those aren't your words. He's controlling you. Fight through it."

Raising a massive, gangly arm in a strike position, he said, "You should have left when you had the chance."

And as his boney fist rocketed toward my head, I couldn't help but think that he was probably right.

34

"Is that all you've got?" Rooster growled, slowly circling me like a brazen predator toying with its wounded prey.

I was bleeding. Badly.

Everything was blurry.

Muted.

Dark.

A deafening buzz of screeching static filled my ears.

My head pulsed with repeated crushing swells of unknowable pain.

I couldn't keep this up.

The deep gash running across my midsection stung like a raging wildfire as blood trickled down my already sullied jeans and pooled at my feet.

He was too strong.

Too fast.

I had to end it — now.

There was no other way.

He'd left me no choice.

That goddamned son of a bitch left me no choice.

Mustering all my strength, I pushed myself off the ground. Not quite ready to get to my feet, I just sat there on my knees and despondently stared at the ground for a long second. This shouldn't be happening — but it was.

"Don't make me do this!" I barked, burying my emotions as I summoned all my unnatural ability and defiantly stood to face him. "I'm begging you."

In response, the mouth of the infernal, fifteen-foot monster standing opposite me curled into a harrowing smile proudly displaying row upon row of barbed, blackened teeth. Seething streams of viscous, ashen drool bubbled from the corners of its massive jaw and steadily oozed down its veiny, sculpted chest like snaking rivers of unnatural lava.

Fixing me with a poisoned glare, the creature's unnerving red eyes danced with a fiery madness as every chiseled, sinewy muscle making up its hulking red frame flexed and bulged from the mocking, guttural laugh that boomed from somewhere deep within its massive throat.

"The *great* Dean Robinson," it taunted, "*begs* me."

His mind was muddled.

Broken.

The man I knew had slipped into the ether.

Only the beast remained.

Tightening the grip on the hilt of my otherworldly gladiator sword, the cloak flared about my shoulders, sending rippling waves of divine Wrath coursing throughout my being.

"You're not thinking straight," I grunted, as my wounds instantly healed themselves and argent metal gauntlets encased my hands in a spectral flash. "Remember who you are."

"And *who* is that?"

"My friend. You're my friend."

"*Friend*," the creature scoffed, as a fine layer of orange flame silhouetted his entire massive physique of scaly blotched skin pulled tautly over a freakish skeletal frame.

"Stand down, goddamn you!"

"*God* has not damned me, my *friend*. Quite the contrary — it is you who are damned."

Holding out one of his impossibly large hands, he mockingly admired the ghastly trio of razor-tipped talons jutting out from its clenched fist.

Composed of jagged ashen bone, and stained deep with streaks of haunting crimson, the grim instruments of eviscerating death forbiddingly gleamed in the moonlight as he loomed over me like an eager executioner waiting to carry out his appointed duty.

"Now, tell me," he growled, frothing at the mouth like a craze-stricken animal, "is that *all* you've got?"

"Not everything," I grumbled. "Not yet."

Letting out another barrage of guttural laughter, he said, "Then let us finish the game."

"Don't do this," I pleaded.

"I am going to end you now, Dean — but take solace in the fact that the rest of your *friends* will not be far behind. I *promise*. They cannot hide from me."

As his words hit me like a raging tidal wave, every muscle in my body tensed in anger. Feeling the mental switch flip to the on position, I pulled in a long, deliberate breath.

Cleared my mind.

Focused my thoughts.

Found the Balance — the perfect equilibrium between wrath and clarity.

As the unfathomable power welled up in the deep recess of my soul and the expected sensation of calmative awareness washed over me, I grumbled, "I really wish you hadn't said that."

And it was right about then when shit got real.

Without so much as another word, his gangly, talon-tipped claws swung toward my head in a blur of motion as he launched at me with a grace and precision that should not have been possible for a creature of such mind-blowing size and strength.

Unfortunately, it no longer mattered.

He was too far gone.

I knew what had to be done.

Right, wrong, or indifferent.

Floating to my left and safely out of the arc of the death blow, his overgrown fingernails ripped into the street as he let out a harrowing, primal scream in clear frustration that I was no longer standing there.

Taking full advantage of the fact he was bent over and off balance, my face curled into a dark scowl as I focused all my supernatural strength and swung my sword toward his massive, heaving pectorals only to have it blocked by a gleaming katana that literally flickered into existence at that exact moment.

"Not so fast, Deano," Double OT said, holding the samurai sword. He was dressed in some ridiculous shogun outfit that looked suspiciously authentic.

"Owen?" I blurted out. "What the hell are you doing?"

"Apparently I'm stopping you from skewering your best butt bud. Der! And besides, do you know how flipping pissed folks are gonna be if you actually cut John Boy's head off? Everybody loves that ginger ass monkey. I mean shit, son, Gilmore's fans wouldn't even read the rest of the damn book!"

"What?" I barked, having no friggin idea what he was talking about, as Rooster boldly rose to his feet and glared at us with a sinister squint.

"Trask," he grunted, evidently less than happy to see Double OT.

"Hey, doucheball," Owen said, with a wolfish grin as he sheathed the katana on his back. "I brought you something."

Reaching into the satchel strapped across his torso and pulling out the oversized, undead cat we'd seen in NecroLord's lair, he muttered a few words under his breath in Enochian before tossing the hissing fuzzball straight into Rooster's chest like a pissed off football. "Say hello to my furry friend!"

Digging its claws into the infernal beast, the fat ass friggin feline proceeded to spit in Rooster's face before sinking its fang-like teeth into his neck, causing him to let out an ear-splitting scream. Staggering backward like he was piss drunk, the mind-blowing creature then simply collapsed to the ground and went limp.

Owen grinned a wide grin. "How's that for a *paw*-some plot twist? I mean like *fur* reals. *Purr*fect, right? Right? Am I right? What? Too soon for cat puns?"

I stood there in a complete and utter loss as to what just happened watching Rooster flop around the street like a beached whale. "What the frig did you do to him?"

"Chillax, monkey man. Johnny'll be fine. He should be back to normal in about three — two — one."

And sure as shit, Rooster began to shift back to his human form as Owen's creepy cat strolled past me and melted into the shadows.

Stunned, I simply said, "How?"

"Simple, whistlebritches, Asshole ain't just your average everyday feline. He's a mau."

"A what?"

"A mau."

"What the hell is that?"

"Sort of like an ancient cat god ... that spits venom ... and's really flipping badass." And when I just stood there gawking at him, he said, "Back in the early days when Johnny and his fugly bros were running wild in the streets, the Sumerians figured out mau venom was the only thing that neutralized lidercs. So, they weaponized it. And then they went to town on those jokers."

"How do you know all this?"

"Well, after me and Johnny had our little *scuffle* in medieval France, I sorta zipped back to 3,102 B.C. and made friends with some liderc hunters that called themselves—"

"The Knights of Uruk," I muttered, putting two and two together.

"That's right. You know of them?"

"Yeah, I hear they're a little short-handed nowadays."

"Hmmmm. That's too bad. They were some cool operators. Anywho, that's where I got Asshole. Figured if I ever ran into John Boy's alter ego again, having a mau would square things up. *And* he's, like, super fuzzy and cuddly. Although he does drink too much and sorta stinks like ass most of the time."

As I did my damnedest to wrap my head around the latest uncanny act of Owen anti-heroism, Rooster completed the transformation from unnatural beastie to lanky ginger and clumsily rose to his feet looking like three bags of shit.

And, unfortunately, he was friggin naked.

With a satisfied smile, Double OT reached into his satchel and pulled out some clothes that he tossed at Rooster. "How you feeling, buddy boy?"

"Better," he said, gazing at us with distended eyes. "Thank you."

More than relieved he was back to normal, I said, "You ready to get back to work?"

He nodded as he slowly put on the black fatigues. "Yes. Yes, I am. And, ah, sorry about trying to rip your head off."

"Back at ya," I muttered.

"Hell yeah!" Owen yelled. "Are we having a *bro*ment here, guys? I, for one, am *totally* feeling it. Bring it in, you crazy sons of bitches. Group hug! I mean after Johnny puts some pants on, of course—"

"Shut up," Rooster and I grumbled in unison.

Shaking his head in defeat, Owen shrugged. "Good feelings gone."

Gazing at the horrific scene laid out around the monument in the not so far distance, Rooster's eyes flashed red. "We need to stop Lucifer."

I nodded. "Yes, we do."

"You got a plan?"

"I fucking hope so," said Roy MacCawill as he fluidly stepped from a portal that flared to life and snapped shut behind him in the literal blink of an eye. He had a sizable gash running down his face.

"Damn, what the hell happened to you?"

"Sons of bitches were waiting for me in Uruguay. Got here as soon as I could after hearing your transmission. Where's everyone else?"

"Wondering the same thing," I muttered.

He glared at Rooster. "Why the fuck doesn't O'Dargan have any pants on? Actually, don't tell me. I don't wanna know."

With a snarky grin, Double OT said, "What's shakin', bacon?"

"What the hell are you still doing here, Trask? Thought you would've pulled your usual disappearing act by now."

"Just sitting on a cornflake. Waiting for the van to come."

And it was right about then when two headlights came barreling toward us from the side street to our immediate left and the Magic Bus pulled to a screeching halt, inches from mowing us down. Somewhat taken aback, MacCawill said, "How'd you know that was gonna happen?"

Owen grinned. "The Beatles are totally prophetic, brah. And I may have skipped ahead a couple pages. I have a very short attention span."

As we all stood there wondering just what in the hell that meant, the driver's side door of the vintage Volkswagen van swung open and a familiar country boy jumped out.

"Coop," I said, as the arcane archer joined our impromptu huddle in the lingering shadows of the bombed-out Smithsonian Castle. "Good to see you."

"It's good to be seen, hoss," he replied, curiously glancing at Rooster, who was frantically trying to pull up his trousers. "Sorry I'm late."

"Stoner let you drive the Bus?"

"Let's just say I drove it like I stole it."

"Where's Mr. Wizard?"

"Getting patched up. We ran into a dagum buzzsaw in London. Barely made it back to the QM after your transmission came through."

"Stoner okay?"

"He'll be all right. Can't say the same for his hairline, though. And he may have a permanent limp."

"And Doc?"

"Wounded clerics are coming back from the field in droves. She agreed to stay at the Quartermaster and get the infirmary spun up." Still awkwardly looking at Rooster, he said, "Ah, Red, where're your pants at?"

"Long story," Rooster grumbled, now fully clothed and seemingly ready for business. "What's the word from Big A?"

"Last I heard, he and Tango were in Third Heaven assembling the remaining Deacons."

"What's their time on target?"

"Your guess is as good as mine. They've been dark since the comms went tits up."

"What about Caveman and Duncan?"

"No telling."

"Fuck," I muttered, as my gaze drifted toward the unnatural gateway steadily burrowing a hole in the sky above the apex of the Washington Monument. "We have any other backup inbound?"

He shrugged. "You mean besides me?"

Following my gaze, MacCawill said, "Looks like Tartarus is within minutes of pairing with the Earth. We need to do something, mancho. Now."

I nodded. "Lew's too strong to take head on — but we can distract the son of a bitch. Buy some time for Abernethy to get here with the cavalry."

"Channeling the power of the Ark requires Lucifer's full focus,"

Rooster said, with his gears clearly turning. "If we can break that focus, it'll weaken the tether. It may even slam the door on Tartarus altogether."

Stuffing a wad of tobacco in his cheek as he peered at the surreal barricade of hulking giants and apocalyptic carnage standing between us and the objective, Coop said, "How we gonna get past the biggins?"

MacCawill turned to me. "Can't you pull some Deacon shit? Rumor has it you took down a whole goddamn realm's worth of anakim — by yourself."

I shook my head. "Bad idea. We're trying to stop a global cataclysmic event. Not cause one."

"Come again?"

"Dean did take down a whole realm's worth of anakim," Rooster said, "but he also kind of reduced the entire realm to infinitesimal pieces of cosmic dust in the process."

"Christ," MacCawill muttered, regretting he asked. "Bad idea then."

I turned to Rooster. "Can you whip up a sticky pad portal? Jump us close to the monument?"

"The Ark's generating too much spectral radiation. Trying to port anywhere near it would be bad."

"How bad?"

"Like having your molecular structure reduced to pork rinds kind of bad."

"Johnny's got a point," Double OT agreed. "Although I do like me some pork rinds. They're delectably crunchalicious while surprisingly low in carbs."

Figuring there was only one thing left to do, I covered my hands in argent metal gauntlets and willed the shotgun into being. "We'll do it the old-fashioned way then. Brute force and ignorance."

Owen burst out in laughter. "You out your monkey man mind? We can't go charging in there on foot like a bunch of jacked up Vikings!"

"Relax. We're not going to charge in there on foot."

To which he happily replied, "Hashtag — groovy."

"We're gonna drive."

To which he defeatedly mumbled, "Shit fire and save the matches."

I glanced at Stoner's yellow mirth mobile. "The Magic Bus doesn't happen to be fit out with any mystical machine guns that I'm not aware of, does it?"

"Nossir," Coop said. "But I'm pretty sure Stoner has a few toys in the back that go boom."

"Then gear up," I said, making the mental note that could be interesting. "Unless anyone plans on pulling a friggin army out of their ass in the next thirty seconds, it looks like we're going in alone."

And much to my surprise, Cyrus Kruger casually emerged from the shadows decked out in his ridiculous fur coat and skinny jeans motif. "Already told you, Deano, an entire army's a stretch. But I'm good for a legion."

"Who the frak is this guy?" Owen asked. "And what the hell's he doing walking around with a legion in his ass?"

"Kruger," I barked, instinctively ripping the shotgun from its holster and swinging the muzzle at his smiling face.

"Whoa, easy there, big guy," he said, throwing his hands in the air.

"What the hell do you want?"

"To help. Just here to help. Figure I owe you a serious solid after that minor *misunderstanding* in Tennessee. Tell him, Roy."

I glared at MacCawill. "What's this about?"

He shrugged. "We made nice. It's a complicated relationship."

"Ah, guys," Double OT piped in. "For those of us not really paying attention. What the flip are y'all jokers talking about?"

"The plan," I muttered, holstering the shotgun. "We're about to crash Lucifer's apocalypse party with six guys, a hippie van, and a give-'em-hell attitude."

"Party?" he scoffed, pointing at the hellish defensive barricade in the not so far distance. "That ain't a *party*, monkey man. That's a grade A shit-show. I'm talking like Shitty Shitterson and the Turdettes opening for Bruce flipping Shitsteen on a random Monday night in Shittsburgh kind of thing."

Coop slapped him on the shoulder. "Come on, cuz. It'll be fun. Just like the old days."

"I don't do fun, Cooper Trooper. Fun does me."

Reaching into his duster, MacCawill tossed Owen a bottle of dark whiskey. "Here. You in or what?"

"I am now, Royboy!" Then he happily uncorked the booze and jumped into the driver's seat of the Magic Bus. "Everybody in. Time to mow down some giant asshats. Let's ride, bitchachos."

As the unlikely strike force piled into the obscure, canary yellow van to undertake perhaps the most audacious frontal assault since Pickett's Charge, Owen popped in an 8-track of *Neil Diamond's Greatest Hits* and started blaring "Girl, You'll Be a Woman Soon" through the speakers mounted on the roof.

And just as I was about the hop in, I felt the ground begin to quake and heard the distinct guttural snort of a certain war pig looming somewhere in the depths of the darkness.

Rooster smiled. "Is that what I think it is?"

"Rhino time," I muttered, as my face curled into a dark grin. "Game on."

35

With a spirited "Hell Yeah!" Owen threw the Bus into gear, and the magical mystery assault vehicle roared to life.

Busting out of the dark shadows like a bat out of hell, we crossed Jefferson Street in a blur of motion and jumped the curb onto the smoldering, ashen lawn of the National Mall. Already driving at breakneck speed, Double OT laid on the brakes and power slid the eclectic van into a Tronesque ninety-degree turn, putting us on a determined beeline toward the Washington Monument located about a mile out.

"Damn, cuz," Coop said, grabbing the dashboard to keep from getting launched out the passenger side window. "Where'd you learn to drive like that?"

"Reruns of *Knight Rider*. Don't hassle the Hoff!"

As the van began to bounce around like we were driving through an earthquake, I slid the side door open to find Duncan galloping alongside us in all his great, white war pig glory. With a furry, muscle-clad rider perched on his mighty back like a supernatural John Wayne, the dynamic duo was covered with streaks of blood and looked exceptionally worse for the wear.

"Hey, Mick!" I yelled, more than happy to see my favorite mansquatch.

"What up, bromando!" he yelled back.

"We were starting to get worried about you guys."

As Duncan let out a harrowing snarl and reared his unnatural tusks, Caveman said, "Yeah, man. Rome was a bitch. Lil' D says sorry we're late."

"You're actually right on time."

"Sweet. We got a plan?"

Holding on for dear life as the Magic Bus rapidly approached the speed of a low flying aircraft, I pointed at the monument and the ridiculous array of anakim surrounding it. Shrugging my shoulders, I said, "Charge?"

He nodded. "Love it."

I tossed him a bandolier of tricked-out grenades that MacCawill dug out of Stoner's stash. "Think you guys can punch a hole through the roadblock?"

Slinging the frags over his shoulder as Duncan snorted plumes of unnatural smoke from his oversized nostrils, he said, "It would be our esteemed pleasure."

And then the terrifying twosome simply kicked it into overdrive and pulled out in front of the Bus like a pissed off battering ram.

"Stay on Duncan's ass," I yelled to Owen, who stomped on the gas and pegged the speedometer as the van's engine whined in protest.

"Weapons," Rooster grunted, suddenly realizing that his unanticipated hiatus in raging infernal beastie mode had left him unarmed. "I need weapons."

Casually puffing on his cigar like we were taking a leisurely Sunday drive and not speeding toward a certain death, MacCawill reached into his enigmatic duster. Producing a ridiculous assortment of guns and knives, he began to nonchalantly flip them at Rooster, like he was a walking arms room.

"I'm gonna want those back," he grumbled.

Quickly decking himself out with his newfound arsenal, Rooster begrudgingly nodded his appreciation and clutched two old school Walther P38 semi-automatics in his hands, now apparently ready for business.

Making the mental note to figure out what the hell MacCawill's deal was at some point down the road, I said, "Stoner have anything else we can put to use?"

Rummaging through the wooden munitions crate in the back of the cargo bay, Kruger pulled out what looked like an archaic rocket launcher etched with several concentric rows of Enochian script. "This looks fun," he said, holding it up and tossing it to MacCawill. "World War II era?"

"Goddamn right," Roy grinned, rubbing the olive drab vintage weapon like it was a swim suit model. "This, boys, is a genuine M1A1 bazooka. Four and a half feet of recoilless, tank snuffing goodness. Made back when folks knew how to reach out and pop a cap in somebody's ass with style."

I chuckled. "Can you operate it?"

"You trying to insult me, slick? I could hit a gnat's ass from three hundred meters with one of these bad boys. How many rounds we got?"

"One," Kruger replied, producing a chunky warhead from the crate and quickly studying it as a mischievous smile curled across his face. "But I'm thinking that'll be enough."

Glancing at the peculiar rocket that looked more like an arcane torpedo, I said, "What the hell is that thing?"

"That, Deano, is a genuine Gomorrah Flare. Weaponized bad mojo forged in the ancient realms of the dark magi. Guaranteed to ruin somebody's day in truly spectacular fashion."

"What'll it do to a juiced-up fallen angel with a serious god complex?"

"At the very least, it should give him a nasty headache."

"That'll do," I muttered.

"Get ready, y'all," Coop bellowed, pulling his seatbelt tightly around his torso as we rapidly approached the unnatural barricade. "It's about to get interesting."

"*And* just as a minor point of clarification," Owen yelled, "what happens *after* we literally drive the van into the army of beasties?"

Bracing for the impending collision of epic proportion, I barked, "Once we get through, follow my lead. Kruger, you spin up the dirt doppelgänger brigade and keep the anakim busy. The rest of you stay close to me. We have one friggin objective — locate Lucifer so MacCawill can get a clear shot at him with the Gomorrah thing. Everybody got it?"

As the team collectively nodded in the affirmative, Owen locked his arms on the steering wheel. "*And* should we happen to die a horrible death *before* that happens?"

Peering out the windshield to get an up close and personal view of the awaiting hellish formation of roaring, armor-clad giants set against a horrifying backdrop of spectral green light raining down from monument, I grumbled, "Walk it off."

"Here we go!" Coop yelled, as our uncanny war pig and mirth mobile caravan was literally seconds from slamming headlong into the unnatural melee.

As Double OT belted out an ear-splitting war cry that sounded like something between a shrieking choir of tone-deaf women and a pack of hyenas having hate sex, the cloak flared out on my shoulders, sending a bolt of divine Wrath pulsing through my system.

All my senses instantly kicked into über overdrive as the expected sensation of calmative awareness drew over me like a warm blanket, and time screeched to a near halt in response.

In what felt like extreme slow motion, I watched with great anticipation as Duncan lowered his massive head and careened with reckless abandon into the mind-blowing blockade.

And for the record — it was pretty goddamn impressive.

Busting through a smoking heap of burned out cars like they were made of cardboard, the great, white war pig plunged into the first rank of anakim with unrivaled violence of action and bloodthirsty fervor. Impaling countless giants on his razor-tipped elephant-sized tusks, Lil D' waded into the masses like a rabid bull in a goddamn china shop while Caveman sunk his battle axe into anything that got remotely close to them.

The mind-blowing phalanx of hulking figures scrambled to close their ranks as the Magic Bus skidded through the breach on Duncan's heels, and a seemingly endless barrage of oversized fists and barbaric weaponry hammered the eclectic van like a nightmarish hailstorm.

Loading his arcane long bow in a blur of motion, Coop kicked out the windshield with both feet and began to launch Holy Flame-laced arrows into the seething hordes of bad guys like a friggin gatling gun.

Rooster, MacCawill, and Kruger held onto anything they could get their hands on to keep from being tossed around like rag dolls, while I ripped the semi-divine Winchester free of its holster and sent a barrage of Judgment fire blasts through the van's side door just for good measure.

Literally plowing our way through the dark gauntlet of thrashing giants, we quickly lost sight of Duncan as Double OT did his damnedest to keep the speeding vehicle under some semblance of control.

Thoroughly enjoying himself as he mowed down anything and everything in our path, he yelled, "Want some? Get some! NecroLord rides again!" Tragically followed by, "Oh shit...hey, guys...you might wanna — hold onto something!"

And then the overzealous time hippie proceeded to swerve around a charging group of spear-bearing anakim and drive the friggin van smack into the cement wall of a moderately-sized building concealed in the deep shadows of the Washington Monument's outer lawn.

Barely managing to pump the brakes before smashing headlong into the immovable obstacle, we screeched to a very abrupt, and rather unfortunate halt, which, in turn, sent all of us in the cargo bay on a violent, very unappreciated one-way trip toward the front seats.

Hurtling into Coop's back, the rest of the crew landed in an inglorious pig pile on top of me while what remained of Stoner's pride and joy quickly filled with billowing black smoke.

Brushing off the rather unfortunate end to our short-lived *Mad Max*-quality joy ride, I muttered, "Everybody okay?"

As an ensuing series of painful grunts indicated nobody was dead, Double OT said, "You think Stoner's got insurance on this thing? That flipping building came out of nowhere, guys. Talk about a public hazard. Anybody know a good personal injury attorney? I think I bit my lip."

And then the driver's side airbag shot out of the mangled steering wheel and socked him squarely in the face. Thank you, karma.

"Owen," I grumbled, as I squirmed out from the bottom of the heaping manwich and retrieved my shotgun.

"Yes, monkey man?" he replied, trying like hell to free himself from the ineffective, yet suffocatingly annoying safety device.

"If we survive the next five minutes, you and me are having a serious talk."

"Heads up, y'all!" Coop yelled, bailing out the passenger side door and slinging arrows at anything that moved in the tormenting green twilight. "We got incoming."

"How many?"

"I reckon pretty much all of 'em are heading this way."

"Fucking perfect," I grumbled as an ear-splitting cacophony of guttural sounds filled the air. "Time to go to work, gents."

A turbo shot of adrenaline raced through my body as I jumped out of the van to find an endless swarm of otherworldly behemoths with bad intentions and a wide array of oversized instruments of death and disfigurement clutched in their colossal hands lumbering toward our impromptu fighting position.

Swinging the shotgun muzzle toward the mob of charging beasties, I focused my will and cocked the lever as the crew pulled up alongside me with weapons at the ready.

"Stand your ground!" I yelled. "Let 'em get nice and close. Kruger, get ready to do your thing. Wait for my signal."

And just as we were about to be engulfed by the grisly sea of massive assailants, something rather unexpected happened.

They stopped.

Like dead in their tracks.

Lowering their weapons and staring at us with eyes as black as pools of oil, a deafening silence fell over the mind-blowing army of monstrous figures as they stood like grotesque statues in the looming, cold darkness.

After a long couple seconds of wondering what the hell was going on, the crowd began to systematically part and a man-sized figure donning an impressive assortment of ornate armor strolled toward us. Despite the fact that I couldn't quite make out his face in the thick shadows, I knew exactly who it was.

"Azazel," I muttered under my breath as the cloak flared out on my shoulders and the smarmy fallen angel pulled to a boasting halt within a few feet of us.

"Hello, *Captain*," he replied. His snake-like eyes danced with elated contempt. "How very nice to see you. And welcome to the revolution, by the way. We couldn't have gotten here without your many contributions."

"Fuck off."

Dismissing my snideness as he admired his freakish legion of super-sized soldiers huddled around us for as far the eye could see, he simply grinned. "Call me curious, but what exactly were you planning to do *after* battering your way through my outer defenses?"

I grinned back. "Before or after I beat the ever-living piss out of you and your merry band of cornfed carnies?" When he offered nothing in response aside from a rather icy stare, I said, "But seriously, after me and my pals make you look like a grade A bitch, my trenchcoated compadre here is going to shove that bazooka up your boss' ass. Figured we'd see where it goes from there. You know the drill. Can't plan too far ahead in these kinds of situations."

"Yes, of course," he said, as he dismissively scanned my five-man crew. "Although, I can't help but notice that your *team* appears tragically understaffed for such an ambitious set of maneuvers."

"Understaffed?" I muttered, scratching my chin. "You think so?"

He smiled like a cat about to inhale a mouse. "I do."

As the distinct sound of booming, throaty laughter permeated the surrounding mob of beasties, I turned to Kruger. "Cyrus, what do you think?"

He casually ran a hand through his highly manicured hair helmet. "Hate to say it, but the man makes a good point, Deano."

"Yeah, I guess he does. Maybe we didn't think this thing through."

He chuckled. "I'm suddenly feeling kinda foolish."

"Same here. What the hell do we do now?"

"Guess there's only one thing left to do."

"Yeah, what's that?"

He winked at Azazel. "Let's dance, bitch."

Then he simply threw both his hands high in the air, causing the frozen landscape to erupt into a swirling maelstrom of unnatural, man-sized funnel clouds that voraciously pulled the surrounding dirt, shrubbery, and anything else in the near vicinity into their whirring columns.

And before our freakishly large adversaries knew what the hell was happening, the endless sea of mini-tornados produced an endless horde of smiling Krugers interspersed within their staggered ranks.

As Azazel's smug façade transformed into something between confounded disbelief and downright outrage, I muttered, "You heard the man, asshole. Let's friggin dance."

36

Toting an impressive array of tricked-out muzzle-loaded rifles and Civil War era cavalry swords, the skinny jean-clad clone army instantly went to work, shooting and hacking their way into the anakim assault force, as a melee of epic proportion erupted around us.

Instinctively jumping into action, Rooster and Coop got back-to-back and started calling out targets as they unloaded relentless volleys of otherworldly arrows and barzel-tipped bullets into the hordes of hulking miscreants. With the loaded bazooka slung on his back, MacCawill popped off rounds with his grenade launcher while Kruger whipped up new golems as quickly as they went down like an unnatural orchestra conductor.

Reverting to stone cold assassin mode, Double OT drew his katana and began to shimmer in and out of existence while cleaving giant body parts with impossible precision as their owners roared and howled in protest.

Letting out a primal scream, Azazel's eyes blazed with maniacal fury as a glinting sword manifested in his hand. A harrowing set of black, feathered wings unfurled from his armored back as he launched at me in a state of unfettered rage. Within seconds of running me through, my face curled into a dark smile as I raised the shotgun and readied to blow a basketball-sized hole through his chest.

And it was right about then when Duncan busted through the surrounding calamity like a pissed off bulldozer and slammed into the demented fallen angel with the force of a runaway train. As Azazel hurtled through the darkness back toward the National Mall, a grinning Caveman yelled, "Boomsicle!"

Glaring at him, I grunted, "What the hell? You know I had that under control, right?"

He shrugged his shoulders as Duncan let loose with a sheepish growl. "Lil' D says he couldn't help himself."

Chuckling despite the situation, I took careful aim at a fifteen-foot behemoth charging in on Rooster's flank before unloading a judgment fire cap in his ass. "You put eyes on Lucifer?"

"Oh, yeah," Caveman said, pointing toward the looming obelisk bathed in haunting green flame. "He's at the monument. You can't miss him."

I made the mental note that that couldn't be a good thing as Kruger yelled, "Go! I got this, Deano. Do what you came here for."

Nodding as the dirt clones continued their Herculean slugfest with the anakim militia, I barked, "Everybody on me. We're moving."

As the crew nodded in acknowledgment, Mick said, "Me and Lil' D will stay here with Kruger. I got an idea."

And then he started lobbing Stoner's mystical grenades into the countless waves of combatants as Duncan snapped back into berserker mode and plunged into the chaos like the war pig version of a bucking bronco.

With Azazel's cronies sufficiently preoccupied for the moment, the rest of the team formed into a tight wedge formation and slipped through the madness with Double OT on point. With no trace remaining of his hipster guitar hero persona, the arcane mercenary moved with the poise of a samurai master, sheathing his fabled katana only to produce a glinting pair of double-edged hatchets.

With the battle raging around us, we successfully skulked past the smoking remains of the Magic Bus and into the eastern boundary of the oval lawn surrounding the monument, as the Krugers continued to throw themselves at the frenzied giants like spider monkeys. Quickly reaching the brink of the frothing fracas, we ducked into the thick shadows of a large makeshift bastion haphazardly cobbled together with chunks of ripped apart buildings and stacks of battered police cars.

Motioning for the crew to sit tight and cover our six, I crept down the long length of the impressively crude barrier until reaching the end. Carefully poking my head around the corner, I finally got my first up close and personal look at the Washington Monument.

And, unfortunately, I about shit myself.

Sitting amidst a literal minefield peppered with heaping stockpiles of smoldering debris and mutilated carnage, the colossal granite edifice blazed in the darkness like a nightmarish torch. The serpentine coils of hissing, spectral green flame that I'd witnessed from afar now completely enveloped the towering structure like a voracious throng of monstrous anacondas. Originating at the base of the monument, they wove their way up to the very tip of the conical apex only to inexplicably meld together into a lava-like stream that spewed into the hellish inter-dimensional portal swirling above.

Trying to wrap my head around what the frig I was actually looking at, Rooster pulled up on my flank and blurted out, "Fucking hell."

After a long couple seconds with the two of us standing there completely awestruck by the inconceivable setting, I grumbled, "Yeah, something like that."

Snapping back into mission mode, I focused my will and projected my Sight across the couple hundred-meter expanse standing between us and the infernal shitshow lying ahead. Like looking through a powerful zoom lens rapidly honing in on its target, my vision slammed to a halt, and the monument's base came into perfect focus.

It didn't take long to zero in on the source of the slithering flame as I locked onto a gold-plated chest sitting atop a rudimentary stone pedestal carefully positioned amongst the tattered American flags encircling the entrance. Pumping out a steady pulse of divine energy like a celestial power plant, the Heavenly artifact glowed and sparked like it was in danger of going thermonuclear.

"I've got eyes on the Ark," I said. "No sign of Lew, though. Where the hell is that son of a bitch?"

Still gawking into the sky, Rooster tapped me on the shoulder and simply pointed upward with a blank look on his face. Following his gaze, I almost shit myself for a second time in as many minutes as a white-cloaked figure inexplicably floating in mid-air adjacent the ghostly silhouette of the monument came into view.

"No fucking way," I muttered.

"Way," he replied.

Again focusing my Sight, I zoomed in on the felonious flying asshole to confirm it was friggin Lucifer.

"Christ," I grumbled, intently watching as he quite literally hovered in a stationary position near the very top of the five-hundred-foot structure.

Apparently in some kind of deep meditative trance, he appeared to be continuously murmuring something under his breath as offshoots of spectral flame danced around him like sentient bolts of lightning.

"What is he doing?" Rooster asked.

"His eyes are closed," I said. "And he's mumbling something."

"It's gotta be the incantation that's powering the gateway. Lucifer's the conduit between the Ark and the monument. If we can break the connection, the gateway closes and Tartarus goes bye-bye."

"Will the Gomorrah Flare do the job?"

"It should."

As my vision instantly returned to normal, I surveyed the distance separating us from our target. "We need to get closer first. I don't care how good MacCawill thinks his damn aim is, there's no fucking way he's making that shot from here with a sixty-year-old rocket launcher and a wannabe wizard warhead."

"Challenge accepted," MacCawill grunted, as Rooster and I spun around to find him standing there with the bazooka propped on his shoulder. Taking careful aim at his former employer, he clenched his teeth on the frayed stub of a cigar hanging out of his mouth. "Who's your daddy..."

As he pulled the trigger, an ungodly boom split the night air like a clap of thunder and the Gomorrah Flare burst from the tube in a flittering haze of fiery apocalypse.

Watching with great anticipation as the peculiar projectile screamed toward the Washington Monument like a psychotic comet, I was more than surprised when the malevolent mojo-laden missile somehow hit its mark and smacked squarely into the levitating Lucifer.

"Fucking Yahtzee," MacCawill muttered, as the Evil Über Deacon plunged toward the ground like a white-cloaked lead balloon.

“Son of bitch!” I happily scoffed. “You did it.”

“Wait,” Rooster said, thoroughly confused. “Shouldn’t there be an explosion?”

With his mouth already curled into an exceptionally mischievous grin, MacCawill reached into his duster and pulled out his signature Oakleys. “Hold that thought,” he said, sliding them on his face and dropping to a knee. “You guys should probably duck.”

Then, as if on cue, the unnatural missile detonated in a blaze of unparalleled glory, sending a mind-boggling explosion of blinding, psychedelic light and palpable waves of blistering heat sprawling across the horizon line. It basically looked like somebody dropped an atomic bomb in the middle of a Pink Floyd laser light show.

Completely mesmerized by the surreal fireworks display, it felt like time screeched to a momentary halt as a caustic mushroom cloud the size of California blasted into the atmosphere, taking the top half of the friggin Washington Monument with it.

“So ... that happened,” Rooster muttered, as our collective jaws hit the ground watching the mammoth fragment of the historic granite edifice hurl into the darkness like a launching Space Shuttle before violently bursting into a gazillion pieces with an ear-splitting boom.

Forming into a horrific cloud of chunky shards, the spine-chilling debris field surged to a staggering height of five thousand or so feet before slowly running out of momentum and plummeting back toward the Earth in a fiery death dive.

And before I had the opportunity to nearly shit myself for the third time in as many minutes, the armageddonesque meteor shower slammed into the ground surrounding the surviving half of the once majestic obelisk with a prolonged series of pelting thuds that, in turn, sent a savage shockwave ripping across the landscape in a hammering blur.

Sort of like somebody unpaused the movie, my concept of reality snapped back into place just in time to get ferociously blown backward several feet as the tidal wave of pissed off energy slammed into Rooster and me with the force of a wrecking ball. Not slowing down in the least, it tore through the legions of anakim and Kruger clones, still locked in mortal combat behind us, until neither man nor beast remained standing for as far as the eye could see.

With my ears ringing and sight blurred, I staggered to my feet as a shellshocked Coop and Double OT stumbled toward me looking like somebody just stole their lunch money.

Picking himself off the ground, a clearly dazed Rooster tried his damnedest to shake off the epic shellacking as MacCawill somehow just stood there sucking on a fresh cigar.

"You didn't duck," he said, smiling at us as he blew a rather elaborate smoke ring.

"Asshole," Rooster muttered, apparently fighting the urge to punch him in the face with every fiber of his being.

Scanning the crew, I grumbled, "Everybody good?"

Still wobbly, Owen said, "Betty? Betty White? Is that you? What the flip are you doing here? Wait, is it my birthday? Did you get me a new bathrobe? And Twinkies? Let's snuggle up and watch some Mr. Rogers. Won't you be my *neighbor* ..." And then he collapsed to the ground and passed out with a creepy smile on his face.

Trying to put that mental image out of mind, I stepped over him. "Is everybody besides NecroDork good?"

Hazily gawking into the smoldering fallout zone, Coop said, "What the hell just happened, y'all?"

"MacCawill happened!" Rooster barked, still pissed.

"We accomplished the mission," MacCawill shot back. "That's what happened."

"And decapitated the goddamn Washington Monument. And apparently laid waste to any structure still standing in the Nation's fucking capital."

"You're welcome."

"You're welcome? Are you serious? Is he serious—"

Figuring we had more important matters at hand, I said, "How much time you think we've got before Lew's back on his feet?"

MacCawill shrugged. "Maybe a couple minutes. Maybe less."

"Well, collateral damage notwithstanding, it seems we momentarily postponed the friggin apocalypse."

And it was right about then when the billows of smoke hovering around us cleared away, and all our gazes collectively drifted upwards to the hellish green portal still swirling in the dark sky above what remained of the jacked-up monument.

"Or not," Coop muttered.

Clearly perplexed as he studied the unnatural vortex which was somehow picking up speed at an exponential rate, Rooster's eyes danced with rapid thought.

"Why didn't the goddamn gate to Tartarus go poof?" I grunted. "We broke the connection between Lucifer and the monument — friggin literally."

Rooster shook his head. "I-I don't know. Somehow it's still drawing power from the Ark."

Peering across the fallout zone, I instantly spotted the glowing silhouette of the divine chest sitting ominously undisturbed amongst the debris field. Still perched on the rustic stone pedestal, it was spitting out bolts of spectral lightning like a Tesla coil on crack.

Gritting my teeth, I grumbled, "Not for long."

"What are you fixin' to do, hoss?" Coop asked.

The cloak flared upon my shoulders like a raging beast sending a jolt of wrathful power coursing through my spine. "Turn the Ark into kindling."

"No!" Rooster yelled. "You can't do that."

I locked gazes with him. "Fucking watch me."

"You don't get it! If you destroy it now, it'll evaporate the entire city... and probably most of the eastern seaboard."

"Bullshit."

"I'm serious, Dean. The fact the Ark's still able to keep that gateway open means it's running full bore. And without Lucifer *or* the obelisk to harness the energy stream, it's highly unstable."

"So, what the hell do we do?"

"We need to figure out how to disable it — make it go dormant."

"Well figure it out fast," MacCawill grumbled. "There's no sign of the cavalry yet, and Lucifer's gonna be pissed when he wakes up."

I turned to Rooster. "All right, what's the plan?"

Starting to pace, he muttered, "I need to think."

"There's no time, John! Just tell me how to turn the fucking thing off."

Stopping mid-stride like he had a major epiphany, he yelled, "That's it! All we have to do is turn it off."

"Turn it off?" Coop scoffed, spitting a wad of tobacco juice on the ground and looking at Rooster like he'd blown a ginger gasket. "You saying the Ark of the Covenant has a dagum kill switch?"

"Yes. Yes, it does. Well, sort of. Actually, I'm pretty sure it doesn't. But that's irrelevant. I have an idea."

"What's the short version?" I grumbled, as a thunderous clamor behind us indicated the anakim army was recovering from the Gomorrah Flare backlash.

Slipping into bloviation mode, he said, "At its most basic level, the Ark's nothing more than a power generator. Now, granted, it's souped up like a celestial freaking Lamborghini with twin turbos running on divine ethanol, *but* just like any other generator, it pumps electrons through a circuit to produce energy. You guys with me?"

Rolling over, Double OT murmured, "I'm with ya, Johnny. Really love your peaches, wanna shake your tree." And then he passed out again.

"Cut to the end!" I grunted.

"The Ark," Rooster said, "is a simple electrical circuit. We just need to add a ground to the return and stop the flow of the current."

"The return?"

Looking at me like I was a complete dumbass, he said, "The point where the electrons leave the circuit to create energy. In the case of the Ark, the *return* is the Mercy Seat."

"The what?"

"You need to get out more, mancho," MacCawill chimed in. "There are two golden angels mounted opposite each other on the Ark's lid. The space between the tips of their wings is called the Mercy Seat."

And as the statement registered with my brain, a lightbulb the size of a hot air balloon went off in my head. "Son a bitch," I muttered, as the prophetic words of Mariel flashed through my thoughts. "Only by embracing mercy will the fate of destiny's design be witnessed." I instantly realized what I had to do.

Rooster raised a ginger eyebrow. "Wait, what did you say?"

"Never mind. Stay here. Hold the anakim off as long as you can."

"And then what?"

"If Big A's not here by then, it might be a swell time to break out the rosary beads and say a couple Hail Marys."

Willing the gauntlets into being, I clenched my fists as the argent metal slowly formed over my hands and forearms.

"Where are you going?" he protested.

My mouth curled into a dark grin. "To embrace mercy."

And then I simply focused on the Ark and took three bold steps.

37

Really hoping I didn't turn into a pork rind, I traversed the smoldering fallout zone in a blur of motion and fluidly manifested directly opposite the Ark of the Covenant.

And, unfortunately, before I had the opportunity to shit myself or go blind, I was bombarded by an overpowering field of otherworldly energy that swirled and hummed around the gilded chest like a spectral swarm of pissed off hornets.

Thinking perhaps this was a really fucking bad idea, I had a brief yet highly ironic Indiana Jones moment as the unrestrained primal power lashed out from the Ark in tenacious, crushing waves that pelted me like a million unseen fists. And somehow, despite the stinging pain that literally screamed through every inch of my body with unrelenting vigor, I convinced myself that my face wasn't going to melt off.

So, at the very least, I had that going for me.

Which was nice.

Burying the pain in a dark corner of my mind, I clenched my fists and summoned all my supernatural strength. Feeding off my raw determination, the cloak flared out on my shoulders as I defiantly fought through the raging, unnatural shitstorm to reach the God box within a half dozen or so labored steps.

Somewhat mesmerized by the surreal artifact in full-on apeshit mode, I was immediately drawn to the two golden cherubim mounted like ever vigilant sentries atop its ornate lid. Silhouetted by pulsing flashes of ethereal green lightning, the majestic statuettes simply gazed at each other with expressions of perfect serenity as a literal maelstrom of unfettered power spun like a centrifuge of imminent destruction between their outstretched wings.

Figuring it was high time to shit or get the hell off the pot, I muttered, “When this is over, I really need to evaluate my life choices.”

And then I raised my metal-encased hands and grasped both tips of the angels' wings with all my friggin might.

I'm pretty sure I started screaming at that point.

I'm also pretty sure my face started melting off.

But, to be fair, it's a bit hard to recollect with any degree of certainty because shortly after I turned myself into a walking circuit breaker for the greatest power source known to mankind, things kind of went to shit.

Real quick like.

Typical.

On the upside, though, Rooster's theory about ‘turning off’ the Ark was right on the friggin money. In fact, after I wrapped my paws around the damn Mercy Seat, it didn't take more than half a second for the entirety of the Ark's divine juice to stop flowing into the gateway to Tartarus.

Mainly because it began to flow into me.

All of it.

Hence the screaming and face melting.

Now, granted, I probably should've seen that coming.

But, in my defense, I was never very good at physics.

At any rate, as I made the mental note to ask Mariel why she left this part out of her cryptic words of wisdom, I felt my legs go limp and instantly collapsed to my knees. With my hands locked into a death grip on the cherubim, the hissing, sparking stream of consummate power literally gushed into my spasming body until even the Deacon's cloak said “screw it” and relented to its divine dominance.

My head rolled back on my shoulders as I fixated on the unnatural portal swirling in the dark sky above. Happily watching it slowly fade from existence, I felt an incredible sigh of relief wash over me.

And then, as my mind began a steady drift into the either, I felt nothing.

No pain.

No guilt.

No remorse.

No nothing.

Apparently about ready to check out and call it an afterlife, a stirring on the periphery of my pain-induced euphoria caught my attention, and a dark figure appeared on the opposite side of the Ark. Unable to really do anything about it, I helplessly watched as the mysterious party crasher glared at me and said, "Dean, I swear to God, if you're fucking dead again, I am *so* kicking your ass."

Wait.

What?

"Doc?"

"It's me. Now, get up. This isn't over."

"What ... what are you doing here?"

"My job," she said, muttering a few words under her breath in Enochian before placing her hands on top of mine.

As my muddled brain churned on overtime trying to figure out what the hell was happening, the crushing torrent of divine energy pouring into me like a firehose instantly stopped.

And it began to pour into Erin instead.

Shit.

That's not good.

Despite my deep-fried, jacked-up condition, I dove into an instant state of panic and tried my damnedest to stand up. When my legs made it pretty clear it wasn't happening anytime soon, I focused all of my remaining will and pulled in a long, deliberate breath.

Cleared my mind.

Focused my thoughts.

Found the Balance — the perfect balance between wrath and clarity.

As the unfathomable power welled up in the deep recesses of my soul, the cloak roared to life and the divine Wrath coursed throughout my being like a turbo shot of diesel-powered adrenaline.

With my strength returned and broken body instantly healed, I boldly rose to my feet and locked gazes with Erin, who was standing opposite me somehow completely unaffected by the Ark's crushing power.

"How are you doing that?" I barked.

With harrowing bolts of spectral green flame dancing around her silhouette like a raging firestorm, she said, "Can we talk about this later?"

"Later?" I protested, trying to pry her hands free of the Mercy Seat. "You need to get out of here! Now!"

Ignoring me as she clamped down even harder with impossible strength, she simply lowered her head and closed her eyes.

Looking up to find the gateway to Tartarus rapidly shriveling into nothing more than a cloudy vapor in the night sky, the Ark began to violently convulse as a deafening human-like screech erupted from somewhere deep within its enigmatic core. The spectral radiation pouring into Doc tripled in intensity as the golden cherubim clutched in our hands began to sizzle like they were within seconds of literally melting.

"Let go!" I yelled, as Erin's eyes shot wide open and bored a hole through me with a cold, empty stare. Saying nothing, she just tightened her grip.

And then something happened that I still haven't got straight in my head.

As I desperately tried to wrestle our hands free of the self-destructing divine relic, Erin's deep brown eyes turned a radiant, almost glowing white.

And I'm not talking like they rolled back in her head.

I'm talking like they literally turned white.

Like a spine chilling — unadulterated — make you piss your pants — white.

As I simply stood there, speechless, the ornate panels of gold plating that covered the four sides of the Ark began to peel off, only to inexplicably morph into an ethereal suit of seamless armor that methodically locked into place around Erin like a jigsaw puzzle.

Smoothly covering her like a glove that hugged every last contour of her body, the otherworldly combat attire completed its surreal manifestation by gliding up her neck and encasing her head in a sleek, full-faced helmet. Almost like a metal ski mask, the menacing headgear coated everything except her eyes, which balefully blazed like sentient orbs set against the featureless golden carapace.

With the Ark reduced to nothing more than an oversized rustic crate, the pint-sized knightress simply removed her armored hands from the cherubim and everything stopped.

The thermonuclear laser light show.

The uncontrollable shaking.

The ear-splitting screeching.

Everything.

Catching a final, fleeting glimpse as the portal to Tartarus disintegrated into nothingness, I spun toward Erin with a look of pure bewilderment across my face.

With a gazillion questions racing through my head, all I managed to blurt out was, "Really?"

Stepping around the fully dormant Ark of the Covenant, her eyes returned to their normal mesmerizing brown as the dauntingly creepy, golden helmet melted from her face. As her mouth curled into a warm grin, she said, "It's okay, Dean."

"Okay?" I scoffed, still awestruck. "No. Hell no! This is not friggin okay! Nothing about this is okay! I mean, look at you for Christ's sake. How in the—"

"It's okay," she repeated, like everything made perfect sense.

Shaking my head and about to launch into an unfiltered, expletive-filled tirade explaining the many reasons to the contrary, the sound of sliding rocks from somewhere in the near vicinity made me stop.

Swinging my attention toward the surviving half of the Washington Monument directly behind us, the cloak rippled anxiously on my shoulders as the mammoth heap of smoldering rubble strewn about its disheveled base began to collapse inward upon itself like something was forcefully burrowing its way out.

"Fuck," I muttered, ripping the shotgun free of its holster before focusing my will and cocking the lever.

Erin's attention swung toward the mini avalanche. "What's happening?"

"Remember yesterday when you wanted to punch Lucifer in the face?"

"Yeah."

"Well, I think you're about to get your chance."

Right on cue, the Evil Über Deacon himself stepped from the mound of crumbling wreckage like he owned the friggin joint. Apparently less than happy about catching a Gomorra Flare in the chest while floating around like an infernal Superman, his white cloak burst into blinding flame as the Wrath of twenty-five Deacons visibly pulsed from his being.

With a batshit crazy glaze over his eyes, Lew methodically scanned the area with a content smile on his face before locking his full attention on Doc and me. Closing the distance between us in a blur of motion, he said, "Greetings and salutations, my pets. It seems the fates have once again brought us together."

"Yeah," I muttered, as my face curled into a dark grin. "Isn't that swell?"

And then I jammed the shotgun muzzle squarely into his chest and pulled the trigger.

My hand blew backward from the recoil as the devastating, point blank blast of judgment fire erupted from the semi-divine Winchester and slammed into my adversary with extreme prejudice.

The smarmy smile vanished from Lucifer's face as the hissing deluge of white flame covered his torso like unnatural napalm, causing him to reel backwards a step.

And just as I was expecting his innards to blow out the back of his cloak before being vaporized in a brilliant flash of wrathful radiance, the fireball harmlessly melted from existence.

Completely friggin dumbfounded by the fact that he somehow shrugged off a blast of judgment fire like it was nothing, I blurted out, "That's not possible."

To which he simply glared at me as his white cloak mockingly billowed upon his shoulders. "You're still not paying attention, Master Robinson. Allow me to provide some further clarity as to the *extent* of my abilities."

Before I knew what the hell was happening, the son of a bitch pulled his left hand into a tight fist and willed a horrifying lance of pure, white flame into being. Without another word spoken, he launched at me with impossible speed and drove it straight through my friggin chest.

All the way through.

Adding insult to certain injury, he thrust the searing pike into the cold ground behind me as I slumped to my knees, impaled like a skewered pig. Giving the infernal weapon a final, forceful shove, he triumphantly loomed over me as a torrent of ineffable pain surged through my body and my perception of time sputtered to a crawl.

Blood leaked out my chest like a friggin sieve as Doc roared a primal scream and her eyes flashed with horror. Overcome with rage, her golden helmet snapped back into place over her face as she ripped the spatha from the scabbard on my back.

In a single motion barely perceptible to the human eye, she leapt at Lucifer with the grace of a ninja and drilled him in the jaw with her armored left hand. Caught off guard by the brazen maneuver, he stumbled backward as Doc continued to unload on his ass. Moving with impossible speed, her white eyes glowed with unfettered fury as she swung the otherworldly sword at Lew's neck, only to have him literally catch the blade mid-arc.

Undeterred, she effortlessly yanked it free and spun to her right, assuming a bold offensive stance as she defiantly held the sword at the ready position.

"Very impressive, poppet," he snidely remarked, seemingly enjoying himself. "You don the Armor with a mastery well beyond your years. But I'm afraid play time is over."

And then he simply waved his left hand and lifted Erin a few feet off the ground with an unseen force. Waving his hand again, the sword flew into the darkness, and she was inexplicably locked into place like a floating mannequin.

Her eyes returned to normal as the metal mask melted from her face and she tried to say something but quickly found herself unable to speak. Snidely smiling at her, Lucifer said, "We have nothing to discuss, my dear Erin. Not as of yet anyway."

"Let her go," I managed to force out, trying like hell to pull the flaming spear out of my chest cavity to no avail. "It's over, asshole."

"Over?" He laughed as his attention shifted back to me. "No, Master

Robinson. It, most certainly, is not over." Glancing at Doc, he said, "Father's great *Witness* has come forth. The script is playing out with uncanny precision. This is splendid news. I'm honestly quite impressed you managed to conceal her identity from me. Very shrewd maneuver on your part. Top marks, Dean."

And when it was pretty clear I had no friggin idea what he was talking about, he said, "Oh, isn't that interesting. Ms. Kelly didn't see fit to disclose to you the nature of her *condition*, did she?"

Stepping toward me, an argent metal gauntlet manifested over his hand as he grasped my chin and pulled my face toward his. As I struggled to keep my eyes open with my life force continuing to drain from my body, he coldly muttered, "I'd say you and the good doctor would have much to discuss, but I don't believe you're going to last long enough to have that particular conversation. You don't look well, Dean."

Spitting a wad of blood in his smarmy face, I grunted. "When I get up, I will fucking end you."

He smiled and callously pushed me away as he strolled toward the Ark. "I think we both know that's simply not going to happen. The Gehenna fire from my lance is devouring the very last of your life essence as we have this enlightened conversation. You've been bested by the very Wrath you were entrusted to wield. The irony is delicious. And yet, the tales of your martyrdom will undoubtedly be etched into the annals of eternal infamy. Perhaps even a nice sonnet will be sung of the mighty *Seventh Deacon of the Seventh Line* and his nobly tragic end at the hand of the Morning Star. I dare say it's almost Shakespearean. And with that parting sentiment, I will bid you adieu, Master Robinson. I'm quite late for my visit with our *friends* in the Heavens."

Ignoring his gloating bullshit as I slumped further down the infernal lance, I muttered, "We slammed the door on Tartarus, asshole. Looks like you're going alone."

"Am I?" he playfully asked, as a fine layer of white flame shimmered into existence on the fringe of his cloak. And then he simply ripped the lid off the Ark and tossed it into the darkness.

As my muddled mind churned to keep focus, the night air filled with an incessant fluttering of unseen, massive wings accompanied by the unnatural shrieking of a thousand, tormented voices.

The unnerving sound rang through my head like a raging nightmare as I looked up in horror to find that Lucifer was no longer alone.

He was standing amidst a legion of angels.

Angels with soulless black eyes infused with countless millennia of crazed madness and sullied, tattered wings that flared from their statuesque frames in seething rage.

The fallen Watchers.

He'd liberated them after all.

Fuck.

Drawing on the last ounce of strength remaining in my body, I lurched forward, only to have the flaming pike rip deeper into my chest.

With nothing more than a contemptuous glance, Lucifer muttered, "And so it begins."

Then he and his army of psychopathic seraphs shot into the night sky like a fleet of shooting stars until they were simply gone.

No longer able to keep my eyes open, I felt my head drop stiffly against my chest as the magnitude of what just happened hit me like a sledgehammer.

Unfortunately, it was right about then when I also came to the bitter conclusion that I had nothing left in the tank. My senses steadily faded to a state of void.

Damn.

Impaled on a flaming spear by the friggin Devil.

If that ain't a hell of a way to go out, I don't know what is.

Yep. Pun intended.

The last thing I heard was yelling.

Actually, it was more like screaming.

Frantic, pissed off screaming.

It was Erin.

I felt her grab me. Shake me.

Then there was just darkness.

Damn the bad luck.

38

"GOOD EVENING, this is Buzz Shea reporting live from Boston's historic Faneuil Hall — or more appropriately, what's left of it. Welcome to tonight's *special* edition of The *Buzz*Source and tonight's *buzz,* as you can well imagine, is the single question on everyone's mind — what's next? By all accounts, it's been roughly forty-eight hours since the unprecedented, global incursion of the barbaric *creatures* that our military leaders are now referring to as Anomalous Genetic Composites — or simply AGCs. While the *intentions* of these so-called *AGCs* remains as much of a mystery as their origin, they seem to have simply vanished as quickly as they appeared. *However,* the questions remain. Where did they go? Will they come back? How will we stop them? *Can* they even be stopped? With every major nation still reeling in the aftermath of their heinous — near unspeakable — atrocities, a unified state of emergency continues to reign throughout the land. *However,* despite the still unquantified levels of death and destruction, several strides toward regaining a semblance of normalcy are well underway in *most* U.S. cities, including the Nation's capital where, *according to unconfirmed reports,* a weapon of mass destruction was detonated. So, what's next? Apparently, only time will tell. In other peculiar, yet seemingly unrelated, news — reports of *giant robots* are also on the rise across the Pacific Northwest. A spokesperson from the..."

"Change the flipping channel," a familiar voice grunted from somewhere in the depths of my mind as the odd sensation of teeth nipping on my ear and a really small tongue licking my face coaxed me into a somewhat lucid state of consciousness.

Slowly opening my eyes, I found myself in a familiar dimly lit room lying on my back, on what felt like an oversized wooden table. Staring at the ceiling in a blurry haze, I became aware of the intense, throbbing pain that raced through every last inch of my body.

With a heartfelt groan, I lifted my head to find a certain brown-spotted, miniature feral hog standing squarely on my bare chest, staring at me with great anticipation. I gave his little head a reassured pat. "Good to see you, Duncan." As the pocket pig responded with an elated squeal, I said, "But if you're licking my face, who the hell's biting my ear?"

And then, unfortunately, I turned my head to find Double OT sitting there in his Spiderman boxer shorts and kittenzilla tee shirt with a shit-eating grin plastered across his bearded face.

"Owen?"

He grinned. "How ya feeling, monkey man?"

"That depends. Am I dead?"

"Don't think so."

"In that case, I feel like shit."

"Yeah, you kinda look like shit. And while we're on the topic, you kinda got this stink—"

"Hey, Owen."

"Yes, monkey man?"

"Why in the fuck where you biting my ear?"

"Is that not a thing?"

"No. That's not a thing."

"So, this is awkward, huh?"

"I'm going to get up now."

"*And* I should probably leave."

Shimmering out of existence only to reappear on the very far side of the Quartermaster with an acoustic guitar in hand, he began to expertly pick an old blues song I couldn't quite place.

Painfully sitting up on the makeshift hospital bed, Duncan excitedly jumped off me and scampered toward the bar. As I looked around through foggy eyes, I found myself surrounded by hundreds of wounded clerics strewn across every available tabletop in the entire friggin Quartermaster.

"Take it slow," Rooster said, pulling up alongside me and placing his hand on my shoulder. "You've had a rough couple days. How you feeling, man?"

Grasping my chest to find one hell of a grotesque, semi-healed wound, I grumbled, "Hazy. How did I—"

"Survive being shish kebab'd by a lance made of Judgment fire?" he said, handing me a black RoosterBragh tee shirt emblazoned with the tagline *The Early Bird Gets the 'Bragh, Brah*. "We're not sure. But you can thank Willa Knightly for patching you up. After we got you back here, she worked some serious vexen mojo. It was — messy."

Making the mental note to figure out what the hell that meant at some point down the road, I muttered, "Lucifer ... he beat us. After all that, the son of bitch still managed to free the Watchers and—"

"I know," he said, hanging his head in frustration. "I know."

"We need to do something."

"Yes. Yes, we do but—"

"How's the team?"

"Everybody's okay. For the most part—"

"Good, then round them up."

"Look, Dean, I need to explain a few things first—"

"Explain it later," I grumbled, painfully throwing my legs off the table. "We need to figure out our next move. Where's Big A?"

His eyes flashed a blazing red. "Stop! That's what I'm trying to tell you. We need to think this through. Things have become — complicated." And when I offered nothing in response besides an icy stare, he said, "*Okay*, so, after Erin pulled Lucifer's skewer out of your chest—"

"Wait," I said, anxiously scanning the makeshift hospital ward. "Doc. Where's Doc? Is she—"

"She's fine. Actually, she's kinda more than fine."

"Then where is she?"

He nervously clearing his throat. "She, ah, left."

"Left? What do you mean she left? Where the hell did she go?"

"To find the *other* one."

And when I gave him the second icy glare in as many minutes, my enigmatic ginger colleague said, "So, apparently, Erin's a—"

"Witness," I muttered, as my mind flashed back to the events at the Washington Monument.

"Wait, you knew?"

"That's what Lucifer called her. What does it mean?"

"Well, according to the Book of Revelations, when the end times are approaching, two prophets arise that bear the Armor of Heaven and are supposedly juiced up with the power to devour their enemies with fire that pours out of their mouths amongst a few other things. They're referred to as Witnesses."

"What are they supposed to do?"

"According to the ancient prophecies, their purpose is to stand against Lucifer and the Four Horsemen. They're supposed to stop the apocalypse."

"Son of a bitch," I grumbled, trying to wrap my head around this more than bizarre twist as I rapidly connected a couple of dots. "Doc's purpose — this is what Mariel was talking about. She knew this was coming. I need to talk to her. I need to talk to Mariel. Right friggin now."

Rooster sighed. "Yeah, and this is the complicated part."

"What do you mean?"

"We can't *talk* to M."

"Why the hell not?"

"Because, hoss," Coop said, joining the discussion with his long bow draped over his shoulder and looking exceptionally worse for the wear, "Heaven's locked up tighter than a clam's ass at high tide. Ain't nobody getting in. Or out."

"What are you talking about?"

"When Lucifer started his shenanigans in D.C.," Rooster said, "the archangels evidently put the Heavens on total lockdown. That's why Skyphos went dark."

"Wait," I grumbled. "Are you saying we're cut off from Skyphos?"

"And Abernethy," Coop added.

"Abernethy?"

Rooster sighed again. "Big A and Tango never made it to the Washington Monument. Because they were gathering the rest of the Deacons in Third Heaven when the doors got slammed shut. They're trapped there."

"Christ," I grumbled. "So, you're telling me that Doc's in the wind, Big's A trapped with half of the Deacons, and Stephen's imprisoned with the other half?"

"And, unless I'm missing something, we have no friggin recourse to do anything about the small fact that Lucifer's raising hell in Heaven. Until, of course, it spills over onto the Earth."

I shook my head in frustration. "What about the friggin anakim?"

"Another conundrum," he muttered. "After Lucifer took the Watchers and headed topside, the anakim just stopped fighting and hauled ass. That was two days ago."

"All of them?"

"Far as we can tell, yes."

"Where the hell did they go?"

"Not sure, hoss," Coop replied. "Yesterday, Crockett and his team tracked a group of biggins into the Grand Canyon, but then the trail went colder than a brass toilet seat in the Yukon."

Shaking off the latest Cooperism, I said, "What could they be doing in the goddamn Grand Canyon?"

He gazed at the droves of wounded clerics scattered throughout the Quartermaster. "Dunno. We've been a little short staffed to figure it out. But whatever it is, all across the dagum globe they're keeping a low profile. For now at least."

Taking a deep breath, I sat back down on the table as an offshoot of pain fired through my torso. "Fuck me. This is complicated."

"Yes. Yes, it is," Rooster muttered. "We need to be smart about our next move."

And it was right about then when the front door to the Quartermaster swung open and a curiously tall figure clad in a blood-soaked tunic and shredded armor staggered through before falling to his knees.

Jumping off the table and willing the cloak into being, I took a bold step forward as the haggard mystery man scanned the room in a panic. Fixating on me, a look of relief washed over his face as he clumsily got back to his feet and stumbled toward us like he was on his last legs. Barely making it to Rooster before face planting on the stone floor in a smoldering heap, he said, "The Heavens are ablaze. The fallen ones have returned ... you must help us ... you must—"

And then he simply went limp.

"Who's this guy?" Coop asked, as Rooster reached down to check his pulse. "Is he dead?"

Pulling back his tunic to reveal the remnants of badly burned and savagely mutilated wings, Rooster said, "No. He's not dead. And he's not a guy. He's an angel. One of Gabriel's foot soldiers, if I had to guess."

I locked gazes with my enigmatic ginger colleague. "And if he figured out a way to get out of Heaven—"

"He can figure out a way to get us in." His eyes danced with rapid thought as they flashed blazing red.

"This isn't over," I said, as the cloak flared on my shoulders and a dark smile curled across my face. "Not yet."

Not by a friggin long shot.

~

The story continues in *Rage of the Heavens*. Read on for an excerpt, or purchase your copy at https://links.liquidmindpublishing.com/9OBx

RAGE OF THE HEAVENS
CHAPTER 1

THE BAR WAS AN ABSOLUTE SHITHOLE.

And I would know.

Mainly because I fashioned myself a faithful connoisseur of the great shithole bar circuit. In my mortal days, I'd patronized just about every kind there was.

Down-and-out shitholes.

Up-and-coming shitholes.

Local no-name shitholes.

Franchise yuppie shitholes.

Backwoods redneck shitholes.

Uptown tourist trap shitholes.

And, of course, my least favorite — hipster bars that tried to pass themselves off as shitholes but they couldn't because they weren't. And everybody knew it. Even the goddamn hipsters.

Making the mental note that the particular establishment I found myself in at the moment had risen to the very top of a yet-to-be-identified shithole bar classification, I curiously watched the muscle-clad bartender coaxing some life into one of the disheveled taps by beating it with a hammer. Realizing I needed a refill, he sauntered over like he owned the joint and grunted something.

"What?" I grunted back, struggling to hear the heavily tattooed beefcake over the blaring seventies rock that crackled and hissed through the series of dilapidated speakers dangling from the ceiling.

"I *said*, do you want another beer?"

"Please. But only if it's flat and warm like the first two."

He scowled. "You some kind of smart ass?"

I grinned. "That depends."

"On what?"

"If you're some kind of dumb ass."

Ignoring my snide commentary, he said, "You want a beer or not, asshole?"

Reaching into the pocket of my sullied jeans, I pulled out an arcane coin and slid it across the bar. "Changed my mind. How about you be a good lad and go fetch me a Black Swan."

His eyes narrowed into an intense squint as he snatched the obscure token. "You got a name?"

"Nope."

"And your friend?"

Glancing at the angel sitting next to me in hex cuffs, I said, "His name's Kerubiel, but you can call him Bobby. And he's not my friend."

Saying nothing more, he waltzed to the far end of the dilapidated wooden bar and placed the coin in front of a peculiar character with an old school black touring cap pulled low over his face.

"Get ready," I muttered, under my breath. "Shit's about to get real."

Trying like hell to ignore the incessant waves of cigarette smoke that rolled through the ramshackle room like a smoldering forest fire, Bobby said, "I don't understand, Dean."

"Understand what?"

"You just told that man I'm not your friend."

"So."

"Are we not friends?"

"We're undercover, Bobby. You're supposed to be my prisoner. Remember the plan?"

"So, you told a lie?"

"Yes. To sell our cover story. You get it?"

He nodded. "I believe I do."

"Just play your part for a little longer, and then it's go-time."

"I understand. I'll play my part. And then we'll leave."

"No, Bobby, we don't *leave* when it's go-time. We *go*. Remember?" Studying his emotionless gaze, I took a healthy gulp from my piss warm beer as he nodded again.

"I remember, Dean," he said. "When it's go-time, we put our shoes in their anuses."

And then I promptly spit the mouthful of beer all over the bar. "What the hell did you just say?"

"That's when we put our shoes in their —"

"Are you about to say anuses again?"

"Yes."

"Please don't. Nobody uses that word in casual conversation. Especially in plural form."

"I'm confused, Dean. Where are we supposed to put our shoes then? You said—"

"I *said*, that's when we put a *boot* in their *ass*. It's a figure of speech... that I really wish I hadn't used. So just forget it, Ok? Forget I ever said it. And keep your shoes on, Bob. I'm friggin serious."

After a long moment, he said, "But how will I know when it's go-time?"

"Well, when we're surrounded by more bad guys than you can count and there's no way out — it's go-time."

"But, Dean, when that happens, we'll be trapped with the bad guys."

My face curled into a dark grin. "No, buddy. They'll be trapped with us."

RAGE OF THE HEAVENS
CHAPTER 2

A Very Long Day or So Earlier

The otherworldly portal spit me from its swirling vortex like a flailing projectile, and despite my best efforts to keep my feet, I careened headfirst into the mangled hood of a smoldering pickup truck.

Slumping to the ground with a splitting headache, I grumbled a few heartfelt expletives under my breath as a misty, yet persistent summer rain drizzled from an overcast sky, and an overpowering stench of gasoline and recent death dominated the warm afternoon air.

Rising to my feet in a momentary haze, I felt a pit form in the bottom of my stomach as I gazed in horror at the harrowing scene laid out before me.

The charmingly rustic downtown street that artfully snaked through an impressive collection of quaint buildings set against a majestic backdrop of sprawling mountains had been turned into nothing short of an apocalyptic fallout zone complete with trashed store fronts, battered vehicles, and butchered body parts.

We were too late — again.

"Bug!" Rooster yelled from across the ransacked street as he unholstered his pair of tricked out Glock pistols and methodically swung them toward the snarling eighteen-foot behemoth charging at him with unnatural speed and bad intentions.

"Bugs?" I yelled back, thinking insects were probably the least of our worries at the moment.

"No, not bugs," my enigmatic ginger colleague replied like I was a complete dumbass as he squeezed off a dozen well-placed rounds that blew out his massive assailants' kneecaps, causing the big bastard to collapse on the sidewalk in a pissed-off heap. "Bug!"

And it was right about then when the cloak rippled anxiously about my shoulders, causing me to instinctively duck and spin to the right as a friggin Volkswagen Beatle careened past my head and obliterated a bus stop behind me.

"Bug," I muttered, shooting Rooster one hell of a dirty look as the voice of a familiar country boy called out, "Heads up, hoss!"

Wiping the stinging rain my from eyes, I turned to the left to find a blurry vision of Cooper Rayfield in his signature maroon hoodie standing a few feet away and about to launch three barzel-tipped arrows from his mighty long bow — at my head.

Dropping to a knee as the arcane bolts rocketed past me like ballistic missiles, I heard as much as felt a guttural howl erupt from my immediate rear as they struck their intended target.

Spinning around to find a highly pissed off fifteen-foot anakim with a tight shot group of arrows sticking out of his gut, I drifted to the right and just barely avoided having my face splattered by an oversized sledgehammer.

The giant lashed out in frustration as his soulless black eyes danced with unfettered fury and double rows of unnaturally large yellow teeth jutted from his gaping mouth in defiance.

Willing the gauntlets into being, my mouth curled into a dark grin as argent metal fluidly coated my hands and forearms. Instinctively pulling my hands into tight fists, I sunk all my weight into a crushing uppercut that landed squarely in my super-sized adversary's super-sized ballsac.

Letting out another cacophonous howl as he dropped to his knees and cradled his nether region, I gave him a quick wink before ripping my otherworldly gladiator sword from the leather scabbard on my back and lopping his head off in a blur of motion. As the unnatural beast vaporized in a brilliant flash of white radiance, I turned to Coop. “How many more?”

Attentively scanning the immediate area while loading his bow, he said, “Aside from the one Rooster’s using as target practice over there, I count three.”

Turning to find another unnaturally large son of a bitch battering his way through the surrounding debris field of jacked-up cars and chunks of asphalt, I sheathed my sword and swapped it out for the semi-divine 1887 Winchester shotgun.

Focusing my will and cocking the lever to chamber a round of judgement fire, I swung the muzzle toward the rampaging beastie and pulled the trigger. As a hissing ball of white flame blew a soccer ball-sized hole through his massive chest and he fizzled out of existence, I muttered, “Make it two.”

Seemingly unimpressed, Coop tucked a healthy wad of tobacco into his cheek and drew back his bow. Without aiming, he sent an explosive-tipped arrow whizzing down the street toward the burned-out hulk of a building at least three hundred yards away. Casually watching it plunge through a window and fade from sight, he said, “Make it one.”

And right on cue, a mammoth silhouette staggered out of the smoldering store front only to have his head literally explode in a burst of white flame.

“Show off,” I grumbled, making the mental note to never piss of Cooper Rayfield. “Speaking of, where the hell is Owen?”

And it was right about then when an angry giant lumbered past us with Owen Octavius Trask perched on his mighty shoulders like a demented howler monkey.

Giving us an energetic thumbs up, Double OT unsheathed one of the dueling katanas crisscrossed on his back and drove the blade through the top of the poor bastard’s skull before launching himself off the now screaming beastie like a long-haired hippie ninja.

Somehow ripping his sword free and decapitating the massive miscreant in midair before effortlessly landing on his feet with feline grace, he yelled, "And the crowd goes wild as Dungeon Master sticks the landing...Boomsicle! Was that killa or what, fellas? Pun!" And then he busted out a series of golf claps while continuously bowing to an imaginary crowd.

I shook my head. "Dungeon Master? I thought you were NecroLord."

"Nah, that was *soooo* last book, monkey man. I've evolved my character based on some focus group feedback."

Wondering what the hell that was supposed to mean, I turned to Coop. "Why exactly do we keep him around?"

He shrugged. "I reckon it's his smooth jazz sensibilities, hoss."

"Yeah. That."

Having apparently dispatched his oversized quarry, Rooster crossed the street while slapping fresh mags into his pistolas. Stopping a few steps from us and pointing at the fiery remnants of the car that nearly pancaked me moments earlier, he said, "Bug."

"I know what the hell it is," I muttered, holstering my shotgun. "Do me a favor, would ya? How about the next time some asshole's about to throw a friggin car at me you say something like '*Holy shit, Dean! Some asshole's about to throw at friggin car at you*' instead of calling out the goddamned make and model."

"You're whiney."

"You think?"

"Yes. Yes, I do."

Panning across the pillaged city block eerily devoid of people, Coop said, "Looks like the Contraption sent us here too late, y'all."

"We must have missed the main hunting party by mere minutes," Rooster muttered, taking in the mind-blowing level of destruction. "There had to a hundred anakim here to do all this. Maybe more."

"Are we still in California?" I asked.

Holstering his Glocks and pulling a slick looking tablet from somewhere in the inner bowels of his battle-scarred, brown leather bomber jacket, Rooster feverishly swiped his fingers across the screen. "No," he said, looking up. "We're in Utah."

"Utah?"

"Yeppers. This is Park City."

"First time the bastards hit Utah."

Joining the conversation, Owen matter-of-factly said, "Guess they got tired of eating people from Arizona and California. Probably 'cause of all the vegans. I bet they taste like cucumbers...and chickpeas...and squash. *Dude*, I hate me some squash. *But* I do like saying it. Squash. Squash! *Squash*?"

Shrugging off the latest Owenism, I muttered, "Let's finish up here. I need a frosty beverage. Or several."

Coop rested his bow on his shoulder. "What's the plan, hoss?"

"Why don't you and Owen—"

"Um, excuse em moi, Deano," Double OT said, "I believe you mean Dungeon Master."

"I'm not friggin calling you that."

"But...it's kinda my name. Dig?"

And when I offered him nothing but a prolonged icy stare in response, he muttered, "Or not. That's coolio. Ha?"

I turned back to Coop. "Take Owen and push out a couple blocks. Make sure there's no more stragglers. Keep an eye out for civilians. And stay on comms. Me and Rooster will sweep the rest of downtown. Meet back here in twenty."

Nodding in acknowledgement, he slapped Double OT on the shoulder. "Let's move, cuz."

As the uncanny duo proceeded to expertly maneuver through the disturbingly quiet urban battlefield before slipping between a couple buildings and fading from sight, Rooster and I began to navigate the surrounding labyrinth of piled up cars and splintered buildings.

Peering into a gutted bookstore, I said, "Hunting parties out in broad daylight. They're getting bolder."

"Yes. Yes, they are," he replied. "And this is the furthest north we've seen them range. But it still fits the pattern."

"The pattern?"

"The pattern," he said, still fixated on his handheld computer. "We know these raids aren't random. They're well-planned. Well-executed. The anakim packs never hit a town with a population greater than ten thousand people because they know the military is concentrated around the large cities. *And,* more importantly, they always stay within a five-hundred-mile radius of the Grand Canyon, where we also know they have some kind of hidey hole."

"That we can't find."

"That we can't find — yet."

"What's your point?"

"My *point* is that they're predictable and the Contraption is very close to—"

"Predictable." I scoffed. "How many towns have the sons of bitches sacked this month?"

"So far, this makes four."

"And how many did your friggin *contraption* send us to in time to stop the bastards from going apeshit on the place and chowing down on some locals?"

"None. But—"

"And just how many attacks did we prevent the last month or the month before that?"

"None."

"Exactly. There's only one thing predictable in this equation — us failing."

"We're getting closer. The Contraption just needs more data and more time."

"Yeah? Tell that to the people of Park City and all the other towns the goddamn anakim laid waste to since the winter. This isn't working."

Pulling to an abrupt halt in front of what used to be a posh coffee shop, his eyes flashed a blazing red as he glared at me. "Do you think I don't know that?"

I glared right back at him. "I know you do. All I'm saying is—"

"I know *exactly* what you're saying," he grumbled, as his skin turned the color of his eyes and the raindrops sizzled as they landed on his face. "Would you like to know how I know *exactly* what you're saying?"

"I really don't give a shit—"

"Go ahead, ask me."

"I'm not asking you."

"*Ask* me."

"Are we really gonna do this?"

"Freaking ask me!"

"Ok, fine," I muttered, realizing I'd apparently popped the cork on the ginger fury and there was no putting it back in the bottle. "How is it that you know exactly what I'm saying?"

"I happen to *know* exactly what you're saying because you've *said it* every fucking day for the last fucking month, you obstinate son of a bitch!"

"Good. Then you should be used to it."

"Used to it? Do you know how tired I am of listening to your brooding bullshit?"

"We're at war, John. And in the event you haven't noticed, we're friggin losing."

"No! We're not losing — not yet."

"Look around." I grunted. "You call this winning?"

"Of course not!" Looking like he was about to blow a gasket, he feverishly paced back and forth, waving his hands around. "We have a *plan*. We just need to be patient."

"Our plan is shit. And patience isn't working. People are dying—"

"And what?" he said, doing his damnedest to hold back the infamous Rooster rage with every ounce of his being. "It's your fault?"

"Maybe it is my fault!"

"Oh, so it's *your* fault that Abernethy and Tango got trapped in Third Heaven with half of the goddamn Deacons when the archangels slammed the gates shut. And I suppose it's also *your* fault that Lucifer captured Stephen and stashed him away with the other half of the Deacons in his freaking collection. Really? Is your ego seriously that big?"

When I offered nothing in response, he said, "Believe it or not, the machinations of angels and giants and all the other unnatural shit that goes bump in the night have been brewing long before Dean *fucking* Robinson came on the scene."

"For Christ's sake," I grumbled, figuring the tensions of the past few weeks had clearly gotten the better of us. "I get it. You're pissed. I'm pissed. Everybody's friggin pissed."

"And?"

"And...I wish Big A was here. He'd know what to do."

"Well, he's not here. And neither is Stephen. And they're both counting on us to set things right. And—"

"And you're right. We need to stick with the plan. For now."

"You're goddamn right I'm right! Wait, I'm right?"

"Yeah. We good? Can we get back to work now?"

As his eyes returned to their normal blue and his jovial ginger demeanor somewhat returned, he said, "Yeah. We're good. Sorry if that was a bit harsh."

"Forget it," I muttered, as we starting moving down the street again. "Needed to be said."

After an awkward couple seconds, he said, "You really are an—"

"Obstinate son of a bitch?"

"Means stubborn."

"I know what it means."

"I was going for effect. Did it work?"

"Oh, yeah. Powerful sentiment."

"Really?"

"No. You sounded like a total jackass."

Unfortunately, we didn't have the opportunity to further debate whether the word 'obstinate' should ever be used in conjunction with the term 'son of a bitch' because at that precise moment, an oddly undersized anakim wearing some grungy sweatpants and matching hoodie staggered out of the smoldering hulk of a liquor store roughly fifty feet in front of us.

With three kegs of beer tucked under his arm, the obscure giant walked headlong into a lamp post and subsequently fell ass over tea kettle on the sidewalk. Clumsily getting back to his feet, the eight- or nine-foot bastard didn't so much as shoot us a passing glance before vaulting over a collection of dilapidated cars and reaching the opposite side of the street in a single, ungraceful bound.

Ripping off the top of a keg with ease and draining the contents into his mouth, he promptly kicked out the oversized glass window of the local bank on the corner and disappeared inside. Oddly, it also seemed he was dragging a chain behind him and had some kind of metal collar around his neck.

Somewhat dumbfounded by what we just witnessed, I said, "That just happened, right?"

"If you're referring to the smallish, beer swilling giant that looks like he just broke out of prison and is apparently trying to rob a bank, then yes. Yes, it did."

"You don't see that every day."

Rooster rubbed his chin a couple times. "Nope. You really don't."

~

MORE FROM STEVE GILMORE

Heaven's Dark Soldiers

Rise of the Giants

Wrath of the Fallen

Rage of the Heavens

Dawn of the After Days

Ride of the Horseman (Coming Soon)

Sign up for Steve's newsletter for updates on deals and new releases!

https://liquidmind.media/steve-gilmore-newsletter-sign-up-1

About the Author

A West Point graduate and former Army Ranger, Steve Gilmore hails from rural New England (the town of Acushnet, MA) and subsequently spent the good majority of his adult life in the southern U.S. resulting from his time in the Army and ensuing misadventures in civilian life. After returning to Massachusetts for a bit, he again retreated to warmer climates and now resides in northern Florida with his beautiful wife, two amazing kiddos, and a yapping triumvirate of slothful canines.

Visit **www.stevegilmore.net** for more information.

Made in the USA
Las Vegas, NV
08 December 2022